King Midas

King Midas

Upton Sinclair

Waking Lion Press

ISBN 978-1-60096-943-0

Published by Waking Lion Press, an imprint of The Editorium

Waking Lion Press™, the Waking Lion Press logo, and The Editorium™ are trademarks of The Editorium, LLC

The Editorium, LLC
West Valley City, UT 84128-3917
wakinglionpress.com
wakinglion@editorium.com

I dreamed that Soul might dare the pain,
Unlike the prince of old,
And wrest from heaven the fiery touch
That turns all things to gold.

Note

In the course of this story, the author has had occasion to refer to Beethoven's Sonata Appassionata as containing a suggestion of the opening theme of the Fifth Symphony. He has often seen this stated, and believed that the statement was generally accepted as true. Since writing, however, he has heard the opinion expressed, by a musician who is qualified to speak as an authority, that the two themes have nothing to do with each other. The author himself is not competent to have an opinion on the subject, but because the statement as first made is closely bound up with the story, he has allowed it to stand unaltered.

The two extracts from MacDowell's "Woodland Sketches," on pages 214 and 291, are reprinted with the kind permission of Professor MacDowell and of Arthur P. Schmidt, publisher.

Part I

In the merry month of May

Chapter I

"O Madchen, Madchen,
Wie lieb' ich dich!"

It was that time of year when all the world belongs to poets, for their harvest of joy; when those who seek the country not for beauty, but for coolness, have as yet thought nothing about it, and when those who dwell in it all the time are too busy planting for another harvest to have any thought of poets; so that the latter, and the few others who keep something in their hearts to chime with the great spring-music, have the woods and waters all for their own for two joyful months, from the time that the first snowy bloodroot has blossomed, until the wild rose has faded and nature has no more to say. In those two months there are two weeks, the ones that usher in the May, that bear the prize of all the year for glory; the commonest trees wear green and silver then that would outshine a coronation robe, and if a man has any of that prodigality of spirit which makes imagination, he may hear the song of all the world.

It was on such a May morning in the midst of a great forest of pine trees, one of those forests whose floors are moss-covered ruins that give to them the solemnity of age and demand humility from those who walk within their silences. There was not much there to tell of the springtime, for the pines are unsympathetic, but it seemed as if all the more wealth had been flung about on the carpeting beneath. Where the moss was not were flowing beds of fern, and the ground was dotted with slender harebells

3

and the dusty, half-blossomed corydalis, while from all the rocks the bright red lanterns of the columbine were dangling.

Of the beauty so wonderfully squandered there was but one witness, a young man who was walking slowly along, stepping as it seemed where there were no flowers; and who, whenever he stopped to gaze at a group of them, left them unmolested in their happiness. He was tall and slenderly built, with a pale face shadowed by dark hair; he was clad in black, and carried in one hand a half-open book, which, however, he seemed to have forgotten.

A short distance ahead was a path, scarcely marked except where the half-rotted trees were trodden through. Down this the young man turned, and a while later, as his ear was caught by the sound of falling water, he quickened his steps a trifle, until he came to a little streamlet which flowed through the forest, taking for its bed the fairest spot in that wonderland of beauty. It fled from rock to rock covered with the brightest of bright green moss and with tender fern that was but half uncurled, and it flashed in the sunlit places and tinkled from the deep black shadows, ever racing faster as if to see what more the forest had to show. The young man's look had been anxious before, but he brightened in spite of himself in the company of the streamlet.

Not far beyond was a place where a tiny rill flowed down from the high rocks above, and where the path broadened out considerably. It was a darkly shadowed spot, and the little rill was gathered in a sunken barrel, which the genius of the place had made haste to cover with the green uniform worn by all else that was to be seen. Beside the spring thus formed the young man seated himself, and after glancing impatiently at his watch, turned his gaze upon the beauty that was about him. Upon the neighboring rocks the columbine and harebell held high revel, but he did not notice them so much as a new sight that flashed upon his eye; for the pool where the two streamlets joined was like a nest which the marsh-marigold had taken for its home. The water was covered with its bright green and yellow, and the young man gazed at the blossoms with eager delight, until finally he knelt and plucked a few of them, which he laid, cool and gleaming, upon the seat by the spring.

The flowers did not hold his attention very long, however; he rose up and turned away towards where, a few steps beyond, the open country could be seen between the tree trunks. Beyond the edge of the woods was a field, through which the footpath and the streamlet both ran, the former to join a road leading to a little town which lay in the distance. The landscape was beautiful in its morning freshness, but it was not that which the young man thought of; he had given but one glance before he started back with a slight exclamation, his face turning paler. He stepped into the concealment of the thick bushes at one side, where he stood gazing out, motionless except for a slight trembling. Down the road he had seen a white-clad figure just coming out of the village; it was too far away to be recognized, but it was a young girl, walking with a quick and springing step, and he seemed to know who it was.

She had not gone very far before she came to a thick hedge which lined the roadside and hid her from the other's view; he could not see her again until she came to the place where the streamlet was crossed by a bridge, and where the little path turned off towards the forest. In the meantime he stood waiting anxiously; for when she reached there he would see her plainly for the first time, and also know if she were coming to the spring. She must have stopped to look at something, for the other had almost started from his hiding place in his eagerness when finally she swept past the bushes. She turned down the path straight towards him, and he clasped his hands together in delight as he gazed at her.

And truly she was a very vision of the springtime, as she passed down the meadows that were gleaming with their first sprinkling of buttercups. She was clad in a dress of snowy white, which the wind swept before her as she walked; and it had stolen one strand of her golden hair to toss about and play with. She came with all the eagerness and spring of the brooklet that danced beside her,

her cheeks glowing with health and filled with the laughter of the morning. Surely, of all the flowers of the May-time there is none so fair as the maiden. And the young man thought as he stood watching her that in all the world there was no maiden so fair as this.

She did not see him, for her eyes were lifted to a little bobolink that had come flying down the wind. One does not hear the bobolink at his best unless one goes to hear him; for sheer glorified happiness there is in all our land no bird like him at the hour of sunrise, when he is drunk with the morning breeze and the sight of the dew-filled roses. At present a shower had just passed and the bobolink may have thought that another dawn had come; or perhaps he saw the maiden. At any rate, he perched himself upon the topmost leaf of the maple tree, still half-flying, as if scorning even that much support; and there he sang his song. First he gave his long prelude that one does not often hear—a few notes a score of times repeated, and growing swift and loud, and more and more strenuous and insistent; as sometimes the orchestra builds up its climax, so that the listener holds his breath and waits for something, he knows not what. Then he paused a moment and turned his head to see if the girl were watching, and filled his throat and poured out his wonderful gushing music, with its watery and bell-like tone that only the streamlet can echo, from its secret places underneath the banks. Again and again he gave it forth, the white patches on his wings flashing in the sunlight and both himself and his song one thrill of joy.

The girl's face was lit up with delight as she tripped down the meadow path. A gust of wind came up behind her, and bowed the grass and the flowers before her and swung the bird upon the tree; and so light was the girl's step that it seemed to lift her and sweep her onward. As it grew stronger she stretched out her arms to it and half leaned upon it and flung her head back for the very fullness of her happiness. The wind tossed her skirts about her, and stole another tress of hair, and swung the lily which she had plucked and which she carried in her hand. It is only when one has heard much music that he understands the morning wind, and knows that it is a living thing about which he can say such things as that; one needs only to train his ear and he can hear its footsteps upon the meadows, and hear it calling to him from the tops of the trees.

The girl was the very spirit of the wind at that moment, and she seemed to feel that some music was needed. She glanced up again at the bobolink, who had ceased his song; she nodded to him once as if for a challenge, and then, still leaning back upon the breeze, and keeping time with the flower in her hand, she broke out into a happy song:

> *"I heard a streamlet gushing*
> *From out its rocky bed,*
> *Far down the valley rushing,*
> *So fresh and clear it sped."*

But then, as if even Schubert were not equal to the fullness of her heart, or because the language of joy has no words, she left the song unfinished and swept on in a wild carol that rose and swelled and made the forest echo. The bobolink listened and then flew on to listen again, while still the girl poured out her breathless music, a mad volley of soaring melody; it seemed fairly to lift her from her feet, and she was half dancing as she went. There came another gust of wind and took her in its arms; and the streamlet fled before her; and thus the three, in one wild burst of happiness, swept into the woodland together.

There in its shadows the girl stopped short, her song cut in half by the sight of the old forest in its majesty. One could not have imagined a greater contrast than the darkness and silence which dwelt beneath the vast canopy, and she gazed about her in rapture, first at the trees and then at the royal carpet of green, starred with its fields of flowers. Her breast heaved, and she stretched out her arms as if she would have clasped it all to her.

"Oh, it is so beautiful!" she cried aloud. "It is so beautiful!"

In the meantime the young man, still unseen, had been standing in the shadow of the bushes, drinking in the sight. The landscape and the figure and the song had all faded from his thoughts, or rather blended themselves as a halo about one thing, the face of this girl. For it was one of those faces that a man may see once in a lifetime and keep as a haunting memory ever afterwards, as a vision of the sweetness and glory of woman; at this moment it was a face transfigured with rapture, and the man who was gazing upon it was trembling, and scarcely aware of where he was.

For fully a minute more the girl stood motionless, gazing about at the forest; then she chanced to look towards the spring, where she saw the flowers upon the seat.

"Why, someone has left a nosegay!" she exclaimed, as she started forward; but that seemed to suggest another thought to her, and she looked around. As she did so she caught sight of the young man and sprang towards him. "Why, Arthur! You here!" she cried.

The other started forward as if he would have clasped her in his arms; but then recollecting himself he came forward very slowly, half lowering his eyes before the girl's beauty.

"So you recollect me, Helen, do you?" he said, in a low voice.

"Recollect you?" was the answer. "Why, you dear, foolish boy, of course I recollect you. But how in the world do you come to be here?"

"I came here to see you, Helen."

"To see me?" exclaimed she. "But pray how—" and then she stopped, and a look of delight swept across her face. "You mean that you knew I would come here the first thing?"

"I do indeed."

"Why, that was beautiful!" she exclaimed. "I am so glad I did come."

The glance which she gave made his heart leap up; for a moment or two they were silent, looking at each other, and then suddenly another thought struck the girl. "Arthur," she cried, "I forgot! Do you mean to tell me that you have come all the way from Hilltown?"

"Yes, Helen."

"And just to see me?"

"Yes, Helen."

"And this morning?"

She received the same answer again. "It is twelve miles," she exclaimed; "who ever heard of such a thing? You must be tired to death."

She put out her hand, which he took tremblingly.

"Let us go sit down on the bench," she said, "and then we can talk about things. I am perfectly delighted that you came," she added when she had seated herself, with the marigolds and the lily in her lap. "It will seem just like old times; just think how long ago it was that I saw you last, Arthur,—three whole years! And do you know, as I left the town I thought of you, and that I might find you here."

The young man's face flushed with pleasure.

"But I'd forgotten you since!" went on the girl, eyeing him mischievously; "for oh, I was so happy, coming down the old, old path, and seeing all the old sights! Things haven't changed a bit, Arthur; the woods look exactly the same, and the bridge hasn't altered a mite since the days we used to sit on the edge and let our feet hang in. Do you remember that, Arthur?"

"Perfectly," was the answer.

"And that was over a dozen years ago! How old are you now, Arthur,—twenty-one—no, twenty-two; and I am just nineteen. To-day is my birthday, you know!"

"I had not forgotten it, Helen."

"You came to welcome me! And so did everything else. Do you know, I don't think I'd ever been so happy in my life as I was just now. For I thought the old trees greeted me, and the bridge, and the stream! And I'm sure that was the same bobolink! They don't have any bobolinks in Germany, and so that one was the first I have heard in three years. You heard him, didn't you, Arthur?"

"I did—at first," said Arthur.

"And then you heard me, you wicked boy! You heard me come in here singing and talking to myself like a mad creature! I don't think I ever felt so like singing before; they make hard work out of singing and everything else in Germany, you know, so I never sang out of business hours; but I believe I could sing all day now, because I'm so happy."

"Go on," said the other, seriously; "I could listen."

"No; I want to talk to you just now," said Helen. "You should have kept yourself hidden and then you'd have heard all sorts of wonderful things that you'll never have another chance to hear. For I was just going to make a speech to the forest, and I think I should have kissed each one of the flowers. You might have put it all into a poem,—for oh, father tells me you're going to be a great poet!"

"I'm going to try," said Arthur, blushing.

"Just think how romantic that would be!" the girl laughed; "and I could write your memoir and tell all I knew about you. Tell me about yourself, Arthur—I don't mean for the memoir, but because I want to know the news."

"There isn't any, Helen, except that I finished college last spring, as I wrote you, and I'm teaching school at Hilltown."

"And you like it?"

"I hate it; but I have to keep alive, to try to be a poet. And that is the news about myself."

"Except," added Helen, "that you walked twelve miles this glorious Saturday morning to welcome me home, which was beautiful. And of course you'll stay over Sunday, now you're here; I can invite you myself, you know, for I've come home to take the reins of government. You never saw such a sight in your life as my poor father has made of our house; he's got the parlor all full of those horrible theological works of his, just as if God had never made anything beautiful! And since I've been away that dreadful Mrs. Dale has gotten complete charge of the church, and she's one of those creatures that wouldn't allow you to burn a candle in the organ loft; and father never was of any use for quarreling about things." (Helen's father, the Reverend Austin Davis, was the rector of the little Episcopal church in the town of Oakdale just across the fields.) "I only arrived last night," the girl prattled on, venting her happiness in that way instead of singing; "but I hunted up two tallow candles in the attic, and you shall see them in church to-morrow. If there's any complaint about the smell, I'll tell Mrs. Dale we ought to have incense, and she'll get so excited about that that I'll carry the candles by default. I'm going to institute other reforms also,—I'm going to make the choir sing in tune!"

"If you will only sing as you were singing just now, nobody will hear the rest of the choir," vowed the young man, who during her remarks had never taken his eyes off the girl's radiant face.

Helen seemed not to notice it, for she had been arranging the marigolds; now she was drying them with her handkerchief before fastening them upon her dress.

"You ought to learn to sing yourself," she said while she bent her head down at that task. "Do you care for music any more than you used to?"

"I think I shall care for it just as I did then," was the answer, "whenever you sing it."

"Pooh!" said Helen, looking up from her marigolds; "the idea of a dumb poet anyway, a man who cannot sing his own songs! Don't you know that if you could sing and make yourself gloriously happy as I was just now, and as I mean to be some more, you could write poetry whenever you wish."

"I can believe that," said Arthur.

"Then why haven't you ever learned? Our English poets have all been ridiculous creatures about music, any how; I don't believe there was one in this century, except Browning, that really knew anything about it, and all their groaning and pining for inspiration was nothing in the world but a need of some music; I was reading the 'Palace of Art' only the other day, and there was that 'lordly pleasure house' with all its modern improvements, and without a sound of music. Of course the poor soul had to go back to the suffering world, if it were only to hear a hand-organ again."

"That is certainly a novel theory," admitted the young poet. "I shall come to you when I need inspiration."

"Come and bring me your songs," added the girl, "and I will sing them to you. You can write me a poem about that brook, for one thing. I was thinking just as I came down the road that if I were a poet I should have beautiful things to say to that brook. Will you do it for me?"

"I have already tried to write one," said the young man, hesitatingly.

"A song?" asked Helen.

"Yes."

"Oh, good! And I shall make some music for it; will you tell it to me?"

"When?"

"Now, if you can remember it," said Helen. "Can you?"

"If you wish it," said Arthur, simply; "I wrote it two or three months ago, when the country was different from now."

He fumbled in his pocket for some papers, and then in a low tone he read these words to the girl:

At Midnight

The burden of the winter
The year has borne too long,
And oh, my heart is weary
For a springtime song!

The moonbeams shrink unwelcomed
From the frozen lake;
Of all the forest voices
There is but one awake

I seek thee, happy streamlet
That murmurest on thy way,

As a child in troubled slumber
Still dreaming of its play;

I ask thee where in thy journey
Thou seeest so fair a sight,
That thou hast joy and singing
All through the winter night.

Helen was silent for a few moments, then she said, "I think that is beautiful, Arthur; but it is not what I want."

"Why not?" he asked.

"I should have liked it when you wrote it, but now the spring has come, and we must be happy. You have heard the springtime song."

"Yes," said Arthur, "and the streamlet has led me to the beautiful sight."

"It *is* beautiful," said Helen, gazing about her with that naive unconsciousness which "every wise man's son doth know" is one thing he may never trust in a woman. "It could not be more beautiful," she added, "and you must write me something about it, instead of wandering around our pasture-pond on winter nights till your imagination turns it into a frozen lake."

The young poet put away his papers rather suddenly at that, and Helen, after gazing at him for a moment, and laughing to herself, sprang up from the seat.

"Come!" she cried, "why are we sitting here, anyway, talking about all sorts of things, and forgetting the springtime altogether? I haven't been half as happy yet as I mean to be."

She seemed to have forgotten her friend's twelve mile walk; but he had forgotten it too, just as he soon forgot the rather wintry reception of his little song. It was not possible for him to remain dull very long in the presence of the girl's glowing energy; for once upon her feet, Helen's dancing mood seemed to come back to her, if indeed it had ever more than half left her. The brooklet struck up the measure again, and the wind shook the trees far above them, to tell that it was still awake, and the girl was the very spirit of the springtime once more.

"Oh, Arthur," she said as she led him down the path, "just think how happy I ought to be, to welcome all the old things after so long, and to find them all so beautiful; it is just as if the country had put on its finest dress to give me greeting, and I feel as if I were not half gay enough in return. Just think what this springtime is, how all over the country everything is growing and rejoicing; *that* is what I want you to put into the poem for me."

And so she led him on into the forest, carried on by joy herself, and taking all things into her song. She did not notice that the young man's forehead was flushed, or that his hand was burning when she took it in hers as they walked; if she noticed it, she chose at any rate to pretend not to. She sang to him about the forest and the flowers, and some more of the merry song which she had sung before; then she stopped to shake her head at a saucy adder's tongue that thrust its yellow face up through the dead leaves at her feet, and to ask that wisest-looking of all flowers what secrets it knew about the spring-time. Later on they came to a place where the brook fled faster, sparkling brightly in the sunlight over its shallow bed of pebbles; it was only her runaway caroling that could keep pace with that, and so her glee mounted higher, the young man at her side half in a trance, watching her laughing face and drinking in the sound of her voice.

How long that might have lasted there is no telling, had it not been that the woods came to an end, disclosing more open fields and a village beyond. "We'd better not go any farther," said Helen, laughing; "if any of the earth creatures should hear us carrying on they would not know it was 'Trunkenheit ohne Wein.'"

She stretched out her hand to her companion, and led him to a seat upon a fallen log nearby. "Poor boy," she said, "I forgot that you were supposed to be tired."

"It does not make any difference," was the reply; "I hadn't thought of it."

"There's no need to walk farther," said Helen, "for I've seen all that I wish to see. How dear this walk ought to be to us, Arthur!"

14

"I do not know about you, Helen," said the young man, "but it has been dear to me indeed. I could not tell you how many times I have walked over it, all alone, since you left; and I used to think about the many times I had walked it with you. You haven't forgotten, Helen, have you?"

"No," said Helen.

"Not one?"

"Not one."

The young man was resting his head upon his hand and gazing steadily at the girl.

"Do you remember, Helen—?" He stopped; and she turned with her bright clear eyes and gazed into his.

"Remember what?" she asked.

"Do you remember the last time we took it, Helen?"

She flushed a trifle, and half involuntarily turned her glance away again.

"Do you remember?" he asked again, seeing that she was silent.

"Yes, I remember," said the girl, her voice lower—"But I'd rather you did not—." She stopped short.

"You wish to forget it, Helen?" asked Arthur.

He was trembling with anxiety, and his hands, which were clasped about his knee, were twitching. "Oh, Helen, how can you?" he went on, his voice breaking. "Do you not remember the last night that we sat there by the spring, and you were going away, no one knew for how long—and how you told me that it was more than you could bear; and the promise that you made me? Oh, Helen!"

The girl gazed at him with a frightened look; he had sunk down upon his knee before her, and he caught her hand which lay upon the log at her side.

"Helen!" he cried, "you cannot mean to forget that? For that promise has been the one joy of my life, that for which I have labored so hard! My one hope, Helen! I came to-day to claim it, to tell you—"

And with a wild glance about her, the girl sprang to her feet, snatching her hand away from his.

15

"Arthur!" she cried; "Arthur, you must not speak to me so!"

"I must not, Helen?"

"No, no," she cried, trembling; "we were only children, and we did not know the meaning of the words we used. You must not talk to me that way, Arthur."

"Helen!" he protested, helplessly.

"No, no, I will not allow it!" she cried more vehemently, stepping back as he started towards her, and holding close to her the hand he had held. "I had no idea there was such a thought in your mind—"

Helen stopped, breathlessly.

"—or you would not have been so kind to me?" the other added faintly.

"I thought of you as an old friend," said Helen. "I was but a child when I went away. I wish you still to be a friend, Arthur; but you must not act in that way."

The young man glanced once at her, and when he saw the stern look upon her face he buried his head in his arms without a sound.

For fully a minute they remained thus, in silence; then as Helen watched him, her chest ceased gradually to heave, and a gentler look returned to her face. She came and sat down on the log again.

"Arthur," she said after another silence, "can we not just be friends?"

The young man answered nothing, but he raised his head and gazed at her; and she saw that there were tears in his eyes, and a look of mute helplessness upon his face. She trembled slightly, and rose to her feet again.

"Arthur," she said gravely, "this must not be; we must not sit here any longer. I must go."

"Helen!" exclaimed the other, springing up.

But he saw her brow knit again, and he stopped short. The girl gazed about her, and the village in the distance caught her eye.

"Listen," she said, with forced calmness; "I promised father that I would go and see old Mrs. Woodward, who was asking for me.

You may wait here, if you like, and walk home with me, for I shall not be gone very long. Will you do it?"

The other gazed at her for a moment or two; he was trying to read the girl's heart, but he saw only the quiet firmness of her features.

"Will you wait, Arthur?" she asked again.

And Arthur's head sank upon his breast. "Yes, Helen," he said. When he lifted it again, the girl was gone; she had disappeared in the thicket, and he could hear her footsteps as she passed swiftly down the hillside.

He went to the edge of the woods, where he could see her a short distance below, hurrying down the path with a step as light and free as ever. The wind had met her at the forest's edge and joined her once more, playing about her skirts and tossing the lily again. As Arthur watched her, the old music came back into his heart; his eyes sparkled, and all his soul seemed to be dancing in time with her light motion. Thus it went until she came to a place where the path must hide her from his view. The young man held his breath, and when she turned a cry of joy escaped him; she saw him and waved her hand to him gaily as she swept on out of his sight.

For a moment afterwards he stood rooted to the spot, then whirled about and laughed aloud. He put his hand to his fore-head, which was flushed and hot, and he gazed about him, as if he were not sure where he was. "Oh, she is so beautiful!" he cried, his face a picture of rapture. "So beautiful!"

And he started through the forest as wildly as any madman, now muttering to himself and now laughing aloud and making the forest echo with Helen's name. When he stopped again he was far away from the path, in a desolate spot, but tho he was staring around him, he saw no more than before. Trembling had seized his limbs, and he sank down upon the yellow forest leaves, hiding his face in his hands and whispering, "Oh, if I should lose her! If I should lose her!" As old Polonius has it, truly it was "the very ecstasy of love."

Chapter II

"A dancing shape, an image gay, To haunt, to startle, and waylay."

The town of Oakdale is at the present time a flourishing place, inhabited principally by "suburbanites," for it lies not very far from New York; but the Reverend Austin Davis, who was the spiritual guardian of most of them, had come to Oakdale some twenty and more years ago, when it was only a little village, with a struggling church which it was the task of the young clergyman to keep alive. Perhaps the growth of the town had as much to do with his success as his own efforts; but however that might have been he had received his temporal reward some ten years later, in the shape of a fine stone church, with a little parsonage beside it. He had lived there ever since, alone with his one child,—for just after coming to Oakdale he had married a daughter of one of the wealthy families of the neighborhood, and been left a widower a year or two later.

A more unromantic and thoroughly busy man than Mr. Davis at the age of forty-five, when this story begins, it would not have been easy to find; but nevertheless people spoke of no less than two romances that had been connected with his life. One of them had been his early marriage, which had created a mild sensation, while the other had come into his life even sooner, in fact on the very first day of his arrival at Oakdale.

Mr. Davis could still bring back to his mind with perfect clearness the first night he had spent in the little wooden cottage which he had hired for his residence; how while busily unpacking his trunk and trying to bring the disordered place into shape, he had opened the door in answer to a knock and beheld a woman stagger in out of the storm. She was a young girl, surely not yet out of her teens, her pale and sunken face showing marks of refinement and of former beauty. She carried in her arms a child of about a year's age, and she dropped it upon the sofa and sank down beside it, half fainting from exhaustion. The young clergyman's anxious inquiries having succeeded in eliciting but incoherent replies, he had left the room to procure some nourishment for the exhausted woman; it was upon his return that the discovery of the romance alluded to was made, for the woman had disappeared in the darkness and storm, and the baby was still lying upon the sofa.

It was not altogether a pleasant romance, as is probably the case with a good many romances in reality. Mr. Davis was destined to retain for a long time a vivid recollection of the first night which he spent in alternately feeding that baby with a spoon, and in walking the floor with it; and also to remember the sly glances which his parishioners only half hid from him when his unpleasant plight was made known.

It happened that the poorhouse at Hilltown near by, to which the infant would have gone if he had left it to the care of the county, was at that time being "investigated," with all that the name implies when referring to public matters; the clergy of the neighborhood being active in pushing the charges, Mr. Davis felt that at present it would look best for him to provide for the child himself. As the investigation came to nothing, the inducement was made a permanent one; perhaps also the memory of the mother's wan face had something to do with the matter. At any rate the young clergyman, tho but scantily provided for himself, managed to spare enough to engage a woman in the town to take care of the young charge. Subsequently when Mr. Davis' wife died the woman became Helen's nurse, and so it was that Arthur, as the baby boy had been christened, became permanently adopted into the clergyman's little family.

It had not been possible to keep from Arthur the secret of his parentage, and the fact that it was known to all served to keep him aloof from the other children of the town, and to drive him still more to the confidence of Helen. One of the phrases which Mr. Davis had caught from the mother's lips had been that the boy was a "gentleman's son;" and Helen was wont to solace him by that reminder. Perhaps the phrase, constantly repeated, had much to do with the proud sensitiveness and the resolute independence which soon manifested itself in the lad's character. He had scarcely passed the age of twelve before, tho treated by Mr. Davis with the love and kindness of a father, he astonished the good man by declaring that he was old enough to take care of himself; and tho Mr. Davis was better situated financially by that time, nothing that he could say could alter the boy's quiet determination to leave school and be independent, a resolution in which he was seconded by Helen, a little miss of some nine years. The two children had talked it over for months, as it appeared, and concluded that it was best to sacrifice in the cause of honor the privilege of going to school together, and of spending the long holidays roaming about the country.

So the lad had served with childish dignity, first as an errand boy, and then as a store clerk, always contributing his mite of "board" to Mr. Davis' household expenses; meanwhile, possibly because he was really "a gentleman's son," and had inherited a taste for study, he had made by himself about as much progress as if he had been at school. Some years later, to the delight of Helen and Mr. Davis, he had carried off a prize scholarship above the heads of the graduates of the Hilltown High School, and still refusing all help, had gone away to college, to support himself there while studying by such work as he could find, knowing well that a true gentleman's son is ashamed of nothing honest.

He spent his vacations at home, where he and Helen studied together,—or such rather had been his hope; it was realized only for the first year.

21

Helen had an aunt upon her mother's side, a woman of wealth and social position, who owned a large country home near Oakdale, and who was by no means inclined to view with the complacency of Mr. Davis the idyllic friendship of the two young people. Mrs. Roberts, or "Aunt Polly" as she was known to the family, had plans of her own concerning the future of the beauty which she saw unfolding itself at the Oakdale parsonage. She said nothing to Mr. Davis, for he, being busy with theological works and charitable organizations, was not considered a man from whom one might hope for proper ideas about life. But with her own more practical husband she had frequently discussed the danger, and the possible methods of warding it off.

To send Helen to a boarding school would have been of no use, for the vacations were the times of danger; so it was that the trip abroad was finally decided upon. Aunt Polly, having traveled herself, had a wholesome regard for German culture, believing that music and things of that sort were paying investments. It chanced, also, that her own eldest daughter, who was a year older than Helen, was about through with all that American teachers had to impart; and so after much argument with Mr. Davis, it was finally arranged that she and Helen should study in Germany together. Just when poor Arthur was returning home with the sublime title of junior, his dream of all things divine was carried off by Aunt Polly, and after a summer spent in "doing" Europe, was installed in a girl's school in Leipzig.

And now, three years having passed, Helen has left her cousin for another year of travel, and returned home in all the glory of her own springtime and of Nature's; which brings us to where we left her, hurrying away to pay a duty call in the little settlement on the hillside.

The visit had not been entirely a subterfuge, for Helen's father had mentioned to her that the elderly person whom she had named to Arthur was expecting to see her when she returned, and Helen had been troubled by the thought that she would never have any peace until she had paid that visit. It was by no means an agreeable one, for old Mrs. Woodward was exceedingly dull, and Helen felt that she was called upon to make war upon dullness. However, it had occurred to her to get her task out of the way at once, while she felt that she ought to leave Arthur.

The visit proved to be quite as depressing as she had expected, for it is sad to have to record that Helen, however sensitive to the streamlet and the flowers, had not the least sympathy in the world for an old woman who had a very sharp chin, who stared at one through two pairs of spectacles, and whose conversation was about her own health and the dampness of the springtime, besides the dreariest gossip about Oakdale's least interesting people. Perhaps it might have occurred to the girl that it is very forlorn to have nothing else to talk about, and that even old Mrs. Woodward might have liked to hear about some of the things in the forest, or to have been offered the lily and the marigold. Unfortunately, however, Helen did not think about any of that, but only moved restlessly about in her chair and gazed around the ugly room. Finally when she could stand it no more, she sprang up between two of Mrs. Woodward's longest sentences and remarked that it was very late and a long way home, and that she would come again some time.

Then at last when she was out in the open air, she drew a deep breath and fled away to the woods, wondering what could be God's reason for such things. It was not until she was half way up the hillside that she could feel that the wind, which blew now upon her forehead, had quite swept away the depression which had settled upon her. She drank in the odors which blew from the woods, and began singing to herself again, and looking out for Arthur.

She was rather surprised not to see him at once, and still more surprised when she came nearer and raised her voice to call him; for she reached the forest and came to the place where she had left him without a reply having come. She shouted his name again and again, until at last, not without a half secret chagrin to have been so quickly forgotten, she was obliged to set out for home alone.

"Perhaps he's gone on ahead," she thought, quickening her pace.

For a time she watched anxiously, expecting to see his darkly clad figure; but she soon wearied of continued failure, and because it was her birthday, and because the brook was still at her side and the beautiful forest still about her, she took to singing again, and was quickly as happy and glorious as before, ceasing her caroling and moderating her woodland pace only when she neared the town. She passed down the main street of Oakdale, not quite without an exulting consciousness that her walk had crowned her beauty and that no one whom she saw was thinking about anything else; and so she came to her home, to the dear old parsonage, with its spreading ivy vines, and its two great elms.

When she had hurried up the steps and shut the door behind her, Helen felt privileged again to be just as merry as she chose, for she was even more at home here than in the woods; it seemed as if everything were stretching out its arms to her to welcome her, and to invite her to carry out her declared purpose of taking the reins of government in her own hands.

Upon one side of the hallway was a parlor, and on the other side two rooms, which Mr. Davis had used as a reception room and a study. The parlor had never been opened, and Helen promised herself a jolly time superintending the fixing up of that; on the other side she had already taken possession of the front room, symbolically at any rate, by having her piano moved in and her music unpacked, and a case emptied for the books she had brought from Germany. To be sure, on the other side was still a dreary wall of theological treatises in funereal black, but Helen was not without hopes that continued doses of cheerfulness might cure her father of such incomprehensible habits, and obtain for her the permission to move the books to the attic.

To start things in that direction the girl now danced gaily into the study where her father was in the act of writing "thirdly, brethren," for his next day's sermon; and crying out merrily,

"Up, up my friend, and quit your books,

24

Or surely you'll grow double!"

she saluted her reverend father with the sweetest of kisses, and then seated herself on the arm of his chair and gravely took his pen out of his hand, and closed his inkstand. She turned over the "thirdly, brethren," without blotting it, and recited solemnly:

"One impulse from a vernal wood
May teach you more of man,
Of moral evil and of good.
Than all the sages can!"

And then she laughed the merriest of merry laughs and added, "Daddy, dear, I am an impulse! And I want you to spare some time for me."

"Yes, my love," said Mr. Davis, smiling upon her, though groaning inwardly for his lost ideas. "You are beautiful this morning, Helen. What have you been doing?"

"I've had a glorious walk," replied the girl, "and all kinds of wonderful adventures; I've had a dance with the morning wind, and a race of a mile or two with a brook, and I've sung duets with all the flowers,—and here you are writing uninteresting things!"

"It's my sermon, Helen," said Mr. Davis.

"I know it," said Helen, gravely.

"But it must be done for to-morrow," protested the other.

"Half your congregation is going to be so excited about two tallow candles that it won't know what you preach about," answered the girl, swinging herself on the arm of the chair; "and I'm going to sing for the other half, and so they won't care either. And besides, Daddy, I've got news to tell you; you've no idea what a good girl I've been."

"How, my love?"

"I went to see Mrs. Woodward."

"You didn't!"

"Yes; and it was just to show you how dutiful I'm going to be. Daddy, I felt so sorry for the poor old lady; it is so beautiful to know that one is doing good and bringing happiness into other people's lives! I think I'll go and see her often, and carry her something nice if you'll let me."

Helen said all that as gravely as a judge; but Mr. Davis was agreeing so delightedly that she feared she was carrying the joke too far. She changed the subject quickly.

"Oh, Daddy!" she cried, "I forgot to tell you—I met a genius to-day!"

"A genius?" inquired the other.

"Yes," said Helen, "and I've been walking around with him all morning out in the woods! Did you never hear that every place like that has a genius?"

"Yes," assented Mr. Davis, "but I don't understand your joke."

"This was the genius of Hilltown High School," laughed Helen.

"Oh, Arthur!"

"Yes; will you believe it, the dear boy had walked all the way from there to see me; and he waited out by the old seat at the spring!"

"But where is he now?"

"I don't know," said Helen. "It's very queer; I left him to go see Mrs. Woodward. He didn't go with me," she added, "I don't believe he felt inclined to charity."

"That is not like Arthur," said the other.

"I'm going to take him in hand, as becomes a clergyman's daughter," said Helen demurely; "I'm going to be a model daughter, Daddy—just you wait and see! I'll visit all your parishioners' lawn-parties and five o'clock teas for you, and I'll play Handel's Largo and Siegfried's Funeral March whenever you want to write sermons. Won't you like that?"

"Perhaps," said Mr. Davis, dubiously.

"Only I know you'll make blots when I come to the cymbals," said Helen; and she doubled up her fists and hummed the passage, and gave so realistic an imitation of the cymbal-clashes in the great dirge that it almost upset the chair. Afterwards she laughed one of her merriest laughs and kissed her father on the forehead.

"I heard it at Baireuth," she said, "and it was just fine! It made your flesh creep all over you. And oh, Daddy, I brought home a souvenir of Wagner's grave!"

"Did you?" asked Mr. Davis, who knew very little about Wagner.

"Yes," said Helen, "just a pebble I picked up near it; and you ought to have seen the custom-house officer at the dock yesterday when he was going through my trunks. 'What's this, Miss?' he asked; I guess he thought it was a diamond in the rough. 'Oh, that's from Wagner's grave,' I said. And what do you think the wretch did?"

"I'm sure I don't know, my love."

"He threw it back, saying it wasn't worth anything; I think he must have been a Brahmsite."

"It took the longest time going through all my treasures," Helen prattled on, after laughing at her own joke; "you know Aunt Polly let us have everything we wanted, bless her heart!"

"I'm afraid Aunt Polly must have spoiled you," said the other.

"She has," laughed Helen; "I really think she must mean to make me marry a rich husband, or else she'd never have left me at that great rich school; Lucy and I were the 'star-boarders' you know, and we just had everybody to spoil us. How in the world could you ever manage to spare so much money, Daddy?"

"Oh, it was not so much," said Mr. Davis; "things are cheaper abroad." (As a matter of fact, the grimly resolute Aunt Polly had paid two-thirds of her niece's expenses secretly, besides distributing pocket money with lavish generosity.)

"And you should see the wonderful dresses I've brought from Paris," Helen went on. "Oh, Daddy, I tell you I shall be glorious! Aunt Polly's going to invite a lot of people at her house next week to meet me, and I'm going to wear the reddest of red, red dresses, and just shine like a lighthouse!"

"I'm afraid," said the clergyman, surveying her with more pride than was perhaps orthodox, "I'm afraid you'll find it hard to be satisfied in this poor little home of ours."

"Oh, that's all right," said Helen; "I'll soon get used to it; and besides, I've got plenty of things to fix it up with—if you'll only get those dreadful theological works out of the front room! Daddy dear, you can't imagine how hard it is to bring the Valkyries and Niebelungs into a theological library."

"I'll see what I can do, my love," said Mr. Davis.

He was silent for a few moments, perhaps wondering vaguely whether it was well that this commanding young lady should have everything in the world she desired; Helen, who had her share of penetration, probably divined the thought, for she made haste to change the subject.

"By the way," she laughed, "we got so interested in our chattering that we forgot all about Arthur."

"Sure enough," exclaimed the other. "Pray where can he have gone?"

"I don't know," Helen said; "it's strange. But poets are such queer creatures!"

"Arthur is a very splendid creature," said Mr. Davis. "You have no idea, Helen, how hard he has labored since you have been away. He carried off all the honors at college, and they say he has written some good poetry. I don't know much about that, but the people who know tell me so."

"It would be gloriously romantic to know a great poet," said Helen, "and perhaps have him write poetry about you,—'Helen, thy beauty is to me,' and 'Sweet Helen, make me immortal with a kiss,' and all sorts of things like that! He's coming to live with us this summer as usual, isn't he, Daddy?"

"I don't know," said the other; "I presume he will. But where can he have gone to-day?"

"He acted very queerly," said the girl; and then suddenly a delighted smile lit up her face. "Oh, Daddy," she added, "do you know, I think Arthur is in love!"

"In love!" gasped Mr. Davis.

"Yes, in love!"

"Pray, with whom?"

"I'm sure I can't imagine," said Helen gravely; "but he seemed so abstracted, and he seemed to have something to tell me. And then he ran away!"

"That is very strange indeed," remarked the other. "I shall have to speak to him about it."

"If he doesn't come back soon, I'll go to look for him," said the girl; "I'm not going to let the water nixies run off with my Arthur; there are such things in that stream, because the song I was singing about it says so." And then she chanted as merrily as ever:

"Why speak I of a murmur?
No murmur can it be;
The Nixies they are singing
'Neath the wave their melody!"

"I will tell you what," said Mr. Davis, rising from his chair as he realized that the sermon had entirely vanished for the present. "You may go part of the way with me, and we'll stop in to see the Vails."

"The Vails!" gasped Helen. (Mr. Vail was the village dairyman, whose farm lay on the outskirts of the town; the village dairyman's family was not one that Helen cared to visit.)

"My love," said Mr. Davis, "poor Mrs. Vail has been very ill, and she has three little children, you know. You told me that you liked to bring joy wherever you could."

"Yes, but, Daddy," protested Helen, "*those* children are *dirty!* Ugh! I saw them as I came by."

"My love," answered the other, "they are God's children none the less; and we cannot always help such things."

"But we *can,* Daddy; there is plenty of water in the world."

"Yes, of course; but when the mother is ill, and the father in trouble! For poor Mr. Vail has had no end of misfortune; he has no resource but the little dairy, and three of his cows have been ill this spring."

And Helen's incorrigible mirth lighted up her face again. "Oh!" she cried. "Is *that* it! I saw him struggling away at the pump as I came by; but I had no idea it was anything so serious!"

Mr. Davis looked grieved; Helen, when her first burst of glee had passed, noticed it and changed her mood. She put her arms around her father's neck and pressed her cheek against his.

29

"Daddy, dear," she said coaxingly, "haven't I done charity enough for one day? You will surfeit me at the start, and then I'll be just as little fond of it as I was before. When I must let dirty children climb all over me, I can dress for the occasion."

"My dear," pleaded Mr. Davis, "Godliness is placed before Cleanliness."

"Yes," admitted Helen, "and of course it is right for you to inculcate the greater virtue; but I'm only a girl, and you mustn't expect sublimity from me. You don't want to turn me into a president of sewing societies, like that dreadful Mrs. Dale!"

"Helen," protested the other, helplessly, "I wish you would not always refer to Mrs. Dale with that adjective; she is the best helper I have."

"Yes, Daddy," said Helen, with the utmost solemnity; "when I have a dreadful eagle nose like hers, perhaps I can preside over meetings too. But I can't now."

"I do not want you to, my love; but—"

"And if I have to cling by the weaker virtue of cleanliness just for a little while, Daddy, you must not mind. I'll visit all your clean parishioners for you,—parishioners like Aunt Polly!"

And before Mr. Davis could make another remark, the girl had skipped into the other room to the piano; as her father went slowly out the door, the echoes of the old house were laughing with the happy melody of Purcell's—

Nymphs and shepherds, come a-way, come a-way,
Nymphs and shepherds, come a-way, come a-way, Come,
come, come, come a-way!

Chapter III

"For you alone I strive to sing,
Oh, tell me how to woo!"

When Helen was left alone, she seated herself before her old music stand which had been brought down to welcome her, and proceeded to glance over and arrange the pieces she had learned and loved in her young girlhood. Most of them made her smile, and when she reflected upon how difficult she used to think them, she realized that now that it was over she was glad for the German regime. Helen had accounted herself an accomplished pianist when she went away, but she had met with new standards and learned to think humbly of herself in the great home of music. She possessed a genuine fondness for the art, however, and had devoted most of her three years to it, so that she came home rejoicing in the possession of a technic that was quite a mastership compared with any that she was likely to meet.

Helen's thoughts did not dwell upon that very long at present, however; she found herself thinking again about Arthur, and the unexpected ending of her walk with him.

"I had no idea he felt that way toward me," she mused, resting her chin in her hand; "what in the world am I going to do? Men are certainly most inconvenient creatures; I thought I was doing everything in the world to make him happy!"

Helen turned to the music once more, but the memory of the figure she had left sunken helplessly upon the forest seat stayed in her mind. "I do wonder if that can be why he did not wait for me," she thought, shuddering,—"if he was too wretched to see me again; what CAN I do?" She got up and began walking restlessly up and down the room for a few minutes.

"Perhaps I ought to go and look for him," she mused; "it was an hour or two ago that I left him there;" and Helen, after thinking the matter over, had half turned to leave, when she heard a step outside and saw the door open quickly. Even before she saw him she knew who it was, for only Arthur would have entered without ringing the bell. After having pictured him overcome by despair, it was rather a blow to her pride to see him, for he entered flushed, and seemingly elated.

"Well, sir, you've treated me nicely!" she exclaimed, showing her vexation in spite of herself.

"You will forgive me," said Arthur, smiling.

"Don't be too sure of it," Helen said; "I looked for you every-where, and I am quite angry."

"I was obeying your high command," the other replied, still smiling.

"My command? I told you to wait for me."

"You told me something else," laughed Arthur. "You spent all the morning instructing me for it, you know."

"Oh!" said Helen. It was a broad and very much prolonged "Oh," for a sudden light was dawning upon the girl; as it came her frown gave place to a look of delight.

"You have been writing me a poem!" she cried, eagerly.

"Yes," said Arthur.

"Oh, you dear boy!" Helen laughed. "Then I do forgive you; but you ought to have told me, for I had to walk home all alone, and I've been worrying about you. I never once thought of the poem."

"The muses call without warning," laughed Arthur, "and one has to obey them, you know."

"Oh, oh!" exclaimed the other. "And so you've been wandering around the woods all this time, making verses! And you've been waving your arms and talking to yourself, and doing all sorts of crazy things, I know!" Then as she saw Arthur flush, she went on:

32

"I was sure of it! And you ran away so that I wouldn't see you! Oh, I wish I'd known; I'd have hunted you up and never come home until I'd found you."

As was usual with Helen, her momentary vexation had gone like April rain, and all her seriousness had vanished with it. She forgot all about the last scene in the woods, and Arthur was once more the friend of her girlhood, whom she might take by the hand when she chose, and with whom she might be as free and happy as when she was alone with the flowers and the wind. It seemed as if Arthur too had vented all his pent up emotion, and returned to his natural cheerful self.

"Tell me," she cried, "did you put in all the things I told you about?"

"I put all I could," said Arthur. "That is a great deal to ask."

"I only want it to be full of life," laughed Helen. "That's all I care about; the man who wants to write springtime poetry for me must be wide awake!"

"Shall I read it to you?" asked Arthur, hesitatingly.

"Yes, of course," said Helen. "And read it as if you meant it; if I like it I'll tell you so."

"I wrote it for nothing but to please you" was the reply, and Arthur took a much bescrawled piece of paper from his pocket; the girl seated herself upon the piano stool again and gazed up at him as he rested his elbow upon the top of the piano and read his lines. There could not have been a situation in which the young poet would have read them with more complete happiness, and so it was a pleasure to watch him. And Helen's eyes kindled, and her cheeks flushed brightly as she listened, for she found that the verses had taken their imagery from her very lips.

In the May-time's golden glory
Ere the quivering sun was high,
I heard the Wind of Morning
Through the laughing meadows fly;

In his passion-song was throbbing

All the madness of the May,
And he whispered: Thou hast labored;
Thou art weary; come away!

Thou shalt drink a fiery potion
For thy prisoned spirit's pain;
Thou shalt taste the ancient rapture
That thy soul has sought in vain.

I will tell thee of a maiden,
One who has thy longing fanned—
Spirit of the Forest Music—
Thou shalt take her by the hand,

Lightly by her rosy fingers
Trembling with her keen delight,
And her flying steps shall lead thee
Out upon the mountain's height;

To a dance undreamed of mortal
To the Bacchanal of Spring,—
Where in mystic joy united
Nature's bright-eyed creatures sing.

There the green things of the mountain,
Million-voiced, newly-born,
And the flowers of the valley
In their beauty's crimson morn;

There the winged winds of morning,
Spirits unresting, touched with fire,
And the streamlets, silver-throated,
They whose leaping steps ne'er tire!

Thou shalt see them, ever circling
Round about a rocky spring,

While the gaunt old forest-warriors
Madly their wide branches fling.

Thou shalt tread the whirling measure,
Bathe thee in its frenzied strife;
Thou shalt have a mighty memory
For thy spirit's after life.

Haste thee while thy heart is burning,
While thine eyes have strength to see;
Hark, behind yon blackening cloud-bank,
To the Storm-King's minstrelsy!

See, he stamps upon the mountains,
And he leaps the valleys high!
Now he smites his forest harp-strings,
And he sounds his thunder-cry:—

Waken, lift ye up, ye creatures,
Sing the song, each living thing!
Join ye in the mighty passion
Of the Symphony of Spring!

And so the young poet finished, his cheeks fairly on fire, and, as he gazed down at Helen, his hand trembling so that he could hardly hold the paper. One glance told him that she was pleased, for the girl's face was flushed like his own, and her eyes were sparkling with delight. Arthur's heart gave a great throb within him.

"You like it!" he exclaimed.

"Oh, Arthur, I do!" she cried. "Oh, how glorious you must have been!" And trembling with girlish delight, she took the paper from his hand and placed it in front of her on the music rack.

"Oh, I should like to write music for it!" she exclaimed; "for those lines about the Storm-King!"

And she read them aloud, clenching her hands and shaking her head, carried away by the image they brought before her eyes. "Oh, I should like music for it!" she cried again.

"I don't know very much about poetry, you know," she added, laughing excitedly. "If it's about the things I like, I can't help thinking it's fine. It's just the same with music,—if a man only makes it swift and strong, so that it leaps and flies and never tires, that is all I care about; and if he just keeps his trombones till the very last, he can carry me off my feet though he makes the worst noise that ever was! It's the same as a storm, you know, Arthur; do you remember how we used to go up on our hillside when the great wind was coming, and when everything was growing still and black; and how we used to watch the big clouds and the sheets of rain, and run for home when we heard the thunder? Once when you were away, Arthur, I didn't run, for I wanted to see what it was like; and I stayed up there and saw it all, singing the 'Ride of the Valkyries,' and pretending I was one of them and could gallop with the wind. For the wind is fine, Arthur! It fills you so full of its power that you stretch out your arms to it, and it makes you sing; and it comes, and it comes again, stronger than ever, and it sweeps you on, just like a great mass of music. And then it howls through the trees and it flies over the valleys,—that was what you were thinking of, weren't you, Arthur?"

And Helen stopped, breathlessly, and gazed at him; her cheeks were flushed, and her hands still tightly clasped.

"Yes," said Arthur, half mechanically, for he had lost himself in the girl's enthusiasm, and felt the storm of his verses once more.

"Your poem made me think of that one time that was so gloriously," Helen went on. "For the rain was almost blinding, and I was drenched, but I did not even know it. For oh, the thunder! Arthur, you've no idea what thunder is like till you're near it! There fell one fearful bolt quite near me, a great white, living thing, as thick as a man's body, and the crash of it seemed to split the air. But oh, I didn't mind it a bit! 'Der Sanger triumphirt in Wettern!' I think I was a real Valkyrie that time, and I only wished that I might put it into music."

The girl turned to the piano, and half in play struck a great rumbling chord, that rolled and echoed through the room; she sounded it once more, laughing aloud with glee. Arthur had sunk down upon a chair beside her, and was bending forward, watching her with growing excitement. For again and again Helen struck the keys with all the power of her arms, until they seemed to give forth real storm and thunder; and as she went on with her reckless play the mood grew upon her, and she lost herself in the vision of the Storm-King sweeping through the sky. She poured out a great stream of his wild music, singing away to herself excitedly in the meantime. And as the rush continued and the fierce music swelled louder, the phantasy took hold of the girl and carried her beyond herself. She seemed to become the very demon of the storm, unbound and reckless; she smote the keys with right royal strength, and the piano seemed a thing of life beneath her touch. The pace became faster, and the thunder rattled and crashed more wildly, and there awoke in the girl's soul a power of musical utterance that she had never dreamed of in her life before. Her whole being was swept away in ecstasy; her lips were moving excitedly, and her pulses were leaping like mad. She seemed no longer to know of the young man beside her, who was bent forward with clenched hands, carried beyond himself by the sight of her exulting power.

And in the meantime, Helen's music was surging on, building itself up into a great climax that swelled and soared and burst in a deafening thunder crash; and while the air was still throbbing and echoing with it, the girl joined to it her deep voice, grown suddenly conscious of new power:

"See, he stamps upon the mountains,
And he leaps the valleys high!
Now he smites his forest harp-strings,
And he sounds his thunder cry!"

And as the cry came the girl laughed aloud, like a very Valkyrie indeed, her laugh part of the music, and carried on by it; and then gradually as the tempest swept on, the rolling thunder was lost in a march that was the very tread of the Storm-King. And the march broadened, and the thunder died out of it slowly, and all the wild confusion, and then it rose, glorious and triumphant, and turned to a mighty pean, a mightier one than ever Helen could have made. The thought of it had come to her as an inspiration, and as a refuge, that the glory of her passion might not be lost. The march had led her to it, and now it had taken her in its arms and swept her away, as it had swept millions by its majesty. It was the great Ninth Symphony Hymn:

"Hail thee, Joy! From Heaven descending,
Daughter from Elysium!
Ecstasy our hearts inflaming,
To thy sacred shrine we come.
Thine enchantments bind together
Those whom custom's law divides;
All are brothers, all united,
Where thy gentle wing abides."

And Helen sang it as one possessed by it, as one made drunk with its glory—as the very Goddess of Joy that she was. For the Storm-King and his legions had fled, and another vision had come into her heart, a vision that every one ought to carry with him when the great symphony is to be heard. He should see the hall in Vienna where it was given for the last time in the great master's life, and see the great master himself, the bowed and broken figure that all musicians worship, standing up to conduct it; and see him leading it through all its wild surging passion, almost too frantic to be endured; and then, when the last towering climax has passed and the music has ceased and the multitude at his back has burst forth into its thundering shout, see the one pathetic figure standing there aloft before all eyes and still blindly beating the time. There must have been tears in the eyes of every man in that place to know the reason for it,—that he from whose heart all their joy had come, he who was lord and master of it, had never heard in his life and could never hope to hear one sound of that music he had written, but must dwell a prisoner in darkness and solitude forever.

That was the picture before Helen's eyes; she did not think of the fearful tragedy of it—she had no feeling for tragedy, she knew no more about suffering than a child just born. But joy she knew, and joy she was; she was the multitude lifted up in its ecstasy, throbbing, burning and triumphant, and she sang the great choruses, one after another, and the piano beneath her fingers thundered and rang with the instrumental part. Surely in all music there is no utterance of joy so sustained and so overwhelming in its intensity as this; it is a frenzy almost more than man can stand; it is joy more than human—the joy of existence:—

"Pleasure every creature living
From kind Nature's breast receives;
Good and evil, all are seeking
For the rosy path she leaves."

And so the torrent of passionate exultation swept Helen onward with it until the very end, the last frantic prestissimo chorus, and then she sprang to her feet and flung up her hands with a cry. She stood thus for a moment, glowing with exultation, and then she sank down again and sat staring before her, the music still echoing through every fiber of her soul, and the shouting multitude still surging before her.

For just how long that lasted, she knew not, but only that her wild mood was gradually subsiding, and that she felt herself sinking back, as a bird sinks after its flight; then suddenly she turned. Arthur was at her side, and she gave a cry, for he had seized her hand in his, and was covering it with burning kisses.

"Arthur! Arthur!" she gasped.

The young man gazed up at her, and Helen remembered the scene in the forest, and realized what she had done. She had shaken him to the very depths of his being by the emotion which she had flung loose before him, and he seemed beside himself

39

at that moment, his hair disordered and his forehead hot and flushed. He made a move as if to clasp the girl in his arms, and Helen tore her hand loose by main force and sprang back to the doorway.

"Arthur!" she cried. "What do you mean?"

He clutched at a chair for support, and stood staring at her. For fully a minute they remained thus, Helen trembling with alarm; then his head sank, and he flung himself down upon the sofa, where he lay sobbing passionately. Helen remained gazing at him with wide open and astonished eyes.

"Arthur!" she exclaimed again.

But he did not hear her, for the cruel sobbing that shook his frame. Helen, as soon as her first alarm had passed, came softly nearer, till she stood by the sofa; but still he did not heed her, and she did not dare even to put her hand upon his shoulder. She was afraid of him, her dearest friend, and she knew not what to make of him.

"Arthur," she whispered again, when he was silent for a moment. "Please speak to me, Arthur."

The other gazed up at her with a look of such helpless despair and longing upon his face that Helen was frightened still more. He had been sobbing as if his heart would break, but his eyes were dry.

"What is the matter?" she cried.

The young man answered her hoarsely: "Can you not see what is the matter, Helen? I love you! And you drive me mad!"

The girl turned very pale, and lowered her eyes before his burning gaze.

"Helen," the other went on impetuously, "you will break my heart if you treat me in this way. Do you not know that for three long years I have been dreaming of you, and of the promise that you gave me? You told me that you loved me, and that you always would love me! You told me that the night before you went away; and you kissed me. All this time I have been thinking of that kiss, and cherishing the memory of it, and waiting for you to return.

I have labored for no other reason, I have had no other hope in the world; I have kept your image before me, and lived in it, and worshiped before it, and the thought of you has been all that I had. When I was tired and worn and ill I could only think of you and remember your promise, and count the days before your return. And, oh, it has been so long that I could not stand it! For weeks I have been so impatient, and so filled with the thought of the day when I might see you again that I have been helpless and half mad; for I thought that I should take your hand in mine and claim your promise. And this morning I wandered about the woods for hours, waiting for you to come. And see how you have treated me!"

He buried his face in his hands again, and Helen stood gazing at him, breathing very fast with alarm, and unable to find a word to say.

"Helen," he groaned, without looking up again, "do you not know that you are beautiful? Have you no heart? You fling your soul bare before me, and you fill me with this fearful passion; you will drive me mad!"

"But, Arthur," she protested, "I could not think of you so; I thought of you as my brother, and I meant to make you happy."

"Tell me, then," he gasped, staring at her, "tell me once for all. You do *not* love me, Helen?"

The girl answered with a frank gaze that was cruel, "No, Arthur."

"And you can never love me? You take back the promise that you made me?"

"I told you that I was only a child, Arthur; it has been a long time since I have thought of it."

The young man choked back a sob. "Oh, Helen, if you only knew what cruel words those are," he groaned. "I cannot bear them."

He gazed at her with his burning eyes, so that the girl lowered hers again. "Tell me!" he exclaimed. "What am I to do?"

41

"Can we not remain friends, just as we used to be?" she asked pleadingly. "Can we not talk together and help each other as before? Oh, Arthur, I thought you would come here to live all summer, and how I should like it! Why can you not? Can you not let me play for you without—without—" and Helen stopped, and flushed a trifle; "I do not know quite what to make of you to-day," she added.

She was speaking kindly, but to the man beside her with his burning heart, her words were hard to hear; he stared at her, shuddering, and then suddenly he clenched his hands and started to his feet.

"Helen," he cried, "there is but one thing. I must go!"

"Go?" echoed Helen.

"If I stay here and gaze at you I shall go mad with despair," he exclaimed incoherently. "Oh, I shall go mad! For I do love you, and you talk to me as if I were a child! Helen, I must get this out of my heart in some way, I cannot stay here."

"But, Arthur," the girl protested, "I told father you would stay, and you will make yourself ill, for you have walked all day."

Every word she uttered was more torment to the other, for it showed him how much his hopes were gone to wreck. He rushed across the room and opened the door; then, however, he paused, as if that had cost him all his resolution. He gazed at the girl with a look of unspeakable yearning, his face white, and his limbs trembling beneath him.

"You wish me to go, Helen?" he exclaimed.

"Wish you!" exclaimed Helen, who was watching him in alarm. "Of course not; I want you to stay and see father, and—"

"And hear you tell me that you do not love me! Oh, Helen, how can you say it again? Can you not see what you have done to me?"

"Arthur!" cried the girl.

"Yes, what you have done to me! You have made me so that I dare not stay near you. You *must* love me, Helen, oh, some time you must!" And he came toward her again, stretching out his arms to her. As she sprang back, frowning, he stopped and stood for an instant, half sinking; then he whirled about and darted out of the door.

Helen was scarcely able to realize at first that he was gone, but when she looked out she saw that he was already far down the street, walking swiftly. For a moment she thought of calling him; but she checked herself, and closed the door quietly instead, after which she walked slowly across the room. In the center of it she stopped still, gazing in front of her thoughtfully, and looking very grave indeed. "That is dreadful," she said slowly. "I had no idea of such a thing. What in the world am I to do?"

There was a tall mirror between the two windows of the room, and Helen went toward it and stood in front of it, gazing earnestly at herself. "Is it true, then, that I am so very beautiful?" she mused. "And even Arthur must fall in love with me!"

Helen's face was still flushed with the glory of her ride with the Storm-King; she smoothed back the long strands of golden hair that had come loose, and then she looked at herself again. "It is dreadful," she said once more, half aloud, "I do not think I ever felt so nervous in my life, and I don't know what to do; everything I did to please him seemed only to make him more miserable. I wanted him to be happy with me; I wanted him to stay with me." And she walked away frowning, and seated herself at the piano and began peevishly striking at the keys. "I am going to write to him and tell him that he must get over that dreadfulness," she muttered after a while, "and come back and be friends with me. Oakdale will be too stupid without him all summer, and I should be miserable."

She was just rising impatiently when the front door opened and her father came in, exclaiming in a cheery voice, "Well, children!" Then he stopped in surprise. "Why, someone told me Arthur was here!" he exclaimed.

"He's gone home again," said Helen, in a dissatisfied tone.

"Home!" exclaimed the other. "To Hilltown?"

"Yes."

"But I thought he was going to stay until tomorrow."

"So did I," said Helen, "but he changed his mind and decided that he'd better not."

"Why, I am really disappointed," said Mr. Davis. "I thought we should have a little family party; I haven't seen Arthur for a month."

"There is some important reason," said Helen—"that's what he told me, anyway." She did not want her father to have any idea of the true reason, or to ask any inconvenient questions.

Mr. Davis would perhaps have done so, had he not something else on his mind. "By the way, Helen," he said, "I must ask you, what in the world was that fearful noise you were making?"

"Noise?" asked Helen, puzzled for a moment.

"Why, yes; I met old Mr. Nelson coming down the street, and he said that you were making a most dreadful racket upon the piano, and shouting, too, and that there were a dozen people standing in the street, staring!"

A sudden wild thought occurred to Helen, and she whirled about. Sure enough, she found the two windows of the room wide open; and that was too much for her gravity; she flung herself upon the sofa and gave vent to peal after peal of laughter.

"Oh, Daddy!" she gasped. "Oh, Daddy!"

Mr. Davis did not understand the joke, but he waited patiently, taking off his gloves in the meantime. "What it is, Helen?" he enquired.

"Oh, Daddy!" exclaimed the girl again, and lifted herself up and turned her laughing eyes upon him. "And now I understand why inspired people have to live in the country!"

"What was it, Helen?"

"It—it wasn't anything, Daddy, except that I was playing and singing for Arthur, and I forgot to close the windows."

"You must remember, my love, that you live in a clergyman's house," said Mr. Davis. "I have no objection to merriment, but it must be within bounds. Mr. Nelson said that he did not know what to think was the matter."

Helen made a wry face at the name; the Nelsons were a family of Methodists who lived across the way. Methodists are people who take life seriously as a rule, and Helen thought the Nelsons were very queer indeed.

"I'll bet he did know what to think," she chuckled, "even if he didn't say it; he thought that was just what to expect from a clergyman who had a decanter of wine on his dinner table."

Mr. Davis could not help smiling. And as for Helen, she was herself all over again; for when her father had come in, she had about reached a point where she could no longer bear to be serious and unhappy. As he went on to ask her to be a little less reckless, Helen put her arms around him and said, with the solemnity that she always wore when she was gayest: "But, Daddy, I don't know what I'm to do; you sent me to Germany to study music, and if I'm never to play it—"

"Yes, but Helen; such frantic, dreadful noise!"

"But, Daddy, the Germans are emotional people, you know; no one would have been in the least surprised at that in Germany; it was a hymn, Daddy!"

"A hymn!" gasped Mr. Davis.

"Yes, honestly," said Helen. "It is a wonderful hymn. Every German knows it nearly by heart."

Mr. Davis had as much knowledge of German music as might be expected of one who had lived twenty years in the country and heard three hymns and an anthem sung every Sunday by a volunteer choir. Helen's musical education, as all her other education, had been superintended by Aunt Polly, and the only idea that came to Mr. Davis' mind was of Wagner, whose name he had heard people talk about in connection with noise and incoherency.

"Helen," he said, "I trust that is not the kind of hymn you are going to sing to-morrow."

"I don't know," was the puzzled reply. "I'll see what I can do, Daddy. It's dreadfully hard to find anything in German music like the slow-going, practical lives that we dull Yankees lead." Then a sudden idea occurred to the girl, and she ran to the piano with a gleeful laugh: "Just see, for instance," she said, fumbling hurriedly amongst her music, "I was playing the Moonlight Sonata this morning, and that's a good instance."

"This is the kind of moonlight they have in Germany," she laughed when she found it. After hammering out a few discords of her own she started recklessly into the incomprehensible "presto," thundering away at every crescendo as if to break her fingers. "Isn't it fine, Daddy?" she cried, gazing over her shoulder.

"I don't see what it has to do with the moon," said the clergyman, gazing helplessly at the open window, and wondering if another crowd was gathering.

"That's what everybody's been trying to find out!" said Helen; then, as she heard the dinner bell out in the hall, she ended with half a dozen frantic runs, and jumping up with the last of them, took her father's arm and danced out of the room with him.

"Perhaps when we come to see the other side of the moon," she said, "we may discover all about it. Or else it's because the moon is supposed to set people crazy." So they passed in to dinner, where Helen was as animated as ever, poor Arthur and his troubles seeming to have vanished completely from her thoughts.

In fact, it was not until the meal was nearly over that she spoke of them again; she noticed that it was growing dark outside, and she stepped to the window just as a distant rumble of thunder was heard.

"Dear me!" she exclaimed. "There's a fearful storm coming, and poor Arthur is out in it; he must be a long way from town by this time, and there is no house where he can go." From the window where she stood she had a view across the hills in back of the town, and could see the black clouds coming swiftly on. "It is like we were imagining this morning," she mused; "I wonder if he will think of it."

The dinner was over soon after that, and she looked out again, just as the first drops of rain were falling; the thunder was rolling louder, bringing to Helen a faint echo of her morning music. She went in and sat down at the piano, her fingers roaming over the keys hesitatingly. "I wish I could get it again," she mused. "It seems like a dream when I think of it, it was so wild and so wonderful. Oh, if I could only remember that march!"

There came a crash of thunder near by, as if to help her, but Helen found that all efforts were in vain. Neither the storm music nor the march came back to her, and even when she played a few chords of the great chorus she had sung, it sounded tame and commonplace. Helen knew that the glory of that morning was gone where goes the best inspiration of all humanity, back into nothingness and night.

"It was a shame," she thought, as she rose discontentedly from the piano. "I never was so carried away by music in my life, and the memory of it would have kept me happy for weeks, if Arthur hadn't been here to trouble me!"

Then, however, as she went to the window again to watch the storm which was now raging in all its majesty, she added more unselfishly: "Poor boy! It is dreadful to think of him being out in it." She saw a bolt of lightning strike in the distance, and she waited breathlessly for the thunder. It was a fearful crash, and it made her blood run faster, and her eyes sparkle. "My!" she exclaimed. "But it's fine!" And then she added with a laugh, "He can correct his poem by it, if he wants to!"

She turned to go upstairs. On the way she stopped with a rather conscience-stricken look, and said to herself, "Poor fellow! It seems a shame to be happy!" She stood for a moment thinking, but then she added, "Yet I declare, I don't know what to do for him; it surely isn't my fault if I am not in love with him in that mad fashion, and I don't see why I should make myself wretched about it!" Having thus silenced her conscience, she went up to unpack her trunks, humming to herself on the way:

"Sir Knight, a faithful sister's love
This heart devotes to thee;
I pray thee ask no other love,
For pain that causes me.

"Quiet would I see thee come,
And quiet see thee go;
The silent weeping of thine eyes
I cannot bear to know."

While she was singing Arthur was in the midst of the tempest, staggering towards his home ten miles away. He was drenched by the cold rain, and shivering and almost fainting from exhaustion— for he had eaten nothing since early dawn; yet so wretched and sick at heart was he that he felt nothing, and scarcely heard the storm or realized where he was.

Chapter IV

"Dosn't thou 'ear my 'erse's legs, as they canters awaay?
Proputty, proputty, proputty—that's what I 'ears 'em saay.
But I knawed a Quaaker feller as often 'as towd ma this:
'Doant thou marry for munny, but goa wheer munny is!'"

Helen had much to do to keep her busy during the next few days. She had in the first place to receive visits from nearly everybody in Oakdale, for she was a general favorite in the town, and besides that everyone was curious to see what effect the trip had had upon her beauty and accomplishments. Then too, she had the unpacking of an incredible number of trunks; it was true that Helen, having been a favored boarder at an aristocratic seminary, was not in the habit of doing anything troublesome herself, but she considered it necessary to superintend the servant. Last of all there was a great event at the house of her aunt, Mrs. Roberts, to be anticipated and prepared for.

It has been said that the marriage of Mr. Davis had been a second romance in that worthy man's career, he having had the fortune to win the love of a daughter of a very wealthy family which lived near Oakdale. The parents had of course been bitterly opposed to the match, but the girl had had her way. Unfortunately, however, the lovers, or at any rate the bride, having been without any real idea of duty or sacrifice, the match had proved one of those that serve to justify the opinions of people who are "sensible;" the young wife, wearying of the lot she had chosen, had sunk into a state of peevish discontent from which death came to relieve her.

Of this prodigal daughter Aunt Polly was the elder, and wiser, sister. She had never ceased to urge upon the other, both before and after marriage, the folly of her conduct, and had lived herself to be a proof of her own more excellent sense, having married a wealthy stockbroker who proved a good investment, trebling his own capital and hers in a few years. Aunt Polly therefore had a fine home upon Madison Avenue in New York, and a most aristocratic country-seat a few miles from Oakdale, together with the privilege of frequenting the best society in New York, and of choosing her friends amongst the most wealthy in the neighborhood of the little town. This superiority to her erring sister had probably been one of the causes that had contributed to develop the most prominent trait in her character—which is perhaps the most prominent trait of high society in general—a complete satisfaction with the world she knew, and what she knew about it, and the part she played in it. For the rest, Aunt Polly was one of those bustling little women who rule the world in almost everything, because the world finds it is too much trouble to oppose them. She had assumed, and had generally succeeded in having recognized, a complete superiority to Mr. Davis in her knowledge about life, with the result that, as has been stated, the education of the one child of the unfortunate marriage had been managed by her.

When, therefore, Helen had come off the steamer, it had been Mrs. Roberts who was there to meet her; and the arrangement announced was that the girl was to have three days to spend with her father, and was then to come for a week or two at her aunt's, who was just opening her country home and who intended to invite a score of people whom she considered, for reasons of her own, proper persons for her niece to meet. Mrs. Roberts spoke very condescendingly indeed of the company which Helen met at her father's, Mr. Davis having his own opinions about the duty of a clergyman toward the non-aristocratic members of his flock.

The arrangement, it is scarcely necessary to say, pleased Helen very much indeed; the atmosphere of luxury and easy superiority which she found at her aunt's was much to her taste, and she looked forward to being a center of attraction there with the keenest delight. In the meantime, however, she slaked her thirst for happiness just as well at Oakdale, accepting with queenly grace the homage of all who came to lay their presents at her feet. Sunday proved to be a day of triumph, for all the town had come to church, and was as much stirred by the glory of her singing as Arthur had predicted. After the service everyone waited to tell her about it, and so she was radiant indeed.

By Tuesday, however, all that had come to seem a trifling matter, for that afternoon Aunt Polly was to come, and a new world was to be opened for her conquest. Helen was amusing herself by sorting out the motley collection of souvenirs and curios which she had brought home to decorate her room, when she heard a carriage drive up at the door, and a minute later heard the voice of Mrs. Roberts' footman in the hall.

Mrs. Roberts herself did not alight, and Helen kept her waiting only long enough to slip on her hat, and to bid her father a hurried farewell. In a minute more she was in the carriage, and was being borne in state down the main street of Oakdale.

"You are beautiful to-day, my dear," said her aunt, beaming upon her; "I hope you are all ready for your triumph."

"I think so," said Helen. "I've about seen everybody and everything I wanted to at home; I've been wonderfully happy, Auntie."

"That is right, my dear," said Aunt Polly. "You have certainly every cause to be, and you would be foolish not to make the most of it. But I should think this town would seem a somewhat less important place to you, after all that you have seen of the world."

"Yes, it does a little," laughed Helen, "but it seemed good to see all the old people again."

"Someone told me they saw Arthur here on Saturday," said the other. "Did you see *him?*"

"Oh, yes," said Helen; "that's what he came for. You can fancy how glad I was to meet him. I spent a couple of hours walking in the woods with him."

Mrs. Roberts' look of dismay may be imagined; it was far too great for her to hide.

"Where is he now?" she asked, hastily.

"Oh, he has gone home," said Helen; and she added, smiling, "he went on Saturday afternoon, because he's writing a poem about thunderstorms, and he wanted to study that one."

The other was sufficiently convinced of the irresponsibility of poets to be half uncertain whether Helen was joking or not; it was very frequently difficult to tell, anyway, for Helen would look serious and amuse herself by watching another person's mystification—a trait of character which would have been intolerable in anyone less fascinating than she.

Perhaps Aunt Polly thought something of that as she sat and watched the girl. Aunt Polly was a little woman who looked as if she herself might have once made some pretense to being a belle, but she was very humble before Helen. "My dear," she said, "every minute that I watch you, I am astonished to see how wonderfully you have grown. Do you know, Helen, you are glorious!"

"Yes," said Helen, smiling delightedly. "Isn't it nice, Aunt Polly? I'm so glad I'm beautiful."

"You funny child," laughed the other. "What a queer thing to say!"

"Am I not to know I am beautiful?" inquired Helen, looking at her with open eyes. "Why, dear me! I can look at myself in the glass and be just as happy as anyone else; I love everything beautiful."

Aunt Polly beamed upon her. "I am glad of it, my dear," she laughed. "I only wish I could say something to you to make you realize what your wonderful beauty means."

"How, Aunt Polly?" asked the girl. "Have you been reading poetry?"

"No," said the other, "not exactly; but you know very well in your heart what hopes I have for you, Helen, and I only wish you could appreciate the gift that has been given you, and not fling it away in any foolish fashion. With your talents and your education, my dear, there is almost nothing that you might not do."

"Yes," said Helen, with all of her seriousness, "I often think of it; perhaps, Auntie, I might become a poetess!"

The other looked aghast. Helen had seen the look on her aunt's face at the mention of her walk with Arthur, and being a young lady of electrical wit, had understood just what it meant, and just how the rest of the conversation was intended to bear upon the matter; with that advantage she was quite in her glory.

"No, indeed, Aunt Polly," she said, "you can never tell; just suppose, for instance, I were to fall in love with and marry a man of wonderful genius, who would help me to devote myself to art? It would not make any difference, you know, if he were poor—we could struggle and help each other. And oh, I tell you, if I were to meet such a man, and to know that he loved me truly, and to have proof that he could remember me and be true to me, even when I was far away, oh, I tell you, nothing could ever keep me—"

Helen was declaiming her glowing speech with real fervor, her hands dramatically outstretched. But she could not get any further, for the look of utter horror upon her auditor's face was too much for her; she dropped her hands and made the air echo with her laughter.

"Oh, Aunt Polly, you goose!" she cried, flinging one arm about her, "have you really forgotten me that much in three years?"

The other was so relieved at the happy denouement of that fearful tragedy that she could only protest, "Helen, Helen, why do you fool me so?"

"Because you fool me, or try to," said Helen. "When you have a sermon to preach on the impropriety of walking in the woods alone with a susceptible young poet, I wish you'd mount formally into the pulpit and begin with the text."

"My dear," laughed the other, "you are too quick; but I must confess—"

"Of course you must," said the girl; and she folded her hands meekly and looked grave. "And now I am ready; and if you meet with any difficulties in the course of your sermon, I've an expert at home who has preached one hundred and four every year for twenty years, all genuine and no two alike."

"Helen," said the other, "I do wish you would talk seriously with me. You are old enough to be your own mistress now, and to do as you please, but you ought to realize that I have seen the world more than you, and that my advice is worth something."

"Tell it to me," said Helen, ceasing to laugh, and leaning back in the carriage and gazing at her aunt. "What do you want me to do, now that I am home? I will be really serious if you wish me to, for that does interest me. I suppose that my education is finished?"

"Yes," said the other, "it ought to be, certainly; you have had every advantage that a girl can have, a great deal more than I ever had. And you owe it all to me, Helen,—you do, really; if it hadn't been for my insisting you'd have gotten all your education at Hilltown, and you'd have played the piano and sung like Mary Nelson across the way."

Helen shuddered, and felt that that was cause indeed for gratitude.

"It is true," said her aunt; "I've taken as much interest in you as in any one of my own children, and you must know it. It was for no reason at all but that I saw what a wonderful woman you promised to become, and I was anxious to help you to the social position that I thought you ought to have. And now, Helen, the chance is yours if you care to take it."

"I am taking it, am I not?" asked Helen; "I'm going with you, and I shall be just as charming as I can."

"Yes, I know," said the other, smiling a little; "but that is not exactly what I mean."

"What do you mean?"

"Of course, my dear, you may enter good society a while by visiting me; but that will not be permanently. You will have to marry into it, Helen dear."

"Marry!" echoed the girl, taken aback. "Dear me!"

"You will wish to marry some time," said the other, "and so you should look forward to it and choose your course. With your charms, Helen, there is almost nothing that you might not hope for; you must know yourself that you could make any man fall in love with you that you wished. And you ought to know also that if you only had wealth you could enter any society; for you have good birth, and you will discover that you have more knowledge and more wit than most of the people you meet."

"I've discovered that already," said Helen, laughing.

"All that you must do, my love," went on the other, "is to realize what is before you, and make up your mind to what you want. You know that your tastes are not those of a poor woman; you have been accustomed to comfort, and you need refinement and wealth; you could never be happy unless you could entertain your friends properly, and live as you pleased."

"But I don't want to marry a man just for his money," protested the girl, not altogether pleased with her aunt's business-like view.

"No one wants you to," the other responded; "you may marry for love if you like; but it is not impossible to love a rich man, is it, Helen?"

"But, Aunt Polly," said Helen, "I am satisfied as I am now. I do not want to marry anybody. The very idea makes me shudder."

"I am not in the least anxious that you should," was the answer. "You are young, and you may choose your own time. All I am anxious for is that you should realize the future that is before you. It is dreadful to me to think that you might throw your precious chance away by some ridiculous folly."

Helen looked at her aunt for a moment, and then the irrepressible smile broke out.

"What is the matter, child?" asked the other.

"Nothing, except that I was thinking about how these thoughts were brought up."

"How do you mean?"

"Apropos of my woodland walk with poor Arthur. Auntie, I do believe you're afraid I'm going to fall in love with the dear fellow."

"No," said Aunt Polly; "it is not exactly that, for I'd never be able to sleep at night if I thought you capable of anything quite so ghastly. But we must have some care of what people will think, my dear Helen."

As a matter of fact, Aunt Polly did have some very serious fears about the matter, as has been hinted before; it was, perhaps, a kind of tribute to the divine fire which even society's leaders pay. If it had been a question of a person of her own sense and experience, the word "genius" would have suggested no danger to Mrs. Roberts, but it was different with a young and probably sentimental person like Helen, with her inflaming beauty.

"As a matter of fact, Aunt Polly," said Helen, "everybody understands my intimacy with Arthur."

"Tell me, Helen dear," said the other, turning her keen glance upon her; "tell me the honest truth."

"About what?"

"You are not in love with Arthur?"

And Helen answered her with her eyes very wide open: "No, I certainly am not in the least."

And the other drew secretly a great breath of relief. "Is he in love with you, Helen?" she asked.

As Helen thought of Arthur's departure, the question could not but bring a smile. "I—I'm afraid he is," she said.—"a very little."

"What a ridiculous impertinence!" exclaimed the other, indignantly.

"Oh, that's all right, Auntie," said Helen; "he really can't help it, you know." She paused for a moment, and then she went on: "Such things used to puzzle me when I was very young, and I used to think them quite exciting; but I'm getting used to them now. All the men seem to fall in love with me,—they do, honestly, and I don't know how in the world to help it. They all will make themselves wretched, and I'm sure it isn't my fault. I haven't told you anything about my German lovers, have I, Auntie?"

"Gracious, no!" said the other; "were there any?"

"Any?" laughed the girl. "I might have robbed the Emperor of a whole colonel's staff, and the colonel at the head of it. But I'll tell you about Johann, the funniest one of all; I think he really loved me more than all the rest."

"Pray, who was Johann?" asked Aunt Polly, thinking how fortunate it was that she learned of these things only after the danger was over.

"I never will forget the first time I met him," laughed the girl, "the first day I went to the school. Johann was a little boy who opened the door for me, and he stared at me as if he were in a trance; he had the most wonderful round eyes, and puffy red cheeks that made me always think I'd happened to ring the bell while he was eating; and every time after that he saw me for three years he used to gaze at me in the same helpless wonder, with all lingers of his fat little hands wide apart."

"What a disagreeable wretch!" said the other.

"Not in the least," laughed Helen; "I liked him. But the funniest part came afterwards, for when I came away Johann had grown a whole foot, and was quite a man. I sent for him to put the straps on my trunks, and guess what he did! He stared at me for a minute, just the same as ever, and then he ran out of the room, blubbering like a baby; and that's the last I ever saw of him."

Helen was laughing as she told the story, but then she stopped and looked a little conscience-stricken. "Do you know, Aunt Polly," she said, "it is really a dreadful thing to make people unhappy like that; I suppose poor Johann had spent three whole years dreaming about the enchanted castle in which I was to be fairy princess."

"It was a good chance for a romantic marriage," said the other.

"Yes," said the girl, laughing again; "I tried to fancy it. He'd have kept a Wirthshaus, I suppose, and I'd have served the guests; and Arthur might have come, and I'd have cut Butterbrod for him and he could have been my Werther! Wouldn't Arthur have made a fine Werther, though, Aunt Polly?"

"And blown his brains out afterwards," added the other.

"No," said Helen, "brains are too scarce; I'd rather have him follow Goethe's example and write a book about it instead. You know I don't believe half the things these poets tell you, for I think they put themselves through their dreadful experiences just to tell about them and make themselves famous. Don't you believe that, Auntie?"

"I don't know," said the other (a statement which she seldom made). "I don't know much about such things. Nobody reads poetry any more, you know, Helen, and it doesn't really help one along very much."

"It doesn't do any harm, does it?" inquired the girl, smiling to herself, "just a little, once in a while?"

"Oh, no, of course not," said the other; "I believe that a woman ought to have a broad education, for she never knows what may be the whims of the men she meets, or what turn a conversation may take. All I'm afraid of, Helen, is that if you fill your mind with sentimental ideas you might be so silly as to fancy that you were doing something romantic in throwing your one great chance away upon some worthless nobody. I want you to realize what you are, Helen, and that you owe something to yourself, and to your family, too; for the Roberts have always had wealth and position until your mother chose to marry a poor man. What I warn you of now is exactly what I warned her of. Your father is a good man, but he had absolutely nothing to make your mother happy; she was cut off from everything she had been used to,—she could not even keep a carriage. And of course she could not receive her old friends, very few of them cared to have anything more to do with her, and so she simply pined away in discontentment and miserable poverty. You have had an easy life, Helen, and you have no idea of what a horrible thing it is to be poor; you have had the best of teachers, and you have lived at an expensive school, and of course you have always had me to rely upon to introduce you to the right people; but if you married a poor man you couldn't expect to keep any of those advantages. I don't speak of your marrying a man who had no money at all, for that would be too fearful to talk about; but suppose you were to take any one of the young men you might meet at Oakdale even, you'd have to live in a mean little house, and do with one or two servants, and worry yourself about the butcher's bills and brush your own dresses and drive your own horse. And how long do you suppose it would be before you repented of that? Think of having to be like those poor Masons, for instance; they are nice people, and I like them, but I hate to go there, for every time I can't help seeing that the parlor furniture is more dingy, and thinking how miserable they must be, not to be able to buy new things. And their servants' liveries are half worn too; and when you dine there you see that Mrs. Mason is eating with a plated fork, because she has not enough of her best silver to go around. All those things are trifles, Helen, but think of the worry they must give those poor people, who are pinching themselves and wearing themselves out soul and body, trying to keep in the station where they belong, or used to. Poor Mrs. Mason is pale and nervous and wrinkled at forty, and those three poor girls, who spend their time making over their old dresses, are so dowdy- looking and uneasy that no man ever glances at them twice. It is such misery as that which I dread for you, Helen, and why I am talking to you. There is no reason why you should take upon you such sorrows; you have a clear head, and you can think for yourself and make up your mind about things if you only won't blind yourself by foolish sentimentality. You have been brought up to a certain station in life, and no man has a right to offer himself to you unless he can maintain you in that station. There is really no scarcity of such men, Helen, and you'd have no trouble in finding one. There are hundreds of men in New York who are worth millions, and who would fling themselves and their wealth at your feet if you would have them. And you would find such a difference between the opportunities of pleasure and command that such a chance would give you and the narrow life that you lead in this little town that you would wonder how you could ever have been satisfied. It is difficult for you to realize what I mean, my dear, because you have only a schoolgirl's knowledge of life and its pleasures, but when you are in the world, and have learned what power is, and what it means to possess such beauty as yours, you will feel your heart swelling with a new pleasure, and you will thank me for what I tell you. I have figured a wonderful triumph for you, Helen, and it is time you knew what is before you. Of what use is your beauty, if you do not carry it into a wide enough sphere, where it can bring you the admiration and homage you deserve? You need such a field, Helen, to discover your own powers in; believe me, my dear, there is really a higher ambition in the world than to be a country clergyman's daughter."

"Is there any higher than being happy, Auntie?" asked Helen.

The importance of that observation was beyond the other's ken, as indeed it was beyond Helen's also; she had thrown it out as a chance remark.

"Mr. Roberts and I were talking about this last night," went on Aunt Polly, "and he told me that I ought to talk seriously to you about it, and get you to realize what a golden future is before you. For it is really true, Helen, as sure as you can trust what I know about the world, that you can have absolutely anything that you want. That is the long and short of the matter—anything that you want! And why should you not have the very best that life can give you? Why should you have to know that other people dwell in finer houses than yours, and are free from cares that make you ill? Why should you have the humiliation of being looked down upon and scorned by other people? Are these other people more entitled to luxury than you, or more able to enjoy it; or could anyone do it more honor than you? You are beautiful beyond telling; you have every gift that a woman can ask to complete enjoyment of life; you are perfect, Helen, you are really perfect! You *must* know that; you must say it to yourself when you are alone, and know that your life ought to be a queenly triumph. You have only to stretch out your arms and everything will come to you; and there is really and truly no end to the happiness you can taste."

Helen was gazing at the other with real earnestness, and the words were sinking deep into her soul, deeper than words generally sunk there. She felt her cheeks burning, and her frame stirred by a new emotion; she had seldom before thought of anything but the happiness of the hour.

"Just think of it, my love," continued Mrs. Roberts, "and know that that is what your old auntie was thinking of when you were only a little tiny girl, sitting upon her knee, and when you were so beautiful that artists used to beg to have you pose for them. I never said anything about it then, because you were too young to understand these things; but now that you are to manage yourself, I have been waiting for a chance to tell you, so that you may see what a prize is yours if you are only wise. And if you wonder why I have cared so much and thought so much of what might be yours, the only reason I can give is that you are my niece, and that I felt that any triumph you might win would be mine. I want you to win a higher place in the world than mine, Helen; I never had such a gift as yours."

Helen was silent for a minute, deeply thoughtful.

"Tell me, Auntie," she asked, "and is it really true, then, that a woman is to train herself and grow beautiful and to have so much trouble and money spent upon her—only for her marriage?"

"Why of course, Helen; what else can a woman do? Unless you have money and a husband you cannot possibly hope to accomplish anything in society. With your talents and your beauty you might go anywhere and rule anywhere, but you have to have money before you can even begin."

"But where am I to meet such a rich man, Aunt Polly?" asked Helen.

"You know perfectly well where. Do you suppose that after I have worried myself about you all this time I mean to desert you now, when you are at the very climax of your glory, when you are all that I ever dared dream of? My dear Helen, I am more interested in you just now than in anything else in the world. I feel as a card player feels when millions are at stake, and when he knows that he holds the perfect hand."

"That is very nice," said Helen, laughing nervously. "But there is always a chance of mistake."

"There is none this time, Helen, for I am an old player, and I have been picking and arranging my hand for long, long years;

and you are the hand, my love, and the greatest glory of it all must be yours."

Helen's heart was throbbing still faster with excitement, as if she were already tasting the wonderful triumph that was before her; her aunt was watching her closely, noting how the blood was mounting to her bright cheeks. The girl felt herself suddenly choking with her pent up excitement, and she stretched out her arms with a strange laugh.

"Auntie," she said, "you tell me too much at once."

The other had been marshaling her forces like a general during the last few minutes, and she felt just then as if there were nothing left but the rout. "All that I tell you, you may see for yourself," she said. "I don't ask you to take anything on my word, for you have only to look in the glass and compare yourself with the women you meet. You will find that all men will turn their eyes upon you when you enter a room."

Helen did not consider it necessary to debate that question. "You have invited some rich man to meet me at your house?" she asked.

"I was going to say nothing to you about it at first," said the other, "and let you find out. But I thought afterwards that it would be better to tell you, so that you could manage for yourself. I have invited all the men whom Mr. Roberts and I thought it would be best for you to meet."

Helen gazed at her aunt silently for a moment, and then she broke into a nervous laugh. "A regular exposition!" she said; "and you'll bring them out one by one and put them through their paces, won't you, Auntie? And have them labeled for comparison,—so that I can tell just what stocks they own and how they stand on the 'Street'! Do you remember the suitor in Moliere?—'J'ai quinze mille livres de rente; j'ai le corps sain; j'ai des beaux dents!_'"

It was a flash of Helen's old merriment, but it did not seem so natural as usual, even to her. She forced herself to laugh, for she was growing more and more excited and uneasy.

"My dear," said Aunt Polly, "please do not begin making fun again."

"But you must let me joke a little, Auntie," said the girl. "I have never been serious for so long before."

"You ought to be serious about it, my dear."

"I will," said Helen. "I have really listened attentively; you must tell me all about these rich men that I am to meet, and what I am to do. I hope I am not the only girl."

"Of course not," was the response; "I would not do anything ridiculous. I have invited a number of other girls—but they won't trouble you in the least."

"No," said Helen. "I am not afraid of other girls; but what's to be done? It's a sort of house-warming, I suppose?"

"Yes," was the reply, "I suppose so, for I only came down last week myself. I have asked about twenty people for a week or two; they all know each other, more or less, so there won't be much formality. We shall amuse ourselves with coaching and golf, and anything else we please; and of course there will be plenty of music in the evening."

Helen smiled at the significant tone of her aunt's voice. "Are the people there now?" she asked.

"Those who live anywhere in the neighborhood are; most of the men will be down on the afternoon train, in time for dinner."

"And tell me who are the men, Auntie?"

"I'm afraid I won't have time," said Mrs. Roberts, glancing out of the carriage. "We are too near home. But I will tell you about one of them, if you like."

"The king-bee?" laughed Helen. "Is there a king-bee?"

"Yes," said Mrs. Roberts; "there is. At any rate, my husband and I think he is, and we are anxious to see what you think. His name is Gerald Harrison, and he comes from Cincinnati."

"Oh, dear," said Helen, "I hate to meet men from the West. He must be a pork-packer, or something horrible."

"No," said the other, "he is a railroad president."

"And why do you think he's the king-bee; is he very rich?"

"He is worth about ten million dollars," said Aunt Polly.

Helen gazed at her wildly. "Ten million dollars!" she gasped.

"Yes," said the other; "about that, probably a little more. Mr. Roberts knows all about his affairs."

Helen was staring into her aunt's face. "Tell me," she asked, very nervously indeed. "Tell me, honestly!"

"What?"

"Is that the man you are bringing me here to meet?"

"Yes, Helen," said the other quietly.

The girl's hands were clasped tightly together just then. "Aunt Polly," she asked, "what kind of a man is he? I will not marry a bad man!"

"A bad man, child? How ridiculous! Do you suppose I would ask you to marry a bad man, if he owned all New York? I want you to be happy. Mr. Harrison is a man who has made his own fortune, and he is a man of tremendous energy. Everyone is obliged to respect him."

"But he must be old, Auntie."

"He is very young, Helen, only about forty."

"Dear me," said the girl, "I could never marry a man as old as forty; and then, I'd have to go out West!"

"Mr. Harrison has come to New York to live," was the other's reply. "He has just bought a really magnificent country seat about ten miles from here—the old Everson place, if you remember it; and he is negotiating for a house near ours in the city. My husband and I both agreed, Helen, that if you could make Mr. Harrison fall in love with you it would be all that we could desire."

"That is not the real problem," Helen said, gazing out of the carriage with a frightened look upon her face; "it is whether I can fall in love with him. Aunt Polly, it is dreadful to me to think of marrying; I don't want to marry! I don't care who the man is!"

"We'll see about that later on," said the other, smiling reassuringly, and at the same time putting her arm about the girl; "there is no hurry, my love, and no one has the least thought of asking you to do what you do not want to do. But a chance like this does not come often to any girl, my dear. Mr. Harrison is in every way a desirable man."

"But he's stupid, Aunt Polly, I know he's stupid! All self-made men are; they tell you about how they made themselves, and what wonderful things they hare made!"

"You must of course not expect to find Mr. Harrison as cultured as yourself, Helen," was the reply; "his education has been that of the world, and not of books. But nobody thinks less of a man for that in the world; the most one can ask is that he does not make pretenses. And he is very far from stupid, I assure you, or he would not have been what he is."

"I suppose not," said Helen, weakly.

"And, besides," observed Aunt Polly, laughing to cheer the girl up, "I assure you it doesn't make any difference. My husband makes no pretense to being a wit, or a musician, or anything like that; he's just a plain, sensible man, but we get along as happily as you could wish. We each of us go our own way, and understand each other perfectly."

"So I'm to marry a plain, sensible man?" asked the girl, apparently not much comforted by the observation.

"A plain, sensible man with ten million dollars, my dear," said Aunt Polly, "who adores you and has nothing to do with his money but to let you make yourself happy and glorious with it? But don't worry yourself, my child, because the first thing for you to feel is that if you don't like him you need not take him. It all rests upon you; he won't be here till after the rest, till the evening train, so you can have time to think it over and calculate whether ten million dollars will buy anything you want." And Mrs. Roberts laughed.

Then the carriage having passed within the gates of her home, she kissed the girl upon her cheek. "By the way," she added, "if you want to meet a romantic person to offset Mr. Harrison, I'll tell you about Mr. Howard. I haven't mentioned him, have I?"

"I never heard of him," said Helen.

"It's a real romance," said the other. "You didn't suppose that your sensible old auntie could have a romance, did you?"

"Tell me about it," laughed Helen.

The carriage was driving up the broad avenue that led to the Roberts house; it was a drive of a minute or two, however, and so Aunt Polly had time for a hasty explanation.

"It was over twenty years ago," she said, "before your mother was married, and when our family had a camp up in the Adirondacks; there were only two others near us, and in each of them there was a young man about my age. We three were great friends for three or four years, but we've never seen each other since till a short while ago."

"And one of them is this man?"

"Yes," said Mrs. Roberts; "his name is David Howard; I met him quite by accident the other day, and recognized him. He lives all alone, in the winter in New York somewheres, and in the summer up at the same place in the mountains; he's the most romantic man you ever met, and I know you'll find him interesting. He's a poet, I fancy, or a musician at any rate, and he's a very great scholar."

"Is he rich too?" asked the girl, laughing.

"I fancy not," was the reply, "but I can't tell; he lives very plainly."

"Aren't you afraid I'll fall in love with him, Auntie?"

"No," said the other, smiling to herself; "I'm not worrying about that."

"Why not?"

"Wait till you see him, my dear," was the reply; "if you choose him for a husband I'll give my consent."

"That sounds mysterious," observed the girl, gazing at her aunt; "tell me, is he here now?"

"Yes," said Aunt Polly; "he's been here a day or two; but I don't think you'll see him at dinner, because he has been feeling unwell today; he may be down a while this evening, for I've been telling him about you, and he's anxious to see you. You must be nice to him, Helen, and try to feel as sorry for him as I do."

"Sorry for him?" echoed the girl with a start.

"Yes, my dear, he is an invalid, with some very dreadful affliction."

And Helen stared at her aunt. "An affliction!" she cried. "Aunt Polly, that is horrible! What in the world did you invite an invalid for at this time, with all the other people? I *hate* invalids!"

"I had asked him before," was the apologetic reply, "and so I couldn't help it. I had great difficulty in getting him to promise to come anyway, for he's a very strange, solitary man. But I wanted to have my little romance, and renew our acquaintance, and this was the only time the third party could come."

"Oh, the third one is here too?"

"He will be in a day or two."

"Who is he?"

"His name is Lieutenant Maynard, and he's in the navy; he's stationed at Brooklyn just now, but he expects to get leave for a while."

"That is a little better," Helen remarked, as the carriage was drawing up in front of the great house. "I'd marry a naval officer."

"No," laughed Aunt Polly; "he leaves a wife and some children in Brooklyn. We three are going to keep to ourselves and talk about old times and what has happened to us since then, and so you young folks will not be troubled by us."

"I hope you will," said the other, "for I can't ever be happy with invalids."

And there, as the carriage door was opened, the conversation ended abruptly. When Helen had sprung out she found that there were six or eight people upon the piazza, to whom the excitement of being introduced drove from her mind for a time all thoughts which her aunt's words had brought.

Chapter V

"If chance will have me king, why chance may crown me,
Without my stir."

Most of the people whom Helen met upon her arrival were of her own sex, so that she did not feel called upon to make special exertions to please them; but she was naturally cheerful and happy with everyone, and the other matters of which Mrs. Roberts had talked took on such vast proportions before her mind that it was a relief to her to put them aside and enjoy herself for a while in her usual way. Helen was glad that most of the men were to arrive later, so that she might make her appearance before them under the most favorable circumstances. When she heard the distant whistle of the afternoon train a couple of hours later, it was with that thought that she retired to her room to rest before dressing.

Aunt Polly, following her plan of accustoming the girl to a proper style of living, had engaged a maid to attend her during her stay; and Helen found therefore that her trunks were unpacked and everything in order. It was a great relief to her to be rid of all care, and she took off her dress and flung herself down upon the bed to think.

Helen had imbided during her Sunday-school days the usual formulas of dogmatic religion, but upon matters of morality her ideas were of the vaguest possible description. The guide of her life had always been her instinct for happiness, her "genial sense of youth." She had never formulated any rule of life to herself, but

that which she sought was joy, primarily for herself, and inciden-
tally for other people, because unhappy people were disturbing
(unless it were possible to avoid them). In debating within herself the arguments which her aunt had brought before her mind,
it was that principle chiefly by which she tested them.

To the girl's eager nature, keenly sensitive to pleasure and
greedy for it, the prospect so suddenly flung wide before her eyes
was so intoxicating that again and again as she thought of it it
made her tremble and burn. So far as Helen could see at that
moment, a marriage with this Mr. Harrison would mean the command of every source of happiness; and upon a scale so magnificent, so belittling of everything she had known before, that she
shrank from it as something impossible and unnatural. Again and
again she buried her heated brow in her hands and muttered: "I
ought to have known it before! I ought to have had time to realize
it."

That which restrained the girl from welcoming such an opportunity, from clasping it to her in ecstasy and flinging herself
madly into the whirl of pleasure it held out, was not so much
her conscience and the ideals which she had formed more or less
vaguely from the novels and poems she had read, as the instinct
of her maidenhood, which made her shrink from the thought of
marriage with a man whom she did not love. So strong was this
feeling in her that at first she felt that she could not even bear to
be introduced to him with such an idea in her mind.

It was Aunt Polly's wisdom and diplomacy which finally overcame her scruples enough to persuade her to that first step; Helen
kept thinking of her aunt's words—that no one wanted to compel
her to marry the man, that she might do just as she chose. She
argued that it was foolish to worry herself, or to be ill at ease. She
might see what sort of a man he was; if he fell in love with her
it would do no harm,—Helen was not long in discovering by the
increased pace of her pulses that she would find it exciting to have
everyone know that a multimillionaire was in love with her. "As
for the rest," she said to herself, "we'll see when the time comes,"

and knew not that one who goes to front his life's temptation with that resolution is a mariner who leaves the steering of his vessel to the tempest.

She had stilled her objection by such arguments, and was just beginning to feel the excitement of the prospect once more, when the maid knocked at the door and asked to know if mademoiselle were ready to dress for dinner. And mademoiselle arose and bathed her face and arms and was once more her old refreshed and rejoicing self, ready for that mysterious and wonderful process which was to send her out an hour or two later a vision of perfectness, compounded of the hues of the rose and the odors of evening, with the new and unutterable magic that is all the woman's own. Besides the prospects her aunt had spoken of, there were reasons enough why Helen should be radiant, for it was her first recognized appearance in high society; and so she sat in front of the tall mirror and criticised every detail of the coiffure which the maid prepared, and eyed by turns her gleaming neck and shoulders and the wonderful dress, as yet unworn, which shone from the bed through its covering of tissue paper; and was all the time so filled with joy and delight that it was a pleasure to be near her. Soon Aunt Polly, clad in plain black as a sign that she retired in favor of Helen, came in to assist and superintend the toilet. So serious at the task, and so filled with a sense of its importance and the issues that were staked upon it was she and the maid also, that one would not dare think of the humor of the situation if Helen herself had not broken the spell by declaring that she felt like an Ashantee warrior being decked out for battle with plumes and war paint, or like Rinaldo, or Amadis donning his armor.

And Helen was in fact going to war, a war for which nature has been training woman since the first fig-tree grew. She carried a bow strong as the one of Ulysses, which no man could draw, and an arrow sharp as the sunbeam and armed with a barb; for a helmet, beside her treasure of golden hair, she wore one rose, set there with the art that conceals art, so that it was no longer a red rose, but one more bright perfection that had come to ripeness

71

about the glowing maiden. Her dress was of the same color, a color which when worn upon a woman is a challenge, crying abroad that here is perfection beyond envy and beyond praise.

When the last touch was finished and Helen gazed upon herself, with her bare shoulders and arms and her throat so soft and white, she knew that she was, compared to all about her, a vision from another world. Chiefest of all, she knew that neither arms and shoulders, nor robe, nor gleaming hair, would ever be thought of when once the face that smiled upon her with its serene perfectness had caught the eye; she knew that as usual, men must start when they saw her, and never take their eyes from her. The thought filled her with an exulting consciousness of power, and reared her form with a new dignity, and made her chest heave and her cheeks burn with yet a new beauty.

When everything was ready, Aunt Polly's husband was called in to gaze upon her. A little man was Aunt Polly's husband, with black side whiskers and a head partly bald; a most quiet and unobtrusive person, looking just what he had been represented,—a "plain, sensible man," who attended to his half of the family affairs, and left the other half to his wife. He gazed upon Helen and blinked once or twice, as if blinded by so much beauty, and then took the end of her fingers very lightly in his and pronounced her "absolutely perfect." "And, my dear," he added, "it's after seven, so perhaps we'd best descend."

So he led the girl down to her triumph, to the handsome parlors of the house where eight or ten men were strolling about. It was quite exciting to Helen to meet them, for they were all strangers, and Aunt Polly had apparently considered Mr. Harrison of so much importance that she had said nothing about the others, leaving her niece at liberty to make what speculations she pleased.

It was a brilliant company which was seated in the dining room a short while later. As it was assembled in Helen's honor, Aunt Polly had taken care to bring those who would please the girl, and represent high life and luxury at its best; all of the guests were young, and therefore perfect. The members of the "smart set," when they have passed the third decade, are apt to show signs of weariness; a little of their beauty and health is gone, and some of their animation, and all of their joy,—so that one may be led to ask himself if there be not really something wrong about their views and ways of living. When they are young, however, they represent the possibilities of the human animal in all things external. In some wonderful way known only to themselves they have managed to manipulate the laws of men so as to make men do for them all the hard and painful tasks of life, so that they have no care but to make themselves as beautiful and as clever and as generally excellent as selfishness can be. Helen, of course, was not in the least troubled about the selfishness, and she was quite satisfied with externals. She saw about her perfect toilets and perfect manners; she saw everyone as happy as she liked everyone to be; and the result was that her spirits took fire, and she was clever and fascinating beyond even herself. She carried everything before her, and performed the real feat of dominating the table by her beauty and cleveness, without being either presumptuous or vain. Aunt Polly replied to the delighted looks of her husband at the other end of the table, and the two only wished that Mr. Harrison had been there then.

As a matter of fact, Helen had forgotten Mr. Harrison entirely, and he did not come back to her mind until the dinner was almost over, when suddenly she heard the bell ring. It was just the time that he was due to arrive, and so she knew that she would see him in another half hour. In the exultation of the present moment all of her hesitation was gone, and she was as ready to meet him as her aunt could have wished.

When the party rose a few minutes later and went into the parlors again, Helen was the first to enter, upon the arm of her neighbor. She was thinking of Mr. Harrison; and as she glanced about her, she could not keep from giving a slight start. Far down at the other end of the room she had caught sight of the figure of a man, and her first thought had been that it must be the millionaire. His frail, slender form was more than half concealed by the cushions of the sofa upon which he was seated, but even so, Helen could discover that he was a slight cripple.

The man rose as the party entered, and Aunt Polly went towards him; she apparently expected her niece to follow and be introduced to the stranger, but in the meantime the truth had occurred to Helen, that it must be the Mr. Howard she had been told of; she turned to one side with her partner, and began remarking the pictures in the room.

When she found opportunity, she glanced over and saw that the man had seated himself on the sofa and was talking to Mrs. Roberts. He looked, as Helen thought, all the invalid her aunt had described him to be, for his face was white and very wan, so that it made her shudder. "Dear me!" she exclaimed to herself, "I don't think such a man ought to go into public." And she turned resolutely away, and set herself to the task of forgetting him, which she very easily did.

A merry party was soon gathered about her, rejoicing in the glory of her presence, and listening to the stories which she told of her adventures in Europe. Helen kept the circle well in hand that way, and was equally ready when one of the young ladies turned the conversation off upon French poetry in the hope of eclipsing her. Thus her animation continued without rest until Mrs. Roberts escorted one of the guests to the piano to sing for them.

"She's keeping me for Mr. Harrison," thought Helen, laughing mischievously to herself; "and I suppose she's picked out the worst musician first, so as to build up a climax."

It seemed as if that might have been the plan for a fact; the performer sang part of Gluck's "J'ai perdu mon Eurydice," in strange French, and in a mournful voice which served very well to display the incompatibility of the melody and the words. As it happened, however, Mistress Helen heard not a word of the song, for it had scarcely begun before she turned her eyes towards the doorway and caught sight of a figure that drove all other ideas from her mind. Mr. Harrison had come at last.

He was a tall, dignified man, and Helen's first feeling was of relief to discover that he was neither coarse-looking, nor even plain. He had rather too bright a complexion, and rather too large a sandy mustache, but his clothes fitted him, and he seemed to be at ease as he glanced about him and waited in the doorway for the young lady at the piano to finish. While the faint applause was still sounding he entered with Mrs. Roberts, moving slowly across the room. "And now!" thought Helen, "now for it!"

As she expected, the two came towards her, and Mr. Harrison was presented; Helen, who was on the watch with all her faculties, decided that he bore that trial tolerably, for while his admiration of course showed itself, he did not stare, and he was not embarrassed.

"I am a little late, I fear," he said; "have I missed much of the music?"

"No," said Helen, "that was the first selection."

"I am glad of that," said the other.

According to the laws which regulate the drifting of conversation, it was next due that Helen should ask if he were fond of singing; and then that he should answer that he was very fond of it, which he did.

"Mrs. Roberts tells me you are a skillful musician," he added; "I trust that I shall hear you?"

Helen of course meant to play, and had devoted some thought to the selection of her program; therefore she answered: "Possibly; we shall see by and by."

"I am told that you have been studying in Germany," was the next observation. "Do you like Germany?"

"Very much," said Helen. "Only they made me work very hard at music, and at everything else."

"That is perhaps why you are a good player," said Mr. Harrison.

"You ought to wait until you hear me," the girl replied, following his example of choosing the most obvious thing to say.

"I fear I am not much of a critic," said the other.

And so the conversation drifted on for several minutes, Mr. Harrison's remarks being so very uninspiring that his companion could find no way to change the subject to anything worth talking about.

"Evidently," the girl thought, during a momentary lull, "he has learned all the rules of talking, and that's why he's at ease. But dear me, what an awful prospect! It would kill me to have to do this often. But then, to be sure I shan't see him in the day time, and in the evenings we should not be at home. One doesn't have to be too intimate with one's husband, I suppose. And then—"

"I think," said Mr. Harrison, "that your aunt is coming to ask you to play."

That was Aunt Polly's mission, for a fact, and Helen was much relieved, for she had found herself quite helpless to lift the conversation out of the slough of despond into which it had fallen; she wanted a little time to collect her faculties and think of something clever to start with again. When in answer to the request of Aunt Polly she arose and went to the piano, the crushed feeling of course left her, and her serenity returned; for Helen was at home at the piano, knowing that she could do whatever she chose, and do it without effort. It was a stimulus to her faculties to perceive that a general hush had fallen upon the room, and that every eye was upon her; as she sat down, therefore, all her old exultation was back.

She paused a moment to collect herself, and gave one easy glance down the room at the groups of people. She caught a glimpse as she did so of Mr. Howard, who was still seated upon the sofa, leaning forward and resting his chin in his hand and fixing his eyes upon her. At another time the sight of his wan face might perhaps have annoyed the girl, but she was carried beyond that just then by the excitement of the moment; her glance came back to the piano, and feeling that everyone was attentive and expectant, she began.

Helen numbered in her repertoire a good many pieces that were hopelessly beyond the technic of the average salon pianist, and she had chosen the most formidable with which to astonish her hearers that evening. She had her full share of that pleasure which people get from concerning themselves with great things: a pleasure which is responsible for much of the reading, and especially the discussing, of the world's great poets, and which brings forth many lofty sentiments from the numerous class of persons who combine idealism with vanity. Helen's selection was the first movement of the "Sonata Appassionata," and she was filled with a pleasing sense of majesty and importance as she began. She liked the first theme especially because it was striking and dignified and never failed to attract attention; and in what followed there was room for every shading of tone, from delicate softness that showed much feeling and sympathy, to stunning fortissimos that made everyone stare. The girl was relieved of any possible fear by the certainty that the composition was completely beyond her hearers' understanding, and so she soon lost herself in her task, and, as her excitement mounted, played with splendid spirit and abandon. Her calculations proved entirely well made, for when she stopped she received a real ovation, having genuinely astonished her hearers; and she crossed the room, beaming radiantly upon everyone and acknowledging their compliments, more assured of triumph than ever before. To cap the climax, when she reached her seat she found Mr. Harrison betraying completely his profound admiration, his gaze being riveted upon the glowing girl as she sat down beside him.

"Miss Davis," he said, with evident sincerity, "that was really wonderful!"

"Thank you very much," said Helen, radiantly.

"It was the most splendid piano playing I have ever heard in my life," the other went on. "Pray what was it that you played—something new?"

"Oh, no," was the answer, "it is very old indeed."

"Ah," said Mr. Harrison, "those old composers were very great men."

"Yes," said Helen, demurely.

"I was astonished to see with what ease you played," the other continued, "and yet so marvelously fast! That must be a fearfully hard piece of music to play."

77

"Yes, it is," said Helen; "but it is quite exciting," she added, fanning herself and laughing.

Helen was at the top of her being just then, and in perfect command of things; she had no idea of letting herself be dragged down into the commonplace again. "I think it's about time I was fascinating him," she said to herself, and she started in, full of merriment and life. Taking her last remark as a cue, she told him funny stories about the eccentricities of the sonata's great composer, how he would storm and rage up and down his room like a madman, and how he hired a boy to pump water over his head by the hour, in case of emergency.

Mr. Harrison remarked that it was funny how all musicians were such queer chaps, but even that did not discourage Helen. She rattled on, quite as supremely captivating as she had been at the dinner table, and as she saw that her companion was yielding to her spell, the color mounted to her cheeks and her blood flowed faster yet.

It is of the nature of such flame to feed itself, and Helen grew the more exulting as she perceived her success,—and consequently all the more irresistible. The eyes of the man were soon riveted upon the gorgeous vision of loveliness before him, and the contagion of the girl's animation showed itself even in him, for he brightened a little, and was clever enough to startle himself. It was a new delight and stimulus to Helen to perceive it, and she was soon swept away in much the same kind of nervous delight as her phantasy with the thunderstorm. The sofa upon which the two were seated had been somewhat apart from the rest, and so they had nothing to disturb them. A short half hour fled by, during which Helen's daring animation ruled everything, and at the end of which Mr. Harrison was quite oblivious to everything about him.

There were others, however, who were watching the affair; the keen-eyed Aunt Polly was comprehending all with joy, but she was as ever calculating and prudent, and she knew that Helen's monopoly of Mr. Harrison would soon become unpleasantly conspicuous, especially as she had so far introduced him to no one else. She felt that little would he lost by breaking the spell, for what the girl was doing then she might do any time she chose; and so after waiting a while longer she made her way unobtrusively over to them and joined their conversation.

Helen of course understood her aunt's meaning, and acquiesced; she kept on laughing and talking for a minute or two more, and then at a lull in the conversation she exclaimed: "But I've been keeping Mr. Harrison here talking to me, and nobody else has seen anything of him." And so Mr. Harrison, inwardly anathematizing the rest of the company, was compelled to go through a long series of handshakings, and finally to be drawn into a group of young persons whose conversation seemed to him the most inane he had ever heard in his life.

In the meantime someone else was giving a piano selection, one which Helen had never heard, but which sounded to every one like a finger exercise after her own meteoric flight; the girl sat half listening to it and half waiting for her aunt to return, which Mrs. Roberts finally did, beaming with gratitude.

"My love," she whispered, "you are an angel; you have done better than I ever dreamed of!"

And Helen felt her blood give a sudden leap that was not quite pleasant; the surging thoughts that were in her mind at that moment brought back the nervous trembling she had felt in the carriage, so that she leaned against the sofa for support.

"Now listen, my dear," the other went swiftly on, perhaps divining the girl's state, "I want you to do a great favor for me."

"Was not that for you, Auntie?" asked Helen, weakly.

"No, my dear, that was for yourself. But this—"

"What is it?"

"I want you to come and talk to my David Howard a little while."

The girl gave a start, and turned a little paler. "Aunt Polly," she exclaimed, "not now! He looks so ill, it makes me nervous even to see him."

"But, Helen, my dear, that is nonsense," was the reply. "Mr. Howard is one of the most interesting men you ever met. He knows more than all the people in this room together, and you will forget he is an invalid when you have talked to him a while."

Helen was, or wished to think herself, upon the heights of happiness just then, and she shrunk more than ever from anything that was wretched. "Not now, Aunt Polly," she said, faintly. "Please wait until—"

"But, my dear," said Aunt Polly, "now is the very time; you will wish to be with Mr. Harrison again soon. And you must meet Mr. Howard, for that is what he came for."

"I suppose then I'll have to," said Helen, knitting her brows; "I'll stroll over in a minute or two."

"All right," said the other; "and please try to get acquainted with him, Helen, for I want you to like him."

"I will do my best," said the girl. "He won't talk about his ailments, will he?"

"No," said the other, laughing, "I fancy not. Talk to him about music—he's a great musician, you know."

And as her aunt left the room, Helen stole a side glance at the man, who was alone upon the sofa just then. His chin was still resting in his hand, and he was looking at Helen as before. As she glanced at him thus he seemed to be all head, or rather all forehead, for his brow was very high and white, and was set off by heavy black hair.

"He does look interesting," the girl thought, as she forced a smile and walked across the room; her aunt entered at the same time, as if by accident, and the two approached Mr. Howard. As he saw them coming he rose, with some effort as Helen noticed, and with a very slight look of pain; it cost her some resolution to give the man her hand. In a minute or two more, however, they were seated alone upon the sofa, Aunt Polly having gone off with the remark to Helen that she had made Mr. Howard promise to talk to her about music, and that they both knew too much about it for her. "You must tell Helen all about her playing," she added to him, laughingly.

And then Helen, to carry on the conversation, added, "I should be very much pleased if you would."

"I am afraid it is an ungracious task Mrs. Roberts has chosen me," the man answered, smiling. "Critics are not a popular race."

"It depends upon the critics," said Helen. "They must be sincere."

"That is just where they get into trouble," was the response.

"It looks as if he were going to be chary with his praise," thought Helen, feeling just the least bit uncomfortable. She thought for a moment, and then said, not without truth, "You pique my curiosity, Mr. Howard."

"My criticism could not be technical," said the other, smiling, again, "for I am not a pianist."

"You play some other instrument?" asked Helen; afterwards she added, mischievously, "or are you just a critic?"

"I play the violin," the man answered.

"You are going to play for us this evening?"

"No," said the other, "I fear I shall not."

"Why not?" Helen inquired.

"I have not been feeling very well to-day," was the response. "But I have promised your aunt to play some evening; we had quite a long dispute."

"You do not like to play in public?" asked Helen.

The question was a perfectly natural one, but it happened unfortunately that as the girl asked it her glance rested upon the figure of her companion. The man chanced to look at her at the same instant, and she saw in a flash that her thought had been misread. Helen colored with the most painful mortification; but Mr. Howard gave, to her surprise, no sign of offense.

"No, not in general," he said, with simple dignity. "I believe that I am much better equipped as a listener."

Helen had never seen more perfect self-possession than that, and she felt quite humbled.

It would have been difficult to guess the age of the man beside her, but Helen noticed that his hair was slightly gray. A closer view had only served to strengthen her first impression of him, that he was all head, and she found herself thinking that if that had been all of him he might have been handsome, tho in a strange, uncomfortable way. The broad forehead seemed more prominent than ever, and the dark eyes seemed fairly to shine from beneath it. The rest of the face, tho wan, was as powerful and massive as the brow, and seemed to Helen, little used as she was to think of such things, to indicate character as well as suffering.

"It looks a little like Arthur's," she thought.

This she had been noticing in the course of the conversation; then, because her curiosity had really been piqued, she brought back the original topic again. "You have not told me about my playing," she smiled, "and I wish for your opinion. I am very vain, you know." (There is wisdom in avowing a weakness which you wish others to think you do not possess.)

"It gave me great pleasure to watch you," said the man, after a moment.

"To watch me!" thought Helen. "That is a palpable evasion. That is not criticising my music itself," she said aloud, not showing that she was a trifle annoyed.

"You have evidently been very well taught," said the other,— "unusually well; and you have a very considerable technic." And Helen was only more uncomfortable than ever; evidently the man would have liked to add a "but" to that sentence, and the girl felt as if she had come near an icicle in the course of her evening's triumph. However, she was now still more curious to hear the rest of his opinion. Half convinced yet that it must be favorable in the end, she said:

"I should not in the least mind your speaking plainly; the admiration of people who do not understand music I really do not care for." And then as Mr. Howard fixed his deep, clear eyes upon her, Helen involuntarily lowered hers a little.

"If you really want my opinion," said the other, "you shall have it. But you must remember that it is yourself who leads me to the bad taste of being serious in company."

That last remark was in Helen's own style, and she looked interested. For the rest, she felt that she had gotten into grave trouble by her question; but it was too late to retreat now.

"I will excuse you," she said. "I wish to know."

"Very well, then," said Mr. Howard; "the truth is that I did not care for your selection."

Helen gave a slight start. "If that is all the trouble, I need not worry," she thought; and she added easily, "The sonata is usually considered one of Beethoven's very greatest works, Mr. Howard."

"I am aware of that," said the other; "but do you know how Beethoven came to compose it?"

Helen had the happy feeling of a person of moderate resources when the conversation turns to one of his specialties. "Yes," she said; "I have read how he said 'So pocht das Schicksal auf die Pforte.'[1] Do you understand that, Mr. Howard?"

"Only partly," said the other, very gently; "do you?" And Helen felt just then that she had made a very awkward blunder indeed.

"Fate is a very dreadful thing to understand, Miss Davis," the other continued, slowly. "When one has heard the knock, he does not forget it, and even the echo of it makes him tremble."

"I suppose then," said Helen, glibly, trying to save herself, "that you think the sonata is too serious to be played in public?"

"Not exactly," was the answer; "it depends upon the circumstances. There are always three persons concerned, you know. In this case, as you have pardoned me for being serious, there is in the first place the great genius with his sacred message; you know how he learned that his life work was to be ruined by deafness, and how he poured his agony and despair into his greatest symphony, and into this sonata. That is the first person, Miss Davis."

He paused for a moment; and Helen took a deep breath, thinking that it was the strangest conversation she had ever been called upon to listen to during an evening's merriment. Yet she did not smile, for the man's deep, resonant voice fascinated her.

"And the second?" she asked.

"The second," said Mr. Howard, turning his dark, sunken eyes full upon the girl, "is another man, not a genius, but one who

---

1. "So knocks Fate upon the door."

has suffered, I fear, nearly as much as one; a man who is very hungry for beauty, and very impatient of insincerity, and who is accustomed to look to the great masters of art for all his help and courage."

Helen felt very uncomfortable indeed.

"Evidently," she said, "I am the third."

"Yes," said Mr. Howard, "the pianist is the third. It is the pianist's place to take the great work and live it, and study it until he knows all that it means; and then—"

"I don't think I took it quite so seriously as that," said Helen, with a poor attempt at humility.

"No," said Mr. Howard, gravely; "it was made evident to me that you did not by every note you played; for you treated it as if it had been a Liszt show-piece."

Helen was of course exceedingly angry at those last blunt words; but she was too proud to let her vexation be observed. She felt that she had gotten herself into the difficulty by asking for serious criticism, for deep in her heart she knew that it was true, and that she would never have dared to play the sonata had she known that a musician was present. Helen felt completely humiliated, her few minutes' conversation having been enough to put her out of humor with herself and all of her surroundings. There was a long silence, in which she had time to think of what she had heard; she felt in spite of herself the folly of what she had done, and her whole triumph had suddenly come to look very small indeed; yet, as was natural, she felt only anger against the man who had broken the spell and destroyed her illusion. She was only the more irritated because she could not find any ground upon which to blame him.

It would have been very difficult for her to have carried on the conversation after that. Fortunately a diversion occurred, the young person who had last played having gone to the piano again, this time with a young man and a violin.

"Aunt Polly has found someone to take your place," said Helen, forcing a smile.

"Yes," said the other, "she told me we had another violinist."

The violinist played Raff's Cavatina, a thing with which fiddlers all love to exhibit themselves; he played it just a little off the key at times, as Helen might have told by watching her companion's eyebrows. She in the meantime was trying to recover her equanimity, and to think what else she could say. "He's the most uncomfortable man I ever met," she thought with vexation. "I wish I'd insisted upon keeping away from him!"

However, Helen was again relieved from her plight by the fact that as the fiddler stopped and the faint applause died out, she saw Mr. Harrison coming towards her. Mr. Harrison had somehow succeeded in extricating himself from the difficulty in which his hostess had placed him, and had no doubt guessed that Helen was no better pleased with her new companion.

"May I join you?" he asked, as he neared the sofa.

"Certainly," said Helen, smiling; she introduced the two men, and Mr. Harrison sat down upon the other side of the girl. Somehow or other he seemed less endurable than he had just before, for his voice was not as soft as Mr. Howard's, and now that Helen's animation was gone she was again aware of the millionaire's very limited attainments.

"That was a very interesting thing we just heard," he said. "What was it? Do you know?"

Helen answered that it was Raff's Cavatina.

"Cavatina?" said Mr. Harrison. "The name sounds familiar; I may have heard it before."

Helen glanced nervously at Mr. Howard; but the latter gave no sign.

"Mr. Howard is himself a violinist," she said. "We must be careful what criticisms we make."

"Oh, I do not make any—I do not know enough about it," said the other, with heartiness which somehow seemed to Helen to fail of deserving the palliating epithet of "bluff."

"Mr. Howard has just been telling me about my own playing," Helen went on, growing a little desperate.

"I hope he admired it as much as I did," said the unfortunate railroad-president.

"I'm afraid he didn't," said Helen, trying to turn the matter into a laugh.

"He didn't!" exclaimed Mr. Harrison, in surprise. "Pray, why not?"

He asked the question of Mr. Howard, and Helen shuddered, for fear he might begin with that dreadful "There are always three persons concerned, you know." But the man merely said, very quietly, "My criticism was of rather a technical nature, Mr. Harrison."

"I'm sure, for my part I thought her playing wonderful," said the gentleman from Cincinnati, to which the other did not reply.

Helen felt herself between two fires and her vexation was increasing every moment; yet, try as she might, she could not think of anything to change the subject, and it was fortunate that the watchful Aunt Polly was on hand to save her. Mrs. Roberts was too diplomatic a person not to see the unwisdom of putting Mr. Harrison in a position where his deficiencies must be so very apparent, and so she came over, determined to carry one of the two men away. She was relieved of the trouble by the fact that, as she came near, Mr. Howard rose, again with some pain as it seemed to Helen, and asked the girl to excuse him. "I have been feeling quite ill today," he explained.

Helen, as she saw him walk away with Mrs. Roberts, sank back with a sigh which was only half restrained. "A very peculiar person," said Mr. Harrison, who was clever enough to divine her vexation."

"Yes," said the girl, "very, indeed."

"He seemed to be lecturing you about something, from what I saw," added the other. The remark was far from being in the best taste, but it pleased Helen, because it went to justify her to herself, and at the same time offered her an opportunity to vent her feelings.

"Yes," she said. "It was about music; he was very much displeased with me."

"So!" exclaimed Mr. Harrison. "I hope you do not let that disturb you?"

"No," said the girl, laughing,—"or at any rate, I shall soon recover my equanimity. It is very hard to please a man who plays himself, you know."

"Or who says he plays," observed Mr. Harrison. "He *didn't* play, you notice."

Helen was pleased to fancy that there might be wisdom in the remark. "Let us change the subject," she said more cheerfully. "It is best to forget things that make one feel uncomfortable."

"I'll leave the finding of a new topic to you," replied the other, with graciousness which did a little more to restore Helen's self-esteem. "I have a very humble opinion of my own conversation."

"Do you like mine?" the girl asked with a laugh.

"I do, indeed," said Mr. Harrison with equally pleasing frankness. "I was as interested as could be in the story that you were telling me when we were stopped."

"Well, we'll begin where we left off!" exclaimed Helen, and felt as if she had suddenly discovered a doorway leading from a prison. She found it easy to forget the recent events after that, and Mr. Harrison grew more tolerable to her every moment now that the other was gone; her self-possession came back to her quickly as she read his admiration in his eyes. Besides that, it was impossible to forget for very long that Mr. Harrison was a multi-millionaire, and the object of the envious glances of every other girl in the room; and so when Aunt Polly returned a while later she found the conversation between the two progressing very well, and in fact almost as much enjoyed by both as it had been the first time. After waiting a few minutes she came to ask Helen to sing for the company, a treat which she had reserved until the last.

Helen's buoyant nature had by that time flung all her doubts behind her, and this last excitement was all that was needed to sweep her away entirely again. She went to the piano as exulting as ever in her command of it and in the homage which it brought her. She sang an arrangement of the "Preislied," and she sang it with all the energy and enthusiasm she possessed; partly because she had a really good voice and enjoyed the song, and partly because an audience appreciates singing more easily than any other kind of music. She really scored the success of the evening. Everybody was as enthusiastic as the limits of good taste allowed, and Helen was compelled, not in the least against her will, to sing again and again. While she was laughing with happiness and triumph, something brought, back "Wohin" to her mind, and she sang it again, quite as gaily as she had sung it by the streamlet with Arthur. It was enough to delight even the dullest, and perhaps if Mr. Howard had been there even he would have applauded a little.

At any rate, as Helen rose from the piano she received a complete ovation, everyone coming to her to thank her and to praise her, and to share in the joy of her beauty; she herself had never been more radiant and more exulting in all her exulting life, drinking in even Mr. Harrison's rapturous compliments and finding nothing exaggerated in them. And in the meantime, Aunt Polly having suggested a waltz to close the festivities, the furniture was rapidly moved to one side, and the hostess herself took her seat at the piano and struck up the "Invitation to the Dance;" Mr. Harrison, who had been at Helen's side since her singing had ceased, was of course her partner, and the girl, flushed and excited by all the homage she had received, was soon waltzing delightedly in his arms. The man danced well, fortunately for him, and that he was the beautiful girl's ardent admirer was by this time evident, not only to Helen, but to everyone else.

In the mood that she was then, the fact was as welcome to her as it could possibly have been, and when, therefore, Mr. Harrison kept her arm and begged for the next dance, and the next in turn, Helen was sufficiently carried away to have no wish to refuse him; when after the third dance she was tired out and sat down to rest, Mr. Harrison was still her companion.

Helen was at the very height of her happiness then, every trace of her former vexation gone, and likewise every trace of her objections to the man beside her. The music was still sounding merrily, and everyone else was dancing, so that her animation did not seem at all out of taste; and so brilliant and fascinating had she become, and so completely enraptured was Mr. Harrison, that he would probably have capitulated then and there if the dancing had not ceased and the company separated when it did. The end of all the excitement was a great disappointment to Helen; she was completely happy just then, and would have gone just as far as the stream had carried her. It being her first social experience was probably the reason that she was less easily wearied than the rest; and besides, when one has thus yielded to the sway of the senses, he dreads instinctively the subsiding of the excitement and the awakening of reason.

The awakening, however, is one that must always come; Helen, having sent away the maid, suddenly found herself standing alone in the middle of her own room gazing at herself in the glass, and seeing a frightened look in her eyes. The merry laughter of the guests ceased gradually, and silence settled about the halls of the great house; but even then Helen did not move. She was standing there still when her aunt came into the room.

Mrs. Roberts was about as excited as was possible in a matron of her age and dignity; she flung her arms rapturously around Helen, and clasped her to her. "My dear," she cried, "it was a triumph!"

"Yes, Auntie," said Helen, weakly.

"You dear child, you!" went on the other, laughing; "I don't believe you realize it yet! Do you know, Helen, that Mr. Harrison is madly in love with you? You ought to be the happiest girl in the land tonight!"

"Yes, Auntie," said Helen again, still more weakly.

"Come here, my dear," said Mrs. Roberts, drawing her gently over to the bed and sitting down beside her; "you are a little dazed, I fancy, and I do not blame you. I should have been beside myself at your age if such a thing had happened to me; do you realize, child, what a fortune like Mr. Harrison's is?"

"No," said Helen, "it is very hard, Aunt Polly. I'm afraid about it; I must have some time to think."

"Think!" laughed the other. "You queer child! My dear, do you actually mean that you could think of refusing this chance of your lifetime?"

"I don't know," said Helen, trembling; "I don't—"

"Everybody'd think you were crazy, child! I know I should, for one." And she added, coaxingly, "Let me tell you what Mr. Roberts said."

"What, Auntie?"

"He sent you in this message; he's a great person for doing generous things, when he takes it into his head. He told me to tell you that if you'd accept Mr. Harrison's offer he would give you the finest trousseau that he could buy. Wasn't that splendid of him?"

"Yes," said Helen, "thank him for me;" and she shuddered. "Don't talk to me any more about it now, tho," she pleaded. "Please don't, Aunt Polly. I was so excited, and it was all like a dream, and I'm half dazed now; I can't think about it, and I must think, somehow! It's too dreadful!"

"You shan't think about it tonight, child," laughed the other, "for I want you to sleep and be beautiful tomorrow. See," she added, beginning to unfasten Helen's dress, "I'm going to be your little mother tonight, and put you to bed."

And so, soothing the girl and kissing her burning forehead and trying to laugh away her fears, her delighted protectress undressed her, and did not leave her until she had seen her in bed and kissed her again. "And promise me, child," she said, "that you won't worry yourself tonight. Go to sleep, and you'll have time to think tomorrow."

Helen promised that she would; but she did not keep her promise. She heard the great clock in the hallway strike many times, and when the darkest hours of the night had passed she was sitting up in bed and gazing about her at the gray shadows in the room, holding the covering tightly about her, because she was very cold; she was muttering nervously to herself, half deliriously: "No, no, I will not do it! They shall not *make* me do it! I must have time to think."

And when at last she fell into a restless slumber, that thought was still in her mind, and those words upon her lips: "I will not do it; I must have time to think!"

[Music: The opening passage of Beethoven's Appassionata Sonata.]

Chapter VI

"And yet methinks I see it in thy face,
What them shouldst be: th' occasion speaks thee; and
My strong imagination sees a crown
Dropping upon thy head."

When Helen awoke upon the following morning, the resolution to withstand her aunt's urging was still strong within her; as she strove to bring back the swift events of the night before, the first discovery she made was a headache and a feeling of weariness and dissatisfaction that was new to her. She arose and looked in the glass, and seeing that she was pale, vowed again, "They shall not torment me in this way! I do not even mean that he shall propose to me; I must have time to realize it!"

And so firm was she in her own mind that she rang the bell and sent the maid to call her aunt. It was then only nine o'clock in the morning, and Helen presumed that neither Mrs. Roberts nor any of the other guests would be awake, they not being fresh from boarding school as she was; but the girl was so nervous and restless, and so weighed upon by her urgent resolution, that she felt she could do nothing else until she had declared it and gotten rid of the matter. "I'm going to tell her once for all," she vowed; "they shall not torment me any more."

It turned out, however, that Mrs. Roberts had been up and dressed a considerable time,—for a reason which, when Helen learned it, prevented her delivering so quickly the speech she had upon her mind; she noticed a worried expression upon her aunt's face as soon as the latter came into the room.

"What is the matter?" she asked, in some surprise.

"A very dreadful misfortune, my dear," said Mrs. Roberts; "I don't know how to tell you, you'll be so put out."

Helen was quite alarmed as she saw her aunt sink down into a chair; but then it flashed over her that Mr. Harrison might have for some reason been called away.

"What is it? Tell me!" she asked eagerly.

"It's Mr. Howard, my dear," said the other; and Helen frowned.

"Oh, bother!" she cried; "what about him?"

"He's been ill during the night," replied Aunt Polly.

"Ill!" exclaimed Helen. "Dear me, what a nuisance!"

"Poor man," said the other, deprecatingly; "he cannot help it."

"Yes," exclaimed Helen, "but he ought not to be here. What is the matter with him?"

"I don't know," was the reply, "but he has been suffering so all night that the doctor has had to give him an opiate."

The wan countenance of Mr. Howard rose up before Helen just then, and she shuddered inwardly.

"Dear me, what a state of affairs!" she exclaimed. "It seems to me as if I were to have nothing but fright and worry. Why should there be such things in the world?"

"I don't know, Helen," said the other, "but it is certainly inopportune for you. Of course the company will all have to leave."

"To leave!" echoed Helen; she had never once thought of that.

"Why, of course," said her aunt. "It would not be possible to enjoy ourselves under such very dreadful circumstances."

"But, Aunt Polly, that is a shame!" cried the girl. "The idea of so many people being inconvenienced for such a cause. Can't he be moved?"

"The doctor declares it would be impossible at present, Helen, and it would not look right anyway, you know. He will certainly have to remain until he is better."

"And how long will that be?"

"A week, or perhaps more," was the reply.

And Helen saw that her promised holiday was ruined; her emotions, however, were not all of disappointment, for though she was vexed at the interruptions, she recollected with sudden relief that she could thus obtain, and without so much effort of her own, the time to debate the problem of Mr. Harrison. Also there was in her mind, if not exactly pity for the invalid, at any rate the nearest to it that Helen had ever learned to feel, an uncomfortable fright at the idea of such suffering.

"I promise you," said Aunt Polly, who had been watching her face and trying to read her emotions, "that we shall only postpone the good time I meant to give you. You cannot possibly be more vexed about it than I, for I was rejoicing in your triumph with Mr. Harrison."

"I'm not worrying on that account," said Helen, angrily.

"Helen, dear," said Mrs. Roberts, pleadingly, "what can be the matter with you? I think anyone who was watching you and me would get the idea that I was the one to whom the fortune is coming. I suppose that was only one of your jokes, my dear, but I truly don't think you show a realization of what a tremendous opportunity you have. You show much more lack of experience than I had any idea could be possible."

"It isn't that, Aunt Polly," protested Helen; "I realize it, but I want time to think."

"To think, Helen! But what is there to think? It seems to be madness to trifle with such a chance."

"Will it be trifling to keep him waiting a while?" asked Helen, laughing in spite of her vexation.

"Maybe not, my dear; but you ought to know that every other girl in this house would snap him up at one second's notice. If you'd only seen them watching you last night as I did."

"I saw a little," was the reply. "But, Aunt Polly, is Mr. Harrison the only man whom I can find?"

"My husband and I have been over the list of our acquaintances, and not found anyone that can be compared with him for an instant, Helen. We know of no one that would do for you that has half as much money."

"I never said *he'd* do for me," said Helen, again laughing. "Understand me, Auntie," she added; "it isn't that I'd not like the fortune! If I could get it without its attachment—"

"But, my dear, you know you can never get any wealth except by marriage; what is the use of talking such nonsense, even in fun?"

"But, listen," objected Helen in turn; "suppose I don't want such a great fortune—suppose I should marry one of these other men?"

"Helen, if you only could know as much as I know about these things," said Mrs. Roberts, "if you only could know the difference between being in the middle and at the top of the social ladder! Dear, why will you choose anything but the best when you can have the best if you want it? I tell you once for all I do not care how clever you are, or how beautiful you are, the great people will look down on you for an upstart if you cannot match them and make just as much of a show. And why can you not discover what your own tastes are? I watched you last night, child; anyone could have seen that you were in your element! You outshone everyone, Helen, and you should do just the same all your life. Can you not see just what that means to you?"

"Yes, Auntie," said Helen, "but then—"

"Were you not perfectly happy last night?" interrupted the other.

"No," protested the other, "that's just what I was going to say."

"The only reason in the world why you are not, my dear, is that you were tormenting yourself with foolish scruples. Can you not see that if you once had the courage to rid yourself of them it would be all that you need. Why are you so weak, Helen?"

"It is not weak!" exclaimed the other.

"Yes," asserted Mrs. Roberts, "I say it is weak. It is weak of you not to comprehend what your life is to be, and what you need for your happiness. It is a shame for you to make no use of the glorious gifts that are yours, and to cramp and hinder all your own progress. I want you to have room to show your true powers, Helen!"

Helen had been leaning over the foot of the bed listening to her aunt, stirred again by all her old emotion, and angry with herself for being stirred; her unspoken resolution was not quite so steady as it had been, tho like all good resolutions it remained in her mind to torment her.

She sprang up suddenly with a very nervous and forced laugh. "I'm glad I don't have to argue with you, Auntie," she said, "and that I'm saved the trouble of worrying myself ill. You see the Fates are on my side,—I must have time to think, whether I want to or not." It was that comfort which saved her from further struggle with herself upon the subject. (Helen much preferred being happy to struggling.) She set hurriedly to work to dress, for her aunt told her that the guests were nearly ready for breakfast.

"Nobody could sleep since all the excitement," she said. "I wonder it did not wake you."

"I was tired," said Helen; "I guess that was it."

"You'll find the breakfast rather a sombre repast," added Mrs. Roberts, pathetically. "I've been up nearly three hours myself, so frightened about poor Mr. Howard; I had neveer seen anyone so dreadfully ill, and I was quite certain he was in his death agony."

"Aunt Polly!" cried Helen with a sudden wild start, "why do you talk like that?"

"I won't say any more about it," was the reply, "only hurry up. And put on your best looks, my dear, for Mr. Harrison to carry away in his memory."

"I'll do that much with pleasure," was the answer; "and please have the maid come up to pack my trunks again; for you won't want me to stay now, of course."

"Oh, no," said Mrs. Roberts, "not unless you want to. Our house won't be a very cheerful place, I fear."

"I'll come back in a week or two, when you are ready for me," Helen added; "in the meantime I can be thinking about Mr. Harrison."

Helen was soon on her way downstairs, for it was terrifying to her to be alone and in the neighborhood of Mr. Howard. She found a sombre gathering indeed, for the guests spoke to each other only in half-whispers, and there were few smiles to be seen. Helen found herself placed opposite Mr. Harrison at the table, and she had a chance to study him by glances through the meal. "He's well dressed, anyway," she mused, "and he isn't altogether bad. I wonder if I'd *dare* to marry him."

After breakfast Helen strolled out upon the piazza, perhaps with some purpose in her mind; for it is not unpleasant to toy with a temptation, even when one means to resist it. At any rate, she was a little excited when she heard Mr. Harrison coming out to join her there.

"Rather a sad ending of our little party, wasn't it, Miss Davis?" he said.

"Yes," answered the girl, "I feel so sorry for poor Mr. Howard."

"He seemed to be rather ill last night," said the other. He was going to add that the fact perhaps accounted for the invalid's severity, but he was afraid of shocking Helen by his levity,—a not entirely necessary precaution, unfortunately.

"You are going back to town this morning, with the others?" Helen asked.

"No," said Mr. Harrison, somewhat to her surprise; "I have a different plan."

"Good Heavens, does he suppose he's going to stay here with me?" thought the girl.

"I received your aunt's permission to ask you," continued Mr. Harrison, "and so I need only yours."

"For what?" Helen inquired, with varied emotions.

"To drive you over to Oakdale with my rig," said the other. "I had it brought down, you know, because I thought there might be a chance to use it."

Helen had turned slightly paler, and was staring in front of her.

"Are you not fond of driving, then, Miss Davis?" asked the other, as she hesitated.

"Yes," said Helen, "but I don't like to trouble you—"

"I assure you it will be the greatest pleasure in the world," said Mr. Harrison; "I only regret that I shall not be able to see more of you, Miss Davis; it is only for the present, I hope."

"Thank you," said Helen, still very faintly.

"And I have a pair of horses that I am rather proud of," added Mr. Harrison, laughing; "I should like you to tell me what you think of them. Will you give me the pleasure?"

And Helen could not hesitate very much longer without being rude. "If you really wish it, Mr. Harrison," she said, "very well." And then someone else came out on the piazza and cut short the conversation; Helen had no time to think any more about the matter, but she had a disagreeable consciousness that her blood was flowing faster again, and that her old agitation was back in all its strength. Soon afterwards Mrs. Roberts came out and joined the two.

"Miss Davis has granted me the very great favor," said Mr. Harrison; "I fear I shall be happier than I ought to be, considering what suffering I leave behind."

"It will do no good to worry about it," said Mrs. Roberts, a reflection which often keeps the world from wasting its sympathy. "I shall have your carriage brought round."

"Isn't it rather early to start?" asked Helen.

"I don't know," said her aunt; "is it?"

"We can take a little drive if it is," said Mr. Harrison; "I mean that Miss Davis shall think a great deal of my horses."

Helen said nothing, but stood gazing in front of her across the lawns, her mind in a tempest of emotions. She could not put away from her the excitement that Mr. Harrison's presence brought; the visions of wealth and power which gleamed before her almost overwhelmed her with their vastness. But she had also the memory of her morning resolve to trouble her conscience; the result was the same confused helplessness, the dazed and frightened feeling which she so rebelled against.

"I do not *want* to be troubled in this way," she muttered angrily to herself, again and again; "I wish to be let alone, so that I can be happy!"

Yet there was no chance just then for her to find an instant's peace, or time for further thought; there were half a dozen people about her, and she was compelled to listen to and answer commonplace remarks about the beauty of the country in front of her, and about her singing on the previous evening.

She had to stifle her agitation as best she could, and almost before she realized it her aunt had come to summon her to get ready for the drive.

Helen hoped to have a moment's quiet then; but there was nothing to be done but put on her hat and gloves, and Mrs. Roberts was with her all the time. "Helen," she said pleadingly, as she watched the girl surveying herself in the glass, "I do hope you will not forget all that I told you."

"I wish you would let me alone about it!" cried Helen, very peevishly.

"If you only knew, my dear girl, how much I have done for you," replied the other, "and how I've planned and looked forward to this time, I don't think you'd answer me in that way."

"It isn't that, Aunt Polly," exclaimed Helen, "but I am so confused and I don't know what to think."

"I am trying my poor, humble best to show you what to think. And you could not possibly feel more worried than I just now; Helen, you could be rid of all these doubts and struggles in one instant, if you chose. Ask yourself if it is not true; you have only to give yourself into the arms of the happiness that calls you. And you never will get rid of the matter in any other way,—indeed you will not! If you should fling away this chance, the memory of it would never leave you all your life; after you knew it was too late, you would torment yourself a thousand times more than ever you can now."

"Oh, dear, dear!" cried Helen, half hysterically; "I can't stand that, Aunt Polly. I'll do anything, only let me alone! My head is aching to split, and I don't know where I am."

"And you will never find another chance like it, Helen," went on the other, with sledge-hammer remorselessness. "For if you behave in this perfectly insane way and lose this opportunity, I shall simply give you up in despair at your perversity."

"But I haven't said I was going to lose it," the girl exclaimed. "He won't be any the less in love with me if I make him wait, Aunt Polly!—"

"Mr. Harrison was going back to Cincinnati in a day or two," put in Mrs. Roberts, swiftly.

"He will stay if I wish him to," was the girl's reply. "There is no need for so much worry; one would think I was getting old."

"Old!" laughed the other. "You are so beautiful this morning, Helen, that I could fall in love with you myself." She turned the girl towards her, seeing that her toilet was finished." I haven't a thought in the world, dear, but to keep you so beautiful," she said; "I hate to see you tormenting yourself and making yourself so pale; why will you not take my advice and fling all these worries aside and let yourself be happy? That is all I want you to do, and it is so easy! Why is it that you do not want to be happy? I like to see you smile, Helen!" And Helen, who was tired of struggling, made a wry attempt to oblige her, and then broke into a laugh at herself. Meanwhile the other picked a rose from a great bunch of them that lay upon the bureau, and pinned it upon her dress.

"There, child," she, said, "he can never resist you now, I know!"

Helen kissed her excitedly upon the cheek, and darted quickly out of the door, singing, in a brave attempt to bring back her old, merry self:—

"The flowers that bloom in the spring, tra-la-la, Have nothing to do with the case."

A moment later, however, she recollected Mr. Howard and his misfortune, and her heart sank; she ran quickly down the steps to get the thought of him from her mind.

It was easy enough to forget him and all other troubles as well when she was once outside upon the piazza; for there were plenty of happy people, and everyone crowded about her to bid her good-by. There too was Mr. Harrison standing upon the steps waiting for her, and there was his driving-cart with two magnificent black horses, alert and eager for the sport. Helen was not much of a judge of horses, having never had one of her own to drive, but she had the eye of a person of aristocratic tastes for what was in good form, and she saw that Mr. Harrison's turnout was all of that, with another attraction for her, that it was daring; for the horses were lithe, restless creatures, thoroughbreds, both of them; and it looked as if they had not been out of the stable in a week. They were giving the groom who held them all that he could do.

Mr. Harrison held out his hand to the girl as she came down the steps, and eyed her keenly to see if her flushed cheeks would betray any sign of fear. But Helen's emotions were surging too strongly for such thoughts, and she had, besides, a little of the thoroughbred nature herself. She laughed gaily as she gave her hand to her companion and sprang into the wagon; he followed her, and as he took the reins the groom sprang aside and the two horses bounded away down the broad avenue. Helen turned once to wave her hand in answer to the chorus of good-bys that sounded from the porch, and then she faced about and sank back into the seat and drank in with delight the fresh morning breeze that blew in her face.

"Oh, I think this is fine!" she cried.

"You like driving, then?" asked the other.

"Yes indeed," was the reply. "I like this kind ever so much."

"Wait until we get out on the high-road," said Mr. Harrison, "and then we will see what we can do. I came from the West, you know, Miss Davis, so I think I am wise on the subject of horses."

The woods on either side sped by them, and Helen's emotions soon began to flow faster. It was always easy for her to forget everything and lose herself in feelings of joy and power, and it was especially easy when she was as much wrought up as she was just then. It was again her ride with the thunderstorm, and soon she felt as if she were being swept out into the rejoicing and the victory once more. She might have realized, if she had thought, that her joy was coming only because she was following her aunt's advice, and yielding herself into the arms of her temptation; but

Helen was thoroughly tired of thinking; she wanted to feel, and again and again she drank in deep breaths of the breeze.

It was only a minute or so before they passed the gates of the Roberts place, and swept out of the woods and into the open country. It was really inspiring then, for Mr. Harrison gave his horses the reins, and Helen was compelled to hold on to her hat. He saw delight and laughter glowing in her countenance as she watched the landscape that fled by them, with its hillsides clad in their brightest green and with its fresh-plowed farm-lands and snowy orchards; the clattering of the horses' hoofs and the whirring of the wheels in the sandy road were music and inspiration such as Helen longed for, and she would have sung with all her heart had she been alone.

As was her way, she talked instead, with the same animation and glow that had fascinated her companion upon the previous evening. She talked of the sights that were about them, and when they came to the top of the hill and paused to gaze around at the view, she told about her trip through the Alps, and pictured the scenery to him, and narrated some of her mountain-climbing adventures; and then Mr. Harrison, who must have been a dull man indeed not to have felt the contagion of Helen's happiness, told her about his own experiences in the Rockies, to which the girl listened with genuine interest. Mr. Harrison's father, so he told her, had been a station-agent of a little town in one of the wildest portions of the mountains; he himself had begun as a railroad surveyor, and had risen step by step by constant exertion and watchfulness. It was a story of a self-made man, such as Helen had vowed to her aunt she could not bear to listen to; yet she did not find it disagreeable just then. There was an exciting story of a race with a rival road, to secure the right to the best route across the mountains; Helen found it quite as exciting as music, and said so.

"Perhaps it is a kind of music," said Mr. Harrison, laughing; "it is the only kind I have cared anything about, excepting yours."

"I had no idea people had to work so hard in the world," said Helen, dodging the compliment.

"They do, unless they have someone else to do it for them," said the other. "It is a, fierce race, nowadays, and a man has to watch and think every minute of the time. But it is glorious to triumph."

Helen found herself already a little more in a position to realize what ten million dollars amounted to, and very much more respectful and awe-stricken in her relation to them. She was sufficiently oblivious to the flight of time to be quite surprised when she gazed about her, and discovered that they were within a couple of miles of home. "I had no idea of how quickly we were going," she said.

"You are not tired, then?" asked the other.

"No indeed," Helen answered, "I enjoyed it ever so much."

"We might drive farther," said Mr. Harrison; "these horses are hardly waked up."

He reined them in a little and glanced at his watch. "It's just eleven," he said, "I think there'd be time," and he turned to her with a smile. "Would you like to have an adventure?" he asked.

"I generally do," replied the girl. "What is it?"

"I was thinking of a drive," said the other; "one that we could just about take and return by lunch-time; it is about ten miles from here."

"What is it?" asked Helen.

"I have just bought a country place near here," said Mr. Harrison. "I thought perhaps you would like to see it."

"My aunt spoke of it," Helen answered; "the Eversons' old home."

"Yes," said the other; "you know it, then?"

"I only saw it once in my life, when I was a very little girl," Helen replied, "and so I have only a dim recollection of its magnificence; the old man who lived there never saw any company."

"It had to be sold because he failed in business," said Mr. Harrison. "Would you like to drive over?"

"Very much," said Helen, and a minute later, when they came to a fork in the road, they took the one which led them to "Fairview," as the place was called.

"I think it a tremendously fine property myself," said Mr. Harrison; "I made up my mind to have it the first time I saw it. I haven't seen anything around here to equal it, and I hope to make a real English country-seat out of it. I'll tell you about what I want to do when we get there, and you can give me your advice; a man never has good taste, you know."

"I should like to see it," answered Helen, smiling; "I have a passion for fixing up things."

"We had an exciting time at the sale," went on Mr. Harrison reminiscently. "You know Mr. Everson's family wanted to keep the place themselves, and the three or four branches of the family had clubbed together to buy it; when the bidding got near the end, there was no one left but the family and myself."

"And you got it?" said Helen. "How cruel!"

"The strongest wins," laughed the other. "I had made up my mind to have it. The Eversons are a very aristocratic family, aren't they?"

"Yes," said Helen, "very, indeed; they have lived in this part of the country since the Revolution." As Mr. Harrison went on to tell her the story of the sale she found herself vividly reminded of what her aunt had told her of the difference between having a good deal of money and all the money one wanted. Perhaps, also, her companion was not without some such vaguely felt purpose in the telling. At any rate, the girl was trembling inwardly more and more at the prospect which was unfolding itself before her; as excitement always acted upon her as a stimulant, she was at her very best during the rest of the drive. She and her companion were conversing very merrily indeed when Fairview was reached.

The very beginning of the place was imposing, for there was a high wall along the roadway for perhaps a quarter of a mile, and then two massive iron gates set in great stone pillars; they were opened by the gate-keeper in response to Mr. Harrison's call. Once inside the two had a drive of some distance through what had once been a, handsome park, though it was a semi-wilderness then. The road ascended somewhat all the way, until the end of the forest was reached, and the first view of the house was gained; Helen could scarcely restrain a cry of pleasure as she saw it, for it was really a magnificent old mansion, built of weather-beaten gray stone, and standing upon a high plateau, surrounded by a lawn and shaded by half a dozen great oaks; below it the lawn sloped in a broad terrace, and in the valley thus formed gleamed a little trout-pond, set off at the back by a thickly-wooded hillside.

"Isn't it splendid!" the girl exclaimed, gazing about her.

"I thought it was rather good," said Mr. Harrison, deprecatingly. "It can be made much finer, of course."

"When you take your last year's hay crop from the lawn, for one thing," laughed she. "But I had no idea there was anything so beautiful near our little Oakdale. Just look at that tremendous entrance!"

"It's all built in royal style," said Mr. Harrison. "The family must have been wealthy in the old days."

"Probably slave-dealers, or something of that kind," observed Helen. "Is the house all furnished inside?"

"Yes," said the other, "but I expect to do most of it over. Wouldn't you like to look?" He asked the question as he saw the gate-keeper coming up the road, presumably with the keys.

The girl gazed about her dubiously; she would have liked to go in, except that she was certain it would be improper. Helen had never had much respect for the proprieties, however, being accustomed to rely upon her own opinions of things; and in the present case, besides, she reflected that no one would ever know anything about it.

"We'd not have time to do more than glance around," continued the other, "but we might do that, if you like."

"Yes," said Helen, after a moment more of hesitation, "I think I should."

Her heart was beating very fast as the two ascended the great stone steps and as the door opened before them; her mind could not but be filled with the overwhelming thought that all that she saw might be hers if she really wanted it. The mere imagining of Mr. Harrison's wealth had been enough to make her thrill and burn, so it was to be expected that the actual presence of some of it would not fail of its effect. It is to be observed that the great Temptation took place upon a high mountain, where the kingdoms of the earth could really be seen; and Helen as she gazed around had the further knowledge that the broad landscape and palatial house, which to her were almost too splendid to be real, were after all but a slight trifle to her companion.

The girl entered the great hallway, with its huge fireplace and its winding stairway, and then strolled through the parlors of the vast house; Helen had in all its fullness the woman's passion for spending money for beautiful things, and it had been her chief woe in all her travels that the furniture and pictures and tapestry which she gazed at with such keen delight must be forever beyond her thoughts. Just at present her fancy was turned loose and madly reveling in these memories, while always above her wildest flights was the intoxicating certainty that there was no reason why they should not all be possible. She could not but recollect with a wondering smile that only yesterday she had been happy at the thought of arranging one dingy little parlor in her country parsonage, and had been trying to persuade her father to the extravagance of re-covering two chairs.

It would have been hard for Helen to keep her emotions from Mr. Harrison, and he must have guessed the reason why she was so flushed and excited. They were standing just then in the center of the great dining-room, with its massive furniture of black mahogany, and she was saying that it ought to be papered in dark red, and was conjuring up the effect to herself. "Something rich, you know, to set off the furniture," she explained.

"And you must take that dreadful portrait from over the mantel," she added, laughing. (It was a picture of a Revolutionary warrior, on horseback and in full uniform, the coloring looking like faded oilcloth.)

"I had thought of that myself," said Mr. Harrison. "It's the founder of the Eversons; there's a picture gallery in a hall back of here, with two whole rows of ancestors in it."

"Why don't you adopt them?" asked Helen mischievously.

"One can buy all the ancestors one wants to, nowadays," laughed Mr. Harrison. "I thought I'd make something more interesting out of it. I'm not much of a judge of art, you know, but I thought if I ever went abroad I'd buy up some of the great paintings that one reads about—some of the old masters, you know."

"I'm afraid you'd find very few of them for sale," said Helen, smiling.

"I'm not accustomed to fail in buying things that I want," was the other's reply. "Are you fond of pictures?"

"Very much indeed," answered the girl. As a matter of fact, the mere mention of the subject opened a new kingdom to her, for she could not count the number of times she had sat before beautiful pictures and almost wept at the thought that she could never own one that was really worth looking at. "I brought home a few myself," she said to her companion,—"just engravings, you know, half a dozen that I thought would please me; I mean to hang them around my music-room."

"Tell me about it," said Mr, Harrison. "I have been thinking of fixing up such a place myself, you know. I thought of extending the house on the side that has the fine view of the valley, and making part a piazza, and part a conservatory or music-room."

"It could be both!" exclaimed the girl, eagerly. "That would be the very thing; there ought not to be anything in a music-room, you know, except the piano and just a few chairs, and the rest all flowers. The pictures ought all to be appropriate—pictures of nature, of things that dance and are beautiful; oh, I could lose myself in such a room as that!" and Helen ran on, completely carried away by the fancy, and forgetting even Mr. Harrison for a moment.

"I have often dreamed of such a place," she said, "where everything would be sympathetic; it's a pity that one can't have a piano taken out into the fields, the way I remember reading that Haydn used to do with his harpsichord. If I were a violinist, that's the way I'd do all my playing, because then one would not need to be afraid to open his eyes; oh, it would be fine—"

Helen stopped; she was at the height of her excitement just then; and the climax came a moment afterwards. "Miss Davis," asked the man, "would you really like to arrange such a music-room?"

The tone of his voice was so different that the girl comprehended instantly; it was this moment to which she had been rushing with so much exultation; but when it came her heart almost stopped beating, and she gave a choking gasp.

"Would you really like it?" asked Mr. Harrison again, bending towards her earnestly.

"Why, certainly," said Helen, making one blind and desperate effort to dodge the issue. "I'll tell you everything that is necessary."

"That is not what I mean, Miss Davis!"

"Not?" echoed Helen, and she tried to look at him with her frank, open eyes; but when she saw his burning look, she could not; she dropped her eyes and turned scarlet.

"Miss Davis," went on the man rapidly, "I have been waiting for a chance to tell you this. Let me tell you now!"

Helen gazed wildly about her once, as if she would have fled; then she stood with her arms lying helplessly at her sides, trembling in every nerve.

"There is very little pleasure that one can get from such beautiful things alone, Miss Davis, and especially when he is as dulled by the world as myself. I thought that some day I might be able to share them with some one who could enjoy them more than I, but I never knew who that person was until last night. I know that I have not much else to offer you, except what wealth and position I have gained; and when I think of all your accomplishments, and all that you have to place you so far beyond me, I almost fear to offer myself to you. But I can only give what I have—my humble admiration of your beauty and your powers; and the promise to worship you, to give the rest of my life to seeing that you have everything in the world that you want. I will put all that I own at your command, and get as much more as I can, with no thought but of your happiness."

Mr. Harrison could not have chosen words more fitted to win the trembling girl beside him; that, he should recognize as well as she did her superiority to him, removed half of his deficiency in her eyes.

"Miss Davis," the other went on, "I cannot know how you will feel toward such a promise, but I cannot but feel that what I possess could give you opportunities of much happiness. You should have all the beauty about you that you wished, for there is nothing in the world too beautiful for you; and you should have every luxury that money can buy, to save you from all care. If this house seemed too small for you, you should have another wherever you desired it, and be mistress of it, and of everything in it; and if you cared for a social career, you should have everything to help you, and it would be my one happiness to see your triumph. I would give a thousand times what I own to have you for my wife."

So the man continued, pleading his cause, until at last he stopped, waiting anxiously for a sign from the girl; he saw that she was agitated, for her breast was heaving, and her forehead flushed, but he could not tell the reason. "Perhaps, Miss Davis," he said, humbly, "you will scorn such things as I have to offer you; tell me, is it that?"

Helen answered him, in a faint voice, "It is not that, Mr. Harrison; it is,—it is,—"

"What, Miss Davis?"

"It has been but a day! I have had no time to know you—to love you."

And Helen stopped, afraid at the words she herself was using; for she knew that for the first time in her life she had stooped to a sham and a lie. Her whole soul was ablaze with longing just then, with longing for the power and the happiness which this man held out to her; and she meant to take him, she had no longer a thought of resistance. It was all the world which offered itself to her, and she meant to clasp it to her—to lose herself quite utterly and forget herself in it, and she was already drunk with the thought. Therefore she could not but shudder as she heard the word "love" upon her lips, and knew that she had used it because she wished to make a show of hesitation.

"I did not need but one day, Miss Davis," went on the other pleadingly, "to know that I loved you—to know that I no longer set any value on the things that I had struggled all my life to win; for you are perfect, Miss Davis. You are so far beyond me that I have scarcely the courage to ask you what I do. But I *must* ask you, and know my fate."

He stopped again and gazed at her; and Helen looked at him wildly, and then turned away once more, trembling. She wished that he would only continue still longer, for the word was upon her lips, and yet it was horror for her to utter it, because she felt she ought not to yield so soon,—because she wanted some delay; she sought for some word that would be an evasion, that would make him urge her more strongly; she wished to be wooed and made to surrender, and yet she could find no pretext.

"Answer me, Miss Davis!" exclaimed the other, passionately.

"What—what do you wish me to say?" asked Helen faintly.

"I wish you to tell me that you will be my wife; I wish you to take me for what I can give you for your happiness and your glory. I ask nothing else, I make no terms; if you will do it, it will make me the happiest man in the world. There is nothing else that I care for in life."

And then as the girl still stood, flushed and shuddering, hovering upon the verge, he took her hand in his and begged her to reply. "You must not keep me in suspense!" he exclaimed. "You must tell me,—tell me."

And Helen, almost sinking, answered him "Yes!" It was such a faint word that she scarcely heard it herself, but the other heard it, and trembling with delight, he caught her in his arms and pressed a burning kiss upon her cheek.

The effect surprised him; for the fire which had burned Helen and inflamed her cheeks had been ambition, and ambition alone. It was the man's money that she wanted and she was stirred with no less horror than ever at the thought of the price to be paid;

therefore the touch of his rough mustache upon her cheek acted upon her as an electric contact, and all the shame in her nature burst into flame. She tore herself loose with almost a scream. "No, no!" she cried. "Stop!"

Mr. Harrison gazed at her in astonishment for a moment, scarcely able to find a word to say. "Miss Davis," he protested, "Helen—what is the matter?"

"You had no right to do that!" she cried, trembling with anger.

"Helen!" protested the other, "have you not just promised to be my wife?" And the words made the girl turn white and drop her eyes in fear.

"Yes, yes," she panted helplessly, "but you should not—it is too soon!" The other stood watching her, perhaps divining a little of the cause of her agitation, and feeling, at any rate, that he could be satisfied for the present with his success. He answered, very humbly, "Perhaps you are right; I am very sorry for offending you," and stood silently waiting until the girl's emotions had subsided a little, and she had looked at him again. "You will pardon me?" he asked.

"Yes, yes," she said, weakly, "only—"

"And you will not forget the promise you have made me?"

"No," she answered, and then she gazed anxiously toward the door. "Let us go," she said imploringly; "it is all so hard for me to realize, and I feel so very faint."

The two went slowly down the hallway, Mr. Harrison not even venturing to offer her his arm; outside they stood for a minute upon the high steps, Helen leaning against a pillar and breathing very hard. She dared not raise her eyes to the man beside her.

"You wish to go now?" he asked, gently.

"Yes, please," she replied, "I think so; it is very late."

Helen scarcely knew what happened during the drive home, for she passed it in a half-dazed condition, almost overwhelmed by what she had done. She answered mechanically to all Mr. Harrison's remarks about his arrangements of the house and his plans elsewhere, but all reference to his wealth seemed powerless to

112

waken in her a trace of the exultation that had swept her away before, while every allusion to their personal relationship was like the touch of fire. Her companion seemed to divine the fact, and again he begged her anxiously not to forget the promise she had given. Helen answered faintly that she would not; but the words were hard for her to say and it was an infinite relief to her to see Oakdale again, and to feel that the strain would soon be over, for the time at any rate.

"I shall stay somewhere in the neighborhood," said Mr. Harrison. "You will let me see you often, Helen, will you not?"

"Yes," answered Helen, mechanically.

"I will come to-morrow," said the other, "and take you driving if you like; I promised to go back and lunch with your aunt to-day, as I thought I was to return to the city." In a moment more the carriage stopped in front of Helen's home, and the girl, without waiting for anyone to assist her, leaped out and with a hasty word of parting, ran into the house. She heard the horses trotting away, and then the door closed behind her, and she stood in the dark, silent hallway. She saw no one, and after gazing about her for a moment she stole into her little music-room and flung herself down upon the couch, where she lay with her head buried in her hands.

It was a long time afterwards when she glanced up again; she was trembling all over, and her face was white.

"In Heaven's name, how can I have done it?" she whispered hoarsely, to herself. "How can I have done it? And what *am* I to do now?"

Nur wer der Minne Macht ent-sagt, nur wer der Liebe Lust verjagt

Chapter VII

"Wie kommt's, dass du so traurig bist,
Da alles froh erscheint?
Man sieht dir's an den Augen an,
Gewiss, du hast geweint."

Helen might have spent the afternoon in that situation, tormenting herself with the doubts and fears that filled her mind, had it not been for the fact that her presence was discovered by Elizabeth, the servant, who came in to clean the room. The latter of course was astonished to see her, but Helen was in no mood to vouchsafe explanations.

"Just leave me alone," she said. "I do not feel very well. And don't tell father I am here yet."

"Your father, Miss Helen!" exclaimed the woman; "didn't you get his letter?"

"What letter?" And then poor Helen was made aware of another trouble.

"Mr. Davis wrote Mrs. Roberts last night," answered the servant. "He's gone away."

"Away!" cried the girl. "Where to?"

"To New York." Then the woman went on to explain that Mr. Davis had been invited to take the place of a friend who was ill, and had left Oakdale for a week. Helen understood that the letter must have reached her aunt after her own departure.

"Dear me!" the girl exclaimed, "How unfortunate! I don't want to stay here alone."

But afterwards it flashed over her that if she did she might be able to have a week of quiet to regain her self-possession. "Mr. Harrison couldn't expect to visit me if I were alone," she thought. "But then, I suppose he could, too," she added hastily, "if I am engaged to him! And I could never stand that!"

"Miss Helen," said the servant, who had been standing and watching her anxiously, "you look very ill; is anything the matter?"

"Nothing," Helen answered, "only I want to rest. Leave me alone, please, Elizabeth."

"Are you going to stay?" the other asked; "I must fix up your room."

"I'll have to stay," said Helen. "There's nothing else to do."

"Have you had lunch yet?"

"No, but I don't want any; just let me be, please."

Helen expected the woman to protest, but she did not. She turned away, and the girl sank back upon the couch and covered her face again.

"Everything has gone wrong!" she groaned to herself, "I know I shall die of despair; I don't want to be here all alone with Mr. Harrison coming here. Dear me, I wish I had never seen him!"

And Helen's nervous impatience grew upon her, until she could stand it no more, and she sprang up and began pacing swiftly up and down the room; she was still doing that when she heard a step in the hall and saw the faithful servant in the doorway with a tray of luncheon. Elizabeth asked no questions about matters that did not concern her, but she regarded this as her province, and she would pay no attention to Helen's protests. "You'll be ill if you don't eat," she vowed; "you look paler than I ever saw you."

And so the girl sat down to attempt to please her, Elizabeth standing by and talking to her in the meantime; but Helen was so wrapped up in her own thoughts that she scarcely heard a word—until the woman chanced to ask one question: "Did you hear about Mr. Arthur?"

And Helen gazed up at her. "Hear about him?" she said, "hear what about him?"

"He's very ill," said Elizabeth. Helen gave a start.

"Ill!" she gasped.

"Yes," said Elizabeth, "I thought you must know; Mr. Davis was over to see him yesterday."

"What is the matter?"

"The doctor said he must have been fearfully run down, and he was out in the storm and caught a cold; and he's been in a very bad way, delirious and unconscious by turns for two or three days."

Helen was staring at the servant in a dumb fright. "Tell me, Elizabeth," she cried, scarcely able to say the words, "he is not dangerously ill?"

"The danger is over now," the other answered, "so the doctor said, or else Mr. Davis would never have left; but he's in a bad way and it may be some time before he's up again."

Perhaps it was the girl's overwrought condition that made her more easily alarmed just then, for she was trembling all over as she heard those words. She had forgotten Arthur almost entirely during the past two days, and he came back to her at that moment as another thorn in her conscience.

"Mr. Davis said he wrote you to go and see him," went on the servant; "shall you, Miss Helen?"

"I—I don't know," said Helen faintly, "I'll see."

As a matter of fact, she knew that she almost certainly would *not* go to see Arthur after what had just passed; even to have him find out about it was something of which she simply could not think. She felt dread enough at having to tell her father of what had occurred with Mr. Harrison, and to see Arthur, even though he did not know about it, she knew was not in her power.

"Perhaps I ought not to have told you about it until after you had had your lunch; you are not eating anything, Miss Helen."

"I don't want anything," said Helen, mournfully; "take it now, please, Elizabeth, and please do not trouble me any more. I have a great deal to worry me."

When the woman had left the room, Helen shut the door and then sat down on a chair, staring blankly before her; there was a

117

mirror just across the room, and her own image caught her eye, startling her by its pale and haggard look.

"Dear me, it's dreadful!" she cried aloud, springing up. "Why *did* I let people trouble me in this way? I can't help Arthur, and I couldn't have helped him in the beginning. It's every bit of it his own fault, and I don't see why I should let it make me ill. And it's the same with the other thing; I could have been happy without all that wealth if I'd never seen it, and now I know I'll never be happy again,—oh, I know it!"

And Helen began once more pacing up and down.

"I never was this way before in my life," she cried with increasing vexation, "and I won't have it!"

She clenched her hands angrily, struggling within herself to shake off what was tormenting her. But she might as well have tried to shake off a mountain from her shoulders; hers had been none of the stern experience that gives power and command to the character, and of the kind of energy that she needed she had none, and not even a thought of it. She tried only to forget her troubles in some of her old pleasures, and when she found that she could not read, and that the music she tried to play sounded hollow and meaningless, she could only fling herself down upon the sofa with a moan. There, realizing her own impotence, she sank into dull despair, unable any longer to realize the difficulties which troubled her, and with only one certainty in her mind— that she was more lost and helpless than she had ever thought it possible for her to be.

Time is not a thing of much consequence under such circumstances, and it was a couple of hours before Helen was aroused. She heard a carriage stop at the door, and sprang up in alarm, with the thought that it might be Mr. Harrison. But as she stood trembling in the middle of the room she heard a voice inquiring for her, and recognized it as that of her aunt; a moment later Mrs. Roberts rushed into the room, and catching sight of Helen, flung her arms eagerly about her.

"My dear girl," she cried, "Mr. Harrison has just told me about what has happened!" And then as she read her niece's state of mind in her countenance, she added, "I expected to find you re-joicing, Helen; what is the matter?"

In point of fact the woman had known pretty well just how she would find Helen, and having no idea of leaving her to her own tormenting fancies, she had driven over the moment she had finished her lunch. "I received your father's letter," she said, without waiting for Helen to answer her, "so I came right over to take you back."

"To take me back!" echoed Helen.

"Yes, my dear; you don't suppose I mean to leave you here all alone by yourself, do you? And especially at such a time as this, when Mr. Harrison wants to see you?"

"But, Aunt Polly," protested Helen, "I don't want to see him!"

"Don't want to see him? Why, my dear girl, you have promised to be his wife!"

Mrs. Roberts saw Helen shudder slightly, and so she went on quickly, "He is going to stay at the hotel in the village; you won't find it the same as being in the house with him. But I do assure you, child, there never was a man more madly in love than he is."

"But, Auntie, dear, that Mr. Howard, too!" protested Helen, trembling.

"He will not interfere with you, for he never makes any noise; and you'll not know he's there. Of course, you won't play the piano, but you can do anything else you choose. And Mr. Harrison will probably take you driving every day." Then seeing how agitated Helen was, her aunt put her arms around her again, and led her to the sofa. "Come, Helen," she said," I don't blame you for being nervous. I know just how you feel, my dear."

"Oh, Aunt Polly!" moaned the girl. "I am so wretched!"

"I know," laughed Aunt Polly; "it's the idea of having to marry him, I suppose; I felt the very same way when I was in your place. But you'll find that wears off very quickly; you'll get used to seeing him. And besides, you know that you've *got* to marry him, if you want any of the other happiness!"

And Mrs. Roberts stopped and gazed about her. "Think, for in-stance, my dear," she went on, "of having to be content with this dingy little room, after having seen that magnificent place of his! Do you know, Helen, dear, that I really envy you; and it seems quite ridiculous to come over here and find you moping around. One would think you were a hermit and did not care anything about life."

"I do care about it," said the other, "and I love beautiful things and all; but, Aunt Polly, I can't help thinking it's dreadful to have to marry."

"Come and learn to like Mr. Harrison," said the other, cheerfully. "Helen, you are really too weak to ruin your peace of mind in this way; for you could see if you chose that all your troubles are of your own making, and that if you were really determined to be happy, you could do it. Why don't you, dear?"

"I don't know," protested the girl, faintly; "perhaps I am weak, but I can't help it."

"Of course not," laughed the other, "if you spend your afternoons shut up in a half-dark room like this. When you come with me you won't be able to do that way; and I tell you you'll find there's nothing like having social duties and an appearance to maintain in the world to keep one cheerful. If you didn't have me at your elbow I really believe you'd go all to pieces."

"I fear I should," said the girl; but she could not help laughing as she allowed herself to be led upstairs, and to have the dust bathed from her face and the wrinkles smoothed from her brow. In the meantime her diplomatic aunt was unobtrusively dropping as many hints as she could think of to stir Helen to a sense of the fact that she had suddenly become a person of consequence; and whether it was these hints or merely the reaction natural to Helen, it is certain that she was much calmer when she went down to the carriage, and much more disposed to resign herself to meeting Mr. Harrison again. And Mrs. Roberts was correspondingly glad that she had been foreseeing enough to come and carry her away; she had great confidence in her ability to keep Helen from foolish worrying, and to interest her in the great future that was before her.

"And then it's just as well that she should be at my house where she can find the comfort that she loves," she reflected. "I can see that she learns to love it more every day."

The great thing, of course, was to keep her ambition as much awake as possible, and so during the drive home Mrs. Roberts' conversation was of the excitement which the announcement of Helen's engagement would create in the social world, and of the brilliant triumph which the rest of her life would be, and of the vast preparations which she was to make for it. The trousseau soon came in for mention then; and what woman could have been indifferent to a trousseau, even for a marriage which she dreaded? After that the conversation was no longer a task, for Helen's animation never failed to build itself up when it was once awake; she was so pleased and eager that the drive was over before she knew it, and before she had had time for even one unpleasant thought about meeting Mr. Harrison.

It proved not to be a difficult task after all, for Mr. Harrison was quiet and dignified, and even a little reserved, as Helen thought, so that it occurred to her that perhaps he was offended at the ve-hemence with which she had repelled him. She did not know, but it seemed to her that perhaps it might have been his right to em-brace her after she had promised to marry him; the thought made her shudder, yet she felt sure that if she had asked her aunt she would have learned that she was very much in the wrong indeed. Helen's conscience was very restless just at that time, and it was pleasant to be able to lull it by being a little more gracious and kind to her ardent lover. The latter of course responded joyfully, so that the remainder of the afternoon passed quite pleasantly.

When Mr. Roberts arrived and had been acquainted with the tidings, he of course sought the first opportunity to see the girl, and to congratulate her upon her wonderful fortune. Helen had always found in her uncle a grave, business-like person, who treated her with indifference, and therefore inspired her with awe; it was not a little stirring to her vanity to find that she was now a person of sufficient consequence to reverse the relation.

This fact did yet a little more to make her realize the vastness of her sudden conquest, and so throughout dinner she was almost as exulting in her own heart as she had been at the same time on the previous day.

Her animation mounted throughout the evening, for Mr. Harrison and her aunt talked of the future—of endless trips abroad, and of palatial houses and royal entertainments at home—until the girl was completely dazed. Afterwards, when she and Mr. Harrison were left alone, Helen fascinated her companion as completely as ever, and was radiant herself, and rejoicing. As if to cap the climax, Mr. Harrison broached the subject of a trip to New York, to see if she could find anything at the various picture dealers to suit her music room, and also of a visit to Fairview to meet an architect and discuss her plan there.

The girl went up to her room just as completely full of exultation as she had been upon the night before, yet more comfortable in the conviction that there would be no repetition of that night's worry. Yet even as the thought occurred to her, it made her tremble; and as if some fiend had arranged it especially for her torment, as she passed down the hall a nurse came silently out of one of the rooms, and through the half open doorway Helen fancied that she heard a low moan. She shuddered and darted into her own room and locked the door; yet that did not exclude the image of the sufferer, or keep it from suggesting a train of thought that plunged the girl into misery. It made her think of Arthur, and of the haggard look that had been upon his face when he left her; and all Helen's angry assertions that it was not her fault could not keep her from tormenting herself after that. Always the fact was before her that however sick he might be, even dying, she could never bear to see him again, and so Arthur became the embodiment of her awakening conscience.

The result was that the girl slept very little that night, spending half of it in fact alternately sitting in a chair and pacing the room in agitation, striving in vain to find some gleam of light to guide her out of the mazes in which she was lost. The gray dawn found her tossing feverishly about upon her pillow, yearning for the time when she had been happy, and upbraiding herself for having been drawn into her present trouble.

When she arose later on, she was more pale and wearied than she had been upon the morning before; then she had at least possessed a resolution, while this time she was only helpless and despairing. Thus her aunt found her when she came in to greet her, and the dismay of the worthy matron may be imagined.

However, being an indefatigable little body, she set bravely to work again; first of all, by rebuking the girl for her weakness she managed to rouse her to effort once more, and then by urging the necessity of seeing people and of hiding her weakness, she managed to obtain at last a semblance of cheerfulness. In the meantime Mrs. Roberts was helping her to dress and to remove all traces of her unhappiness, so that when Helen descended to breakfast she had received her first lesson in one of the chief tasks of the social regime:

> *"Full many in the silent night*
> *Have wept their grief away;*
> *And in the morn you fancy*
> *Their hearts were ever gay."*

And Helen played her part so well that Mrs. Roberts was much encouraged, and beamed upon her across the table. As a, matter of fact, because her natural happiness was not all crushed, and because playing a part was not easy to the girl, she was very soon interested in the various plans that were being discussed. When Mr. Harrison called later on and proposed a drive, she accepted with genuine pleasure.

To be sure, she found it a trifle less thrilling than on the day before, for the novelty was gone; but that fact did not cause her much worry. In all her anticipations of the pleasure before her, it had occurred to her as little as it occurs to others in her situation to investigate the laws of the senses through which the pleasure is to be obtained. There is a whole moral philosophy to be extracted from the little word "ennui" by those who know; but Helen was not of the knowing. She believed that when she was tired of the horses she could delight herself with her beautiful house, and that when she was tired of the house she could have a new one. All her life she had been deriving ecstasy from beautiful things, from dresses, and flowers, and books, and music, and pictures; and of course it was only necessary to have an infinite quantity of such things in order to be infinitely happy. The way to have the infinite quantity was to marry Mr. Harrison, or at any rate that was Helen's view, and she was becoming more and more irritated because it did not work well in practice, and more and more convinced that her aunt must be right in blaming her weakness.

In the meantime, being in the open air and among all the things that she loved, she was bound to rejoice once more; and rejoice she did, not even allowing herself to be hindered by Mr. Harrison's too obvious failures to comprehend her best remarks. Helen argued that she was not engaged to the man because of his cleverness, and that when she had come to the infinite happiness towards which she was traveling so fast, she would have inspiration enough for two. She had enough for the present to keep them both happy throughout the drive, and when she returned she found that some of the neighbors had driven over to see her, and to increase her excitement by their congratulations. The Machiavellian Aunt Polly had told the news to several friends on the day before, knowing full well that it would spread during the night, and that Helen would have her first taste of triumph the next day.

And so it continued, and exactly as on the night before, the feverish excitement swept Helen on until the bedtime hour arrived. Then she went up into her room alone, to wrestle with the same dreadful specter as before.

The story of that day was the story of all that followed; Helen was destined to find that she might sweep herself away upon the wings of her ambition as often as she chose, and revel all she pleased in the thought of Mr. Harrison's wealth; but when the excitement was over, and she came to be all alone, she could think only of the one dreadful fact of the necessity of marrying him. She was paying a Faustus price for her happiness; and in the night time the price stared at her, and turned all her happiness to misery.

A state of mind such as this was so alien to Helen that it would have been strange indeed if she had sunk into it without protest and rebellion; as day after day passed, and the misery continued, her dissatisfaction with everything about her built itself into a climax; more and more plainly she was coming to see the widening of the gulf between the phantom she was pursuing and the place, where she stood. Finally there came one day, nearly a week after her engagement, when Helen was so exhausted and so wretched that she had made up her mind to remain in her room, and had withstood all her aunt's attempts to dissuade her. She had passed the morning in bed, between equally vain attempts to become interested in a book and to make up for the sleep she had missed during the night, and was just about giving up both in despair when the maid entered to say that Elizabeth wished to see her. Helen gave a start, for she knew that something must be wrong; when the woman entered she asked breathlessly what it was.

"It's about Mr. Arthur," was the hurried reply, and Helen turned paler than ever, and clutched the bedclothing in her trembling hands.

"What is it?" she cried.

"Why you know, Miss Helen," said Elizabeth, "your father wrote me to go and see him whenever I could, and I've just come from there this morning."

"And how is he?"

"He looked dreadful, but he had gotten up to-day, and he was sitting by the window when I came in. He was hardly a shadow of himself."

Helen was trembling. "You have not been to see him?" asked the woman.

"No," said Helen, faintly, "I—" and then she stopped.

"Why not?" Elizabeth inquired anxiously.

"He did not ask for me, did he?" asked the girl, scarcely able to utter the words.

"No," said the woman, "but you know, everybody told me you were engaged to a rich man—"

And Helen started forwrard with a cry. "Elizabeth!" she gasped, "you—you didn't—!"

"Yes," said the other, "I told him." And then seeing the girl's look of terror, she stopped short. Helen stared at her for fully half a minute without uttering a word; and then the woman went on, slowly, "It was very dreadful, Miss Helen; he went almost crazy, and I was so frightened that I didn't know what I should do. Please tell me what is the matter."

Helen was still gazing dumbly at the woman, seeming not to have heard the last question. "I—I can't tell you," she said, when it was repeated again; "you ought not to have told him, Elizabeth."

"Miss Helen," cried the woman, anxiously, "you *must* do something! For I am sure that I know what is the matter; he loves you, and you must know it, too. And it will certainly kill him; weak as he was, he rushed out of the house, and I could not find him anywhere. Miss Helen, you *must* go and see him!"

The girl sat with the same look of helpless fright upon her face, and with her hands clenched tightly between her knees; the other went on talking hurriedly, but Helen scarcely heard anything after that; her mind was too full of its own thoughts. It was several minutes more before she even noticed that the woman was still insisting that she must go to see Artheur. "Please leave me now!" she cried wildly; "please leave me! I cannot explain anything,— I want to be alone!" And when the door was shut she became once more dumb and motionless, staring blankly ahead of her, a helpless victim of her own wretched thoughts.

"That is the end of it," she groaned to herself; "oh, that is the end of it!"

Winkt dir nicht hold die hehre Burg?

Chapter VIII

Thou would'st be happy,
Endlessly happy,
Or endlessly wretched.

Helen was quite powerless to do anything whatever after that last piece of misfortune; it seemed as if she could have remained just where she was for hours, shuddering at the sight of what was happening, yet utterly helpless before it. The world was taking a very serious aspect indeed to the bright and laughing girl, who had thought of it as the home of birds and flowers; yet she knew not what to make of the change, or how she was to blame for it, and she could only sit still and tremble. She was in the same position and the same state of mind when her aunt entered the room some minutes later.

Mrs. Roberts stood watching her silently, and then as Helen turned her gaze of pleading misery upon her, she came forward and sat down in a chair by the bedside, and fixed her keen eyes upon the girl.

"Oh, Aunt Polly!" cried Helen; "what am I to do? I am so wretched!"

"I have just been talking to Elizabeth," said Mrs. Roberts, with some sternness, "and she's been telling you about Arthur—is that what is the matter with you, Helen?"

"Yes," was the trembling response, "what can I do?"

"Tell me, Helen, in the first place," demanded the other. "When you saw Arthur that day in the woods, what did you do? Did you make him any promises?"

"No, Auntie."

"Did you hold out any hopes to him? Did you say anything to him at all about love?"

"I—I told him it was impossible," said Helen, eagerly, clutching at that little crumb of comfort.

"Then in Heaven's name, child," cried the other in amazement, "what is the matter with you? If Arthur chooses to carry on in this fashion, why in the world should you punish yourself in this horrible way? What is the matter with you, Helen? Are you responsible to him for your marriage? I don't know which is the most absurd, the boy's behavior, or your worrying about it."

"But, Auntie," stammered the girl, "he is so ill—he might die!"

"Die, bosh!" exclaimed Mrs. Roberts; "he frightened Elizabeth by his ravings; it is the most absurd nonsense,—he a penniless school-teacher, and the Lord only knows what besides! I only wish I'd been there to talk to him, for I don't think he'd have frightened me! What in the world do you suppose he wants, anyway? Is he mad enough to expect you to marry him?"

"I don't know, Aunt Polly," said Helen, weakly.

"I'd never have believed that Arthur could be capable of anything so preposterous as this behavior," vowed Mrs. Roberts; "and then to come up here and find you wearing yourself to a skeleton about it!"

"It isn't only that, Auntie," protested Helen, "there is so much else; I am miserable!"

"Yes," said the other, grimly; "I see it as well as you, and there's just about as much reason in any of it as in the matter of Arthur." Then Mrs. Roberts moved her chair nearer, and after gazing at Helen for a moment, began again. "I've been meaning to say something to you, and it might just as well be said now. For all this matter is coming to a climax, Helen; it can't go on this way very much longer, for you'll kill yourself. It's got to be settled one way or the other, once and for all." And Mrs. Roberts stopped and took a deep breath, preparing for one more struggle; Helen still gazed at her helplessly.

"I'm not going to say anything more about Arthur," declared the woman; "if you choose to torment yourself about such absurdities, I can't help it. Arthur's behavior is not the least your fault, and you know it; but all the other trouble is your fault, and there's nobody else to blame. For the question is just as simple as the day, Helen, and you must see it and decide it; you've got to choose between one of two things, either to marry Mr. Harrison or to give him up; and there's no excuse for your hesitating and tormenting yourself one day longer."

Then the indomitable woman set to work at her old task of conjuring up before the girl's eyes all the allurements that had so often made her heart throb; she, pictured Fairview and all its luxuries, and the admiration and power that must be hers when she was mistress of it; and she mentioned every other source of pleasure that she knew would stir Helen's eager thirst. After having hammered away at that theme until she saw signs of the effect she desired, she turned to the other side of the picture.

"Helen," she demanded, "is it really possible for you to think of giving up these things and going back to live in that miserable little house at Oakdale? Can you not see that you would be simply burying yourself alive? You might just as well be as ugly as those horrible Nelson girls across the way. Helen, you *know* you belong to a different station in life than those people! You know you have a right to some of the beautiful things in the world, and you know that after this vision of everything perfect that you have seen, you can never possibly be happy in your ignorant girlish way again. You have promised Mr. Harrison to marry him, and made him go to all the expense that he has; and you've told everybody you know, and all the world is talking about your triumph; and you've had Mr. Roberts go to all the trouble he has about your trousseau,—surely, Helen, you cannot dream of changing your mind and giving all this up. It is ridiculous to talk about it."

"I don't want to give it up," protested the girl, moaning, "but, oh, I can't—"

"I know!" exclaimed the other. "I've heard all that a thousand times. Don't you see, Helen, that you've simply *got* to marry him!

There is no other possibility to think of, and all of your weakness is that you don't perceive that fact, and make up your mind to it. Just see how absurd you are, to make yourself ill in this way."

"But I can't help it, Auntie, indeed I can't!"

"You could help it if you wanted to," vowed the other. "I am quite disgusted with you. I have told you a thousand times that this is all an imaginary terror that you are conjuring up for yourself, to ruin your health and happiness. When you have married him you will see that it's just as I tell you, and you'll laugh at yourself for feeling as you did."

"But it's in the, meantime, Aunt Polly—it's having to think about it that frightens me."

"Well, let me tell you one thing," said Mrs. Roberts; "if I found that I couldn't cure myself of such weakness as this, sooner than let it ruin my life and make everyone about me wretched, I'd settle the matter right now and forever; I'd marry him within a week, Helen!" And the resolute little woman clenched her hands grimly. "Yes, I would," she exclaimed, "and if I found I hadn't strength enough to hold my resolution, I'd marry him to-morrow, and there'd be an end to it!"

"You don't realize, Helen, how you treat Mr. Harrison," she went on, as the girl shuddered; "and how patient he is. You'd not find many men like him in that respect, my dear. For he's madly in love with you, and you treat him as coldly as if he were a stranger. I can see that, for I watch you, and I can see how it offends him. You have promised to be his wife, Helen, and yet you behave in this ridiculous way. You are making yourself ill, and you look years older every day, yet you make not the least attempt to conquer yourself."

So she went on, and Helen began to feel more and more that she was doing a very great wrong indeed. Mrs. Roberts' sharp questioning finally drew from her the story of her reception of Mr. Harrison's one kiss, and Helen was made to seem quite ridiculous and even rude in her own eyes; her aunt lectured her with such unaccustomed sternness that she was completely frightened, and came to look upon her action as the cause of all the rest of her misery.

"It's precisely on that account that you still regard him as a stranger," Mrs. Roberts vowed; "of course he makes no more advances, and you might go on forever in that way." Helen promised that the next time she was alone with Mr. Harrison she would apologize for her rudeness, and treat him in a different manner.

"I wish," Mrs. Roberts went on, "that I could only make you see as plainly as I see, Helen, how very absurd your conduct is. Day by day you are filling your mind with the thought of the triumph that is to be yours, so that it takes hold of you and becomes all your life to you; and all the time you know that to possess it there is one thing which you have got to do. And instead of realizing the fact and reconciling yourself to it, you sit down and torment yourself as if you were a creature without reason or will. Can you not see that you must be wretched?"

"Yes, I see," said Helen, weakly.

"You see it, but you make no effort to do anything else! You make me almost give you up in despair. You will not see that this weakness has only to be conquered once, and that then your life can be happy!"

"But, Auntie, dear," exclaimed Helen, "it is so hard!"

"Anything in life would be hard for a person who had no more resolution than you," responded the other. "Because you know nothing about the world, you fancy you are doing something very unusual and dreadful; but I assure you it's what every girl has to do when she marries in society. And there's no one of them but would laugh at your behavior; you just give Mr. Harrison up, and see how long it would be before somebody else would take him! Oh, child, how I wish I could give you a little of my energy; you would go to the life that is before you in a very different way, I promise you! For really the only way that you can have any happiness in the world is to be strong and take it, and if you once had a purpose and some determination you would feel like a different person. Make up your mind what you wish to do, Helen, and go and do it, and take hold of yourself and master yourself, and show what you are made of!"

Aunt Polly was quite sublime as she delivered that little exordium; and to the girl, anxious as she was for her old strength and happiness, the words were like music. They made her blood flow again, and there was a light in her eyes.

"Oh, Auntie," she said, "I'll try to."

"Try!" echoed the other, "what comes of all your trying? You have been reveling for a week in visions of what is to be yours; and that ought surely to have been enough time for you to make up your mind; and yet every time that I find you alone, all your resolution is gone; you simply have no strength, Helen!"

"Oh, I will have it!" cried the girl; "I don't mean to do this way any more; I never saw it so plainly."

"You see it now, because I'm talking to you, and you always do see it then. But I should think the very terror of what you have suffered would serve as a motive, and make you quite desperate. Can you not see that your very safety depends upon your taking this resolution and keeping it, and not letting go of it, no matter what happens? From what I've seen of you, Helen, I know that if you do not summon all your energies together, and fling aside every purpose but this, and act upon it *now,* while you feel it so keenly, you will surely fail. For anybody can withstand a temptation for a while, when his mind is made up; all the trouble is in keeping it made up for a long time. I tell you if I found I was losing, sooner than surrender I would do anything, absolutely anything!"

Mrs. Roberts had many more words of that heroic kind; she was a vigorous little body, and she was quite on fire with enthusiasm just then, and with zeal for the consummation of the great triumph. Perhaps there is no occupation of men quite without its poetry, and even a society leader may attain to the sublime in her devotion to life as she sees it. Besides that the over-zealous woman was exalted to eloquence just then by a feeling that she was nearer her goal than ever before, and that she had only to spur Helen on and keep her in her present glow to clinch the matter; for the girl was very much excited indeed, and showed both by what she said and by the change in her behavior that she was determined to have an end to her own wretchedness and to conquer her shrinking from her future husband at any cost. During all the time that she was dressing, her aunt was stirring her resolution with the same appeal, so that Helen felt that she had never seen her course so clearly before, or had so much resolution to follow it. She spread out her arms and drank deep breaths of relief because she was free from her misery, and knew how to keep so; and at the same time, because she still felt tremblings of fear, she clenched her hands in grim earnestness. When she was ready to descend she was flushed and trembling with excitement, and quite full of her resolution. "She won't have to go very far," Mrs. Roberts mused, "for the man is madly in love with her."

"I want you to look as beautiful as you can, dear," she said aloud, by way of changing the subject; "besides Mr. Harrison, there'll be another visitor at lunch to-day."

"A stranger?" echoed Helen.

"You remember, dear, when I told you of Mr. Howard I spoke of a third person who was coming—Lieutenant Maynard?"

"Oh, yes," said the girl; "is he here?"

"Just until the late train this evening," answered the other. "He got his leave as he expected, but of course he didn't want to come while Mr. Howard was so ill."

Helen remembered with a start having heard someone say that Mr. Howard was better. "Auntie," she cried, "he won't be at lunch, will he? I don't want to see him."

"He won't, dear," was the reply; "the doctor said he could leave his room to-day, but it will be afterwards, when you have gone driving with Mr. Harrison."

"And will he leave soon?" asked Helen, shuddering; the mention of the invalid's name had instantly brought to her mind the thought of Arthur.

"He will leave to-morrow, I presume; he probably knows he has caused us trouble enough," answered Mrs. Roberts; and then

133

reading Helen's thought, and seeing a sign upon her face of the old worry, she made haste to lead her down the stairs.

Helen found Mr. Harrison in conversation with a tall, distinguished-looking man in naval uniform, to whom she was introduced by her aunt; the girl saw that the officer admired her, which was only another stimulant to her energies, so that she was at her cleverest during the meal that followed. She accepted the invitation of Mr. Harrison to go with him to Fairview during the afternoon, and after having been in her room all the morning, she was looking forward to the drive with no little pleasure, as also—to the meeting with the architect whom Mr. Harrison said would be there.

It seemed once as if the plan were to be interrupted, and as if her excitement and resolution were to come to naught, for a telegram arrived for Mr. Harrison, and he announced that he was called away to New York upon some business. But as it proved, this was only another circumstance to urge her on in carrying out her defiant resolution, for Mr. Harrison added that he would not have to leave until the evening, and her aunt gazed at the girl significantly, to remind her of how little time there was. Helen felt her heart give a sudden leap, and felt a disagreeable trembling seize upon her; her animation became more feverish yet in consequence.

After the luncheon, when she ran up for her hat and gloves, her aunt followed her, but Helen shook her off with a laughing assurance that everything would be all right, and then ran out into the hallway; she did not go on, however, for something that she saw caused her to spring quickly back, and turn pale.

"What is it?" whispered her aunt, as Helen put her finger to her lips.

"It's *he!*" replied the girl, shuddering; "wait!"

"He" was the unfortunate invalid, who was passing down the hallway upon the arm of Lieutenant Maynard; Helen shook her head at all her aunt's laughing protests, and could not be induced to leave the room until the two had passed on; then she ran down, and leaving the house by another door, sprang into the carriage with Mr. Harrison and was whirled away, waving a laughing good-by to her aunt.

The fresh air and the swift motion soon completed the reaction from Helen's morning unhappiness; and as generally happened when she was much excited, her imagination carried her away in one of her wild flights of joy, so that her companion was as much lost as ever in admiration and delight. Helen told him countless stories, and made countless half-comprehended witticisms, and darted a great many mischievous glances which were comprehended much better; when they had passed within the gates of Fairview, being on private land she felt even less need of restraint, and sang "Dich, theure Halle, gruss' ich wieder!" and laughed at her own cleverness quite as much as if her companion had understood it all.

After that it was a new delight to discover that work was progressing rapidly upon the trimming of the forest and the turning of the grass-grown road into a broad avenue; likewise the "hay crop" was in, and the lawn plowed and raked and ready for grass seed, and the undesirable part of the old furniture carted away,— all of which things Helen knew had been done according to her commands. And scarcely had all this been appreciated properly before the architect arrived; Helen was pleased with him because for one thing he was evidently very much impressed by her beauty, and for another because he entered so understandingly into all her ideas. He and the girl spent a couple of the happiest hours in discussing the details of the wonderful music room, a thing which seemed to her more full of delightful possibilities than any other in all her radiant future; it was a sort of a child's dream to her, with a fairy godmother to make it real, and her imagination ran riot in a vision of banks of flowers, and of paintings of all things that embody the joys of music, the "shapes that haunt thought's wildernesses." At night the whole was to be illuminated in such a way as to give these verisimilitude, and in the daytime it would be no less beautiful, because it was to be almost all glass upon two sides. Helen was rejoiced that the architect realized the importance of the fact that "a music room ought to be out of doors;"

and then as she made the further welcome discovery that the moon would shine into it, she vowed eagerly that there would be no lights at all in her music room at those times. Afterwards she told a funny story of how Schumann had been wont to improvise under such circumstances, until his next-door neighbor was so struck by the romance of it that he proceeded to imitate it, and to play somebody or other's technical studies whenever the moon rose; at which narrative Helen and the architect laughed very heartily, and Mr. Harrison with them, though he would not have known the difference between a technical study and the "Moonlight Sonata."

Altogether, Helen was about as happy as ever throughout that afternoon, tho one who watched her closely might have thought there was something nervous about her animation, especially later on, when the talk with the architect was nearing its end; Helen's eyes had once or twice wandered uneasily about the room, and when finally the man rose to leave, she asked him with a sudden desperate resolution to look over the rest of the rooms and see what he thought of her suggestions. The latter expressed himself as pleased to oblige her, but he would probably have been somewhat chagrined had he known how little Helen really attended to his remarks; her mind was in a whirl, and all that he said sounded distant and vague; her one wish was that he might stay and give her time to think.

But Helen found the uselessness of shrinking, and the time came at last when she saw to her despair that there was no more to say, and that the man must go. In a few minutes more he was actually gone, and she was left all alone in the great house with Mr. Harrison.

The two went back into the dining room, where Mr. Harrison stood leaning his hand upon the table, and Helen stood in front of him, her lips trembling. Twice she made a faint attempt to speak, and then she turned and began pacing up and down the room in agitation. Mr. Harrison was watching her, seeing that there was something on her mind, and also that her emotion made her more beautiful and more disturbing to him than ever.

At last Helen went and sat down upon a sofa at one side, and clenching her hands very tightly about her knees, looked up at him and said, in a faint voice, "I had something to say to you, Mr. Harrison." Then she stopped, and her eyes fell, and her breath came very hard.

"What is it, dear?" asked Mr. Harrison gently.

And Helen's lips trembled more than ever, and her voice sank still lower as she said, "I—I don't know how to begin."

The other was silent for a few moments more, after which he came slowly across the room and sat down beside her.

"Helen," he said, "I had something to say to you also; suppose I say it first?"

The girl's chest was heaving painfully, and her heart throbbing violently, but she gazed into his eyes, and smiled, and answered him "Very well." He took one of her burning hands in his, and she made no resistance.

"Helen, dear," he said, "do you remember it was nearly a week ago that we stood in this same room, and that you promised to be my wife? You were very cold to me then. I have been waiting patiently for you to change a little, not venturing to say anything for fear of offending you. But it is very hard—"

He had bent forward pleadingly, and his face was very close to hers, trying to read her heart. Perhaps it was well that he could not, for it would have frightened him. The moment was one of fearful suffering for Helen, tho there was no sign of it, except that she was trembling like a leaf, and that her lips were white. There was just a moment of suspense, and then with a cruel effort she mastered herself and gazed up at the man, a smile forcing itself to her lips again.

"What is it that you wish?" she asked.

"I want you to care for me," the other said—"to love me just a little, Helen; will you?"

"I—I think so," was the reply, in a scarcely audible voice.

And Mr. Harrison pressed her hand in his and bent forward eagerly. "Then I may kiss you, dear?" he asked; "you will not mind?"

And Helen bowed her head and answered, "No." In this same instant, as she sank forward the man clasped her in his arms; he pressed her upon his bosom, and covered her cheeks and forehead with his passionate, burning kisses. Helen, crushed and helpless in his grasp, felt a revulsion of feeling so sudden and so overwhelming that it was an agony to her, and she almost screamed aloud. She was choking and shuddering, and her cheeks were on fire, while in the meantime Mr. Harrison, almost beside himself with passion, pressed her tighter to him and poured out his protestations of devotion. Helen bore it until she was almost mad with the emotion that had rushed over her, and then she made a wild effort to tear herself free. Her hair was disordered, and her face red, and her whole being throbbing with shame, but he still held her in his tight embrace.

"You are not angry, Helen dear?" he asked.

"No," the girl gasped

"You told me that I might kiss you," he said; and she was so choking with her emotion that she could not answer a word, she could only shudder and submit to his will. And Mr. Harrison, supposing that her emotions were very different from what they were, rested her head upon his shoulder, smoothing back her tangled hair and whispering into her ear how beautiful she was beyond any dream of his, and how the present moment was the happiest of his lifetime.

"I thought it would never come, dear," he said, kissing her forehead again, "you were so very cold." Helen had not yet ceased fighting the fearful battle in her own heart, and so as he looked into her eyes, she gazed up at him and forced another ghastly smile to her lips: they looked so very beautiful that Mr. Harrison kissed them again and again, and he would probably have been content to kiss them many times more, and to forget everything else in the bliss, had Helen been willing.

But she felt just then that if the strain continued longer she would go mad; with a laugh that was half hysterical, she tore herself loose by main force, and sprang up, reminding the other that he had a train to catch. Mr. Harrison demurred, but the girl would hear no more, and she took him by the hand and led him to the door, still laughing, and very much flushed and excited, so that he thought she was happier than ever. It would have startled him could he have seen her as he went to call for the horses,— how she staggered and clung to a pillar for support, as white as the marble she leaned against.

He did not see her, however, and when the two were driving rapidly away she was as vivacious as ever; Helen had fought yet one more conflict, and her companion was not skilled enough in the study of character to perceive that it was a desperate and hysterical kind of animation. Poor Helen was facing gigantic shadows just then, and life wore its most fearful and menacing look to her; she had plunged so far in her contest that it was now a battle for life and death, and with no quarter. She had made the choice of "Der Atlas," of endless joy or endless sorrow, and in her struggle to keep the joy she was becoming more and more frantic, more and more terrified at the thought of the other possibility. She knew that to fail now would mean shame and misery more overwhelming than she could bear, and so she was laughing and talking with frenzied haste; and every now and then she would stop and shudder, and then race wildly on,—

> "Like one, that on a lonesome road
> Doth walk in fear and dread,
> And having once turned round walks on,
> And turns no more his head;
> Because he knows a frightful fiend
> Doth close behind him tread."

And so all through the ride, because the girl's shame and fear haunted her more and more, she became more and more hysterical, and more and more desperate; and Mr. Harrison thought that he had never seen her so brilliant, and so daring, and so inspired; nor did he have the least idea how fearfully overwrought she was,

until suddenly as they came to a fork in the road he took a different one than she expected, and she clutched him wildly by the
arm. "Why do you do that?" she almost screamed. "Stop!"

"What?" he asked in surprise. "Take this road?"

"Yes!" exclaimed Helen. "Stop! Stop!"

"But it's only half a mile or so farther," said Mr. Harrison, rein-
ing up his horses, "and I thought you'd like the change."

"Yes," panted Helen, with more agitation than ever. "But I
can't,—we'd have to go through Hilltown!"

The wondering look of course did not leave the other's face at
that explanation. "You object to Hilltown?" he asked.

"Yes," said Helen, shuddering; "it is a horrible place."

"Why, I thought it was a beautiful town," laughed he. "But of
course it is for you to say." Then he gazed about him to find a
place to turn the carriage. "We'll have to go on a way," he said.
"The road is too narrow here. I'm sorry I didn't ask you, but I had
no idea it made any difference."

They continued, however, for fully a mile, and the road remained narrow, so that there was danger of upsetting in the ditch
if they tried to turn. "What do you wish me to do?" Mr. Harrison
asked with a smile. "The more we go on the longer it will take us
if we are to go back, and I may miss my train; is your prejudice
against Hilltown so very strong, Miss Davis?"

"Oh, no," Helen answered, with a ghastly smile. "Pray go on;
it's of no consequence."

As a matter of fact, it was of the greatest consequence; for
that incident marked the turning point of the battle in Helen's
heart. Her power seemed to go from her with every turn of the
wheels that brought her nearer to that dreaded place, and she
became more and more silent, and more conscious of the fearful
fact that her wretchedness was mastering her again. It seemed to
her terrified imagination as if everything was growing dark and
threatening, as before the breaking of a thunderstorm.

"You must indeed dislike Hilltown, Miss Davis," said her companion, smiling. "Why are you so very silent?"

Helen made no reply; she scarcely heard him, in fact, so taken up was she with what was taking place in her own mind; all her thoughts then were about Arthur and what had become of him, and what he was thinking about her; and chiefest of all, because her cheeks and forehead had a fearfully conscious feeling, what he would think, could he know what she had just been doing. Thus it was that as the houses of Hilltown drew near, remorse and shame and terror were rising, and her frantic protests against them were weakening, until suddenly every emotion was lost in suspense, and the shadows of the great elm-trees that arched the main street of the town closed them in. Helen knew the house where Arthur lodged, and knew that she should pass it in another minute; she could do nothing but wait and watch and tremble.

The carriage rattled on, gazed at by many curious eyes, for everyone in Hilltown knew about the young beauty and the prize she had caught; but Helen saw no one, and had eyes for only one thing, the little white house where Arthur lodges. The carriage swept by and she saw no one, but she saw that the curtain of Arthur's room was drawn, and she shuddered at the thought, "Suppose he should be dying!" Yet it was a great load off her mind to have escaped seeing him, and she was beginning to breathe again and ask herself if she still might not win the battle, when the carriage came to the end of the town, and to a sight that froze her blood.

There was a tavern by the roadside, a low saloon that was the curse of the place, and she saw from the distance a figure come out of the door. Her heart gave a fearful throb, for it was a slender figure, clad in black, hatless and with disordered hair and clothing. In a moment more, as Helen clutched the rail beside her and stared wildly, the carriage had swept on and come opposite the man; and he glanced up into Helen's eyes, and she recognized the face, in spite of all its ghastly whiteness and its sunken cheeks; it was Arthur!

There was just an instant's meeting of their looks, and then the girl was whirled on; but that one glance was enough to leave her as if paralyzed. She made no sound, nor any movement, and so her companion did not even know that anything had happened until they had gone half a mile farther; then as he chanced to glance at her he reined up his horses with a cry.

"Helen!" he exclaimed. "What is the matter?" The girl clutched his arm so tightly that he winced, powerful man that he was. "Take me home," she gasped. "Oh, quick, please take me home!"

Chapter IX

"Peace! Sit you down,
And let me wring your heart; for so I shall,
If it be made of penetrable stuff."

Helen ran up to her room when she reached home, and shut herself in, and after that she had nothing to do but suffer. All of her excitement was gone from her then, and with it every spark of her strength; the fiends that had been pursuing her rose up and seized hold of her, and lashed her until she writhed and cried aloud in agony. She was helpless to resist them, knowing not which way to turn or what to do,—completely cowed and terrified. But there was no more sinking into the dull despair that had mastered her before; the face of Arthur, as she had seen it in that one glimpse, had been burned into her memory with fire, and she could not shut it from her sight; when the fact that he had come from the tavern, and what that must mean rose before her, it was almost more than she could bear, cry out as she might that she could not help it, that she never could have helped it, that she had nothing to do with it. Moreover, if there was any possibility of the girl's driving out that specter, there was always another to take its place. It was not until she was alone in her room, until all her resolution was gone, and all of her delusions, that she realized the actual truth about what she had done that afternoon; it was like a nightmare to her then. She seemed always to feel the man's arms clasping her, and whenever she thought of his kisses her forehead burned her like fire, so that she flung herself down by the bedside, and buried it in the pillows.

It was thus that her aunt found her when she came in to call Helen to dinner; and this time the latter's emotions were so real and so keen that there was no prevailing over them, or persuading her to anything. "I don't want to eat!" she cried again and again in answer to her aunt's alarmed insistence. "No, I am not coming down! I want to be alone! Alone, Aunt Polly—please leave me alone!"

"But, Helen," protested Mrs. Roberts, "won't you please tell me what is the matter? What in the world can have happened to you?"

"I can't tell you," the girl cried hysterically. "I want you to go and leave me alone!" And she shut the door and locked it, and then began pacing wildly up and down the room, heedless of the fact that her aunt was still standing out in the hallway; the girl was too deeply shaken just then to have any thought about appearances.

She was thinking about Arthur again, and about his fearful plight; there rushed back upon her all the memories of their childhood, and of the happiness which they had known together. The thought of the broken figure which she had seen by the roadside became more fearful to her every moment. It was not that it troubled her conscience, for Helen could still argue to herself that she had done nothing to wrong her friend, that there had been nothing selfish in her attitude towards him; she had wished him to be happy. It seemed to her that it was simply a result of the cruel perversity of things that she had been trampling upon her friend's happiness in order to reach her own, and that all her struggling had only served to make things worse. The fact that it was not her fault, however, did not make the situation seem less tragic and fearful to her; it had come to such a crisis now that it drove her almost mad to think about it, yet she was completely helpless to know what to do, and as she strode up and down the room, she clasped her hands to her aching head and cried aloud in her perplexity.

Then too her surging thoughts hurried on to another unhappiness,—to her father, and what he would say when he learned the dreadful news. How could she explain it to him? And how could she tell him about her marriage? At the mere thought of that the other horror seized upon her again, and she sank down in a chair by the window and hid her face in her hands.

"Oh, how can I have done it?" she gasped to herself. "Oh, it was so dreadful! And what am I to do now?"

That last was the chief question, the one to which all others led; yet it was one to which she could find no answer. She was completely confused and helpless, and she exclaimed aloud again and again, "Oh, if I could only find some one to tell me! I do not know how I can keep Arthur from behaving in that dreadful way, and I know that I cannot ever marry Mr. Harrison!"

The more she tortured herself with these problems, the more agitated she became. She sat there at the window, clutching the sill in her hands and staring out, seeing nothing, and knowing only that the time was flying, and that her anxiety was building itself up and becoming an agony which she could not bear.

"Oh, what am I to do?" she groaned again and again; and she passed hours asking herself the fearful question; the twilight had closed about her, and the moon had risen behind the distant hills.

So oblivious to all things about her was she, that she failed at first to notice something else, something which would ordinarily have attracted her attention at once,—a sound of music which came to her from somewhere near. It was the melody of Grieg's "An den Frubling" played upon a violin, and it had stolen into Helen's heart and become part of her own stormy emotion before she had even thought of what it was or whence it came. The little piece is the very soul of the springtime passion, and to the girl it was the very utterance of all her yearning, lifting her heart in a great throbbing prayer. When it had died away her hands were clenched very tightly, and her breath was coming fast.

She remained thus for a minute, forgetful of everything; then at last she found herself thinking "it must be Mr. Howard," and waiting to see if he would play again. But he did not do so, and Helen sat in silence for a long time, her thoughts turned to him. She found herself whispering "so he is a wonderful musician after all," and noticing that the memory of his wan face frightened her no longer; it seemed just then that there could be no one in the world more wretched than herself. She was only wishing that he would begin again, for that utterance of her grief had seemed like a victory, and now in the silence she was sinking back into her despair. The more she waited, the more impatient she grew, until suddenly she rose from her seat.

"He might play again if I asked him," she said to herself. "He would if he knew I was unhappy; I wonder where he can be?"

Helen's window was in the front of the house, opening upon a broad lawn whose walks were marked in the moonlight by the high shrubbery that lined them. Some distance beyond, down one of the paths, were two summer-houses, and it seemed to her that the music had come from one of them, probably the far one, for it had sounded very soft. No sooner had the thought come to her than she turned and went quietly to the door. She ran quickly down the steps, and seeing her aunt and Mr. Roberts upon the piazza, she turned and passed out by one of the side doors.

Helen had yielded to a sudden impulse in doing thus, drawn by her yearning for the music. When she thought about it as she walked on it seemed to her a foolish idea, for the man could not possibly know of her trouble, and moreover was probably with his friend the lieutenant. But she did not stop even then, for her heart's hunger still drove her on, and she thought, "I'll see, and perhaps he will play again without my asking; I can sit in the near summer-house and wait."

She went swiftly on with that purpose in mind, not going upon the path, because she would have been in the full moonlight, and in sight of the two upon the piazza. She passed silently along by the high hedge, concealed in its shadows, and her footsteps deadened by the grass. She was as quiet as possible, wishing to be in the summer-house without anyone's knowing it.

And she had come very close to it indeed, within a few yards, when suddenly she stopped short with an inward exclamation; the silence of the twilight had been broken by a voice—one that seemed almost beside her, and that startled her with a realization of the mistake she had made. The two men were themselves in the house to which she had been going.

It was Mr. Howard's voice which she heard; he was speaking very low, almost in a whisper, yet Helen was near enough to hear every word that he uttered.

"Most people would think it simply a happy and beautiful piece of music," he said. "Most people think that of the springtime; but when a man has lived as I, he may find that the springtime too is a great labor and a great suffering,—he does not forget that for the thousands of creatures that win the great fight and come forth rejoicing, there are thousands and tens of thousands that go down, and have their mite of life crushed out, and find the law very stern indeed. Even those that win do it by a fearful effort, and cannot keep their beauty long; so that the springtime passion takes on a kind of desperate intensity when one thinks of it."

The voice ceased again for a moment, and Helen stood gazing about her; the words were not without a dimly-felt meaning to her just then, and the tone of the man's voice seemed like the music she had heard him play. She would have liked to stay and listen, tho she knew that she had no right to. She was certain that she had not been seen, because the little house was thickly wrapped about with eglantine; and she stood, uncertain as to whether she ought to steal back or go out and join the two men. In the meantime the voice began again:

"It gives a man a new feeling of the preciousness of life to know keenly what it means to fail, to be like a tiny spark, struggling to maintain itself in the darkness, and finding that all it can do is not sufficient, and that it is sinking back into nothingness forever. I think that is the meaning of the wild and startled look that the creatures of the forest wear; and it is a very tragic thing indeed to realize, and makes one full of mercy. If he knows his own heart he can read the same thing in the faces of men, and he no longer even laughs at their pride and their greediness, but sees them quite infinitely wretched and pitiable. I do not speak merely of the poor and hopeless people, the hunted creatures of society; for this terror is not merely physical. It is the same imperative of life that makes conscience, and so every man knows it who has made himself a slave to his body, and sees the soul within him helpless and sinking; and every man who has sinned and sees his evil stamped upon the face of things outside him, in shapes of terror that must be forever. Strange as it may seem, I think the man who lives most rightly, the man of genius, knows the feeling most of all, because his conscience is the quickest. It is his task to live from his own heart, to take the power that is within him and wrestle with it, and build new universes from it,—to be a pioneer of the soul, so to speak, and to go where no man has ever been before; and yet all his victory is nothing to him, because he knows so well what he might have done. Every time that he shrinks, as he must shrink, from what is so hard and so high in his own vision, he knows that yet another glory is lost forever, and so it comes that he stands very near indeed to the'tears of things.'"

Mr. Howard stopped again, and Helen found herself leaning forward and wondering.

"I know more about those tears than most people," the man went on slowly, after a long pause, "for I have had to build my own life in that way; I know best of all the failure, for that has been my lot. When you and I knew each other, I was very strong in my own heart, and I could always find what joy and power I needed for the living of my life; but there have come to me since, in the years that I have dwelt all alone with my great trial, times when I think that I have stood face to face with this thing that we speak of, this naked tragedy and terror of existence. There have been times when all the yearning and all the prayer that I had could not save me, when I have known that I had not an ounce of resource left, and have sat and watched the impulse of my soul die within me, and all my strength go from me, and seen myself with fearful plainness as a spark of yearning, a living thing in all its pitifulness and hunger, helpless and walled up in darkness. To feel that is to be very near indeed to the losing creatures and their sorrow, and the memory of one such time is enough to keep a man merciful forever. For it is really the deepest fact about life that a man can know;—how it is so hazardous and so precious, how it keeps its head above the great ocean of the infinite only by all the force it can exert; it happens sometimes that a man does not discover that truth until it is too late, and then he finds life very cruel and savage indeed, I can tell you."

Mr. Howard stopped, and Helen drew a deep breath; she had been trembling slightly as she stood listening; then as he spoke again, her heart gave a violent throb. "Some day," he said, "this girl that we were talking about will have to come to that part of her life's journey; it is a very sad thing to know."

"She will understand her sonata better," said the officer.

"No," was the reply; "I wish I could think even that; I know how sorrow affects a person whose heart is true, how it draws him close to the great heart of life, and teaches him its sacredness, and sends him forth merciful and humble. But selfish misery and selfish fear are no less ugly than selfish happiness; a person who suffers ignobly becomes only disgusted and disagreeable, and more selfish than ever. . . . But let us not talk any more about Miss Davis, for it is not a pleasant subject; to a man who seeks as I do to keep his heart full of worship the very air of this place is stifling, with its idleness and pride. It gives the lie to all my faith about life, and I have only to go back into my solitude and forget it as soon as I can."

"That ought not to be a difficult thing to do," said the officer.

"It is for me," the other answered; "it haunts my thoughts all the time." He paused for a while, and then he added, "I happened to think of something I came across this morning, in a collection of French verse I was reading; William, did you ever read anything of Auguste Brizeux?"

The other answered in the negative.

"He has some qualities that are very rare in French poetry," went on Mr. Howard. "He makes one think of Wordsworth. I happened to read a homely little ballad of his,—a story of some of that tragedy of things that we spoke of; one could name hundreds of such poems quite as good, I suppose, but this happened to be the one I came across, and I could not help thinking of Miss Davis and wondering if she were really so cold and so hard that she could have heard this story without shuddering. For it really shook me very much."

"What is it?" the other asked.

"I can tell you the story in a few words," said Mr. Howard. "To me it was one of those flashes of beauty that frighten one and haunt him long afterwards; and I do not quite like to think about it again."

The speaker's voice dropped, and the girl involuntarily crept a little nearer to hear him; there was a tree in front of her, and she leaned against it, breathing very hard, tho making no sound.

"The ballad is called 'Jacques the Mason,'" said Mr. Howard, "There are three little pictures in it; in the first of them you see two men setting off to their work together, one of them bidding his wife and children good-by, and promising to return with his friend for an evening's feast, because the great building is to be finished. Then you see them at work, swarming upon the structure and rejoicing in their success; and then you hear the shouts of the crowd as the scaffolding breaks, and see those two men hanging over the abyss, clinging to a little plank. It is not strong enough to hold them both, and it is cracking, and that means a fearful death; they try to cling to the stones of the building and cannot, and so there comes one of those fearful moments that makes a man's heart break to think of. Then in the fearful silence you hear one of the men whisper that he has three children and a wife; and you see the other gaze at him an instant with terror in his eyes, and then let go his hold and shoot down to the street below. And that is all of the story."

Mr. Howard stopped, and there followed a long silence; afterwards he went on, his voice trembling: "That is all," he said, "except of course that the man was killed. And I can think of nothing but that body hurled down through the air, and the crushed figure and the writhing limbs. I fancy the epic grandeur of soul of that poor ignorant laborer, and the glory that must have flamed up in his heart at that great instant; so I find it a dreadful poem, and wonder if it would not frighten that careless girl to read it."

Mr. Howard stopped again, and the officer asked if the story were true.

"I do not know that," answered the other, "nor do I care; it is enough to know that every day men are called upon to face the shuddering reality of existence in some such form as that. And the question which it brought to my heart is, if it came to me, as terrible as that, and as sudden and implacable, would I show myself the man or the dastard? And that filled me with a fearful awe and humility, and a guilty wonder whether somewhere in the world there might not be a wall from which I should be throwing myself, instead of nursing my illness as I do, and being content to read about greatness. And oh, I tell you, when I think of such things as that, and see the pride and worthlessness of this thing that men call 'high life,' it seemed to me no longer heedless folly, but dastardly and fiendish crime, so that one can only bury his face in his hands and sob to know of it. And William, the more I realized it, the more unbearable it seemed to me that this glorious girl with all her God-given beauty, should be plunging herself into a stream so foul. I felt as if it were cowardice of mine that I did not take her by the hand and try to make her see what madness she was doing."

"Why do you not?" asked the lieutenant.

"I think I should have, in my more Quixotic days," replied the other, sadly; "and perhaps some day I may find myself in a kind of high life where royal sincerity is understood. But in this world even an idealist has to keep a sense of humor, unless he happens to be dowered with an Isaiah's rage."

Mr. Howard paused for a moment and laughed slightly; then, however, he went on more earnestly: "Yet, as I think of it, I know that I could frighten her; I think that if I should tell her of some of the days and nights that I have spent in tossing upon a bed of fire, she might find the cup of her selfishness a trifle less pleasant to drink. It is something that I have noticed with people, that they may be coarse or shallow enough to laugh at virtue and earnestness, but there are very few who do not bow their heads before suffering. For that is something physical; and they may harden their conscience if they please, but from the possibility of bodily pain they know that they can never be safe; and they seem to know that a man who has walked with that demon has laid his hand upon the grim reality of things, before which their shams and vanities shrink into nothingness. The sight of it is always a kind of warning of the seriousness of life, and so even when people feel no sympathy, they cannot but feel fear; I saw for instance, that the first time this girl saw me she turned pale, and she would not come anywhere near me."

As the speaker paused again, Lieutenant Maynard said, very quietly: "I should think that would be a hard cross to bear, David."

"No," said Mr. Howard, with a slight smile, "I had not that thought in my mind. I have seen too much of the reality of life to trouble myself or the the world with vanity of that very crude kind; I can sometimes imagine myself being proud of my serenity, but that is one step beyond at any rate. A man who lives in his soul very seldom thinks of himself in an external way; when I look in the glass it is generally to think how strange it is that this form of mine should be that which represents me to men, and I cannot find anything they might really learn about me, except the one physical fact of suffering."

"They can certainly not fail to learn that," said the other.

"Yes," replied Mr. Howard sadly, "I know, if any man does, what it is to earn one's life by suffering and labor. That is why I have so mastering a sense of life's preciousness, and why I cannot reconcile myself to this dreadful fact of wealth. It is the same thing, too, that makes me feel so keenly about this girl and her beauty, and keeps her in my thoughts. I don't think I could tell you how the sight of her affected me, unless you knew how I have lived all these lonely years. For I have had no friends and no strength for any of the world's work, and all my battle has been with my own soul, to be brave and to keep my self-command through all my trials; I think my illness has acted as a kind of nervous stimulus upon me, as if it were only by laboring to dwell upon the heights of my being night and day that I could have strength to stand against despair. The result is that I have lived for days in a kind of frenzy of effort, with all my faculties at white heat; and it has always been the artist's life, it has always been beauty that brought me the joy that I needed, and given me the strength to go on. Beauty is the sign of victory, and the prize of it, in this heart's battle; the more I have suffered and labored, the more keenly I have come to feel that, until the commonest flower has a song for me. And William, the time I saw this girl she wore a rose in her hair, but she was so perfect that I scarcely saw the flower; there is that in a man's heart which makes it that to him the fairest and most sacred of God's creatures must always be the maiden. When I was young, I walked about the earth half drunk with a dream of love; and even now, when I am twice as old as my years, and burnt out and dying, I could not but start when I saw this girl. For I fancied that she must carry about in that maiden's heart of hers some high notion of what she meant in the world, and what was due to her. When a man gazes upon beauty such as hers, there is a feeling that comes to him that is quite unutterable, a feeling born of all the weakness and failure and sin of his lifetime. For every true man's life is a failure; and this is the vision that he sought with so much pain, the thing that might have been, had he kept the faith with his own genius. It is so that beauty is the conscience of the artist; and that there must always be something painful and terrible about high perfection. It was that way that I felt when I saw this girl's face, and I dreamt my old dream of the sweetness and glory of a maiden's heart. I thought of its spotlessness and of its royal scorn of baseness; and I tell you, William, if

153

I had found it thus I could have been content to worship and not even ask that the girl look at me. For a man, when he has lived as I have lived, can feel towards anything more perfect than himself a quite wonderful kind of humility; I know that all the trouble with my helpless struggling is that I must be everything to myself, and cannot find anything to love, and so be at peace. That was the way I felt when I saw this Miss Davis, all that agitation and all that yearning; and was it not enough to make a man mock at himself, to learn the real truth? I was glad that it did not happen to me when I was young and dependent upon things about me; is it not easy to imagine how a young man might make such a woman the dream of his life, how he might lay all his prayer at her feet, and how, when he learned of her fearful baseness, it might make of him a mocking libertine for the rest of his days?"

"You think it baseness?" asked Lieutenant Maynard.

"I tried to persuade myself at first that it must be only blindness; I wondered to myself, 'Can she not see the difference between the life of these people about her and the music and poetry her aunt tells me she loves?' I never waste any of my worry upon the old and hardened of these vulgar and worldly people; it is enough for me to know why the women are dull and full of gossip, and to know how much depth there is in the pride and in the wisdom of the men. But it was very hard for me to give up my dream of the girl's purity; I rememher I thought of Heine's 'Thou art as a flower,' and my heart was full of prayer. I wondered if it might not be possible to tell her that one cannot combine music and a social career, and that one cannot really buy happiness with sin; I thought that perhaps she might be grateful for the warning that in cutting herself off from the great deepening experience of woman she was consigning herself to stagnation and wretchedness from which no money could ever purchase her ransom; I thought that possibly she did not see that this man knew nothing of her pre-ciousness and had no high thoughts about her beauty. That was the way I argued with myself about her innocence, and you may fancy the kind of laughter that came over me at the truth. It is a ghastly thing, William, the utter hardness, the grim and determined worldliness, of this girl. For she knew very well what she was doing, and all the ignorance was on my part. She had no care about anything in the world until that man came in, and the short half hour that I watched them was enough to tell her that her life's happiness was won. But only think of her, William, with all her God-given beauty, allowing herself to be kissed by him! Try to fancy what new kind of fiendishness must lie in her heart! I remember that she is to marry him because he pays her millions, and the word prostitution keeps haunting my memory; when I try to define it, I find that the millions do not alter it in the least. That is a very cruel thought,—a thought that drives away everything but the prayer—and I sit and wonder what fearful punishment the hand of Fate will deal out for such a thing as that, what hatefulness it will stamp upon her for a sign to men. And then because the perfect face still haunts my memory, I have a very Christ-like feeling indeed,—that I could truly die to save that girl from such a horror."

There was another long silence, and then suddenly, Mr. Howard rose from his seat. "William," he said in a different voice, "it is all useless, so why should we talk so? The girl has to live her own life and learn these things for herself. And in the meantime, perhaps I am letting myself be too much moved by her beauty, for there are many people in the world who are not beautiful, but who suffer things they do not deserve to suffer, and who really deserve our sympathy and help."

"I fancy you'd not be much thanked for it in this case," said the other, with a dry laugh.

Mr. Howard stood for some moments in silence, and then turned away to end the conversation. "I fear," he said, "that I have kept you more than I have any right to. Let us go back to the house; it is not very polite to our hostess to stay so long."

"It must be nearly time for my train, anyhow," said the officer, and a moment later the two had passed out of the summer-house and up the path, Lieutenant Maynard carrying Mr. Howard's violin-case in his hand.

The two did not see Helen as they passed her; the reason was that Helen was stretched out upon the ground by the side of the hedge. It was not that she was hiding,—she had no thought of that; it was because she had been struck there by the scathing words that she had heard. Some of them were so bitter that they could only have filled her with rage had she not known that they were true, and had she not been awed by what she had learned of this man's heart. She could feel only terror and fiery shame, and the cruel words had beaten her down, first upon her knees, and then upon her face, and they lashed her like whips of flame and tore into her flesh and made her writhe. She dared not cry out, or even sob; she could only dig into the ground with her quivering fingers, and lie there, shuddering in a fearful way. Long after the two men were gone her cruel punishment still continued, for she still seemed to hear his words, seared into her memory with fire as they had been. What Mr. Howard had said had come like a flash of lightning in the darkness to show her actions as they really were; the last fearful sentences which she had heard had set all her being aflame, and the thought of Mr. Harrison's embraces filled her now with a perfect spasm of shame and loathing.

"I sold myself to him for money!" she panted. "Oh, God, for money!"

But then suddenly she raised herself up and stared about her, crying out, half-hysterically, "No, no, it is not true! It is not true! I could never have done it—I should have gone mad!" And a moment later Helen had staggered to her feet. "I must tell him," she gasped. "He must not think so of me!"

Mr. Howard had come to her as a vision from a higher world, making all that she had known and admired seem hideous and base; and her one thought just then was of him. "He will still scorn me," she thought, "but I must tell him I really did suffer." And heedless of the fact that her hair was loose about her shoulders and her dress wet with the dew of the grass, the girl ran swiftly up the lawn towards the house, whispering again and again, "I must tell him!"

It was only a minute more before she was near the piazza, and could see the people upon it as they stood in the lighted doorway. Mr. Howard was one of them, and Helen would have rushed blindly up to speak to him, had it not been that another thought came to her to stop her.

"Suppose he should know of Arthur!" she muttered, clenching her hands until the nails cut her flesh. "Oh, what would he think then? And what could I tell him?" And she shrank back into the darkness, like a black and guilty thing. She crept around the side of the house and entered by another door, stealing into one of the darkened parlors, where she flung herself down upon a sofa and lay trembling before that new terror. When a few minutes had passed and she heard a carriage outside, she sprang up wildly, with the thought that he might be going. She had run half way to the door before she recollected that the carriage must be for the lieutenant, and then she stopped and stood still in the darkness, twisting her hands together nervously and asking herself what she could do.

It occurred to her that she could look down the piazza from the window of the room, and so she went swiftly to it. The officer was just descending to the carriage, Mr. Roberts with him, and her aunt and Mr. Howard standing at the top of the steps, the latter's figure clearly outlined in the moonlight. Helen's heart was so full of despair and yearning just then that she could have rushed out and flung herself at his feet, had he been alone; but she felt a new kind of shrinking from her aunt. She stood hesitating, therefore, muttering to herself, "I must let him know about it somehow, and he will tell me what to do. Oh, I MUST! And I must tell him now, before it is too late!"

She stood by the window, panting and almost choking with her emotion, kneading her hands one upon the other in frenzied agitation; and then she heard Mr. Howard say to her aunt, "I shall have to ask you to excuse me now, for I must not forget that I am an invalid." And Helen clutched her burning temples, seeing him turn to enter the house, and seeing that her chance was going.

She glanced around her, almost desperate, and then suddenly her heart gave a great leap, for just beside her was something that had brought one resource to her mind. She had seen the piano in the dim light, and had thought suddenly of the song that Mr. Howard had mentioned.

"He will remember!" she thought swiftly, as she ran to the instrument and sat down before it. With a strength born of her desperation she mastered the quivering of her hands, and catching her breath, began in a weak and trembling voice the melody of Rubenstein:

"Thou art as a flower,
So pure and fair thou art;
I gaze on thee, and sorrow
Doth steal into my heart.

"I would lay my hands upon thee,
Upon thy snowy brow,
And pray that God might keep thee
So pure and fair as now."

Helen did not know how she was singing, she thought only of telling her yearning and her pain; she was so choked with emotion that she could scarcely utter a sound at all, and the song must have startled those who heard it. It was laden with all the tears that had been gathering in Helen's heart for days.

She did not finish the song; she was thinking, "Will he understand?" She stopped suddenly as she saw a shadow upon the porch outside, telling her that Mr Howard had come nearer. There was a minute or so of breathless suspense and then, as the shadow began to draw slowly backwards, Helen clenched her hands convulsively, whispering to herself, "He will think it was only an accident! Oh, what can I do?"

There are some people all of whose emotions take the form of music; there came into Helen's mind at that instant a melody that was the very soul of her agitation and her longing—MacDowell's "To a Water Lily;" the girl thought of what Mr. Howard had said about the feeling that comes to suffering mortals at the sight of something perfect and serene, and she began playing the little piece, very softly, and with trembling hands.

It is quite wonderful music; to Helen with her heart full of grief and despair, the chords that floated so cold and white and high were almost too much to be borne. She played desperately on, however, because she saw that Mr. Howard had stopped again, and she did not believe that he could fail to understand that music.

So she continued until she came to the pleading song of the swan. The music is written to a poem of Geibel's which tells of the snow-white lily, and of the bird which wonders at its beauty; afterwards, because there is nothing in all nature more cold and unapproachable than a water-lily, and because one might sing to it all day and never fancy that it heard him, the first melody rises again, as keen and as high as ever, and one knows that his yearning is in vain, and that there is nothing for him but his old despair. When Helen came to that she could go no farther, for her wretchedness had been heaping itself up, and her heart was bursting. Her fingers gave way as she struck the keys, and she sank down and hid her face in her arms, and broke into wild and passionate sobbing. She was almost choking with her pent-up emotions, so shaken that she was no longer conscious of what went on about her. She did not hear Mr. Howard's voice, as he entered, and she did not even hear the frightened exclamations of her aunt, until the latter had flung her arms about her. Then she sprang up and tore herself loose by main force, rushing upstairs and locking herself in her own room, where she flung herself down upon the bed and wept until she could weep no more, in the meantime not even hearing her aunt's voice from the hallway, and altogether unconscious of the flight of time.

When she sat up and brushed away her tangled hair and gazed about her, everything in the house was silent. She herself was exhausted, but she rose, and after pacing up and down the room a few minutes, seated herself at the writing desk, and in spite of her trembling fingers, wrote a short note to Mr. Gerald Harrison; then with a deep breath of relief, she rose, and going to the window knelt down in front of it and gazed out.

The moon was high in the sky by that time, and the landscape about her was flooded with its light. Everything was so calm and still that the girl held her breath as she watched it; but suddenly she gave a start, for she heard the sound of a violin again, so very faint that she at first thought she was deluding herself. As she listened, however, she heard it more plainly, and then she realized in a flash that Mr. Howard must have heard her long-continued sobbing, and that he was playing something for her. It was Schumann's "Traumerei;" and as the girl knelt there her soul was borne away upon the wings of that heavenly melody, and there welled up in her heart a new and very different emotion from any that she had ever known before; it was born, half of the music, and half of the calm and the stillness of the night,— that wonderful peace which may come to mortals either in victory or defeat, when they give up their weakness and their fear, and become aware of the Infinite Presence. When the melody had died away, and Helen rose, there was a new light in her eyes, and a new beauty upon her countenance, and she knew that her soul was right at last.

Chapter X

"Our acts our angels are, or good or ill,
Our fatal shadows that walk by us still."

Naturally there was considerable agitation in the Roberts family on account of Helen's strange behavior; early the next morning Mrs. Roberts was at her niece's door, trying to gain admittance. This time she did not have to knock but once, and when she entered she was surprised to see that Helen was already up and dressing. She had been expecting to find the girl more prostrated than ever, and so the discovery was a great relief to her; she stood gazing at her anxiously.

"Helen, dear," she said, "I scarcely know how to begin to talk to you about your extraordinary—"

"I wish," interrupted Helen, "that you would not begin to talk to me about it at all."

"But you must explain to me what in the world is the matter," protested the other.

"I cannot possibly explain to you," was the abrupt reply. Helen's voice was firm, and there was a determined look upon her face, a look which quite took her aunt by surprise.

"But, my dear girl!" she began once more.

"Aunt Polly!" said the other, interrupting her again, "I wish instead of talking about it you would listen to what I have to say for a few moments. For I have made up my mind just what I am going to do, and I am going to take the reins in my own hands and not do any arguing or explaining to anyone. And there is no use of asking me a word about what has happened, for I could not hope to make you understand me, and I do not mean to try."

As Helen uttered those words she fixed her eyes upon her aunt with an unflinching gaze, with the result that Mrs. Roberts was quite too much taken aback to find a word to say.

Without waiting for anything more Helen turned to the table. "Here is a letter," she said, "which I have written to Mr. Harrison; you know his address in New York, I suppose?"

"His address?" stammered the other; "why,—yes, of course. But what in the world—"

"I wish this letter delivered to him at once, Aunt Polly," Helen continued. "It is of the utmost importance, and I want you to do me the favor to send someone into the city with it by the next train."

"But, Helen, dear—"

"Now please do not ask me anything about it," went on the girl, impatiently. "I have told you that you must let me manage this affair myself. If you will not send it I shall simply have to get someone to take it. He must have it, and have it at once."

"Will it not do to mail it, Helen?"

"No, because I wish him to get it this morning." And Helen put the letter into her aunt's hands, while the latter gazed helplessly, first at it, and then at the girl. There is an essay of Bacon's in which is set forth the truth that you can bewilder and master anyone if you are only sufficiently bold and rapid; Mrs. Roberts was so used to managing everything and being looked up to by everyone that Helen's present mood left her quite dazed.

Nor did the girl give her any time to recover her presence of mind. "There is only one thing more," she said, "I want you to have breakfast as soon as you can, and then to let me have a carriage at once."

"A carriage?" echoed the other.

"Yes, Aunt Polly, I wish to drive over to Hilltown immediately."

"To Hilltown!" gasped Aunt Polly with yet greater consternation, and showing signs of resistance at last; "pray what—"

But Helen only came again to the attack, with yet more audacity and confidence. "Yes," she said, "to Hilltown; I mean to go to see Arthur."

For answer to that last statement, poor Mrs, Roberts had simply no words whatever; she could only gaze, and in the meantime, Helen was going calmly on with her dressing, as if the matter were settled.

"Will Mr. Howard be down to breakfast?" she asked.

"As he is going away to-day, I presume he will be down," was the reply, after which Helen quickly completed her toilet, her aunt standing by and watching her in the meantime.

"Helen, dear," she asked at last, after having recovered her faculties a trifle, "do you really mean that you will not explain to me a thing of what has happened, or of what you are doing?"

"There is so much, Aunt Polly, that I cannot possibly explain it now; I have too much else to think of. You must simply let me go my way, and I will tell you afterwards."

"But, Helen, is that the right way to treat me? Is it nothing to you, all the interest that I have taken in this and all that I have done for you, that you should think so little of my advice?"

"I do not need any advice now," was the answer. "Aunt Polly, I see exactly what I should do, and I do not mean to stop a minute for anything else until I have done it. If it seems unkind, I am very sorry, but in the meantime it must be done."

And while she was saying the words, Helen was putting on her hat; then taking up her parasol and gloves she turned towards her aunt. "I am ready now," she said, "and please let me have breakfast just as soon as you can."

The girl was so much preoccupied with her own thoughts and purposes that she scarcely even heard what her aunt said; she went down into the garden where she could be alone, and paced up and down impatiently until she heard the bell. Then she went up into the dining room, where she found her aunt and uncle in conversation with Mr. Howard.

Helen had long been preparing herself to meet him, but she could not keep her cheeks from flushing or keep from lowering her eyes; she bit her lips together, however, and forced herself to look at him, saying very resolutely, "Mr. Howard, I have to drive over to Hilltown after breakfast, and I wish very much to talk to you about something; would you like to drive with me?"

"Very much indeed," said he, quietly, after which Helen said not a word more. She saw that her aunt and uncle were gazing at her and at each other in silent wonder, but she paid no attention to it. After eating a few hurried mouthfuls she excused herself, and rose and went outside, where she saw the driving-cart which had been bought for her use, waiting for her. It was not much longer before Mr. Howard was ready, for he saw her agitation.

"It is rather a strange hour to start upon a drive," she said to him, "but I have real cause for hurrying; I will explain about it." And then she stopped, as her aunt came out to join them.

It was only a moment more before Mr. Howard had excused himself, and the two were in the wagon, Helen taking the reins. She waved a farewell to her aunt and then started the horse, and they were whirled swiftly away down the road.

All the morning Helen's mind had been filled with things that she wished to say to Mr. Howard. But now all her resolution seemed to have left her, and she was trembling very much, and staring straight ahead, busying herself with guiding the horse. When they were out upon the main road where they might go as fast as they pleased without that necessity, she swallowed the lump in her throat and made one or two nervous attempts to speak.

Mr. Howard in the meantime had been gazing in front of him thoughtfully. "Miss Davis," he said suddenly, turning his eyes upon her, "may I ask you a question?"

"Yes," said Helen faintly.

"You heard all that I said about you last night?"

And Helen turned very red and looked away. "Yes, I heard it all," she said; and then there was a long silence.

It was broken by the man, who began in a low voice: "I scarcely know how, Miss Davis, I can apologize to you—"

And then he stopped short, for the girl had turned her glance upon him, wonderingly. "Apologize?" she said; she had never once thought of that view of it, and the word took her by surprise.

"Yes," said Mr. Howard; "I said so many hard and cruel things that I cannot bear to think of them."

Helen still kept her eyes fixed upon him, as she said, "Did you say anything that was not true, Mr. Howard?"

The man hesitated a moment, and then he answered: "I said many things that I had no right to say to you."

"That is not it," said Helen simply. "Did you say anything that was not true?"

Again Mr. Howard paused. "I am quite sure that I did," he said at last. "Most of what I said I feel to have been untrue since I have seen how it affected you."

"Because it made me so ashamed?" said Helen. And then some of the thoughts that possessed her forced their way out, and she hurried on impetuously: "That was the first thing I wanted to tell you. It is really true that you were wrong, for I am not hard-hearted at all. It was something that my—that people were making me do, and all the time I was wretched. It was dreadful, I know, but I was tempted, because I do love beautiful things. And it was all so sudden, and I could not realize it, and I had nobody to advise me, for none of the people I meet would think it was wrong. You must talk to me and help me, because I've got to be very strong; my aunt will be angry, and when I get back perhaps Mr. Harrison will be there, and I shall have to tell him."

Then the girl stopped, out of breath and trembling with excitement; Mr. Howard turned abruptly and fixed his dark eyes upon her.

"Tell him," he said. "Tell him what?"

"That I shall not marry him, of course," answered Helen; the other gave a start, but she was so eager that she did not even notice it. "I could not lose a minute," she said. "For it was so very dreadful, you know."

"And you really mean not to marry him?" asked the other.

"Mean it!" echoed the girl, opening her eyes very wide. "Why, how in the world could you suppose—" And then she stopped short, and laughed nervously. "Of course," she said, "I forgot; you might suppose anything. But, oh, if I could tell you how I have suffered, Mr. Howard, you would understand that I could never have such a thought again in the world. Please do understand me, for if I had really been so base I should not come to you as I do after what I heard. I cannot tell you how dreadfully I suffered while I was listening, but after I had cried so much about it, I felt better, and it seemed to me that it was the best thing that could have happened to me, just to see my actions as they seemed to someone else,—to someone who was good. I saw all at once the truth of what I was doing, and it was agony to me to know that you thought so of me. That was why I could not rest last night until I had told you that I was really unhappy; for it was something that I was unhappy, wasn't it, Mr. Howard?"

"Yes," said the other, "it was very much indeed."

"And oh, I want you to know the truth," Helen went on swiftly. "Perhaps it is just egotism on my part, and I have really no right to tell you all about myself in this way; and perhaps you will scorn me when you come to know the whole truth. But I cannot help telling you about it, so that you may advise me what to do; I was all helpless and lost, and what you said came last night like a wonderful light. And I don't care what you think about me if you will only tell me the real truth, in just the same way that you did; for I realized afterwards that it was that which had helped me so. It was the first time in my life that it had ever happened to me; when you meet people in the world, they only say things that they know will please you, and that does you no good. I never realized before how a person might go through the world and really never meet with another heart in all his life; and that one can be fearfully lonely, even in a parlor full of people. Did you ever think of that, Mr. Howard?"

Mr. Howard had fixed his keen eyes upon the girl as she went breathlessly on; she was very pale, and the sorrow through which she had passed had left will think I have been so cold and wicked, that you will soon scorn me altogether."

"I do not think that is possible," said her companion, gently, as he saw the girl choking back a sob.

"Well, listen then," Helen began; but then she stopped again. "Do you wish me to tell you?" she asked. "Do you care anything about it at all, or does it seem—"

"I care very much about it, indeed," the other answered.

"However dreadful it may seem," said Helen. "Oh, please know that while I have been doing it, it has made me utterly wretched, and that I am so frightened now that I can scarcely talk to you; and that if there is anything that I can do—oh, absolutely anything—I will do it!" Then the girl bit her lips together and went on with desperate haste, "It's what you said about what would happen if there were someone else to love me, and to see how very bad I was!"

"There is some such person?" asked the man, in a low voice.

"Yes," said she. "It is someone I have known as long as I can remember. And he loves me very much indeed, I think; and while I was letting myself be tempted in this way he was very sick, and because I knew I was so bad I did not dare go near him; and yesterday when he heard I was going to marry this man, it almost killed him, and I do not know what to fear now."

Then, punishing herself very bravely and swallowing all her bitter shame, Helen went on to tell Mr. Howard of Arthur, and of her friendship with him, and of how long he had waited for her; she narrated in a few words how he had left her, and then how she had seen him upon the road. Afterwards she stopped and sat very still, trembling, and with her eyes lowered, quite forgetting that she was driving.

"Miss Davis," said the other, gently, seeing how she was suffering, "if you wish my advice about this, I should not worry myself too much; it is better, I find in my own soul's life, to save most of the time that one spends upon remorse, and devote it to action."

"To action?" asked Helen.

"Yes," said the other. "You have been very thoughtless, but you may hope that nothing irrevocable has happened; and when you have seen your friend and told him the truth just as you have told it to me, I fancy it will bring him joy enough to compensate him for what he has suffered."

"That was what I meant to do," the girl went on. "But I have been terrified by all sorts of fancies, and when I remember how much pain I caused him, I scarcely dare think of speaking to him. When I saw him by the roadside, Mr. Howard, he seemed to me to look exactly like you, there was such dreadful suffering written in his face."

"A man who lives as you have told me your friend has lived," said the other, "has usually a very great power of suffering; such a man builds for himself an ideal which gives him all his joy and his power, and makes his life a very glorious thing; but when anything happens to destroy his vision or to keep him from seeking it, he suffers with the same intensity that he rejoiced before. The great hunger that was once the source of his power only tears him to pieces then, as steam wrecks a broken engine."

"It's very dreadful," Helen said, "how thoughtless I was all along. I only knew that he loved me very much, and that it was a vexation to me."

Mr. Howard glanced at her. "You do not love him?" he asked.

"No," said Helen, quickly. "If I had loved him, I could never have had a thought of all these other things. But I had no wish to love anybody; it was more of my selfishness."

"Perhaps not," the other replied gently. "Some day you may come to love him, Miss Davis."

"I do not know," Helen said. "Arthur was very impatient."

"When a man is swift and eager in all his life," said Mr. Howard, smiling, "he cannot well be otherwise in his love. Such devotion ought to be very precious to a woman, for such hearts are not easy to find in the world."

Helen had turned and was gazing anxiously at Mr. Howard as he spoke to her thus. "You really think," she said, "that I should learn to appreciate Arthur's love?"

"I cannot know much about him from the little you have told me," was the other's answer. "But it seems to me that it is there you might find the best chance to become the unselfish woman that you wish to be."

"It is very strange," the girl responded, wonderingly, "how differently you think about it. I should have supposed I was acting very unwisely indeed if I loved Arthur; everyone would have told me of his poverty and obscurity, and of how I must give up my social career."

"I think differently, perhaps," Mr. Howard said, "because I have lived so much alone. I have come to know that happiness is a thing of one's own heart, and not of externals; the questions I should ask about a marriage would not be of wealth and position. If you really wish to seek the precious things of the soul, I should think you would be very glad to prove it by some sacrifice; and I know that two hearts are brought closer, and all the memories of life made dearer, by some such trial in the early days. People sneer at love in a cottage, but I am sure that love that could wish to live anywhere else is not love. And as to the social career, a person who has once come to know the life of the heart soon ceases to care for any kind of life that is heartless; a social career is certainly that, and in comparison very vulgar indeed."

Helen looked a little puzzled, and repeated the word "vulgar" inquiringly. Mr Howard smiled.

"That is the word I always use when I am talking about high life," he said, laughing. "You may hurl the words 'selfish' and 'worldly' at it all you please, and never reach a vital spot; but the word 'vulgar' goes straight to the heart."

"You must explain to me why it is that," said Helen, with so much seriousness that the other could not help smiling again.

"Perhaps I cannot make anyone else see the thing as I do," was his reply. "And yet it seems rery simple. When a man lives a while in his own soul, he becomes aware of the existence of a certain spiritual fact which gives life all its dignity and meaning; he learns that this sacred thing demands to be sought for, and worshiped;

and that the man who honors it and seeks it is only hailed as gentleman, and aristocrat, and that he who does not honor it and seek it is vulgar, tho he be heir of a hundred earls, and leader of all society, and lord of millions. Every day that one lives in this presence that I speak of, he discovers a little more how sacred a thing is true nobility, and how impertinent is the standard that values men for the wealth they win, or for the ribbons they wear, or for anything else in the world. I fancy that you, if you came once to love your friend, would find it very easy to do without the admiration of those who go to make up society; they would come to seem to you very trivial and empty people, and afterwards, perhaps, even very cruel and base."

Mr. Howard stopped; but then seeing that Helen was gazing at him inquiringly once more he added, gravely, "One could be well content to let vain people strut their little hour and be as wonderful as they chose, if it were not for the painful fact that they are eating the bread of honest men, and that millions are toiling and starving in order that they may have ease and luxury. That is such a very dreadful thing to know that sometimes one can think of nothing else, and it drives him quite mad."

The girl sat very still after that, trembling a little in her heart; finally she asked, her voice shaking slightly, "Mr. Howard, what can one do about such things?"

"Very little," was the reply, "for they must always be; but at least one can keep his own life earnest and true. A woman who felt such things very keenly might be an inspiration to a man who was called upon to battle with selfishness and evil."

"You are thinking of Arthur once more?" asked the girl.

"Yes," answered the other, with a slight smile. "It would be a happy memory for me, to know that I have been able to give you such an ideal. Some of these days, you see, I am hoping that we shall again have a poet with a conviction and a voice, so that men may know that sympathy and love are things as real as money. I am quite sure there never was a nation so ridiculously sodden as our own just at present; all of our maxims and ways of life are as if we were the queer little Niebelung creatures that dig for treasure in the bowels of the earth, and see no farther than the ends of their shovels; we live in the City of God, and spend all our time scraping the gold of the pavements. Your uncle told me this morning that he did not see why a boy should go to college when he can get a higher salary if he spends the four years in business. I find that there is nothing to do but to run away and live alone, if one wants really to believe that man is a spiritual nature, with an infinite possibility of wonder and love; and that the one business of his life is to develop that nature by contact with things about him; and that every act of narrow selfishness he commits is a veil which he ties about his own eyes, and that when he has tied enough of them, not all the pearl and gold of the gorgeous East can make him less a pitiable wretch."

Mr. Howard stopped again, and smiled slightly; Helen sat gazing thoughtfully ahead, thinking about his way of looking at life, and how very strange her own actions seemed in the light of it. Suddenly, however, because throughout all the conversation there had been another thought in her consciousness, she glanced ahead and urged the horse even faster. She saw far in the distance the houses of the place to which she was bound, and she said nothing more, her companion also becoming silent as he perceived her agitation.

Helen had been constantly growing more anxious, so that now the carriage could not travel fast enough; it seemed to her that everything depended upon what she might find at Hilltown. It was only the thought of Arthur that kept her from feeling completely free from her wretchedness; she felt that she might remedy all the wrong that she had done, and win once more the prize of a good conscience, provided only that nothing irretrievable had happened to him. Now as she came nearer she found herself imagining more and more what might have happened, and becoming more and more impatient. There was a balance dangling before her eyes, with utter happiness on one side and utter misery on the other; the issue depended upon what she discovered at Hilltown.

The two sat in silence, both thinking of the same thing, as they whirled past the place where Helen had seen Arthur before. The girl trembled as she glanced at it, for all of the previous day's suffering rose before her again, and made her fears still more real and importunate. She forced herself to look, however, half thinking that she might see Arthur again; but that did not happen, and in a minute or two more the carriage had come to the house where he lived. She gave the reins to Mr. Howard, and sprang quickly out; she rang the bell, and then stood for a minute, twitching her fingers, and waiting.

The woman who kept the house, and whom Helen knew personally, opened the door; the visitor stepped in and gasped out breathlessly, "Where is Arthur?" Her hands shook visibly as she waited for the reply.

"He is not in, Miss Davis," the woman answered.

"Where is he?" Helen cried.

"I do not know," was the response. "He has gone."

"Gone!" And the girl started back, catching at her heart. "Gone where?"

"I do not know, Miss Davis."

"But what—" began the other.

"This will tell you all I know," said the woman, as she fumbled in her apron, and put a scrap of crumpled paper into Helen's trembling hands.

The girl seized it and glanced at it; then she staggered back against the wall, ghastly pale and almost sinking. The note, in Arthur's hand, but so unsteady as to be almost illegible, ran thus: "You will find in this my board for the past week; I am compelled to leave Hilltown, and I shall not ever return."

And that was all. Helen stared at it and stared again, and then let it fall and gazed about her, echoing, in a hollow voice, "And I shall not ever return!"

"That is all I can tell you about it," went on the woman. "I have not seen him since Elizabeth was here yesterday morning; he came back late last night and packed his bag and went away."

Helen sank down upon a chair and buried her face in her hands, quite overwhelmed by the suddenness of that discovery. She remained thus for a long time, without either sound or motion, and the woman stood watching her, knowing full well what was the matter. When Helen looked up again there was agony written upon her countenance. "Oh, are you sure you have no idea where I can find him?" she moaned.

"No, Miss Davis," said the woman. "I was asounded when I got this note."

"But someone must know, oh, surely they must! Someone must have seen him,—or he must have told someone!"

"I think it likely that he took care not to," was the reply.

The thought was a death-knell to Helen's last hope, and she sank down, quite overcome; she knew that Arthur could have had but one motive in acting as he had,—that he meant to cut himself off entirely from all his old life and surroundings. He had no friends in Hilltown, and having lived all alone, it would be possible for him to do it. Helen remembered Mr. Howard's saying of the night before, how the sight of her baseness might wreck a man's life forever, and the more she thought of that, the more it made her tremble. It seemed almost more than she could bear to see this fearful consequence of her sin, and to know that it had become a fact of the outer world, and gone beyond her power. It seemed quite too cruel that she should have such a thing on her conscience, and have it there forever; most maddening of all was the thought that it had depended upon a few hours of time.

"Oh, how can I have waited!" she moaned. "I should have come last night, I should have stopped the carriage when I saw him! Oh, it is not possible!"

Perhaps there are no more tragic words in human speech than "Too late." Helen felt just then as if the right even to repentance were taken from her life. It was her first introduction to that fearful thing of which Mr. Howard had told her upon their first meeting; in the deep loneliness of her own heart Helen was face to face just then with FATE. She shrank back in terror, and she struggled frantically, but she felt its grip of steel about her wrist; and while she sat there with her face hidden, she was learning to gaze into its eyes, and front their fiery terror. When she looked up again her face was very white and pitiful to see, and she rose from her chair and went toward the door so unsteadily that the woman put her arm about her.

"You will tell me," she gasped faintly—"you will tell me if you hear anything?"

"Yes," said the other gently, "I will."

So Helen crept into the carriage again, looking so full of wretchedness that her companion knew that the worst must have happened, and took the reins and silently drove towards home, while the girl sat perfectly still. They were fully half way home before she could find a word in which to tell him of her misery. "I shall never be happy in my life again!" she whispered. "Oh, Mr. Howard, never in my life!"

When the man gazed at her, he was frightened to see how grief and fear had taken possession of her face; and yet there was no word that he could say to soothe her, and no hope that he could give her. When the drive was ended, she stole silently up to her room, to be alone with her misery once more.

Chapter XI

"Thou majestic in thy sadness."

Upon the present occasion there was no violent demonstration of emotion to alarm the Roberts household, for Helen's grief was not of the kind to vent itself in a passionate outburst and pass away. To be sure, she wept a little, but the thoughts which haunted her were not of a kind to be forgotten, and afterwards she was as wretched as ever. What she had done seemed to her so dreadful that even tears were not right, and she felt that she ought only to sit still and think of it, and be frightened; it seemed to her just then as if she would have to do the same thing for the rest of her days. She spent several hours in her room without once moving, and without being disturbed, for her aunt was sufficiently annoyed at her morning's reception not to visit her again. The lunch hour passed, therefore, unthought of by Helen, and it was an hour or two later before she heard her aunt's step in the hall, and her knock upon the door.

Mrs. Roberts entered and stood in the center of the room, gazing at Helen, and at the look of helpless despair which she turned towards her; the woman's own lips were set very tightly.

"Well?" she said abruptly, "have you had your wish, and are you happy?"

Helen did not answer, nor did she half realize the question, so lost was she in her own misery. She sat gazing at her aunt, while the latter went on: "You have had your way in one thing, at any rate, Helen; Mr. Harrison is downstairs to see you."

The girl gave a slight start, but then she answered quietly: "Thank you, Auntie; I shall go down and see him."

"Helen," said Mrs. Roberts, "do you still refuse to tell me anything of what I ask you?"

Helen was quite too much humbled to wish to oppose anyone just then; and she answered mournfully, "What is it that you wish?"

"I wish to know in the first place why you wanted to see Mr. Harrison."

"I wanted to see him to tell him that I could not marry him, Aunt Polly."

And Mrs. Roberts sat down opposite Helen and fixed her gaze upon her. "I knew that was it," she said grimly. "Now, Helen, what in the world has come over you to make you behave in this fashion?"

"Oh, it is so much to tell you," began the girl; "I don't know—"

"What did you find at Hilltown?" went on her aunt persistently. "Did you see Arthur?"

"No, Aunt Polly, that is what is the matter; he has gone."

"Gone! Gone where?"

"Away, Aunt Polly! Nobody saw him go, and he left a note saying that he would never return. And I am so frightened—"

Mrs. Roberts was gazing at her niece with a puzzled look upon her face. She interrupted her by echoing the word "frightened" inquiringly.

"Yes, Auntie!" cried the girl; "for I may never be able to find him again, to undo what I have done!"

And Mrs. Roberts responded with a wondering laugh, and observed, "For my part, I should think you'd be very glad to be rid of him so."

She saw Helen give a start, but she could not read the girl's mind, and did not know how much she had done to estrange her by those words. It was as if Helen's whole soul had shrunk back in horror, and she sat staring at her aunt with open eyes.

"I suppose you think," the other went on grimly, "that I am going to share all this wonderful sentimentality with you about that boy; but I assure you that you don't know me! He may get you to weep over him because he chooses to behave like a fool, but not me."

Helen was still for a moment, and then she said, in an awe-stricken voice: "Aunt Polly, I have wrecked Arthur's life!" Mrs. Roberts responded with a loud guffaw, which was to the other so offensive that it was like a blow in the face.

"Wrecked his life!" the woman cried scornfully. "Helen, you talk like a baby! Can't you know in the first place that Arthur is doing all this high-tragedy acting for nothing in the world but to frighten you? Wrecked his life! And there you were, I suppose, all ready to get down on your knees to him, and beg his pardon for daring to be engaged, and to promise to come to his attic and live off bread and water, if he would only be good and not run away!"

Mrs. Roberts' voice was bitter and mocking, and her words seemed to Helen almost blasphemy; it had never occurred to her that such grief as hers would not be sacred to anyone. Yet there was no thought of anger in her mind just then, for she had been chastened in a fiery furnace, and was too full of penitence and humility for even that much egotism. She only bowed her head, and said, in a trembling voice: "Oh, Aunt Polly, I would stay in an attic and live off bread and water for the rest of my days, if I could only clear my conscience of the dreadful thing I have done."

"A beautiful sentiment indeed!" said Mrs. Roberts, with a sniff of disgust; and she stood surveying her niece in silence for a minute or two. Then smothering her feelings a little, she asked her in a quieter voice, "And so, Helen, you are really going to fling aside the life opportunity that is yours for such nonsense as this? There is no other reason?"

"There is another reason, Aunt Polly," said Helen; "it is so dreadful of you to ask me in that way. How CAN you have expected me to marry a man just because he was rich?"

"Oh," said the other, "so that is it! And pray what put the idea into your head so suddenly?" She paused a moment, and then, as the girl did not raise her head, she went on, sarcastically, "I fancy I know pretty well where you got all of these wonderful new ideas; you have not been talking with Mr. Howard for nothing, I see."

"No, not for nothing," said Helen gently.

"A nice state of affairs!" continued the other angrily; "I knew pretty well that his head was full of nonsense, but when I asked him here I thought at least that he would know enough about good manners to mind his own affairs. So he has been talking to you, has he? And now you cannot possibly marry a rich man!"

Mrs. Roberts stopped, quite too angry to find any more words; but as she sat for a minute or two, gazing at Helen, it must have occurred to her that she would not accomplish anything in that way. She made an effort to swallow her emotions.

"Helen, dear," she said, sitting down near her niece, "why will you worry me in this dreadful way, and make me speak so crossly to you? I cannot tell you, Helen, what a torment it is to me to see you throwing yourself away in this fashion; I implore you to stop and think before you take this step, for as sure as you are alive you will regret it all your days. Just think of it how you will feel, and how I will feel, when you look back at the happiness you might have had, and know that it is too late! And, Helen, it is due to nothing in the world but to your inexperience that you have let yourself be carried away by these sublimities. You *must* know, child, and you can see if you choose, that they have nothing to do with life; they will not butter your bread, Helen, or pay your coachman, and when you get over all this excitement, you will find that what I tell you is true. Look about you in the world, and where can you find anybody who lives according to such ideas?"

"What ideas do you mean, Aunt Polly?" asked Helen, with a puzzled look.

"Oh, don't you suppose," answered the other, "that I know perfectly well what kind of stuff it is that Mr. Howard has talked to you? I used to hear all that kind of thing when I was young, and I believed some of it, too,—about how beautiful it was to marry for love, and to have a fine scorn of wealth and all the rest of it; but it wasn't very long before I found out that such opinions were of no use in the world."

"Then you don't believe in love, Aunt Polly?" asked Helen, fixing her eyes on the other.

"What's the use of asking such an absurd question?" was the answer. "Of course I believe in love; I wanted you to love Mr. Harrison, and you might have, if you had chosen. I learned to love Mr. Roberts; naturally, a couple have to love each other, or how would they ever live happily together? But what has that to do with this ridiculous talk of Mr. Howard's? As if two people had nothing else to do in the world but to love each other! It's all very well, Helen, for a man who chooses to live like Robinson Crusoe to talk such nonsense, but he ought not to put it in the mind of a sentimental girl. He would very soon find, if he came out into life, that the world isn't run by love, and that people need a good many other things to keep them happy in it. You ought to have sense enough to see that you've got to live a different sort of a life, and that Mr. Howard knows nothing in the world about your needs. I don't go alone and live in visions, and make myself imaginary lives, Helen; I look at the world as it is. You will have to learn some day that the real way to find happiness is to take things as you find them, and get the best out of life you can. I never had one-tenth of your advantages, and yet there aren't many people in the world better off than I am; and you could be just as happy, if you would only take my advice about it. What I am talking to you is common sense, Helen, and anybody that you choose to ask will tell you the same thing."

So Mrs. Roberts went on, quite fairly under way in her usual course of argument, and rousing all her faculties for this last struggle. She was as convinced as ever of the completeness of her own views, and of the effect which they must have upon Helen; perhaps it was not her fault that she did not know to what another person she was talking.

In truth, it would not be easy to tell how great a difference there was in the effect of those old arguments upon Helen; while she had been sitting in her room alone and suffering so very keenly, the girl had been, though she did not know it, very near indeed to the sacred truths of life, and now as she listened to her aunt, she was simply holding her breath. The climax came suddenly, for as the other stopped, Helen leaned forward in her chair, and gazing deep into her eyes asked her, "Aunt Polly, can it really be that you do not know that what you have been saying to me is dreadfully *wicked?*"

There was perhaps nothing that the girl could have done to take her complacent relative more by surprise; Mrs. Roberts sat for a moment, echoing the last word, and staring as if not quite able to realize what Helen meant. As the truth came to her she turned quite pale.

"It seems to me," she said with a sneer, "that I remember a time when it didn't seem quite so wicked to you. If I am not mistaken you were quite glad to do all that I told you, and to get as much as ever you could."

Helen was quite used to that taunt in her own heart, and to the pain that it brought her, so she only lowered her eyes and said nothing. In the meantime Mrs. Roberts was going on in her sarcastic tone:

"Wicked indeed!" she ejaculated, "and I suppose all that I have been doing for you was wicked too! I suppose it was wicked of me to watch over your education all these years as I have, and to plan your future as if you were my own child, so that you might amount to something in the world; and it was wicked of me to take all the trouble that I have for your happiness, and wicked of Mr. Roberts to go to all the trouble about the trousseau that he has! The only right and virtuous thing about it all is the conduct of our niece who causes us to do it all, and who promises herself to a man and lets him go to all the trouble that he has, and then gets her head full of sanctimonious notions and begins to preach about wickedness to her elders!"

Helen had nothing to reply to those bitter words, for it was only too easy just then to make her accuse herself of anything. She sat meekly suffering, and thinking that the other was quite justified in all her anger. Mrs. Roberts was, of course, quite incapable of appreciating her mood, and continued to pour out her sarcasm, and to grow more and more bitter. To tell the truth, the worthy matron had not been half so unselfish in her hopes about Helen as she liked to pretend, and she showed then that like most people of the world who are perfectly good-natured on the surface, she could display no little ugliness when thwarted in her ambitions and offended in her pride.

It was not possible, however, for her to find a word that could seem to Helen unjust, so much was the girl already humbled. It was only after her aunt had ceased to direct her taunts at her, and turned her spite upon Mr. Howard and his superior ideas, that it seemed to Helen that it was not helping her to hear any more; then she rose and said, very gently, "Aunt Polly, I am sorry that you feel so about me, and I wish that I could explain to you better what I am doing. I know that what I did at first was all wrong, but that is no reason why I should leave it wrong forever. I think now that I ought to go and talk to Mr. Harrison, who is waiting for me, and after that I want you to please send me home, because father will be there to-day, and I want to tell him about how dreadfully I have treated Arthur, and beg him to forgive me."

Then, without waiting for any reply, the girl left the room and went slowly down the steps. The sorrow that possessed her lay so deep upon her heart that everything else seemed trivial in comparison, and she had put aside and forgotten the whole scene with her aunt before she had reached the parlor where Mr. Harrison was waiting; she did not stop to compose herself or to think what to say, but went quickly into the room.

Mr. Harrison, who was standing by the window, turned when he heard her; she answered his greeting kindly, and then sat down and remained very still for a moment or two, gazing at her hands in her lap. At last she raised her eyes to him, and asked: "Mr. Harrison, did you receive the letter I wrote you?"

"Yes," the other answered quickly, "I did. I cannot tell you how much pain it caused me. And, Helen—or must I call you Miss Davis?"

"You may call me Helen," said the girl simply. "I was very sorry to cause you pain," she added, "but there was nothing else that I could do."

"At least," the other responded, "I hope that you will not refuse to explain to me why this step is necessary?"

"No, Mr. Harrison," said Helen, "it is right that I should tell you all, no matter how hard it is to me to do it. It is all because of a great wrong that I have done; I know that when I have told you, you will think very badly of me indeed, but I have no right to do anything except to speak the truth."

She said that in a very low voice, not allowing her eyes to drop, and wearing upon her face the look of sadness which seemed now to belong to it always. Mr. Harrison gazed at her anxiously, and said: "You seem to have been ill, Helen."

"I have been very unhappy, Mr. Harrison," she answered, "and I do not believe I can ever be otherwise again. Did you not notice that I was unhappy?"

"I never thought of it until yesterday," the other replied.

"Until the drive," said Helen; "that was the climax of it. I must tell you the reason why I was so frightened then,—that I have a friend who was as dear to me as if he were my brother, and he loved me very much, very much more than I deserve to be loved by anyone; and when I was engaged to you he was very ill, and because I knew I was doing so wrong I did not dare to go and see him. That was why I was afraid to pass through Hilltown. The reason I was so frightened afterwards is that I caught a glimpse of him, and he was in such a dreadful way. This morning I found that he had left his home and gone away, no one knows where, so that I fear I shall never see him again."

Helen paused, and the other, who had sat down and was leaning forward anxiously, asked her, "Then it is this friend that you love?"

"No," the girl replied, "it is not that; I do not love anybody."

"But then I do not understand," went on Mr. Harrison, with a puzzled look. "You spoke of its having been so wrong; was it not your right to wish to marry me?"

And Helen, punishing herself as she had learned so bravely to do, did not lower her eyes even then; she flushed somewhat, however, as she answered: "Mr. Harrison, do you know WHY I wished to marry you?"

The other started a trifle, and looked very much at a loss indeed. "Why?" he echoed. "No, I do not know—that is—I never thought—"

"It hurts me more than I can tell you to have to say this to you," Helen said, "for you were right and true in your feeling. But did you think that I was that, Mr. Harrison? Did you think that I really loved you?"

Probably the good man had never been more embarrassed in his life than he was just then. The truth to be told, he was perfectly well aware why Helen had wished to marry him, and had been all along, without seeing anything in that for which to dislike her; he was quite without an answer to her present question, and could only cough and stammer, and reach for his handkerchief. The girl went on quickly, without waiting very long for his reply.

"I owe it to you to tell you the truth," she said, "and then it will no longer cause you pain to give me up. For I did not love you at all, Mr. Harrison; but I loved all that you offered me, and I allowed myself to be tempted thus, to promise to marry you. Ever afterwards I was quite wretched, because I knew that I was doing something wicked, and yet I never had the courage to stop. So it went on until my punishment came yesterday. I have suffered fearfully since that."

Helen had said all that there was to be said, and she stopped and took a deep breath of relief. There was a minute or two of silence, after which Mr. Harrison asked: "And you really think that it was so wrong to promise to marry me for the happiness that I could offer you?"

Helen gazed at him in surprise as she echoed, "Was it so wrong?" And at the same moment even while she was speaking, a memory flashed across her mind, the memory of what had occurred at Fairview the last time she had been there with Mr. Harrison. A deep, burning blush mantled her face, and her eyes dropped, and she trembled visibly. It was a better response to the other's question than any words could have been, and because in spite of his contact with the world he was still in his heart a gentleman, he understood and changed color himself and looked away, feeling perhaps more rebuked and humbled than he had ever felt in his life before.

So they sat thus for several minutes without speaking a word, or looking at each other, each doing penance in his own heart. At last, in a very low voice, the man said, "Helen, I do not know just how I can ever apologize to you."

The girl answered quietly: "I could not let you apologize to me, Mr. Harrison, for I never once thought that you had done anything wrong."

"I have done very wrong indeed," he answered, his voice trembling, "for I do not think that I had any right even to ask you to marry me. You make me feel suddenly how very coarse a world I have lived in, and how much lower than yours all my ways of thinking are. You look surprised that I say that," he added, as he saw that the girl was about to interrupt him, "but you do not know much about the world. Do you suppose that there are many women in society who would hesitate to marry me for my money?"

"I do not know," said Helen, slowly; "but, Mr. Harrison, you could certainly never be happy with a woman who would do that."

"I do not think now that I should," the man replied, earnestly, "but I did not feel that way before. I did not have much else to offer, Helen, for money is all that a man like me ever tries to get in the world."

"It is so very wrong, Mr. Harrison," put in the other, quickly. "When people live in that way they come to lose sight of all that is right and beautiful in life; and it is all so selfish and wicked!" (Those were words which might have made Mr. Howard smile a

184

trifle had he been there to hear them; but Helen was too much in earnest to think about being original.)

"I know," said Mr. Harrison, "and I used to believe in such things; but one never meets anyone else that does, and it is so easy to live differently. When you spoke to me as you did just now, you made me seem a very poor kind of a person indeed."

The man paused, and Helen sat gazing at him with a worried look upon her face. "It was not that which I meant to do," she began, but then she stopped; and after a long silence, Mr. Harrison took up the conversation again, speaking in a low, earnest voice.

"Helen," he said, "you have made me see that I am quite unworthy to ask for your regard,—that I have really nothing fit to offer you. But I might have one thing that you could appreciate,—for I could worship, really worship, such a woman as you; and I could do everything that I could think of to make myself worthy of you,—even if it meant the changing of all my ways of life. Do you not suppose that you could quite forget that I was a rich man, Helen, and still let me be devoted to you?"

There was a look in Mr. Harrison's eyes as he gazed at her just then which made him seem to her a different sort of a man,—as indeed he was. She answered very gently. "Mr. Harrison," she said, "it would be a great happiness to me to know that anyone felt so about me. But I could never marry you; I do not love you."

"And you do not think," asked the other, "that you could ever come to love me, no matter how long I might wait?"

"I do not think so," Helen said in a low voice. "I wish that you would not ever think of me so."

"It is very easy to say that," the man answered, pleadingly, "but how am I to do it? For everything that I have seems cheap compared with the thought of you. Why should I go on with the life I have been leading, heaping up wealth that I do not know how to use, and that makes me no better and no happier? I thought of you as a new motive for going on, Helen, and you must know that a man cannot so easily change his feelings. For I really loved you, and I do love you still, and I think that I always must love you."

Helen's own suffering had made her alive to other people's feelings, and the tone of voice in which he spoke those words moved her very much. She leaned over and laid her hand upon his,—something which she would not have thought she could ever do.

"Mr. Harrison," she said, "I cannot tell you how much it hurts me to have you speak to me so, for it makes me see more than ever how cruelly unfeeling I have been, and how much I have wronged you. It was for that I wished to beg you to forgive me, to forgive me just out of the goodness of your heart, for I cannot offer any excuse for what I did. It makes me quite wretched to have to say that, and to know that others are suffering because of my selfishness; if I had any thought of the sacredness of the beauty God has given me, I would never have let you think of me as you did, and caused you the pain that I have. But you must forgive me, Mr. Harrison, and help me, for to think of your being unhappy about me also would be really more than I could bear. Sometimes when I think of the one great sorrow that I have already upon my conscience, I feel that I do not know what I am to do; and you must go away and forget about me, for my sake if not for your own. I really cannot love anyone; I do not think that I am fit to love anyone; I only do not want to make anyone else unhappy."

And Helen stopped again, and pressed her hand upon Mr. Harrison's imploringly. He sat gazing at her in silence for a minute, and then he said, slowly: "When you put it so, it is very hard for me to say anything more. If you are only sure that that is your final word—that there is really no chance that you could ever love me,—"

"I am perfectly sure of it," the girl answered; "and because I know how cruel it sounds, it is harder for me to say than for you to hear. But it is really the truth, Mr. Harrison. I do not think that you ought to see me again until you are sure that it will not make you unhappy."

The man sat for a moment after that, with his head bowed, and then he bit his lip very hard and rose from his chair. "You can never know," he said, "how lonely it makes a man feel to hear words like those." But he took Helen's hand in his and held it for an instant, and then added: "I shall do as you ask me. Good-by." And he let her hand fall and went to the door. There he stopped to gaze once again for a moment, and then turned and disappeared, closing the door behind him.

Helen was left seated in the chair, where she remained for several minutes, leaning forward with her head in her hands, and gazing steadily in front of her, thinking very grave thoughts. She rose at last, however, and brushed back the hair from her forehead, and went slowly towards the door. It would have seemed lack of feeling to her, had she thought of it, but even before she had reached the stairs the scene through which she had just passed was gone from her mind entirely, and she was saying to herself, "If I could only know where Arthur is this afternoon!"

Her mind was still full of that thought when she entered the room, where she found her aunt seated just as she had left her, and in no more pleasant humor than before.

"You have told him, I suppose?" she inquired.

"Yes," Helen said, "I have told him, Aunt Polly."

"And now you are happy, I suppose!"

"No, indeed, I am very far from that," said Helen, and she went to the window; she stood there, gazing out, but with her thoughts equally far away from the scene outside as from Mrs. Roberts' warnings and sarcasms. The latter had gone on for several minutes before her niece turned suddenly. "Excuse me for interrupting you, Aunt Polly," she said; "but I want to know whether Mr. Howard has gone yet."

"His train goes in an hour or so," said Mrs. Roberts, not very graciously.

"I think I will see if he is downstairs," Helen responded; "I wish to speak to him before he goes." And so she descended and found Mr. Howard seated alone upon the piazza.

Taking a seat beside him, she said, "I did not thank you when I left you in the carriage, Mr. Howard, for having been so kind to me; but I was so wrapped up in my worry—"

"I understood perfectly," put in the other. "I saw that you felt too keenly about your discovery to have anything to say to me."

"I feel no less keenly about it now," said Helen; "but I could not let you go away until I had spoken to you." She gazed very earnestly at him as she continued: "I have to tell you how much you have done for me, and how I thank you for it from the bottom of my heart. I simply cannot say how much all that you have shown me has meant to me; I should have cared for nothing but to have you tell me what it would be right for me to do with my life,—if only it had not been for this dreadful misfortune of Arthur's, which makes it seem as if it would be wicked for me to think about anything."

Mr. Howard sat gazing in front of him for a moment, and then he said gently, "What if the change that you speak of were to be accomplished, Miss Davis, without your ever thinking about it? For what is it that makes the difference between being thoughtless and selfish, and being noble and good, if it be not simply to walk reverently in God's great temple of life, and to think with sorrow of one's own self? Believe me, my dear friend, the best men that have lived on earth have seen no more cause to be pleased with themselves than you."

"That may be true, Mr. Howard," said Helen, sadly, "but it can do me no good to know it. It does not make what happens to Arthur a bit less dreadful to think of."

"It is the most painful fact about all our wrong," the other answered, "that no amount of repentance can ever alter the consequences. But, Miss Davis, that is a guilt which all creation carries on its shoulders; it is what is symbolized in the Fall of Man—that he has to realize that he might have had infinite beauty and joy for his portion, if only the soul within him had never weakened and failed. Let me tell you that he is a lucky man who can look back at all his life and see no more shameful guilt than yours, and no consequence worse than yours can be." As Mr. Howard spoke he saw a startled look cross the girl's face, and he added, "Do not suppose that I am saying that to comfort you, for it is really the truth. It oftens happens too, that the natures that are strongest and most ardent in their search for righteousness have the worst sins to remember."

Helen did not answer for several moments, for the thought was strange to her; then suddenly she gazed at the other very earnestly and said: "Mr. Howard, you are a man who lives for what is beautiful and high,—suppose that YOU had to carry all through your life the burden of such guilt as mine?"

The man's voice was trembling slightly as he answered her: "It is not hard for me to suppose that, Miss Davis; I HAVE such a burden to carry." As he raised his eyes he saw a still more wondering look upon her countenance.

"But the consequences!" she exclaimed. "Surely, Mr. Howard, you could not bear to live if you knew—"

"I have never known the consequences," said the man, as she stopped abruptly; "just as you may never know them; but this I know, that yours could not be so dreadful as mine must be. I know also that I am far more to blame for them than you."

Helen could not have told what caused the emotion which made her shudder so just then as she gazed into Mr. Howard's dark eyes. Her voice was almost a whisper as she said, "And yet you are GOOD!"

"I am good," said the man gently, "with all the goodness that any man can claim, the goodness of trying to be better. You may be that also."

Helen sat for a long time in silence after that, wondering at what was passing in her own mind; it was as if she had caught a sudden glimpse into a great vista of life. She had always before thought of this man's suffering as having been physical; and the deep movement of sympathy and awe which stirred her now was one step farther from her own self-absorption, and one step nearer to the suffering that is the heart of things.

But Helen had to keep that thought and dwell upon it in solitude; there was no chance for her to talk with Mr. Howard any more, for she heard her aunt's step in the hall behind her. She had only time to say, "I am going home myself this afternoon; will you come there to see me, Mr. Howard? I cannot tell you how much pleasure it would give me."

"There is nothing I should like to do more," the man answered; "I hope to keep your friendship. "When would you like me to come?"

"Any time that you can," replied Helen. "Come soon, for I know how unhappy I shall be."

That was practically the last word she said to Mr. Howard, for her aunt joined them, and after that the conversation was formal. It was not very long before the carriage came for him, and Helen pressed his hand gratefully at parting, and stood leaning against a pillar of the porch, shading her eyes from the sun while she watched the carriage depart. Then she sat down to wait for it to return from the depot for her, which it did before long; and so she bid farewell to her aunt.

It was a great relief to Helen; and while we know not what emotions it may cause to the reader, it is perhaps well to say that he may likewise pay his last respects to the worthy matron, who will not take part in the humble events of which the rest of our story must be composed.

For Helen was going home, home to the poor little parsonage of Oakdale! She was going with a feeling of relief in her heart second only to her sorow; the more she had come to feel how shallow and false was the splendor that had allured her, the more she had found herself drawn to her old home, with its memories that were so dear and so beautiful. She felt that there she might at least think of Arthur all that she chose, and meet with nothing to affront her grief; and also she found herself thinking of her father's love with a new kind of hunger.

When she arrived, she found Mr. Davis waiting for her with a very anxious look upon his countenance; he had stopped at Hilltown on his way, and learned about Arthur's disappearance, and then heard from Elizabeth what she knew about Helen's engagement. The girl flung herself into his arms, and afterwards, quite overcome by the emotions that surged up within her, sank down upon her knees before him and sobbed out the whole story, her heart bursting with sorrow and contrition; as he lifted her up and kissed her and whispered his beautiful words of pardon and comfort, Helen found it a real homecoming indeed.

Mr. Davis was also able to calm her worry a little by telling her that he did not think it possible that Arthur would keep his whereabouts secret from him very long. "When I find him, dear child," he said, "it will all be well again, for we will believe in love, you and I, and not care what the great world says about it. I think I could be well content that you should marry our dear Arthur."

"But, father, I do not love him," put in Helen faintly.

"That may come in time," said the other, kissing her tenderly, and smiling. "There is no need to talk of it, for you are too young to marry, anyway. And in the meantime we must find him."

There was a long silence after that. Helen sat down on the sofa beside her father and put her arms about him and leaned her head upon his bosom, drinking in deep drafts of his pardon and love. She told him about Mr. Howard, and of the words of counsel which he had given her, and how he was coming to see her again. Afterwards the conversation came back to Arthur and his love for Helen, and then Mr. Davis went on to add something that caused Helen to open her eyes very wide and gaze at him in wonder.

"There is still another reason for wishing to find him soon," he said, "for something else has happened to-day that he ought to know about."

"What is it?" asked Helen.

"I don't know that I ought to tell you about it just now," said the other, "for it is a very sad story. But someone was here to see Arthur this morning—someone whom I never expected to see again in all my life."

"To see Arthur?" echoed the girl in perplexity. "Who could want to see Arthur?" As her father went on she gave a great start.

"It was his mother," said Mr. Davis.

And Helen stared at him, gasping for breath as she echoed the words, "His mother!"

"You may well be astonished," said the clergyman. "But the woman proved beyond doubt that she was really the person who left Arthur with me."

"You did not recognize her?"

"No, Helen; for it has been twenty-one or two years since I saw her, and she has changed very much since then. But she told me that in all that time she has never once lost sight of her boy, and has been watching all that he did."

"Where has she been?"

"She did not tell me," the other answered, "but I fancy in New York. The poor woman has lived a very dreadful life, a life of such wretched wickedness that we cannot even talk about it; I think I never heard of more cruel suffering. I was glad that you were not here to see her, or know about it until after she was gone; she said that she had come to see Arthur once, because she was going away to die."

"To die!" exclaimed the girl, in horror.

"Yes," said Mr. Davis, "to die; she looked as if she could not live many days longer. I begged her to let me see that she was provided for, but she said that she was going to find her way back to her old home, somewhere far off in the country, and she would hear of nothing else. She would not tell the name of the place, nor her own name, but she left a letter for Arthur, and begged me to find him and give it to him, so that he might come and speak to her once if he cared to do so. She begged me to forgive her for the trouble she had caused me, and to pray that God would forgive her too; and then she bade me farewell and dragged herself away."

Mr. Davis stopped, and Helen sat for a long time staring ahead of her, with a very frightened look in her eyes, and thinking, "Oh, we MUST find Arthur!" Then she turned to her father, her lips trembling and her countenance very pale. "Tell me," she said, in a low, awe-stricken voice, "a long time ago someone must have wronged that woman."

"Yes, dear," said Mr. Davis, "when she was not even as old as you are. And the man who wronged her was worth millions of dollars, Helen, and could have saved her from all her suffering with a few of them if he cared to. No one but God knows his name, for the woman would not tell it."

Helen sat for a moment or two staring at him wildly; and then suddenly she buried her head in his bosom and burst into tears, sobbing so cruelly that her father was sorry he had told her what he had. He knew why that story moved her so, and it wrung his heart to think of it,—that this child of his had put upon her own shoulders some of that burden of the guilt of things, and must suffer beneath it, perhaps for the rest of her days.

When Helen gazed up at him again there was the old frightened look upon her face, and all his attempts to comfort her were useless. "No, no!" she whispered. "No, father! I cannot even think of peace again, until we have found Arthur!"

Freundliches Voglein!

Chapter XII

"A fugitive and gracious light he seeks,
Shy to illumine; and I seek it too.
This does not come with houses or with gold,
With place, with honor, and a flattering crew;
'Tis not in the world's market bought and sold."

Three days passed by after Helen had returned to her father, during which the girl stayed by herself most of the time. When the breaking off of her engagement was known, many of her old friends came to see her, but the hints that they dropped did not move her to any confidences; she felt that it would not be possible for her to find among them any understanding of her present moods. Her old life, or rather the life to which she had been looking forward, seemed to her quite empty and shallow, and there was nothing useful that she knew of to do except to offer to help her father in such ways as she could. She drew back into her own heart, giving most of her time to thinking about Mr. Howard and Arthur, and no one but her father knew why it was that she was so subdued and silent.

It was only on the third morning, when there came a letter from Mr. Howard saying that he was coming out that afternoon to see her, that Helen seemed to be interested and stirred again. She went to the window more than once to look for him; and when at last her friend had arrived, and the two were seated in the parlor, she said to him without waiting for any circumstance, "I have been wishing very much to see you, Mr. Howard, because there is something I am anxious to talk to you about, if you will let me."

"I am sorry to say that it is about myself," she went on, when the other had expressed his willingness to hear her, "for I want to ask you to help me, and to give me some advice. I ought to have asked you the questions I am going to before this, but the last time I saw you I could think about nothing but Arthur. They only came to me after you had gone."

"What are they?" asked the man.

"You must knew, Mr. Howard," said Helen, "that it is you who have shown me the wrongness of all that I was doing in my life, and stirred me with a desire to do better. I find now that such thoughts have always been so far from me that the wish to be right is all that I have, and I do not know at all what to do. It seemed to me that I would rather talk to you about it than to anyone, even my own father. I do not know whether that is just right, but you do not mind my asking you, do you?"

"It is my wish to help you in every way that I can," was the gentle response.

"I will tell you what I have been thinking," said Helen. "I have been so unhappy in the last three days that I have done nothing at all; but it seemed to me somehow that it must be wrong of me to let go of myself in that way—as if I had no right to pamper myself and indulge my own feelings. It was not that I wished to forget what wrong things I have done, or keep from suffering because of them; yet it seemed to me that the fact that I was wretched and frightened was no excuse for my doing no good for the rest of my life. When I have thought about my duty before, it has always been my school-girl's task of studying and practicing music, but that is not at all what I want now, for I cannot bear to think of such things while the memory of Arthur is in my mind. I need something that is not for myself, Mr. Howard, and I find myself thinking that it should be something that I do not like to do."

Helen paused for a moment, gazing at the other anxiously; and then she went on: "You must know that what is really behind what

196

I am saying is what you said that evening in the arbor, about the kind of woman I ought to be because God has made me beautiful. My heart is full of a great hunger to be set right, and to get a clearer sight of the things that are truly good in life. I want you to talk to me about your own ideals, and what you do to keep your life deep and true; and then to tell me what you would do in my place. I promise you that no matter how hard it may be I shall feel that just what you tell me to do is my duty, and at least I shall never be happy again until I have done it. Do you understand how I feel, Mr. Howard?"

"Yes," the man answered, in a quiet voice, "I understand you perfectly." And then as he paused, watching the girl from beneath his dark brows, Helen asked, "You do not mind talking to me about yourself?"

"When a man lives all alone and as self-centered as I," the other replied, smiling, "it is fatally easy for him to do that; he may blend himself with his ideals in such a curious way that he never talks about anything else. But if you will excuse that, I will tell you what I can."

"Tell me why it is that you live so much alone," said the girl. "Is it that you do not care for friends?"

"It is very difficult for a man who feels about life as I do to find many friends," he responded. "If one strives to dwell in deep things, and is very keen and earnest about it, he is apt to find very little to help him outside of himself; perhaps it is because I have met very few persons in my life, but it has not happened to me to find anyone who thinks about it as I do, or who cares to live it with my strenuousness. I have met musicians, some who labored very hard at their art, but none who felt it a duty to labor with their own souls, to make them beautiful and strong; and I have met literary men and scholars, but they were all interested in books, and were willing to be learned, and to classify and plod; I have never found one who was swift and eager, and full of high impatience for what is real and the best. There should come times to a man, I think, when he feels that books are an impertinence, when he knows that he has only the long-delayed battle with his own heart to fight, and the prize of its joy to win. When such moods come upon him he sees that he has to live his life upon his knees, and it is rarely indeed that he knows of anyone who can follow him and share in his labor. So it is that I have had to live all my life by myself, Miss Davis."

"You have always done that?" Helen asked, as he stopped.

"Yes," he answered, "or for very many years. I have a little house on the wildest of lakes up in the mountains, wyhere I play the hermit in the summer, and where I should have been now if it had not been that I yielded to your aunt's invitation. When I spoke of having no friends I forgot the things of Nature, which really do sympathize with an artist's life; I find that they never fail to become full of meaning whenever my own spirit shakes off its bonds. It has always been a belief of mine that there is nothing that Nature makes that is quite so dull and unfeeling as man,— with the exception of children and lovers, I had much rather play my violin for the flowers and the trees."

"You like to play it out of doors?" Helen asked, with a sudden smile.

"Yes," laughed the other, "that is one of my privileges as a hermit. It seems quite natural to the wild things, for they have all a music of their own, a wonderful, silent music that the best musicians cannot catch; do you not believe that, Miss Davis?"

"Yes," Helen said, and sat gazing at her companion silently for a minute. "I should think a life of such effort would be very hard," she said finally. "Do you not ever fail?"

"I do not do much else," he replied with a sad smile, "and get up and stumble on. The mastership of one's heart is the ideal, you know; and after all one's own life cannot be anything but struggle and failure, for the power he is trying to conquer is infinite. When I find my life very hard I do not complain, but know that the reason for it is that I have chosen to have it real, and that the essence of the soul is its effort. I think that is a very important thing to feel about life, Miss Davis."

"That is why I do not wish to be idle," said Helen.

"It is just because people do not know this fact about the soul," the other continued, "and are not willing to dare and suffer, and overcome dullness, and keep their spiritual faculties free, that they sink down as they grow older, and become what they call practical, and talk very wisely about experience. It is only when God sends into the world a man of genius that no mountains of earth can crush, and who keeps his faith and sweetness all through his life that we learn the baseness of the thought that experience necessarily brings cynicism and selfishness. There is to me in all this world nothing more hateful than this disillusioned worldliness, and nothing makes me angrier than to see it taking the name of wisdom. If I were a man with an art, there is nothing, I think, that I should feel more called to make war upon; it is a very blow in the face of God. Nothing makes me sadder than to see the life that such people live,—to see for instance how pathetic are the things they call their entertainments; and when one knows himself that life is a magic potion, to be drank with rapture and awe,—that every instance of it ought to be a hymn of rejoicing, and the whole of it rich and full of power, like some majestic symphony. I often find myself wishing that there were some way of saving the time that people spend in their pleasures;

"Life piled on life
Were all too little, and of one to me
Little remains.'

As I kneel before God's altar of the heart I know that if I had infinite time and infinite energy there would be beauty and joy still to seek, and so as I look about me in the world and see all the sin and misery that is in it, it is my comfort to know that the reason for it is that men are still living the lives of the animals, and have not even dreamed of the life that belongs to them as men. That is something about which I feel very strongly myself,— that is part of my duty as a man who seeks worship and rightness to mark that difference in my own life quite plainly."

Mr. Howard paused for a moment, and Helen said very earnestly, "I wish that you would tell me about that."

"I consider it my duty," the other replied, "to keep all the external circumstances of my life as simple and as humble as I should have to if I were quite poor. If I were not physically unable, I should feel that I ought to do for my own self all that I needed to have done, for I think that if it is necessary that others should be degraded to menial service in order that my soul might be beautiful and true, then life is bad at the heart of it, and I want none of its truth and beauty. I do not have to look into my heart very long, Miss Davis, to discover that what I am seeking in life is something that no millions of money can buy me; and when I am face to face with the sternness of what I call that spiritual fact, I see that fine houses and all the rest are a foolish kind of toy, and wonder that any man should think that he can please me by giving the labor of his soul to making them. It is much the same thing as I feel, for instance, when I go to hear a master of music, and find that he has spent his hours in torturing himself and his fingers in order to give me an acrobatic exhibition, when all the time what I wish him to do, and what his genius gave him power to do, was to find the magic word that should set free the slumbering demon of my soul. So I think that a man who wishes to grow by sympathy and worship should do without wealth, if only because it is so trivial; but of course I have left unmentioned what is the great reason for a self-denying life, the reason that lies at the heart of the matter, and that includes all the others in it,—that he who lives by prayer and joy makes all men richer, but he who takes more than his bare necessity of the wealth of the body must know that he robs his brother when he does it. The things of the soul are everywhere, but wealth stands for the toil and suffering of human beings, and thousands must starve and die so that one rich man may live at ease. That is no fine rhetoric that I am indulging in, but a very deep and earnest conviction of my soul; first of all facts of morality stands the law that the life of man is labor, and that he who chooses to live otherwise is a dastard. He may chase the phantom of happiness all his days and not find it, and yet never guess the reason,—that joy is a melody of the heart, and that he is playing upon an instrument that is out of tune. Few people choose to think of that at all, but I cannot afford ever to forget it, for my task is to live the artist's life, to dwell close to the heart of things; it is something that I simply cannot understand how any man who pretends to do that can know of the suffering and starving that is in the world, and can feel that he who has God's temple of the soul for his dwelling, has right to more of the pleasures of earth than the plainest food and shelter and what tools of his art he requires. If it is otherwise it can only be because he is no artist at all, no lover of life, but only a tradesman under another name, using God's high gift to get for himself what he can, and thinking of his sympathy and feeling as things that he puts on when he goes to work, and when he is sure that they will cost him no trouble."

Mr. Howard had been speaking very slowly, and in a deep and earnest voice; he paused for a moment, and then added with a slight smile, "I have been answering your question without thinking about it, Miss Davis, for I have told you all that there is to tell about my life."

Helen did not answer, but sat for a long time gazing at him and thinking very deeply; then she said to him, her voice shaking slightly: "You have answered only half of my question, Mr. Howard; I want you to tell me what a woman can do to bring those high things into her life—to keep her soul humble and strong. I do not think that I have your courage and self-reliance."

The man's voice dropped lower as he answered her, "Suppose that you were to find this friend of yours that knows you so well, and loves you so truly; do you not think that there might be a chance for you to win this prize of life that I speak of?" Helen did not reply, but sat with her eyes still fixed upon the other's countenance; as he went on, his deep, musical voice held them there by a spell.

"Miss Davis," he said, "a man does not live very long in the kingdom of the soul before there comes to be one thing that he loves more than anything else that life can offer; that thing is love. For love is the great gateway into the spiritual life, the stage of life's journey when human beings are unselfish and true to their hearts, if ever the power of unselfishness and truth lies in them. As for man, he has many battles to fight and much of himself to kill before the great prizes of the soul can be his—but the true woman has but one glory and one duty in life, and sacredness and beauty are hers by the free gift of God. If she be a true woman, when her one great passion takes its hold upon her it carries all her being with it, and she gives herself and all that she has. Because I believe in unselfishness and know that love is the essence of things, I find in all the world nothing more beautiful than that, and think that she has no other task in life, except to see that the self which she gives is her best and Inghest, and to hold to the thought of the sacredness of what she is doing. For love is the soul's great act of worship, and the heart's great awakening to life. If the man be selfish and a seeker of pleasure, what I say of love and woman is not for him; but if he be one who seeks to worship, to rouse the soul within him to its vision of the beauty and preciousness of life, then he must know that this is the great chance that Nature gives him, that no effort of his own will ever carry him so far towards what he seeks. The woman who gives herself to him he takes for his own with awe and trembling, knowing that the glory which he reads in her eyes is the very presence of the spirit of life; and because she stands for this precious thing to him he seeks her love more than anything else upon earth, feeling that if he has it he has everything, and if he has it not, he has nothing. He cherishes the woman as before he cherished what was best in his own soul; he chooses all fair and noble actions that may bring him still more of her love; all else that life has for him he lays as an offering at the shrine of her heart, all his joy and all his care, and asks but love in return; and because the giving of love is the woman's joy and the perfectness of her sacrifice, her glory, they come to forget themselves in each other's being, and to live their lives in each other's hearts. The joy that each cares for is no longer his own joy, but the other's; and so they come to stand for the sacredness of God to each other, and for perpetual inspiration. By and by, perhaps, from long dwelling out of themselves and feeding their hearts upon things spiritual, they learn the deep and mystic religion of love, that is the last lesson life has to teach; it is given to no man to know what is the source of this mysterious being of ours, but men who come near to it find it so glorious that they die for it in joy; and the least glimpse of it gives a man quite a new feeling about a human heart. So at last it happens that the lovers read a fearful wonder in each other's eyes, and give each other royal greeting, no longer for what they are, but for that which they would like to be. They come to worship together as they could never have worshiped apart; and always that which they worship and that in which they dwell, is what all existence is seeking with so much pain, the sacred presence of wonder that some call Truth, and some Beauty,—but all Love. When you ask me how unselfishness is to be made yours in life, that is the answer which I give you."

Mr. Howard's voice had dropped very low; as he stopped Helen was trembling within herself. She was drinking still more from the bottomless cup of her humiliation and remorse, for she was still haunted by the specter of what she had done. The man went on after an interval of silence.

"I think there is no one," he said, "whom these things touch more than the man who would live the life of art that I have talked of before; for the artist seeks experience above all things, seeks it not only for himself but for his race. And it must come from his own heart; no one can drive him to his task. All artists tell that the great source of their power is love; and the wisest of them makes of his love an art-work, as he makes an art-work of his life. He counts his power of loving most sacred of all his powers, and guards it from harm as he guards his life itself; he gives all his soul to the dreaming of that dream, and lays all his prayer before it; and when he meets with the maiden who will honor such effort, he forgets everything else in his life, and gives her all his heart, and studies to 'worship her by years of noble deeds.' For a woman who loves love, the heart of such a man is a lifetime's treasure; for his passion is of the soul, and does not die; and all that he has done has been really but a training of himself for that great consecration. If he be a true artist, all his days have been spent in learning to wrestle with himself, to rouse himself and master his own heart; until at last his very being has become a prayer, and his soul like a great storm of wind that sweeps everything away in its arms. Perhaps that hunger has possessed him so that he never even wakens in the dead of night without finding it with him in all its strength; it rouses him in the morning with a song, and when midnight comes and he is weary, it is a benediction and a hand upon his brow. All the time, because he has a man's heart and knows of his life's great glory, his longing turns to a dream of love, to a vision of the flying perfect for which all his life is a search. There is a maiden who dwells in all the music that he hears, and who calls to him in the sunrise, and flings wide the flowers upon the meadows; she treads before him on the moonlit waters and strews them with showers of fire. If his soul be only strong enough, perhaps he waits long years for that perfect woman, that woman who loves not herself, but loves love; and all the time the yearning of his heart is growing, so that those who gaze at him wonder why his eyes are dark and sunken. He knows that his heart is a treasure-house which he himself cannot explore, and that in all the world he seeks nothing but some woman before whom he might fling wide its doors."

Helen had been leaning on the table, holding her hands in front of her; towards the end they were trembling so much that she took them away and clasped them in her lap. When he ceased her eyes were lowered; she could not see how his were fixed upon her, but she knew that her bosom was heaving painfully, and that there were hot tears upon her cheeks. He added slowly: "I have told you all that I think about life, my dear friend, and all that I think about love; so I think I have told you all that I know." And Helen lifted her eyes to his and gazed at him through her tears.

"You tell *me* of such things?" she asked. "You give such advice to *me!*"

"Yes," said the other, gently, "why not to you?"

"Mr. Howard," Helen answered, "do you not know what I have done, and how I must feel while I listen to you? It is good that I should hear such things, because I ought to suffer; but when I asked you for your advice I wished for something hard and stern to do, before I dared ever think of love, or feel myself right again."

Mr. Howard sat watching her for a moment in silence, and then he answered gently, "I do not think, my dear friend, that it is our duty as struggling mortals to feel ourselves right at all; I am not even sure that we ought to care about our rightness in the least. For God has put high and beautiful things in the world, things that call for all our attention; and I am sure that we are never so close to rightness as when we give all our devotion to them and cease quite utterly to think about ourselves. And besides that, the love that I speak of is not easy to give, Miss Davis. It is easy to give up one's self in the first glow of feeling; but to forget one's self entirely, and one's comfort and happiness in all the little things of life; to consecrate one's self and all that one has to a lifetime of patience and self-abnegation; and to seek no reward and ask for no happiness but love,—do you not think that such things would cost one pain and bring a good conscience at last?"

Helen's voice was very low as she answered, "Perhaps, at last." Then she sat very still, and finally raised her deep, earnest eyes and leaned forward and gazed straight into her companion's. "Mr. Howard," she said, "you must know that YOU are my conscience; and it is the memory of your words that causes me all my suffering. And now tell me one thing; suppose I were to say to you that I could beg upon my knees for a chance to earn such a life as that; and suppose I should ever come really to love someone, and should give up everything to win such a treasure, do you think that I could clear my soul from what I have done, and win rightness for mine? Do you think that you—that YOU could ever forget that I was the woman who had wished to sell her love for money?"

Mr. Howard answered softly, "Yes, I think so."

"But are you sure of it?" Helen asked; and when she had received the same reply she drew a long breath, and a wonderful expression of relief came upon her face; all her being seemed to rise,—as if all in an instant she had flung away the burden of shame and fear that had been crushing her soul. She sat gazing at the other with a strange look in her eyes, and then she sank down and buried her head in her arms upon the table.

And fully a minute passed thus without a sound. Helen was just lifting her head again, and Mr. Howard was about to speak, when an unexpected interruption caused him to stop. The front door was opened, and as Helen turned with a start the servant came and stood in the doorway.

"What is it, Elizabeth?" Helen asked in a faint voice.

"I have just been to the post office," the woman answered; "here is a letter for you."

"Very well," Helen answered; "give it to me."

And she took it and put it on the table in front of her. Then she waited until the servant was gone, and in the meantime, half mechanically, turned her eyes upon the envelope. Suddenly the man saw her give a violent start and turn very pale; she snatched up the letter and sprang to her feet, and stood supporting herself by the chair, her hand shaking, and her breath coming in gasps.

"What is it?" Mr. Howard cried.

Helen's voice was hoarse and choking as she answered him: "It is from Arthur!" As he started and half rose from his chair the girl tore open the letter and unfolded the contents, glancing at it once very swiftly, her eyes flying from line to line; the next instant she let it fall to the floor with a cry and clutched with her hands at her bosom. She tried to speak, but she was choking with her emotion; only her companion saw that her face was transfigured with delight; and then suddenly she sank down upon the sofa beside her, her form shaken with hysterical laughter and sobbing.

Mr. Howard had risen from his chair in wonder; but before he could take a step toward her he heard someone in the hall, and

Mr. Davis rushed into the room. "Helen, Helen!" he exclaimed, "what is the matter?" and sank down upon his knees beside her; the girl raised her head and then flung herself into his arms, exclaiming incoherently: "Oh, Daddy, I am free! Oh, oh—can you believe it—I am free!"

Long after her first ecstasy had passed Helen still lay with her head buried in her father's bosom, trembling and weeping and repeating half as if in a dream that last wonderful word, "Free!" Meanwhile Mr. Davis had bent down and picked up the paper to glance over it.

Most certainly Arthur would have wondered had he seen the effect of that letter upon Helen; for he wrote to her with bitter scorn, and told her that he had torn his love for her from his heart, and made himself master of his own life again. He bid her go on in the course she had chosen, for a day or two had been enough for him to find the end of her power over him, and of his care for her; and he added that he wrote to her only that she might not please herself with the thought of having wrecked him, and that he was going far away to begin his life again.

The words brought many emotions to Mr. Davis, and suggested many doubts; but to Helen they brought but one thought. She still clung to her father, sobbing like a child and muttering the one word "Free!" When at last the fit had vented itself and she looked up again, she seemed to Mr. Howard more like a girl than she ever had before; and she wiped away her tears laughingly, and smoothed back her hair, and was wonderfully beautiful in her emotion. She introduced Mr. Howard to her father, and begged him to excuse her for her lack of self-control. "I could not help it," she said, "for oh, I am so happy—so happy!" And she leaned her head upon her father's shoulder again and gazed up into his face. "Daddy dear," she said, "and are you not happy too?"

"My dear," Mr Davis protested, "of course I am glad to hear that Arthur is himself again. But that is not finding him, and I fear—"

"Oh, oh, please don't!" Helen cried, the frightened look coming back upon her face in a flash. "Oh please do not tell me that—no, no! Do let me be happy just a little while—think of it, how wretched I have been! And now to know he is safe! Oh, please, Daddy!" And the tears had welled up in Helen's eyes again. She turned quickly to Mr. Howard, her voice trembling. "Tell me that I may be happy," she exclaimed. "You know all about it, Mr. Howard. Is it not right that I should be happy just a little?"

As her friend answered her gently that he thought it was, she sat looking at him for a moment, and then the cloud passed over. She brushed away her tears, and put her arms about her father again.

"I cannot help it," she went on, quickly, "I must be happy whether I want to or not! You must not mind anything I do! For oh, think what it means to have been so wretched, so crushed and so frightened! I thought that all my life was to be like that, that I could never sing again, because Arthur was ruined. Nobody will ever know how I felt,—how many tears I shed; and now think what it means to be free—to be free,—oh, free! And to be able to be good once more! I should go mad if I thought about it!"

Helen had risen as she spoke, and she spread out her arms and flung back her head and drank in a deep breath of joy. She began singing, half to herself; and then as that brought a sudden idea into her mind she ran to the window and shut it quickly. "I will sing you my hymn!" she laughed, "*that* is the way to be happy!"

And she went to the piano; in a minute more she had begun the chorus she had sung to Arthur, "Hail thee Joy, from Heaven descending!" The flood of emotion that was pent up within her poured itself out in the wild torrent of music, and Helen seemed happy enough to make up for all the weeks of suffering. As she swept herself on she proved what she had said,—that she would go mad if she thought much about her release; and Mr. Howard and her father sat gazing at her in wonder. When she stopped she was quite exhausted and quite dazed, and came and buried her head in her father's arms, and sat waiting until the heaving of her bosom had subsided, and she was calm once more,—in the meantime murmuring faintly to herself again and again that she was happy and that she was free.

When she looked up and brushed away her tangled hair again, perhaps she thought that her conduct was not very conventional, for she begged Mr. Howard's pardon once more, promising to be more orderly by and by. Then she added, laughing, "It is good that you should see me happy, though, because I have always troubled you with my egotisms before." She went on talking merrily, until suddenly she sprang up and said, "I shall have to sing again if I do not run away, so I am going upstairs to make myself look respectable!" And with that she danced out of the room, waking the echoes of the house with her caroling:

"Merrily, merrily, shall I live now,
Under the blossom that hangs on the bough!"
Lus-tig im Leid, sing'ich von Lieb-e!

Chapter XIII

"Some one whom I can court
With no great change of manner,
Still holding reason's fort,
Tho waving fancy's banner."

Several weeks had passed since Helen had received the letter from Arthur, the girl having in the meantime settled quietly down at Oakdale She had seen few of her friends excepting Mr. Howard, who had come out often from the city.

She was expecting a visit from him one bright afternoon, and was standing by one of the pillars of the vine-covered porch, gazing up at the blue sky above her and waiting to hear the whistle of the train. When she saw her friend from the distance she waved her hand to him and went to meet him, laughing, "I am going to take you out to see my stream and my bobolink to-day. You have not seen our country yet, you know."

The girl seemed to Mr. Howard more beautiful that afternoon than he had ever known her before, for she was dressed all in white and there was the old spring in her step, and the old joy in her heart. When they had passed out of the village, she found the sky so very blue, and the clouds so very white, and the woods and meadows so very green, that she was radiantly happy and feared that she would have to sing. And she laughed:

"Away, away from men and towns,
To the wild wood and the downs!"

And then interrupted herself to say, "You must not care, Mr. Howard, if I chatter away and do all the talking. It has been a long time since I have paid a visit to my friends out here, and they will all be here to welcome me."

Even as Helen spoke she looked up, and there was the bobolink flying over her head and pouring out his song; also the merry breeze was dancing over the meadows, and everything about her was in motion.

"Do you know," she told her companion, "I think most of the happiness of my life has been out in these fields; I don't know what made me so fond of the country, but even when I was a very little thing, whenever I learned a new song I would come out here and sing it. Those were times when I had nothing to do but be happy, you know, and I never thought about anything else. It has always been so easy for me to be happy, I don't know why. There is a fountain of joy in my heart that wells up whether I want it to or not, so that I can always be as merry as I choose. I am afraid that is very selfish, isn't it, Mr. Howard? I am trying to be right now, you know."

"You may consider you are being merry for my sake at present," said the man with a laugh. "It is not always so easy for me to be joyful."

"Very well, then," smiled Helen; "I only wish that you had brought your violin along. For you see I always think of these things of Nature with music; when I was little they were all creatures that danced with me. These winds that are so lively were funny little fairy-men, and you could see all the flowers shake as they swept over them; whenever I heard any music that was quick and bright I always used to fancy that some of them had hold of my hands and were teaching me to run. I never thought about asking why, but I used to find that very exciting. And then there was my streamlet—he's just ahead here past the bushes—and I used to like him best of all. For he was a very beautiful youth, with a crown of flowers upon his head; there was a wonderful light in his eyes, and his voice was very strong and clear, and his step very swift, so it was quite wonderful when you danced with him. For he was the lord of all the rest, and everything around you got into motion then; there was never any stopping, for you know the streamlet always goes faster and faster, and gets more and more joyous, until you cannot bear it any more and have to give up. We shall have to play the Kreutzer Sonata some time, Mr. Howard.'

"I was thinking of that," said the other, smiling.

"I think it would be interesting to know what people imagine when they listen to music," went on Helen. "I have all sorts of queer fancies for myself; whenever it gets too exciting there is always one last resource, you can fly away to the top of the nearest mountain. I don't know just why that is, but perhaps it's because you can see so much from there, or because there are so many winds; anyway, there is a dance—a wonderfully thrilling thing, if only the composer knows how to manage it. There is someone who dances with me—I never saw his face, but he's always there; and everything around you is flying fast, and there comes surge after surge of the music and sweeps you on,—perhaps some of those wild runs on the violins that are just as if the wind took you up in its arms and whirled you away in the air! That is a most tremendous experience when it happens, because then you go quite beside yourself and you see that all the world is alive and full of power; the great things of the forest begin to stir too, the trees and the strange shapes in the clouds, and all the world is suddenly gone mad with motion; and so by the time you come to the last chords your hands are clenched and you can hardly breathe, and you feel that all your soul is throbbing!"

Helen was getting quite excited then, just over her own enthusiasm; perhaps it was because the wind was blowing about her. "Is that the way music does with you?" she laughed, as she stopped.

"Sometimes," said Mr. Howard, smiling in turn; "but then again while all my soul is throbbing I feel my neighbor reaching to put on her wraps, and that brings me down from the mountains so quickly that it is painful; afterwards you go outside among the cabs and cable-cars, and make sad discoveries about life."

"You are a pessimist," said the girl.

"Possibly," responded the other, "but try to keep your fountain of joy a while, Miss Davis. There are disagreeable things in life to be done, and some suffering to be borne, and sometimes the fountain dries up very quickly indeed."

Helen was much more ready to look serious than she would have been a month before; she asked in a different tone, "You think that must always happen?"

"Not quite always," was the reply; "there are a few who manage to keep it, but it means a great deal of effort. Perhaps you never took your own happiness so seriously," he added with a smile.

"No," said Helen, "I never made much effort that I know of."

"Some day perhaps you will have to," replied the other, "and then you will think of the creatures of nature as I do, not simply as rejoicing, but as fighting the same battle and daring the same pain as you."

The girl thought for a moment, and then asked: "Do you really believe that as a fact?"

"I believe something," was the answer, "that makes me think when I go among men and see their dullness, that Nature is flinging wide her glory in helpless appeal to them; and that it is a dreadful accident that they have no eyes and she no voice." He paused for a moment and then added, smiling, "It would take metaphysics to explain that; and meanwhile we were talking about your precious fountain of joy."

"I should think," answered Helen, thoughtfully, "that it would be much better to earn one's happiness."

"Perhaps after you had tried it a while you would not think so," replied her companion; "that is the artist's life, you know, and in practice it is generally a very dreadful life. Real effort is very hard to make; and there is always a new possibility to lure the artist, so that his life is always restless and a cruel defeat."

"It is such a life that you have lived, Mr. Howard?" asked Helen, gazing at him.

"There are compensations," he replied, smiling slightly, "or there would be no artists. There comes to each one who persists some hour of victory, some hour when he catches the tide of his being at the flood, and when he finds himself master of all that his soul contains, and takes a kind of fierce delight in sweeping himself on and in breaking through everything that stands in his way. You made me think of such things by what you said of your joy in music; only perhaps the artist discovers that not only the streamlets and the winds have motion and meaning, but that the planets also have a word for his soul; and his own being comes suddenly to seem to him a power which it frightens him to know of, and he sees the genius of life as a spirit with eyes of flame. It lifts him from his feet and drags him away, and the task of his soul takes the form of something that he could cry out to escape. He has fought his way into the depths of being at last, and lie stands alone in all his littleness on the shore of an ocean whose waves are centuries—and then even while he is wondering and full of fear, his power begins to die within him and to go he knows not how; and when he looks at himself again he is like a man who has had a dream, and wakened with only the trembling left; except that he knows it was no dream but a fiery reality, and that the memory of it will cast a shadow over all the rest of his days and make them seem trivial and meaningless. No one knows how many years he may spend in seeking and never find that lost glory again."

Mr. Howard had been speaking very intensely, and when he stopped Helen did not reply at once, but continued gazing at him. "What is the use of such moments," she asked at last, "if they only make one wretched?"

"At least one may keep the memory," he replied with a smile, "and that gives him a standard of reality. He learns to be humble, and learns how to judge men and men's glory, and the wonderful things of men's world,—so that while they are the most self-occupied and self-delighted creatures living he may see them as dumb cattle that are grazing while the sunrise is firing the hill-tops."

"You have had such moments yourself?" asked Helen.

"A long time ago," said the other, smiling at the seriousness with which she spoke. "When you were telling me about your musical fancies you made me remember how once when I was young I climbed a high hill and had an adventure with a wind that was very swift and eager. At first I recollect I tried not to heed it, because I had been dull and idle and unhappy; but I found that I could not be very long in the presence of so much life without being made ashamed, and that brave windstorm put me through a course of repentance of the very sternest kind before it let me go. I tried just to promise that I would be more wide-awake and more true, but it paid not the least attention to that; and it would hear no arguments as to the consequences,—it came again and again with a furious burst, and swept me away every time I tried to think; it declared that I had been putting off the task of living my life long enough, and that I was to attend to it then and there. And when I gave myself up as demanded, it had not the least mercy upon me, and each time that I protested that I was at the end of my power it simply whirled me away again like a mad thing. When at last I came down from the hillside I had quite a new idea of what living meant, and I have been more respectful before the winds and other people of genius ever since."

Helen felt very much at home in that merry phantasy of her companion's, but she did not say anything; after a moment's waiting the other went on to tell her of something else that pleased her no less. "I remember," he said, "how as I came down I chanced upon a very wonderful sight, one which made an impression upon me that I have not forgotten. It was a thicket of wild roses; and I have always dreamed that the wild rose was a creature of the wind and fire, but I never knew so much about it before. After that day I have come seriously to believe it would be best if we prudent and timid creatures, who neither dare nor care anything for the sake of beauty,—if we simply did not ever see the wild rose. For it lives only for a day or two, Miss Davis, and yet, as I discovered then, we may live all our years and never get one such burst of glory, one such instant of exultation and faith as that. And also I

216

seriously think that among men and all the wonderful works of men there is nothing so beautiful and so precious as that little flower that none of them heeds."

Mr. Howard glanced at the girl suddenly; she had half stopped in her walk, and she was gazing at him with a very eager look in her bright eyes. "What is it?" he asked her, and Helen exclaimed, "Oh, I am so glad you mentioned it! I had forgotten—actually forgotten!"

As her friend looked puzzled, the girl went on with her merriest laugh, "I must tell you all about it, and we shall be happy once more; for you turn down this path towards the woods, and then you must go very quietly and hold your breath, and prepare yourself just as if you were going into a great cathedral; for you want all your heart to be full of expectation and joy! It is for only about one week in the year that you may see this great sight, and the excitement of the first rapture is best of all. It would be so dreadful if you were not reverent; you must fancy that you are coming to hear a wonderful musician, and you know that he'll play for you, but you don't know just when. That's what I used to pretend, and I used to come every day for a week or two, and very early in the morning, when the dew was still everywhere and the winds were still gay. Several times you go back home disappointed, but that only makes you more eager for the next time; and when you do find them it is wonderful—oh, most wonderful! For there is a whole hedge of them along the edge of the wood; and you may be just as madly happy as you choose and never be half happy enough, because they are so beautiful!"

"These are wild roses?" asked the other, smiling.

"Yes," said Helen, "and oh, think how many days I have forgotten them, and they may have bloomed! And for three years I have not been here, and I was thinking about it all the way over on the steamer." They had come to the path that turned off to the woods, and Helen led her companion down it, still prattling away in the meantime; when they came to the edge of the woods she began walking upon tip toe, and put her fingers upon her lips in fun.

Then suddenly she gave a cry of delight, for there were the roses for a fact, a whole hedge of them as she had said, glowing in the bright sun and making a wonderful vision.

The two stopped and stood gazing at them, the girl's whole soul dancing within her. "Oh do you know," she cried suddenly, "I think that I could get drunk with just looking at roses! There is a strange kind of excitement that comes over one, from drinking in the sight of their rich red, and their gracefulness and perfume; it makes all my blood begin to flow faster, and I quite forget everything else." Helen stood for a few moments longer with her countenance of joy; afterwards she went towards the flowers and knelt down in front of them, choosing a bud that was very perfect. "I always allow myself just one," she said, "just one for love," and then she bent over it, whispering softly:

"Hush,'tis the lullaby time is singing,
Hush and heed not, for all things pass."

She plucked it and held it up before her, while the wind came up behind her and tossed it about, and tossed her skirts; Helen, radiant with laughter, glanced at her companion, saying gaily, "You must hold it very lightly, just like this, you know, with one finger and a thumb; and then you may toss it before you and lose yourself in its perfectness, until it makes all your soul feel gracious. Do you know, Mr. Howard, I think one could not live with the roses very long without becoming beautiful?"

"That was what Plato thought," said the other with a smile, "and many other wise people."

"I only wish that they might bloom forever," said the girl, "I should try it."

Her companion had been lost in watching her, and now as she paused he said: "Sometimes, I have been happy with the roses, too, Miss Davis. Here is some music for your flower." She gazed at him eagerly, and he recited, half laughingly:

"Wild rose, wild rose, sing me thy song,
Come, let us sing it together!—

I hear the silver streamlet call
From his home in the dewy heather."

"Let us sing the wild dance with the mountain breeze,
The rush of the mountain rain,
And the passionate clasp of the glowing sun
When the clouds are rent again."

"They tell us the time for the song is short,
That the wings of joy are fleet;
But the soul of the rose has bid me sing
That oh, while it lasts 'tis sweet!"

Afterwards Helen stood for a moment in silence; then a happy idea came to her mind, and she turned towards the hedge of roses once more and threw back her head upon the wind and took a deep breath and began singing a very beautiful melody.

As it swelled out Helen's joy increased until her face was alight with laughter, and very wonderful to see; she stood with the rose tossing in one of her hands, and with the other pressed upon her bosom,—"singing of summer in full-throated ease." One might have been sure that the roses knew what she was saying, and that all about her loved her for her song.

Yet the girl had just heard that the wings of joy are fleet; and she was destined to find even then that it was true. For when she stopped she turned to her companion with a happy smile and said, "Do you know what that is that I was singing?" When he said "No," she went on, "It is some wild-rose music that somebody made for me, I think. It is in the same book as the 'Water Lily' that I played you." And then in a flash the fearful memory of that evening came over the girl, and made her start back; for a moment she stood gazing at her friend, breathing very hard, and then she lowered her eyes and whispered faintly to herself, "And it was not a month ago!"

There was a long silence after that, and when Helen looked up again the joy was gone out of her face, and she was the same

219

frightened soul as before. Her lips were trembling a little as she said, "Mr. Howard, I feel somehow that I have no right to be quite happy, for I have done nothing to make myself good." Then, thinking of her friend, she added, "I am spoiling your joy in the roses! Can you forgive me for that?" As he answered that he could, Helen turned away and said, "Let us go into the woods, because I do not like to see them any more just now."

They passed beneath the deep shadows of the trees, and Helen led Mr. Howard to the spring where she had been with Arthur. She sat down upon the seat, and then there was a long silence, the girl gazing steadfastly in front of her; she was thinking of the last time she had been there, and how it was likely that the pale, wan look must still be upon Arthur's face. Mr. Howard perhaps divined her thought, for he watched her for a long time without speaking a word, and then at last he said gently, as if to divert her attention, "Miss Davis, I think that you are not the first one whom the sight of the wild rose has made unhappy."

Helen turned and looked at him, and he gazed gravely into her eyes. For at least a minute he said nothing; when he went on his voice was much changed, and Helen knew not what to expect "Miss Davis," he said, "God has given to the wild rose a very wonderful power of beauty and joy; and perhaps the man who looks at it has been dreaming all his life that somewhere he too might find such precious things and have them for his own. When he sees the flower there comes to him the fearful realization that with all the effort of his soul he has never won the glory which the wild rose wears by Heaven's free gift; and that perhaps in his loneliness and weakness he has even forgotten all about such high perfection. So there rises within him a yearning of all his being to forget his misery and his struggling, and to lay all his worship and all his care before the flower that is so sweet; he is afraid of his own sin and his own baseness, and now suddenly he finds a way of escape,—that he will live no longer for himself and his own happiness, but that his joy shall be the rose's joy, and all his life the rose's life. Do you think, my dear friend, that that might please the flower?"

"Yes," said Helen wonderingly, "it would be beautiful, if one could do it."

The other spoke more gently still as he answered her, his voice trembling slightly: "And do you not know, Miss Davis, that God has made *you* a rose?"

The girl started visibly; she whispered, "You say that to me, Mr. Howard? Why do you say that to *me?*"

And he fixed his dark eyes upon her, his voice very low as he responded: "I say it to you,—because I love you."

And Helen shrank back and stared at him; and then as she saw his look her own dropped lower and lower and the color mounted to her face. Mr. Howard paused for a moment or two and then very gently took one of her hands in his, and went on:

"Helen," he said,—"you must let me call you Helen—listen to me a while, for I have something to tell you. And since we both of us love the roses so much, perhaps it will be beautiful to speak of them still. I want to tell you how the man who loves the flower needs not to love it for his own sake, but may love it for the flower's; how one who really worships beauty, worships that which is not himself, and the more he worships it the less he thinks of himself. And Helen, you can never know how hard a struggle my life has been, just to keep before me something to love,—how lonely a struggle it has been, and how sad. I can only tell you that there was very little strength left, and very little beauty, and that it was all I could do to remember there was such a thing as joy in the world, and that I had once possessed it. The music that moved me and the music that I made was never your wild-rose singing, but such yearning, restless music as you heard in the garden. I cannot tell you how much I have loved that little piece that I played then; perhaps it is my own sad heart that finds such breathing passion in it, but I have sent it out into the darkness of many a night, dreaming that somewhere it might waken an echo. For as long as the heart beats it never ceases to hunger and to hope, and I felt that somewhere in the world there must be left some living creature that was beautiful and pure, and that might be loved. So it was that when I saw you all my soul was roused within me; you were the fairest of all God's creatures that I had ever seen. That was why I was so bitter at first, and that was why all my heart went out to you when I saw your suffering, and why it is to me the dearest memory of my lifetime that I was able to help you. Afterwards when I saw how true you were, I was happier than I had ever dared hope to be again; for when I went back to my lonely little home, it was no longer to think about myself and my sorrow and my dullness, but to think about you,—to rejoice in your salvation, and to pray for you in your trouble, and to wait for the day when I might see you again. And so I knew that something had happened to me for which I had yearned, oh so long and so painfully!—that my heart had been taken from me, and that I was living in another life; I knew, dear Helen, that I loved you. I said to myself long ago, before you got Arthur's letter, that I would wait for the chance to say this to you, to take your hand in mine and say: Sweet girl, the law of my life has been that all my soul I must give to the best thing that ever I know; and that thing is you. You must know that I love you, and how I love you; that I lay myself at your feet and ask to help you and watch over you and strengthen you all that I may. For your life is young and there is much to be hoped for in it, and to my own poor self there is no longer any duty that I owe. My heart is yours, and I ask for nothing but that I may love you. Those were the words that I first meant to say to you, Helen; and to ask you if it pleased you that I should speak to you thus."

Mr. Howard stopped, and after he had waited a minute, the girl raised her eyes to his face. She did not answer him, but she put out her other hand and laid it very gently in his own.

There was a long silence before the man continued; at last he said, "Dear Helen, that was what I wished to say to you, and no more than that, because I believed that I was old, and that my heart was dying within me. But oh, when that letter came from Arthur, it was as if I heard the voice of my soul crying out to me that my life had just begun, that I had still to love. As I came out here into the forest with you to-day, my soul was full of a wondrous thought, a thought that brought more awe and rapture than words have power to tell; it was that this precious maiden was not made to be happy alone, but that some day she and all her being would go out to someone, to someone who could win her heart, who could love her and worship her as she deserved. And my soul cried out to me that *I* could worship you; the thought wakened in me a wilder music than ever I had heard in my life before. Here as I kneel before you and hold your hands in mine, dear Helen, all my being cries out to you to come to me; for in your sorrow your heart has been laid bare to my sight, and I have seen only sweetness and truth. To keep it, and serve it, and feed it upon thoughts of beauty, would be all that I could care for in life; and the thought of winning you for mine, so that all your life I might cherish you, is to me a joy which brings tears into my eyes. Oh, dearest girl, I must live before you with that prayer, and tell me what you will, I must still pray it. Nor do I care how long you ask me to wait; my life has now but one desire, to love you in such a way as best may please you, to love you as much as you will let me. Helen, I have told all myself to you, and here as we gaze into each other's eyes our souls are bare to each other. As I say those words they bring to me a thought that sweeps away all my being,—that perhaps the great sorrow you have known has chastened your heart so that you too wish to forget yourself, and worship at the shrine of love; I see you trembling, and I think that perhaps it may be that, and that it needs only a word of mine to bring your soul to me! What that thought is I cannot tell you; but oh, it has been the dream of my life, it has been the thing for which I have lived, and for which I was dying. If I could win you for mine, Helen, for mine—and take you away with me, away from all else but love! The thought of it chokes me, and fills me with mighty anguish of yearning; and my soul burns for you, and I stretch out my arms to you; and I cry out to you that the happiness of my life is in your hands—that I love you—oh, that I love you!"

As the man had been speaking he had sunk down before Helen, still clasping her hands in his own. A great trembling had seized upon the girl and her bosom was rising and falling swiftly; but she mastered herself with a desperate effort and looked up, staring at him. "You tell me that you love me," she gasped, "you tell me that I am perfect! And yet you know what I have done—you have seen all my wrongness!"

Her voice broke, and she could not speak a word more; she bowed her head and the trembling came again, while the other clasped her hands more tightly and bent towards her. "Helen," he said, "I call you to a sacred life that forgets all things but love. Precious girl, my soul cries out to me that I have a right to you, that you were made that I might kneel before you; it cries out to me, 'Speak the word and claim her, claim her for your own, for no man could love her more than you love her. Tell her that all your life you have waited for this sacred hour to come; tell her that you have power and life, and that all your soul is hers!' And oh, dear heart, if only you could tell me that you might love me, that years of waiting might win you, it would be such happiness as I have never dared to dream. Tell me, Helen, tell me if it be true!"

And the girl lifted her face to him, and he saw that all her soul had leaped into her eyes. Her bosom heaved, and she flung back her head and stretched wide her arms, and cried aloud, "Oh, David, I do love you!"

He clasped her in his arms and pressed her upon his bosom in an ecstasy of joy, and kissed the lips that had spoken the wonderful words. "Tell me," he exclaimed, "you will be mine?" And she answered him, "Yours!"

For that there was no answer but the clasp of his love. At last he whispered, "Oh, Helen, a lifetime of worship can never repay you for words like those. My life, my soul, tell me once more, for you cannot be mine too utterly; tell me once more that you are mine!"

And suddenly she leaned back her head and looked into his burning eyes, and began swiftly, her voice choking: "Oh, listen,

listen to me!—if it be a pleasure to you to know how you have this heart. I tell you, wonderful man that God has given me for mine, that I loved you the first word that I heard you speak in the garden. You were all that I knew of in life to yearn for—you were a wonderful light that had flashed upon me and blinded me; and when I saw my own vileness in it I flung myself down on my face, and felt a more fearful despair than I had ever dreamed could torture a soul. I would have crawled to you upon my knees and groveled in the dirt and begged you to have mercy upon me; and afterwards when you lifted me up, I could have kissed the ground that you trod. But oh, I knew one thing, and it was all that gave me courage ever to look upon you; I heard the sacred voice of my womanhood within me, telling me that I was not utterly vile, because it was in my ignorance that I had done my sin; and that if ever I had known what love really was, I should have laughed at the wealth of empires. To win your heart I would fling away all that I ever cared for in life—my beauty, my health, my happiness—yes, I would fling away my soul! And when you talked to me of love and told me that its sacrifice was hard, I—I, little girl that I am—could have told you that you were talking as a child; and I thought, 'Oh, if only this man, instead of urging me to love another and win my peace, if only *he* were not afraid to trust me, if only he were willing that I should love *him!*' And this afternoon when I set out with you, do you know what was the real thing that lay at the bottom of my heart and made me so happy? I said to myself, 'It may take months, and it may take years, but there is a crown in life that I may win—that I may win forever! And this man shall tell me my duty, and night and day I shall watch and pray to do it, and do more; and he will not know why I do it, but it shall be for nothing but the love of him; and some day the worship that is in his heart shall come to me, tho it find me upon my death-bed.' And now you take me and tell me that I have only to love you; and you frighten me, and I cannot believe that it is true! But oh, you are pilot and master, and you know, and I will believe you—only tell me this wonderful thing again that I may be sure—that in spite of all my weakness and my helplessness and my failures, you love me—and you trust me—and you ask for me. If that is really the truth, David,—tell me if that is really the truth!"

David whispered to her, "Yes, yes; that is the truth;" and the girl went on swiftly, half sobbing with her emotion:

"If you tell me that, what more do I need to know? You are my life and my soul, and you call me. For the glory of your wonderful love I will leave all the rest of the world behind me, and you may take me where you will and when you will, and do with me what you please. And oh, you who frightened me so about my wrongness and told me how hard it was to be right—do you know how easy it is for me to say those words? And do you know how happy I am—because I love you and you are mine? David— my David—my heart has been so full,—so wild and thirsty,—that now when you tell me that you want all my love, it is a word of glory to me, it tells me to be happy as never in my life have I been happy before!"

And David bent towards her and kissed her upon her beautiful lips and upon her forehead; and he pressed the trembling form closer upon him, so that the heaving of her bosom answered to his own. "Listen, my love, my precious heart," he whispered, "I will tell you about the vision of my life, now when you and I are thus heart to heart. Helen, my soul cries out that this union must be perfect, in mind and soul and body a blending of all ourselves; so that we may live in each other's hearts, and seek each other's perfection; so that we may have nothing one from the other, but be one and the same soul in the glory of our love. That is such a sacred thought, my life, my darling; it makes all my being a song! And as I clasp you to me thus, and kiss you, I feel that I have never been so near to God. I have worshiped all my days in the great religion of love, and now as the glory of it burns in my heart I feel lifted above even us, and see that it is because of Him that we love each other so; because He is one, our souls may be one, actually and really one, so that each loses himself and lives the other's life. I know that I love you so that I can fling my whole self away, and give up every thought in life but you. As I tell you that, my heart is bursting; oh! drink in this passion of mine, and tell me once more that you love me!"

Helen had still been leaning back her head and gazing into his eyes, all her soul uplifted in the glory of her emotion; there was a wild look upon her face,—and her breath was coming swiftly. For a moment more she gazed at him, and then she buried her face on his shoulder, crying, "Mine—mine!" For a long time she clung to him, breathing the word and quite lost in the joy of it; until at last she leaned back her head and gazed up into his eyes once more.

"Oh, David," she said, "what can I answer you? I can only tell you one thing, that here I am in your arms, and that I am yours—yours! And I love you, oh, before God I love you with all my soul! And I am so happy—oh, David, so happy! Dearest heart, can you not see how you have won me, so that I cannot live without you, so that anything you ask of me you may have? I cannot tell you any more, because I am trembling so, and I am so weak; for this has been more than I can bear, it is as if all my being were melting within me. But oh, I never thought that a human being could be so happy, or that to love could be such a world of wonder and joy."

Helen, as she had been speaking, had sunk down exhaustedly, letting her head fall forward upon her bosom; she lay quite limp in David's arms, while little by little the agitation that had so shaken her subsided. In the meantime he was bending over the golden hair that was so wild and so beautiful, and there were tears in his eyes. When at last the girl was quiet she leaned back her head upon his arm and looked up into his face, and he bent over her and pressed a kiss upon her mouth. Helen gazed into his eyes and asked him:

"David, do you really know what you have done to this little maiden, how fearfully and how madly you have made her yours? I never dreamed of what it could mean to love before; when men talked to me of it I laughed at them, and the touch of their hands made me shrink. And now here I am, and everything about me is changed. Take me away with you, David, and keep me—I do not care what becomes of me, if only you let me have your heart."

The girl closed her eyes and lay still again for a long time; when she began to speak once more it was softly, and very slowly, and half as if in a dream: "David," she whispered, "*my* David, I am tired; I think I never felt so helpless. But oh, dear heart, it seems a kind of music in my soul,—that I have cast all my sorrow away, and that I may be happy again, and be at peace—at peace!" And the girl repeated the words to herself more and more gently, until her voice had died away altogether; the other was silent for a long time, gazing down upon the perfect face, and then at last he kissed the trembling eyelids till they opened once again.

"Sweet girl," he whispered, "as God gives me life you shall never be sorry for that beautiful faith, or sorry that you have laid bare your heart to me." Long afterwards, having watched her without speaking, he went on with a smile, "I wonder if you would not be happier yet, dearest, if I should tell you all the beautiful things that I mean to do with you. For now that you are all mine, I am going to carry you far away; you will like that, will you not, precious one?"

He saw a little of an old light come back into Helen's eyes as he asked that question. "What difference does it make?" she asked, gently.

David laughed and went on: "Very well then, you shall have nothing to do with it. I shall take you in my arms just as you are. And I have a beautiful little house, a very little house among the wildest of mountains, and there we shall live this wonderful summer, all alone with our wonderful love. And there we shall have nature to worship, and beautiful music, and beautiful books to read. You shall never have anything more to think about all your life but making yourself perfect and beautiful."

The girl had raised herself up and was gazing at him with interest as he spoke thus. But he saw a swift frown cross her features at his last words, and he stopped and asked her what was the matter. Helen's reply was delivered very gravely. "What I was to think about," she said, "was settled long ago, and I wish you would not say wicked things like that to me."

A moment later she laughed at herself a little; but then, pushing back her tangled hair from her forehead, she went on seriously: "David, what you tell me of is all that I ever thought of enjoying in life; and yet I am so glad that you did not say anything about it before! For I want to love you because of *you,* and I want you to know that I would follow you and worship you and live in your love if there were nothing else in life for you to offer me. And, David, do you not see that you are never going to make this poor, restless creature happy until you have given her something stern to do, something that she may know she is doing just for your love and for nothing else, bearing some effort and pain to make you happy?"

The girl had put her hands upon his shoulders, and was gazing earnestly into his eyes; he looked at her for a moment, and then responded in a low voice: "Helen, dearest, let us not play with fearful words, and let us not tempt sorrow. My life has not been all happiness, and you will have pain enough to share with me, I fear, poor little girl." She thought in a flash of his sickness, and she turned quite pale as she looked at him; but then she bent forward gently and folded her arms about him, and for a minute more there was silence.

There were tears standing in David's eyes when she looked at him again. But he smiled in spite of them and kissed her once more, and said: "Sweetheart, it is not wrong that we should be happy while we can; and come what may, you know, we need not ever cease to love. When I hear such noble words from you I think I have a medicine to make all sickness light; so be bright and beautiful once more for my sake."

Helen smiled and answered that she would, and then her eye chanced to light upon the ground, where she saw the wild rose lying forgotten; she stooped down and picked it up, and then knelt on the grass beside David and pressed it against his bosom while she gazed up into his face. "Once," she said, smiling tenderly, "I read a pretty little stanza, and if you will love me more for it, I will tell it to you.

> *"'The sweetest flower that blows*
> *I give you as we part,*
> *To you, it is a rose,*
> *To me, it is a heart.'"*

And the man took the flower, and took the hands too, and kissed them; then a memory chanced to come to him, and he glanced about him on the moss-covered forest floor. He saw some little clover-like leaves that all forest-lovers love, and he stooped and picked one of the gleaming white blossoms and laid it in Helen's hands. "Dearest," he said, "it is beautiful to make love with the flowers; I chanced to think how I once *wrote* a pretty little poem, and if you will love me more for it, I will tell it to *you*." Then while the girl gazed at him happily, he went on to add, "This was long before I knew you, dear, and when I worshiped the flowers. One of them was this little wood sorrel.

> *I found it in the forest dark,*
> *A blossom of the snow;*
> *I read upon its face so fair,*
> *No heed of human woe.*
>
> *Yet when I sang my passion song*
> *And when the sun rose higher,*
> *The flower flung wide its heart to me,*
> *And lo! its heart was fire."*

Helen gazed at him a moment after he finished, and then she took the little flower and laid it gently back in the group from which he had plucked it; afterwards she looked up and laughed. "I want that poem for myself," she said, and drew closer to him, and put her arms about him; he gazed into her upraised face, and there was a look of wonder in his eyes.

"Oh, precious girl," he said, "I wonder if you know what a vision of beauty God has made you! I wonder if you know how fair your eyes are, if you know what glory a man may read in your face! Helen, when I look upon you I know that God has meant to pay me for all my years of pain; and it is all that I can do to think that you are really, really mine. Do you not know that to gaze upon you will make me a mad, mad creature for years and years and years?"

Helen answered him gravely: "With all my beauty, David, I am really, really yours; and I love you so that I do not care anything in the world about being beautiful, except because it makes you happy; to do that I shall be always just as perfect as I may, thro all those mad years and years and years!" Then, as she glanced about her, she added: "We must go pretty soon, because it is late; but oh, before we do, sweetheart, will you kiss me once more for all those years and years and years?"

And David bent over and clasped her in his arms again,

Sie ist mir ewig, ist mir
immer, Erb und Eigen, ein und all!

Part II

"When summer gathers up her robes of glory,
And like a dream of beauty glides away."

Chapter I

"Across the hills and far away,
Beyond their utmost purple rim,
And deep into the dying day
The happy princess follow'd him."

It was several months after Helen's marriage. The scene was a little lake, in one of the wildest parts of the Adirondacks, surrounded by tall mountains which converted it into a basin in the land, and walled in by a dense growth about the shores, which added still more to its appearance of seclusion. In only one place was the scenery more open, where there was a little vale between two of the hills, and where a mountain torrent came rushing down the steep incline. There the underbrush had been cleared away, and beneath the great forest trees a house constructed, a little cabin built of logs, and in harmony with the rest of the scene.

It was only large enough for two or three rooms downstairs, and as many above, and all were furnished in the plainest way. About the main room there were shelves of books, and a piano and a well-chosen music-library. It was the little home which for a dozen years or more David Howard had occupied alone, and where he and Helen had spent the golden summer of their love.

It was late in the fall then, and the mountains were robed in scarlet and orange. Helen was standing upon the little piazza, a shawl flung about her shoulders, because it was yet early in the morning. She was talking to her father, who had been paying them a few days' visit, and was taking a last look about him at the fresh morning scene before it was time for him to begin his long homeward journey.

Helen was clad in a simple dress, and with the prettiest of white sun bonnets tied upon her head; she was browned by the sun, and looked a picture of health and happiness as she held her father's arm in hers. "And then you are quite sure that you are happy?" he was saying, as he looked at her radiant face.

She echoed the word—"Happy?" and then she stretched out her arms and took a deep breath and echoed it again. "I am so happy," she laughed, "I never know what to do! You did not stay long enough for me to tell you, Daddy!" She paused for a moment, and then went on, "I think there never was anybody in the world so full of joy. For this is such a beautiful little home, you know, and we live such a beautiful life; and oh, we love each other so that the days seem to fly by like the wind! I never even have time to think how happy I am."

"Your husband really loves you as much as he ought," said the father, gazing at her tenderly.

"I think God never put on earth another such man as David," replied, the girl, with sudden gravity. "He is so noble, and so un-selfish in every little thing; I see it in his eyes every instant that all his life is lived for nothing but to win my love. And it just draws the heart right out of me, Daddy, so that I could live on my knees before him, just trying to tell him how much I love him. I cannot ever love him enough; but it grows—it grows like great music, and every day my heart is more full!"

Helen was standing with her head thrown back, gazing ahead of her; then she turned and laughed, and put her arm about her father again, saying: "Haven't you just seen what a beautiful life we live? And oh, Daddy, most of the time I am afraid because I married David, when I see how much he knows. Just think of it,— he has lived all alone ever since he was young, and done nothing but read and study. Now he brings all those treasures to me, to make me happy with, and he frightens me." She stopped for a moment and then continued earnestly: "I have to be able to go

234

with him everywhere, you know, I can't expect him to stay back all his life for me; and that makes me work very hard. David says that there is one duty in the world higher than love, and that is the duty of labor,—that no soul in the world can be right for one instant if it is standing still and is satisfied, even with the soul it loves. He told me that before he married me, but at first when we came up here he was so impatient that he quite frightened me; but now I have learned to understand it all, and we are wonderfully one in everything. Daddy, dear, isn't it a beautiful way to live, to be always striving, and having something high and sacred in one's mind? And to make all of one's life from one's own heart, and not to be dependent upon anything else? David and I live away off here in the mountains, and we never have anything of what other people call comforts and enjoyments—we have nothing but a few books and a little music, and Nature, and our own love; and we are so wonderfully happy with just those that nothing else in the world could make any difference, certainly nothing that money could buy us."

"I was worried when you wrote me that you did not even have a servant," said Mr. Davis.

"It isn't any trouble," laughed Helen. (David's man lived in the village half a mile away and came over every day to bring what was necessary.) "This is such a tiny little cottage, and David and I are very enthusiastic people, and we want to be able to make lots of noise and do just as we please. We have so much music, you know, Daddy, and of course David is quite a wild man when he gets excited with music."

Helen stopped and looked at her father and laughed; then she rattled merrily on: "We are both of us just two children, for David is so much in love with me that it makes him as young as I am; and we are away off from everything, and so we can be as happy with each other as we choose. We have this little lake all to ourselves, you know; it's getting cold now, and pretty soon we'll have to fly away to the south, but all this summer long we used to get up in the morning in time to see the sun rise, and to have a wonderful swim. And then we have so many things to read and study;

and David talks to me, and tells me all that he knows; and besides all that we have to tell each other how much we love each other, which takes a fearful amount of time. It seems that neither of us can ever quite realize the glory of it, and when we think of it, it is a wonder that nobody ever told. Is not that a beautiful way to live, Daddy dear, and to love?"

"Yes," said Mr. Davis, "that is a very beautiful way indeed. And I think that my little girl has all that I could wish her to have."

"Oh, there is no need to tell me that!" laughed Helen. "All I wish is that I might really be like David and be worth his love; I never think about anything else all day." The girl stood for a moment gazing at her father, and then, looking more serious, she put her arm about him and whispered softly: "And oh, Daddy, it is too wonderful to talk about, but I ought to tell you; for some day by and by God is going to send us a new, oh, a new, new wonder!" And Helen blushed beautifully as her father gazed into her eyes.

He took her hand tenderly in his own, and the two stood for some time in silence. When it was broken it was by the rattling of the wagon which had come to take Mr. Davis away.

David came out then to bid his guest good-by, and the three stood for a few minutes conversing. It was not very difficult for, Helen to take leave of her father, for she would see him, so she said, in a week or two more. She stood waving her hands to him, until the bumping wagon was lost to sight in the woods, and then she turned and took David's hand in hers and gazed across the water at the gorgeous-colored mountains. The lake was sparkling in the sunlight, and the sky was bright and clear, but Helen's thoughts took a different turn from that.

All summer long she had been rejoicing in the glory of the landscape about her, in the glowing fern and the wild-flowers underfoot, and in the boundless canopy of green above, with its unresting song-birds; now there were only the shrill cries of a pair of blue-jays to be heard, and every puff of wind that came brought down a shower of rustling leaves to the already thickly-covered ground.

"Is it not sad, David," the girl said, "to think how the beauty should all be going?"

David did not answer her for a moment. "When I think of it," he said at last, "it brings me not so much sadness as a strange feeling of mystery. Only stop, and think of what that vanished springtime meant—think that it was a presence of living, feeling, growing creatures,—infinite, unthinkable masses of them, robing all the world; and that now the life and the glory of it all is suddenly gone back into nothingness, that it was all but a fleeting vision, a phantom presence on the earth. I never realize that without coming to think of all the other things of life, and that they too are no more real than the springtime flowers; and so it makes me feel as if I were walking upon air, and living in a dream."

Helen was leaning against a post of the piazza, her eyes fixed upon David intently. "Does that not give a new meaning to the vanished spring-time?" he asked her; and she replied in a wondering whisper, "Yes," and then gazed at him for a long time.

"David," she said at last, "it is fearful to think of a thing like that. What does it all mean? What causes it?"

"Men have been asking that helpless question since the dawn of time," he answered, "we only know what we see, this whirling and weaving of shadows, with its sacred facts of beauty and love."

Helen looked at him thoughtfully a moment, and then, recollecting something she had heard from her father, she said, "But, David, if God be a mystery like that, how can there be any religion?"

"What we may fancy God to be makes no difference," he answered. "That which we know is always the same, we have always the love and always the beauty. All men's religion is but the assertion that the source of these sacred things must be infinitely sacred, and that whatever may happen to us, that source can suffer no harm; that we live by a power stronger than ourselves, and that has no need of us."

Helen was looking at her husband anxiously; then suddenly she asked him, "But tell me then, David; you do not believe in heaven? You do not believe that our souls are immortal?" As he answered her in the negative she gave a slight start, and knitted her brows; and after another pause she demanded, "You do not believe in revealed religion then?"

David could not help smiling, recognizing the voice of his clerical father-in-law; when he answered, however, he was serious again. "Some day, perhaps, dear Helen," he said, "I will tell you all about what I think as to such things. But very few of the world's real thinkers believe in revealed religions any more—they have come to see them simply as guesses of humanity at God's great sacred mystery, and to believe that God's way of revealing Himself to men is through the forms of life itself. As to the question of immortality that you speak of, I have always felt that death is a sign of the fact that God is infinite and perfect, and that we are but shadows in his sight; that we live by a power that is not our own, and seek for beauty that is not our own, and that each instant of our lives is a free gift which we can only repay by thankfulness and worship."

He paused for a moment, and the girl, who had still been gazing at him thoughtfully, went on, "Father used to talk about those things to me, David, and he showed me how the life of men is all spent in suffering and struggling, and that therefore faith teaches us—"

"Yes, dearest," the other put in, "I know all that you are going to say; I have read these arguments very often, you know. But suppose that I were to tell you that I think suffering and struggling is the very essence of the soul, and that what faith teaches us is that the suffering and struggling are sacred, and not in the least that they are some day to be made as nothing? Dearest, if it is true that the soul makes this life what it is, a life of restless seeking for an infinite, would it not make the same life anywhere else? Do you remember reading with me Emerson's poem about Uriel, the seraph who sang before God's throne,—how even that could not please him, and how he left it to plunge into the struggle of things imperfect; and how ever after the rest of the seraphim were afraid of Uriel? Do you think, dearest, that this life of love and labor that you and I live our own selves needs anything else to justify it? The life that I lived all alone was much harder and more full of pain than this, but I never thought that it needed any rewarding."

David stopped and stood gazing ahead of him thoughtfully; when he continued his voice was lower and more solemn. "These things are almost too sacred to talk of, Helen," he said; "but there is one doubt that I have known about this, one thing that has made me wonder if there ought not to be another world after all. I never sympathized with any man's longing for heaven, but I can understand how a man might be haunted by some fearful baseness of his own self,—something which long years of effort had taught him he could not ever expiate by the strength of his own heart,—and how he could pray that there might be some place where rightness might be won at last, cost what it would."

The man's tone had been so strange as he spoke that it caused Helen to start; suddenly she came closer to him and put her hands upon his shoulders and gazed into his eyes. "David," she whispered, "listen to me a moment."

"Yes, dear," he said, "what is it?"

"Was it because of yourself that you said those words?"

He was silent for a moment, gazing into her anxious eyes; then he bowed his head and said in a faint voice, "Yes, dear, it was because of myself."

And the girl, becoming suddenly very serious, went on, "Do you remember, David, a long time ago—the time that I was leaving Aunt Polly's—that you told me how you knew what it was to have something very terrible on one's conscience? I have not ever said anything about that, but I have never forgotten it. Was it that that you thought of then?"

"Yes, dear, it was that," answered the other, trembling slightly.

Helen stooped down upon her knees and put her arms about him, gazing up pleadingly into his face. "Dearest David," she whispered, "is it right to refuse to tell me about that sorrow?"

There was a long silence, after which the man replied slowly, "I have not ever refused to tell you, sweetheart; it would be very fearful to tell, but I have not any secrets from you; and if you wished it, you should know. But, dear, it was long, long ago, and nothing can ever change it now. It would only make us sad to know it, so why should we talk of it?"

He stopped, and Helen gazed long and earnestly into his face. "David," she said, "it is not possible for me to imagine you ever doing anything wrong, you are so good."

"Perhaps," said David, "it is because you are so good yourself." But Helen interrupted him at that with a quick rejoinder: "Do you forget that I too have a sorrow upon my conscience?" Afterwards, as she saw that the eager remark caused the other to smile in spite of himself, she checked him gravely with the words, "Have you really forgotten so soon? Do you suppose I do not ever think now of how I treated poor Arthur, and how I drove away from me the best friend of my girlhood? He wrote me that he would think of me no more, but, David, sometimes I wonder if it were not just an angry boast, and if he might not yet be lonely and wretched, somewhere in this great cold world where I cannot ever find him or help him."

The girl paused; David was regarding her earnestly, and for a long time neither of them spoke. Then suddenly the man bent down, and pressed a kiss upon her forehead. "Let us only love each other, dear," he whispered, "and try to keep as right as we can while the time is given us."

There was a long silence after that while the two sat gazing out across the blue lake; when Helen spoke again it was to say, "Some day you must tell me all about it, David, because I can help you; but let us not talk about these dreadful things now." She stopped again, and afterwards went on thoughtfully, "I was thinking still of what you said about immortality, and how very strange it is to think of ceasing to be. Might it not be, David, that heaven is a place not of reward, but of the same ceaseless effort as you spoke of?"

"Ah, yes," said the other, "that is the thought of 'the wages of going on.' And of course, dear, we would all like those wages; there is no thought that tempts me so much as the possibility of being able to continue the great race forever; but I don't see how we have the least right to demand it, or that the facts give us the least reason to suppose that we will get it. It seems to me simply a fantastic and arbitrary fancy; the re-creating of a worn-out life in that way. I do not think, dearest, that I am in the least justified in claiming an eternity of vision because God gives me an hour; and when I ask Him the question in my own heart I learn simply that I am a wretched, sodden creature that I do not crowd that hour with all infinity and go quite mad at the sight of the beauty that He flings wide before me."

Helen did not reply for a while, and then she asked: "And you think, David, that our life justifies itself no matter how much suffering may be in it?"

"I think, dearest," was his reply, "that the soul's life is struggle, and that the soul's life is sacred; and that to be right, to struggle to be right, is not only life's purpose, but also life's reward; and that each instant of such righteousness is its own warrant, tho the man be swept out of existence in the next." Then David stopped, and when he went on it was in a lower voice. "Dear Helen," he said, "after I have told you what I feel I deserve in life, you can understand my not wishing to talk lightly about such things as suffering. Just now, as I sit here at my ease, and in fact all through my poor life, I have felt about such sacred words as duty and righteousness that it would be just as well if they did not ever pass my lips. But there have come to me one or two times, dear, when I dared a little of the labor of things, and drank a drop or two of the wine of the spirit; and those times have lived to haunt me and make me at least not a happy man in my unearned ease. There come to me still just once in a while hours when I get sight of the gleam, hours that make me loathe all that in my hours of comfort I loved; and there comes over me then a kind of Titanic rage, that I should go down a beaten soul because I have not the iron strength of will to lash my own self to life, and tear out of my own heart a little of what power is in it. At such times, Helen, I find just this one wish in my mind,—that God would send to me, cost what it might, some of the fearful experience that rouses a man's soul within him, and makes him live his life in spite of all his dullness and his fear."

David had not finished, but he halted, because he saw a strange look upon the girl's face. She did not answer him at once, but sat gazing at him; and then she said in a very grave voice, "David, I do not like to hear such words as that from you."

"What words, dearest?"

"Do you mean actually that it sometimes seems to you wrong to live happily with me as you have?"

David laid his hand quietly upon hers, watching for a minute her anxious countenance. Then he said in a low voice: "You ought not to ask me about such things, dear, or blame me for them. Sometimes I have to face the very cruel thought that I ought not ever to have linked my fate to one so sweet and gentle as you, because what I ought to be doing in the world to win a right conscience is something so hard and so stern that it would mean that I could never be really happy all my life."

David was about to go on, but he stopped again because of Helen's look of displeasure. "David," she whispered, "that is the most unloving thing that I have ever heard from you!"

"And you must blame me, dear, because of it?" he asked.

"I suppose," Helen answered, "that you would misunderstand me as long as I chose to let you. Do you not suppose that I too have a conscience,—do you suppose that I want any happiness it is wrong for us to take, or that I would not dare to go anywhere that your duty took you? And do you suppose that anything could be so painful to me as to know that you do not trust me, that you are afraid to live your life, and do what is your duty, before me?"

David bent down suddenly and pressed a kiss upon the girl's forehead. "Precious little heart," he whispered, "those words are very beautiful."

"I did not say them because they were beautiful," answered Helen gravely; "I said them because I meant them, and because I wanted you to take them in earnest. I want to know what it is that you and I ought to be doing, instead of enjoying our lives; and after you have told me what it is I can tell you one thing— that I shall not be happy again in my life until it is done."

David watched her thoughtfully a while before he answered, because he saw that she was very much in earnest. Then he said sadly, "Dearest Helen, perhaps the reason that I have never been able all through my life to satisfy my soul is the pitiful fact that I have not the strength to dare any of the work of other men; I have had always to chafe under the fact that I must choose between nourishing my poor body, or ceasing to live. I have learned that all my power—and more too, as it sometimes seemed,—was needed to bear bravely the dreadful trials that God has sent to me."

Helen paled slightly; she felt his hand trembling upon hers, and she remembered his illness at her aunt's, about which she had never had the courage to speak to him. "And so, dear heart," he went on slowly, "let us only be sure that we are keeping our lives pure and strong, that we are living in the presence of high thoughts and keeping the mastery of ourselves, and saying and really meaning that we live for something unselfish; so that if duty and danger come, we shall not prove cowards, and if suffering comes we should not give way and lose our faith. Does that please you, dear Helen?"

The girl pressed his hand silently in hers. After a while he went on still more solemnly: "Some time," he said, "I meant to talk to you about just that, dearest, to tell you how stern and how watchful we ought to be. It is very sad to me to see what happens when the great and fearful realities of life disclose themselves to good and kind people who have been living without any thought of such things. I feel that it is very wrong to live so, that if we wished to be right we would hold the high truths before us, no matter how much labor it cost."

"What truths do you mean?" asked Helen earnestly; and he answered her: "For one, the very fearful fact of which I have just been talking—that you and I are two bubbles that meet for an instant upon the whirling stream of time. Suppose, sweetheart, that I were to tell you that I do not think you and I would be living our lives truly, until we were quite sure that we could bear to be parted forever without losing our faith in God's righteousness?"

Helen turned quite white, and clutched the other's hands in hers; she had not once thought of actually applying what he had said to her. "David! David!" she cried, "No!"

The man smiled gently as he brushed back the hair from her forehead and gazed into her eyes. "And when you asked for stern- ness, dear," he said, "was it that you did not know what the word meant? Life is real, dear Helen, and the effort it demands is real effort."

The girl did not half hear these last words; she was still staring at her husband. "Listen to me, David," she said at last, still holding his hand tightly in hers, her voice almost a whisper; "I could bear anything for you, David, I know that I could bear *anything;* I could really die for you, I say that with all my soul,—that was what I was thinking of when you spoke of death. But David, if you were to be taken from me,—if you were to be taken from me—" and she stopped, unable to find a word more.

"Perhaps it will be just as well not to tell me, dear heart," he said to her, gently.

"David," she went on more strenuously yet, "listen to me—you must not ever ask me to think of that! Do you hear me? For, oh, it cannot be true, it cannot be true, David, that you could be taken from me forever! What would I have left to live for?"

"Would you not have the great wonderful God?" asked the other gently—"the God who made me and all that was lovable in me, and made you, and would demand that you worship him?" But Helen only shook her head once more and answered, "It could not be true, David,—no, no!" Then she added in a faint voice, "What would be the use of my having lived?"

The man bent forward and kissed her again, and kissed away a little of the frightened, anxious look upon her face. "My dear," he said with a gentle smile, "perhaps I was wrong to trouble you with such fearful things after all. Let me tell you instead a thought that once came to my mind, and that has stayed there as the one I should like to call the most beautiful of all my life; it may help to answer that question of yours about the use of having lived. Men love life so much, Helen dear, that they cannot ever have enough of it, and to keep it and build it up they make what we call the arts; this thought of mine is about one of them, about music, the art that you and I love most. For all the others have been derived from things external, but music was made out of nothing, and exists but for its one great purpose, and therefore is the most spiritual of all of them. I like to say that it is time made beautiful, and so a shadow picture of the soul; it is this, because it can picture different degrees of speed and of power, because it can breathe and throb, can sweep and soar, can yearn and pray,—because, in short, everything that happens in the heart can happen in music, so that we may lose ourselves in it and actually live its life, or so that a great genius can not merely tell us about himself, but can make all the best hours of his soul actually a part of our own. This thought that I said was beautiful came to me from noticing how perfectly the art was one with that which it represented; so that we may say not only that music is life, but that life is music. Music exists because it is beautiful, dear Helen, and because it brings an instant of the joy of beauty to our hearts, and for no other reason whatever; it may be music of happiness or of sorrow, of achievement or only of hope, but so long as it is beautiful it is right, and it makes no difference, either, that it cost much labor of men, or that when it is gone it is gone forever. And dearest, suppose that the music not only was beautiful, but knew that it was beautiful; that it was not only the motion of the air, but also the joy of our hearts; might it not then be its own excuse, just one strain of it that rose in the darkness, and quivered and died away again forever?"

When David had spoken thus he stopped and sat still for a while, gazing at his wife; then seeing the anxious look still in possession of her face, he rose suddenly by way of ending their talk. "Dearest," he said, smiling, "it is wrong of me, perhaps, to worry you about such very fearful things as those; let us go in, and find something to do that is useful, and not trouble ourselves with them any more."

Chapter II

"O Freude, habe Acht!
Sprich leise,
Dass nicht der Schmerz erwacht!"

It was late on the afternoon of the day that Helen's father had left for home, and David was going into the village with some letters to mail. Helen was not feeling very well herself and could not go, but she insisted upon his going, for she watched over his exercise and other matters of health with scrupulous care. She had wrapped him up in a heavy overcoat, and was kneeling beside his chair with her arms about him.

"Tell me, dear," she asked him, for the third or fourth time, "are you sure this will be enough to keep you warm?—for the nights are so very cold, you know; I do not like you to come back alone anyway."

"I don't think you would be much of a protection against danger," laughed David.

"But it will be dark when you get back, dear."

"It will only be about dusk," was the reply; "I don't mind that."

Helen gazed at him wistfully for a minute, and then she went on: "Do you not know what is the matter with me, David? You frightened me to-day, and I cannot forget what you said. Each time that it comes to my mind it makes me shudder. Why should you say such fearful things to me?"

"I am very sorry," said the other, gently.

"You simply must not talk to me so!" cried the girl; "if you do you will make me so that I cannot bear to leave you for an instant. For those thoughts make my love for you simply desperate, David; I cry out to myself that I never have loved you enough, never told you enough!" And then she added pleadingly, "But oh, you know that I love you, do you not, dear? Tell me."

"Yes, I know it," said the other gently, taking her in his arms and kissing her.

"Come back soon," Helen went on, "and I will tell you once more how much I do; and then we can be happy again, and I won't be afraid any more. Please let me be happy, won't you, David?"

"Yes, love, I will," said the man with a smile. "I do not think that I was wise ever to trouble you."

Helen was silent for a while, then as a sudden thought occurred to her she added: "David, I meant to tell you something—do you know if those horrible thoughts keep haunting me, it is just this that they will make me do; you said that God was very good, and so I was thinking that I would show him how very much I love you, how I could really never get along without you, and how I care for nothing else in the world. It seems to me to be such a little thing, that we should only just want to love; and truly, that is all I do want,—I would not mind anything else in the world,—I would go away from this little house and live in any poor place, and do all the work, and never care about anything else at all, if I just might have you. That is really true, David, and I wish that you would know it, and that God would know it, and not expect me to think of such dreadful things as you talk of."

As David gazed into her deep, earnest eyes he pressed her to him with a sudden burst of emotion. "You have me now, dearest," he whispered, "and oh, I shall trust the God who gave me this precious heart!"—He kissed her once more in fervent love, and kissed her again and again until the clouds had left her face. She leaned back and gazed at him, and was radiant with delight again. "Oh—oh—oh!" she cried. "David, it only makes me more full of

wonder at the real truth! For it is the truth, David, it is the truth—
that you are all mine! It is so wonderful, and it makes me so
happy,—I seem to lose myself more in the thought every day!"

"You can never lose yourself too much, little sweetheart," David
whispered; "let us trust to love, and let it grow all that it will.
Helen, I never knew what it was to live until I met you,—never
knew how life could be so full and rich and happy. And never,
never will I be able to tell you how much I love you, dearest
soul."

"Oh, but I believe you without being told!" she said, laughing.
"Do you know, I could make myself quite mad just with saying
over to myself that you love me all that I could ever wish you to
love me, all that I could imagine you loving me! Isn't that true,
David?"

"Yes, that is true," the man replied.

"But you don't know what a wonderful imagination I have,"
laughed the girl, "and how hungry for your love I am." And she
clasped him to her passionately and cried, "David, you can make
me too happy to live with that thought! I shall have to think about
it all the time that you are gone, and when you come back I shall
be so wonderfully excited,—oh—oh, David!"

Then she laughed eagerly and sprang up. "You must not stay
any longer," she exclaimed, "because it is getting late; only hurry
back, because I can do nothing but wait for you." And so she led
him to the door, and kissed him again, and then watched him as
he started up the road. He turned and looked at her, as she leaned
against the railing of the porch, with the glory of the sunset falling
upon her hair; she made a radiant picture, for her cheeks were
still flushed, and her bosom still heaving with the glory of the
thought she had promised to keep. There was so much of her
love in the look which she kept upon David that it took some
resolution to go on. and leave her.

As for Helen, she watched him until he had quite disappeared
in the forest, after which she turned and gazed across the lake
at the gold and crimson mountains. But all the time she was still

thinking the thought of David's love; the wonder of it was still upon her face, and it seemed to lift her form; until at last she stretched wide her arms, and leaned back her head, and drank a deep draft of the evening air, whispering aloud, "Oh, I do not dare to be as happy as I can!" And she clasped her arms upon her bosom and laughed a wild laugh of joy.

Later on, because it was cold, she turned and went into the house, singing a song to herself as she moved. As she went to the piano and sat down she saw upon the rack the little springtime song of Grieg's that was the first thing she had ever heard upon David's violin; she played a few bars of it to herself, and then she stopped and sat still, lost in the memory which it brought to her mind of the night when she had sat at the window and listened to it, just after seeing Arthur for the last time. "And to think that it was only four or five months ago!" she whispered to herself. "And how wretched I was!"

"I do not believe I could ever be so unhappy again," she went on after a while, "I know that I could not, while I have David!" after which her thoughts came back into the old, old course of joy. When she looked at the music again the memory of her grief was gone, and she read in it all of her own love-glory. She played it through again, and afterwards sat quite still, until the twilight had begun to gather in the room.

Helen then rose and lit the lamp, and the fire in the open fireplace; she glanced at the clock and saw that more than a quarter of an hour had passed, and she said to herself that it could not be more than that time again before David was back.

"I should go out and meet him if I were feeling quite strong," she added as she went to the door and looked out; then she exclaimed suddenly: "But oh, I know how I can please him better!" And the girl went to the table where some of her books were lying, and sat down and began very diligently studying, glancing every half minute at the clock and at the door. "I shall be too busy even to hear him!" she said, with a sudden burst of glee; and quite delighted with the effect that would produce she listened eagerly every time she fancied she heard a step, and then fixed her eyes upon the book, and put on a look of most complete absorption.

Unfortunately for Helen's plan, however, each time it proved to be a false alarm; and so the fifteen minutes passed completely, and then five, and five again. The girl had quite given up studying by that time, and was gazing at the clock, and listening to its ticking, and wondering very much indeed. At last when more than three-quarters of an hour had passed since David had left, she got up and went to the door once more to listen; as she did not hear anything she went out on the piazza, and finally to the road. All about her was veiled in shadow, which her eyes strove in vain to pierce; and so growing still more impatient she raised her voice and called, "David, David!" and then stood and listened to the rustling of the leaves and the faint lapping of the water on the shore.

"That is very strange," Helen thought, growing very anxious indeed; "it is fearfully strange! What in the world can have happened?" And she called again, with no more result that before; until with a sudden resolution she turned and passed quickly into the house, and flinging a wrap about her, came out and started down the road. Occasionally she raised her voice and shouted David's name, but still she got no reply, and her anxiety soon changed into alarm, and she was hurrying along, almost in a run. In this way she climbed the long ascent which the road made from the lake shore; and when she had reached the top of it she gathered her breath and shouted once more, louder and more excitedly than ever.

This time she heard the expected reply, and found that David was only a few rods ahead of her. "What is the matter?" she called to him, and as he answered that it was nothing, but to come to him, she ran on more alarmed than ever.

There was just light enough for her to see that David was bending down; and then as she got very near she saw that on the ground in front of him was lying a dark, shadowy form. As Helen cried out again to know what was the matter, her husband said,

"Do not be frightened, dear; it is only some poor woman that I have found here by the roadside."

"A woman!" the girl echoed in wonder, at the same time giving a gasp of relief at the discovery that her husband was not in trouble. "Where in the world can she have come from, David?"

"I do not know," he answered, "but she probably wandered off the main road. It is some poor, wretched creature, Helen; she has been drinking, and is quite helpless."

And Helen stood still in horror, while David arose and came to her. "You are out of breath, dear," he exclaimed, "why did you come so fast?"

"Oh, I was so frightened!" the girl panted. "I cannot tell you, David, what happens in my heart whenever I think of your coming to any harm. It was dreadful, for I knew something serious must be the matter."

David put his arm about her and kissed her to quiet her fears; then he said, "You ought not to have come out, dear; but be calm now, for there is nothing to worry you, only we must take care of this poor woman. It is such a sad sight, Helen; I wish that you had not come here."

"What were you going to do?" asked the girl, forgetting herself quickly in her sympathy.

"I meant to come down and tell you," was David's reply; "and then go back to town and get someone to come and take her away."

"But, David, you can never get back over that rough road in the darkness!" exclaimed Helen in alarm; "it is too far for you to walk, even in the daytime—I will not let you do it, you must not!"

"But dear, this poor creature cannot be left here; it will be a bitter cold night, and she might die."

Helen was silent for a moment in thought, and then she said in a low, trembling voice: "David, there is only one thing to do."

"What is that, dear?" asked the other.

"We will have to take her home with us."

"Do you know what you are saying?" asked the other with a start; "that would be a fearful thing to do, Helen."

"I cannot help it," she replied, "it is the only thing. And it would be wicked not to be willing to do that, because she is a woman."

"She is in a fearful way, dear," said the other, hesitatingly; "and to ask you to take care of her—"

"I would do anything sooner than let you take that walk in such darkness as this!" was the girl's reply; and with that statement she silenced all of his objections.

And so at last David pressed her hand, and whispered, "Very well, dear, God will bless you for it." Then for a while the two stood in silence, until Helen asked, "Do you think that we can carry her, poor creature?"

"We may try it," the other replied; and Helen went and knelt by the prostrate figure. The woman was muttering to herself, but she seemed to be quite dazed, and not to know what was going on about her. Helen did not hesitate any longer, but bent over and strove to lift her; the woman was fortunately of a slight build, and seemed to be very thin, so that with David's help it was easy to raise her to her feet. It was a fearful task none the less, for the poor wretch was foul with the mud in which she had been lying, and her wet hair was streaming over her shoulders; as Helen strove to lift her up the head sunk over upon her, but the girl bit her lips together grimly. She put her arm about the woman's waist, and David did the same on the other side, and so the three started, stumbling slowly along in the darkness.

"Are you sure that it is not too much for you?" David asked; "we can stop whenever you like, Helen."

"No, let us go on," the girl said; "she has almost no weight, and we must not leave her out here in the cold. Her hands are almost frozen now."

They soon made their way on down to where the lights of the little cottage shone through the trees. David could not but shrink back as he thought of taking their wretched burden into their little home, but he heard the woman groan feebly, and he was ashamed of his thought. Nothing more was said until they had climbed the steps, not without difficulty, and had deposited their burden upon the floor of the sitting room; after which David rose and sank back into a chair, for the strain had been a heavy one for him.

Helen also sprang up as she gazed at the figure; the woman was foul with every misery that disease and sin can bring upon a human creature, her clothing torn to shreds and her face swollen and stained. She was half delirious, and clawing about her with her shrunken, quivering hands, so that Helen exclaimed in horror: "Oh God, that is the most dreadful sight I have ever seen in my life!"

"Come away," said the other, raising himself from the chair; "it is not right that you should look at such things."

But with Helen it was only a moment before her pity had overcome every other emotion; she knelt down by the stranger and took one of the cold hands and began chafing it. "Poor, poor woman!" she exclaimed; "oh, what misery you must have suffered! David, what can a woman do to be punished like this? It is fearful!"

It was a strange picture which the two made at that moment, the woman in her cruel misery, and the girl in her pure and noble beauty. But Helen had no more thought of shrinking, for all her soul had gone out to the unfortunate stranger, and she kept on trying to bring her back to consciousness. "Oh, David," she said, "what can we do to help her? It is too much that any human being should be like this,—she would have died if we had not found her." And then as the other opened her eyes and struggled to lift herself, Helen caught an incoherent word and said, "I think she is thirsty, David; get some water and perhaps that will help her. We must find some way to comfort her, for this is too horrible to be. And perhaps it is not her fault, you know,—who knows but perhaps some man may have been the cause of it all? Is it not dreadful to think of, David?"

So the girl went on; her back was turned to her husband, and she was engrossed in her task of mercy, and did not see what he was doing. She did not see that he had started forward in his chair and was staring at the woman; she did not see him leaning forward, farther and farther, with a strange look upon his face. But there was something she did see at last, as the woman lifted herself again and stared first at Helen's own pitying face, and then vaguely about the room, and last of all gazing at David. Suddenly she stretched out her arms to him and strove to rise, with a wild cry that made Helen leap back in consternation:—"David! It's David!"

And at the same instant David sprang up with what was almost a scream of horror; he reeled and staggered backwards against the wall, clutching with his hands at his forehead, his face a ghastly, ashen gray; and as Helen sprang up and ran towards him, he sank down upon his knees with a moan, gazing up into the air with a look of agony upon his face. "My God! My God!" he gasped; "it is my Mary!"

And Helen sank down beside him, clutching him by the arm, and staring at him in terror. "David, David!" she whispered, in a hoarse voice. But the man seemed not to hear her, so overwhelmed was he by his own emotion. "It is Mary," he cried out again,—"it is my Mary!—oh God, have mercy upon my soul!" And then a shudder passed over him, and he buried his face in his arms and fell down upon the floor, with Helen, almost paralyzed with fright, still clinging to him.

In the meantime the woman had still been stretching out her trembling arms to him, crying his name again and again; as she sank back exhausted the man started up and rushed toward her, clutching her by the hand, and exclaiming frantically, "Mary, Mary, it is I—speak to me!" But the other's delirium seemed to have returned, and she only stared at him blankly. At last David staggered to his feet and began pacing wildly up and down, hiding his face in his hands, and crying helplessly, "Oh, God, that this should come to me now! Oh, how can I bear it—oh, Mary, Mary!"

He sank down upon the sofa again and burst into fearful sobbing; Helen, who had still been kneeling where he left her, rushed toward him and flung her arms about him, crying out, "David, David, what is the matter? David, you will kill me; what is it?"

And he started and stared at her wildly, clutching her arm. "He-len," he gasped, "listen to me! I ruined that woman! Do you hear me?—do you hear me? It was I who betrayed her—I who made her what she is! *I—I!* Oh, leave me,—leave me alone—oh, what can I do?"

Then as the girl still clung to him, sobbing his name in terror, the man went on, half beside himself with his grief, "Oh, think of it—oh, how can I bear to know it and live? Twenty-three years ago,—and it comes back to curse me now! And all these years I have been living and forgetting it—and been happy, and talk-ing of my goodness—oh God, and this fearful madness upon the earth! And I made it—I—and *she* has had to pay for it! Oh, look at her, Helen, look at her—think that that foulness is mine! She was beautiful,—she was pure,—and she might have been happy, she would have been good, but for me! Oh God in heaven, where can I hide myself, what can I do?"

Helen was still clutching at his arm, crying to him, "David, spare me!" He flung her off in a mad frenzy, holding her at arm's length, and staring at her with a fearful light in his eyes. "Girl, girl!" he cried, "do you know who I am—do you know what I have done? This girl was like you once, and I made her love me— made her love me with the sacred fire that God had given me, made her love me as I made *you* love me! And she was beautiful like you—she was younger than you, and as happy as you! And she trusted me as you trusted me, she gave herself to me as you did, and I took her, and promised her my love—and now look at her! Can you wish to be near me, can you wish to see me? Oh, Helen, I cannot bear myself—oh, leave me, I must die!"

He sank down once more, weeping, all his form shaking with his grief; Helen flung her arms about his neck again, but the man seemed to forget her presence. "Oh, think where that woman has been," he moaned; "think what she has seen, and done, and suffered—and what she is! Was there ever such a wreck of wom-anhood, ever such a curse upon earth? And, oh, for the years that she has lived in her fearful sin, and I have been happy—great

256

God, what can I do for those years,—how can I live and gaze upon this crime of mine? I, who sought for beauty, to have made this madness; and it comes now to curse me, now, when it is too late; when the life is wrecked,—when it is gone forever!"

David's voice had sunk into a moan; and then suddenly he heard the woman crying out, and he staggered to his feet. She was sitting up again, her arms stretched out; David caught her in his own, gazing into her face and crying, "Mary, Mary! Look at me! Here I am—I am David, the David you loved."

He stopped, gasping for breath, and the woman cried in a faint voice, "Water, water!" David turned and called to Helen, and the poor girl, tho scarcely able to stand, ran to get a glass of it; another thought came to the man in the meantime, and he turned to the other with a sudden cry. "If there were a child!" he gasped, "a child of mine somewhere in the world, alone and helpless!" He stared into the woman's eyes imploringly.

She was gazing at him, choking and trying to speak; she seemed to be making an effort to understand him, and as David repeated his agonizing question she gave a sign of assent, causing a still wilder look to cross the man's face. He called to her again to tell him where; but the woman seemed to be sinking back into her raving, and she only gasped faintly again for water.

When Helen brought it they poured it down her throat, and then David repeated his question once more; but he gave a groan as he saw that it was all in vain; the wild raving had begun again, and the woman only stared at him blankly, until at last the wretched man, quite overcome, sank down at her side and buried his head upon her shrunken bosom and cried like a child, poor Helen in the meantime clinging to him still.

It was only when David had quite worn himself out that he seemed to hear her pleading voice; then he looked at her, and for the first time through his own grief caught sight of hers. There was such a look of helpless woe upon Helen's face that he put out his hand to her and whispered faintly, "Oh, poor little girl, what have *you* done that you should suffer so?" As Helen drew closer to him, clinging to his hand in fright, he went on, "Can you ever forgive me for this horror—forgive me that I dared to forget it, that I dared to marry you?"

The girl's answer was a faint moan, "David, David, have mercy on me!" He gazed at her for a moment, reading still more of her suffering.

"Helen," he asked, "you see what has come upon me—can you ask me not to be wretched, can you ask me still to live? What can I do for such a crime,—when I look at this wreck of a soul, what comfort can I hope to find?" And the girl, her heart bursting with grief, could only clasp his hands in hers and gaze into his eyes; there was no word she could think of to say to him, and so for a long time the two remained in silence, David again fixing his eyes upon the woman, who seemed to be sinking into a kind of stupor.

When he looked up once more it was because Helen was whispering in his ear, a new thought having come to her, "David, perhaps *I* might be able to help you yet."

The man replied in a faint, gasping voice, "Help me? How?" And the girl answered, "Come with me," and rose weakly to her feet, half lifting him also. He gazed at the woman and saw that she was lying still, and then he did as Helen asked. She led him gently into the other room, away from the fearful sight, and the two sat down, David limp and helpless, so that he could only sink down in her arms with a groan. "Poor, poor David," she whispered, in a voice of infinite pity; "oh, my poor David!"

"Then you do not scorn me, Helen?" the man asked in a faint, trembling voice, and went on pleading with her, in words so abject and so wretched that they wrung the girl's heart more than ever.

"David, how can you speak to me so?" she cried, "you who are all my life?" And then she added with swift intensity, "Listen to me, David, it cannot be so bad as that, I know it! Will you not tell me, David? Tell me all, so that I may help you!" So she went on pleading with him gently, until at last the man spoke again, in faltering words.

"Helen," he said, "I was only a boy; God knows that is one excuse, if it is the only one. I was only seventeen, and she was no more."

"Who was she, David?" the girl asked.

"She lived in a village across the mountains from here, near where our home used to be. She was a farmer's daughter, and she was beautiful—oh, to think that that woman was once a beautiful girl, and innocent and pure! But we were young, we loved each other, and we had no one to warn us; it was so long ago that it seems like a dream to me now, but we sinned, and I took her for mine; then I went home to tell my father, to tell him that she was my wife, and that I must marry her. And oh, God, she was a farmer's daughter, and I was a rich man's son, and the cursed world knows nothing of human souls! And I must not marry her— I found all the world in arms against it—"

"And you let yourself be persuaded?" asked the girl, in a faint whisper.

"Persuaded?" echoed David, his voice shaking; "who would have thought of persuading a mad boy? I let myself be commanded and frightened into submission, and carried away. And then five or six miserable months passed away and I got a letter from her, and she was with child, and she was ruined forever,— she prayed to me in words that have haunted me night and day all my life, to come to her and keep my promise."

And David stopped and gave a groan; the other whispered, "You could not go?"

"I went," he answered; "I borrowed money, begged it from one of my father's servants, and ran away and went up there; and oh, I was two days too late!"

"Too late?" exclaimed Helen wonderingly.

"Yes, yes," was the hoarse reply, "for she was a weak and helpless girl, and scorned of all the world; and her parents had turned her away, and she was gone, no one knew where. Helen, from that day to this I have never seen her, nor ever heard of her; and now she comes to curse me,—to curse my soul forever. And it is more than I can bear, more than I can bear!"

David sank down again, crying out, "It is too much, it is too much!" But then suddenly he caught his wife's hand in his and stared up at her, exclaiming, "And she said there was a child, Helen! Somewhere in the world there is another soul suffering for this sin of mine! Oh, somehow we must find out about that—something must be done, I could not have two such fearful things to know of. We must find out, we must find out!"

As the man stopped and stared wildly about him he heard the woman's voice again, and sprang up; but Helen, terrified at his suffering, caught him by the arm, whispering, "No, no, David, let me go in, I can take care of her." And she forced her husband down on the sofa once more, and then ran into the next room. She found the woman again struggling to raise herself upon her trembling arms, staring about her and calling out incoherently. Helen rushed to her and took her hands in hers, trying to soothe her again.

But the woman staggered to her feet, oblivious of everything about her. "Where is he? Where is he?" she gasped hoarsely; "he will come back!" She began calling David's name, and a moment later, as Helen tried to keep her quiet, she tore her hands loose and rushed blindly across the room, shrieking louder yet, "David, where are you? Don't you know me, David?"

As Helen turned she saw that her husband had heard the cries and come to the doorway again; but it was all in vain, for the woman, though she looked at him, knew him no more; it was to a phantom of her own brain that she was calling, in the meantime pacing up and down, her voice rising higher and higher. She was reeling this way and that, and Helen, frightened at her violence, strove to restrain her, only to be flung off as if she had been a child; the woman rushed on, groping about her blindly and crying still, "David! Tell me where is David!"

Then as David and Helen stood watching her in helpless misery her delirious mood changed, and she clutched her hands over her bosom, and shuddered, and moaned to herself, "It is cold, oh, it is cold!" Afterwards she burst into frantic sobbing, that choked her and shook all her frame; and again into wild peals of laughter; and then last of all she stopped and sprang back, staring in front of her with her whole face a picture of agonizing fright; she gave one wild scream after another and staggered and sank down at last upon the floor. "Oh, it is he, it is he!" she cried, her voice sinking into a shudder; "oh, spare me,—why should you beat me? Oh God, have mercy—have mercy!" Her cries rose again into a shriek that made Helen's blood run cold; she looked in terror at her husband, and saw that his face was white; in the meantime the wretched woman had flung herself down prostrate upon the floor, where she lay groveling and writhing.

That again, however, was only for a minute or two; she staggered up once more and rushed blindly across the room, crying, "I cannot bear it, I cannot bear it! Oh, what have I done?" Then suddenly as she flung up her arms imploringly and staggered blindly on, she lurched forward and fell, striking her head against the corner of the table.

Helen started forward with a cry of alarm, but before she had taken half a dozen steps the woman had raised herself to her feet once more, and was staring at her, blinded by the blood which poured from a cut in her forehead. Her clothing was torn half from her, and her tangled hair streamed from her shoulders; she was a ghastly sight to behold, as, delirious with terror, she began once more rushing this way and that about the room. The two who watched her were powerless to help her, and could only drink in the horror of it all and shudder, as with each minute the poor creature became more frantic and more desperate. All the while it was evident that her strength was fast leaving her; she staggered more and more, and at last she sank down upon her knees. She strove to rise again and found that she could not, but lurched and fell upon the floor; as she turned over and Helen saw her face, the sight was too much for the girl's self-control, and she buried her face in her hands and broke into frantic sobbing.

David in the meantime was crouching in the doorway, his gaze fixed upon the woman; he did not seem even to notice Helen's outburst, so lost was all his soul in the other sight. Fie saw that the stranger's convulsive efforts were weakening, and he staggered forward with a cry, and flung himself forward down on his knees beside her. "Mary, Mary!" he called; but she did not heed him, tho he clasped her hands and shook her, gazing into her face imploringly. Her eyes were fixed upon him, but it was with a vacant stare; and then suddenly he started back with a cry of horror—"Great God, she is dying!"

The woman made a sudden fearful effort to lift herself, struggling and gasping, her face distorted with fierce agony; as it failed she sank back, and lay panting hard for breath; then a shudder passed over her, and while David still stared, transfixed, a hoarse rattle came from her throat, and her features became suddenly set in their dreadful passion. In a moment more all was still; and David buried his face in his hands and sank down upon the corpse, without even a moan.

Afterwards, for a full minute there was not a sound in the room; Helen's sobbing had ceased, she had looked up and sat staring at the two figures,—until at last, with a sudden start of fright she sprang up and crept silently toward them. She glanced once at the woman's body, and then bent over David; as she felt that his heart was still beating, she caught him to her bosom, and knelt thus in terror, staring first into his white and tortured features, and then at the body on the floor.

Finally, however, she nerved herself, and tho she was trembling and exhausted, staggered to her feet with her burden; holding it tightly in her arms she went step by step, slowly and in silence out of the room. When she had passed into the next one she shut the door and, sinking down upon the sofa, lifted David's broken figure beside her and locked it in her arms and was still. Thus she sat without a sound or a motion, her heart within her torn with fear and pain, all through the long hours of that night; when the cold, white dawn came up, she was still pressing him to her bosom, sobbing and whispering faintly, "Oh, David! Oh, my poor, poor David!"

*Hast du im Venusburg geweilt, So bist nun
ewig du verdammt!*

Chapter III

"Then said I, 'Woe is me! For I am undone; . . . for mine eyes have seen the King, the Lord of Hosts.'"

David'S servant drove out early upon the following morning to tell him of a strange woman who had been asking for him in the village; they sent the man back for a doctor, and it was found that the poor creature was really dead.

They wished to take the body away, but David would not have it; and so, late in the afternoon, a grave was dug by the lake-shore near the little cottage, and what was left of Mary was buried there. David was too exhausted to leave the house, and Helen would not stir from his side, so the two sat in silence until the ceremony was over, and the men had gone. The servant went with them, because the girl said they wished to be alone; and then the house settled down to its usual quietness,—a quietness that frightened Helen now.

For when she looked at her husband her heart scarcely beat for her terror; he was ghastly white, and his lips were trembling, and though he had not shed a tear all the day, there was a look of mournful despair on his face that told more fearfully than any words how utterly the soul within him was beaten and crushed. All that day he had been so, and as Helen remembered the man that had been before so strong and eager and brare, her whole soul stood still with awe; yet as before she could do nothing but cling to him, and gaze at him with bursting heart.

But at last when the hours had passed and not a move had been made, she asked him faintly, "David, is there no hope? Is it to be like this always?"

The man raised his eyes and gazed at her helplessly. "Helen," he said, his voice sounding hollow and strange, "what can you ask of me? How can I bear to look about me again, how can I think of living? Oh, that night of horror! Helen, it burns my brain—it tortures my soul—it will drive me mad!" He buried his face in his hands again, shaking with emotion. "Oh, I cannot ever forget it," he whispered hoarsely; "it must haunt me, haunt me until I die! I must know that after all my years of struggle it was this that I made, it is this that stands for my life—and it is over, and gone from me forever and finished! Oh, God, was there ever such a horror flashed upon a guilty soul—ever such fiendish torture for a man to bear? And Helen, there was a child, too—think how that thought must goad me—a child of mine, and I cannot ever aid it—it must suffer for its mother's shame. And think, if it were a woman, Helen—this madness must go on, and go on forever! Oh, where am I to hide me; and what can I do?"

There came no tears, but only a fearful sobbing; poor Helen whispered frantically, "David, it was not your fault, you could not help it—surely you cannot be to blame for all this."

He did not answer her, but after a long silence he went on in a deep, low voice, "Helen, she was so beautiful! She has lived in my thoughts all these years as the figure that I used to see, so bright and so happy; I used to hear her singing in church, and the music was a kind of madness to me, because I knew that she loved me. And her home was a little farm-house, half buried in great trees, and I used to see her there with her flowers. Now— oh, think of her now—think of her life of shame and agony— think of her turned away from her home, and from all she loved in the world,—deserted and scorned, and helpless—think of her with child, and of the agony of her degradation! What must she not have suffered to be as she was last night—oh, are there tears enough in the world to pay for such a curse, for that twenty years' burden of wretchedness and sin? And she was beaten—oh, she was beaten—Mary, my poor, poor Mary! And to die in such horror, in drunkenness and madness! And now she is gone, and it is over; and oh, why should I live, what can I do?"

His voice dropped into a moan, and then again there was a long silence. At last Helen whispered, in a weak, trembling voice, "David, you have still love; can that be nothing to you?"

"I have no right to love," he groaned, "no right to love, and I never had any. For oh, all my life this vision has haunted me—I knew that nothing but death could have saved her from shame! Yes, and I knew, too, that some day I must find her. I have carried the terror of that in my heart all these years. Yet I dared to take your love, and dared to fly from my sin; and then there comes this thunderbolt—oh, merciful heaven, it is too much to bear, too much to bear!" He sank down again; poor Helen could find no word of comfort, no utterance of her own bursting heart except the same frantic clasp of her love.

So the day went by over that shattered life; and each hour the man's despair grew more black, his grief and misery more hopeless. The girl watched him and followed him about as if she had been a child, but she could get him to take no food, and to divert his mind to anything else she dared not even try. He would sit for hours writhing in his torment, and then again he would spring up and pace the room in agitation, though he was too weak to bear that very long. Afterwards the long night came on, and all through it he lay tossing and moaning, sometimes shuddering in a kind of paroxysm of grief,—Helen, though she was weary and almost fainting, watching thro the whole night, her heart wild with her dread.

And so the morning came, and another day of misery; and in the midst of it David flung himself down upon the sofa and buried his face in his arms and cried out, "Oh God, my God, I cannot stand it, I cannot stand it! Oh, let me die! I dare not lift my head—there is no hope for me—there is no life for me—I dare not pray! It is more than I can bear—I am beaten, I am lost forever!"

267

And Helen fell down upon her knees beside him, and tore away his hands from his face and stared at him frantically, exclaiming, "David, it is too cruel! Oh, have mercy upon me, David, if you love me!"

He stopped and gazed long and earnestly into her face, and a look of infinite pity came into his eyes; at last he whispered, in a low voice, "Poor, poor little Helen; oh, Helen, God help you, what can I do?" He paused and afterwards went on tremblingly, "What have you done that you should suffer like this? You are right that it is too cruel—it is another curse that I have to bear! For I knew that I was born to suffering—I knew that my life was broken and dying—and yet I dared to take yours into it! And now, what can I do to save you, Helen; can you not see that I dare not live?"

"David, it is you who are killing yourself," the girl moaned in answer. He did not reply, but there came a long, long silence, in which he seemed to be sinking still deeper; and when he went on it was in a shuddering voice that made Helen's heart stop. "Oh, it is no use," he gasped, "it is no use! Listen, Helen, there was another secret that I kept from you, because it was too fearful; but I can keep it no more, I can fight no more!"

He stopped; the girl had clutched his arm, and was staring into his face, whispering his name hoarsely. At last he went on in his cruel despair, "I knew this years ago, too, and I knew that I was bringing it upon you—the misery of this wretched, dying body. Oh, it hurts—it hurts now!" And he put his hand over his heart, as a look of pain came into his face. "It cannot stand much more, my heart," he panted; "the time must come—they told me it would come years ago! And then—and then—"

The man stopped, because he was looking at Helen; she had not made a sound, but her face had turned so white, and her lips were trembling so fearfully that he dared not go on; she gave a loud, choking cry and burst out wildly, "Oh, David—David—it is fiendish—you have no right to punish me so! Oh, have mercy upon me, for you are killing me! You have no right to do it, I tell you it is a crime; you promised me your love, and if you loved me you would live for my sake, you would think of me! A thing so cruel ought not to be—it cannot be right—God could never have meant a human soul to suffer so! And there must be pardon in the world, there must be light—it cannot all be torture like this!" She burst into a flood of tears and flung herself upon David's bosom, sobbing again and again, "Oh, no, no, it is too fearful, oh, save me, save me!"

He did not answer her; as she looked up at him again she saw the same look of fearful woe, and read the cruel fact that there was no help, that her own grief and pleadings were only deepening the man's wretchedness. She stared at him for a long time; and when she spoke to him again it was with a sudden start, and in a strange, ghastly voice,—"And then, David, there is no God?"

He trembled, but the words choked him as he tried to respond, and his head dropped; then at last she heard him moan, "Oh, how can God free my soul from this madness, how can he deliver me from such a curse?" Helen could say no more—could only cling to him and sob in her fright.

So the day passed away, and another night came; and still the crushed and beaten soul was writhing in its misery, lost in blackness and despair; and still Helen read it all in his white and tortured features, and drank the full cup of his soul's fiery pain.

They took no heed of the time; but it was long after darkness had fallen; and once when the girl had gone upstairs for a moment she heard David pacing about, and then heard a stifled cry. She rushed down, and stopped short in the doorway. For the man was upon his knees, his face uplifted in wild entreaty. "Oh God, oh merciful God!" he sobbed; "all the days of my life I have sought for righteousness, labored and suffered to keep my soul alive! And oh, was it all for this—was it to go down in blackness and night, to die a beaten man, crushed and lost? Oh, I cannot bear it, I cannot bear it! It cannot—it must not be!"

He sank forward upon the sofa, and buried his head in his arms, and the girl could hear his breathing in the stillness; at last she crept across the room and knelt down beside him, and whispered softly in his ear, "You do not give me your heart any more, David?"

It was a long time before he answered her, and then it was to moan, "Oh, Helen, my heart is broken, I can give it to no one. Once I had strength and faith, and could love; but now I am lost and ruined, and there is nothing that can save me. I dare not live, and I dare not die, and I know not where to turn!"

He started up suddenly, clasping his hands to his forehead and staggering across the room, crying out, "Oh no, it cannot be, oh, it cannot be! There must be some way of finding pardon, some way of winning Tightness for a soul! Oh God, what can I do for peace?" But then again he sank down and hid his face and sobbed out: "In the face of this nightmare,—with this horror fronting me! *She* cried for pardon, and none came."

After that there was a long silence, with Helen crouching in terror by his side. She heard him groan: "It is all over, it is finished—I can fight no more," and then again came stillness, and when she lifted him and gazed into his face she knew not which was worse, the silent helpless despair that was upon it, or the torment and the suffering that had gone before. She tried still to soothe him, begging and pleading with him to have mercy upon her. He asked her faintly what he could do, and the poor girl, seeing how weak and exhausted he was, could think of only the things of the body, and begged him to try to rest. "It has been two nights since you have slept, David," she whispered.

"I cannot sleep with this burden upon my soul," he answered her; but still she pleaded with him, begging him as he loved her; and he yielded to her at last, and broken and helpless as he was, she half carried him upstairs and laid him upon the bed as if he had been a little child. That seemed to help little, however, for he only lay tossing and moaning, "Oh, God, it must end; I cannot bear it!"

Those were the last words Helen heard, for the poor girl was exhausted herself, almost to fainting; she lay down, without undressing, and her head had scarcely touched the pillow before she was asleep. In the meantime, through the long night-watches David lay writhing and crying out for help.

The moon rose dim and red behind the mountains,—it had mounted high in the sky, and the room was bright with it, when at last the man rose from the bed and began swiftly pacing the room, still muttering to himself. He sank down upon his knees by the window and gazed up at the silent moon. Then again he rose and turned suddenly, and after a hurried glance at Helen went to the door and passed out, closing it silently behind him, and whispered to himself, half deliriously, "Oh, great God, it must end! It must end!"

It was more than an hour afterwards that the girl awakened from her troubled sleep; she lay for an instant half dazed, trying to bring back to her mind what had happened; and then she put out her hand and discovered that her husband was no longer by her. She sat up with a wild start, and at the same instant her ear was caught by a sound outside, of footsteps pacing swiftly back and forth, back and forth, upon the piazza. The girl leaped up with a stifled cry, and ran out of the room and down the steps. The room below was still half lighted by the flickering log-fire, and Helen's shadow loomed up on the opposite wall as she rushed across the room and opened the door.

The gray light of dawn was just spreading across the lake, but the girl noticed only one thing, her husband's swiftly moving figure. She rushed to him, and as he heard her, he turned and stared at her an instant as if dazed, and then staggered with a cry into her arms. "David, David!" she exclaimed, "what is the matter?" Then as she clasped him to her she found that his body was trembling convulsively, and that his hand as she took it was hot like fire; she called to him again in yet greater anxiety: "David, David! What is it? You will kill me if you treat me so!"

He answered her weakly, "Nothing, dear, nothing," and she caught him to her, and turned and half carried him into the house. She staggered into a chair with him, and then sat gazing in terror at his countenance. For the man's forehead was burning and moist, and his frame was shaking and broken; he was completely prostrated by the fearful agitation that had possessed him. Helen cried to him once more, but he could only pant, "Wait, wait," and sink back and let his head fall upon her arm; he lay with his eyes closed, breathing swiftly, and shuddering now and then. "It was God!" he panted with a sudden start, his voice choking; "He has shown me His face! He has set me free!"

Then again for a long time he lay with heaving bosom, Helen whispering to him pleadingly, "David, David!" As he opened his eyes, the girl saw a wonderful look upon his face; and at last he began speaking, in a low, shaking voice, and pausing often to catch his breath: "Oh, Helen," he said, "it is all gone, but I won, and my life's prayer has not been for nothing! I was never so lost, so beaten; but all the time there was a voice in my soul that cried to me to fight,—that there was glory enough in God's home for even me! And oh, to-night it came—it came!"

David sank back, and there was a long silence before he went on: "It was wonderful, Helen," he whispered, "there has come nothing like it to me in all my life; for I had never drunk such sorrow before, never known such fearful need. It seems as if all the pent-up forces of my nature broke loose in one wild, fearful surge, as if there was a force behind me like a mighty, driving storm, that swept me on and away, beyond self and beyond time, and out into the life of things. It was like the surging of fierce music, it was the great ocean of the infinite bursting its way into my heart. And it bore me on, so that I was mad with it, so that I knew not where I was, only that I was panting for breath, and that I could bear it no more and cried out in pain!"

David as he spoke had been lifting himself, the memory of his vision taking hold of him once more; but then he sank down again and whispered, "Oh, I have no more strength, I can do no more; but it was God, and I am free!"

He lay trembling and breathing fast again, but sinking back from his effort and closing his eyes exhaustedly. After a long time he went on in a faint voice, "I suppose if I had lived long ago that would have been a vision of God's heaven; and yet there was not an instant of it—even when I fell down upon the ground and when I struck my hands upon the stones because they were numb and burning—when I did not know just what it was, the surging passion of my soul flung loose at last! It was like the voices of the stars and the mountains, that whisper of that which is and which conquers, of That which conquers without sound or sign; Helen, I thought of that wonderful testament of Pascal's that has haunted me all my lifetime,—those strange, wild, gasping words of a soul gone mad with awe, and beyond all utterance except a cry,—'Joy, joy, tears of joy!' And I thought of a still more fearful story, I thought that it must have been such thunder-music that rang through the soul of the Master and swept Him away beyond scorn and pain, so that the men about Him seemed like jeering phantoms that He might scatter with His hand, before the glory of vision in which it was all one to live or die. Oh, it is that which has brought me my peace! God needs not our help, but only our worship; and beside His glory all our guilt is nothing, and there is no madness like our fear. And oh, if we can only hold to that and fight for it, conquer all temptation and all pain—all fear because we must die, and cease to be—"

The man had clenched his hands again, and was lifting himself with the wild look upon his countenance; he seemed to the girl to be delirious, and she was shuddering, half with awe and half with terror. She interrupted him in a sudden burst of alarm: "Yes, yes,—but David, David, not now, not now—it is too much—you will kill yourself!"

"I can die," he panted, "I can die, but I cannot ever be mastered again, never again be blind! Oh, Helen, all my life I have been lost and beaten—beaten by my weakness and my fear; but this once, this once I was free, this once I knew, and I lived; and now I can die rejoicing! Listen to me, Helen; while I am here there can be no more delaying,—no more weakness! Such sin and doubt as that of yesterday must never conquer my soul again, I will not any more be at the mercy of chance. I love you, Helen, God knows that I love you with all my soul; and this much for love I will do, if God spares me a day,—take you, and tear the heart out of you, if need be, but only teach you to live, teach you to hold by this Truth. It is a fearful thing, Helen; it is madness to me to know that at any instant I may cease to be, and that you may be left alone in your terror and your weakness. Oh, look at me,—look at me! There is no more tempting fate, there is no more shirking the battle—there is life, there is life to be lived! And it calls to you now,—*now!* And now you must win,—cost just what it may in blood and tears! You have the choice between that and ruin, and before God you shall choose the right! Listen to me, Helen—it is only prayer that can do it, it is only by prayer that you can fight this fearful battle—bring before you this truth of the soul, and hold on to it,—hold on to it tho it kill you! For He was through all the ages, His glory is of the skies; and we are but for an instant, and we have to die; and this we must know, or we are lost! There comes pain, and calls you back to fear and doubt; and you fight— oh, it is a cruel fight, it is like a wild beast at your vitals,—but still you hold on—you hold on!"

The man had lifted himself with a wild effort, his hands clenched and his teeth set. He had caught the girl's hands in his, and she screamed in fear: "David, David! You will kill yourself!"

"Yes, yes!" he answered, and rushed on, chokingly; "it is coming just so; for I have just force enough left to win—just force enough to save you,—and then it will rend this frame of mine in two! It comes like a clutch at my heart—it blinds me, and the sky seems to turn to fire—"

He sank back with a gasp; Helen caught him to her bosom, exclaiming frantically, "Oh, David, spare me—wait! Not now— you cannot bear it—have mercy!"

He lay for a long time motionless, seemingly half dazed; then he whispered faintly, "Yes, dear, yes; let us wait. But oh, if you could know the terror of another defeat, of sinking down and letting one's self be bound in the old chains—I must not lose, Helen, I dare not fail!"

"Listen, David," whispered Helen, beginning suddenly with desperate swiftness; "why should you fail? Why can you not listen to me, pity me, wait until you are strong? You have won, you will not forget—and is there no peace, can you not rest in this faith, and fear no more?" The man seemed to Helen to be half out of his mind for the moment; she was trying to manage him with a kind of frenzied cunning. As she went on whispering and imploring she saw that David's exhaustion was gradually overcoming him more and more, and that he was sinking farther and farther back from his wild agitation. At last after she had continued thus for a while he closed his eyes and began breathing softly. "Yes, dear," he whispered; "yes; I will be quiet. There has come to my soul to-night a peace that is not for words; I can be still, and know that He is God, and that He is holy."

His voice dropped lower each instant, the girl in the meantime soothing him and stroking his forehead and pleading with him in a shuddering voice, her heart wild with fright. When at last he was quite still, and the fearful vision, that had been like a nightmare to her, was gone with all its storm and its madness, she took him upon her lap, just as she had done before, and sat there clasping him in her arms while the time fled by unheeded. It was long afterwards—the sun was gleaming across the lake and in at the window—before at last her trembling prayer was answered, and he sank into an exhausted slumber.

She sat watching him for a long time still, quite white with fear and weariness; finally, however, she rose, and carrying the frail body in her arms, laid it quietly upon the sofa in the next room. She knelt watching it for a time, then went out upon the piazza, closing the door behind her.

And there the fearful tension that the dread of wakening him had put upon her faculties gave way at last, and the poor girl buried her face in her hands, and sank down, sobbing convulsively: "Oh, God, oh, God, what can I do, how can I bear it?" She gazed about her wildly, exclaiming, "I cannot stand it, and there is no one to help me! What *can* I do?"

Perhaps it was the first real prayer that had ever passed Helen's lips; but the burden of her sorrow was too great just then for her to bear alone, even in thought. She leaned against the railing of the porch with her arms stretched out before her imploringly, her face uplifted, and the tears running down her cheeks; she poured out one frantic cry, the only cry that she could think of:—"Oh, God, have mercy upon me, have mercy upon me! I cannot bear it!"

So she sobbed on, and several minutes passed, but there came to her no relief; when she thought of David, of his breaking body and of his struggling soul, it seemed to her as if she were caught in the grip of a fiend, and that no power could save her. She could only clasp her hands together and shudder, and whisper, "What shall I do, what shall I do?"

Thus it was that the time sped by; and the morning sun rose higher in front of her, and shone down upon the wild and wan figure that seemed like a phantom of the night. She was still crouching in the same position, her mind as overwrought and hysterical as ever, when a strange and unexpected event took place, one which seemed to her at first in her state of fright like some delusion of her mind.

Except for her own emotion, and for the faint sound of the waves upon the shore, everything about her had been still; her ear was suddenly caught, however, by the noise of a footstep, and she turned and saw the figure of a man coming down the path from the woods; she started to her feet, gazing in surprise.

It was broad daylight then, and Helen could see the person plainly; she took only one glance, and reeled and staggered back as if it were a ghost at which she was gazing. She crouched by a pillar of the porch, trembling like a leaf, and scarcely able to keep her senses, leaning from side to side and peering out, with her whole attitude expressive of unutterable consternation, and even fright. At last when she had gazed until it was no longer possible for her to think that she was the victim of madness, she stared suddenly up into the air, and caught her forehead in her hands, at the same time whispering to herself in an almost fainting voice: "Great heaven, what can it mean? Can it be real—can it be true? *It is Arthur!*"

Chapter IV

I am Merlin
And I am dying,
"I am Merlin,
Who follow the Gleam."

Helen stood gazing at the figure in utter consternation for at least half a minute before she could find voice; then she bent forward and called to him wildly—"Arthur!"

It was the other's turn to be startled then, and he staggered backward; as he gazed up at Helen his look showed plainly that he too was half convinced that he was gazing at a phantom of his own mind, and for a long time he stood, pressing his hands to his heart and unable to make a sound or a movement. When finally he broke the silence his voice was a hoarse whisper. "Helen," he panted, "what in heaven's name are you doing here?"

And then as the girl answered, "This is my home, Arthur," he gave another start.

"You live here with him?" he gasped.

"With him?" echoed Helen in a low voice. "With whom, Arthur?"

He answered, "With that Mr. Harrison." A look of amazement crossed Helen's face, tho followed quickly by a gleam of comprehension. She had quite forgotten that Arthur knew nothing about what she had done.

"Arthur," she said, "I did not marry Mr. Harrison;" then, seeing that he was staring at her in still greater wonder, she went on hastily: "It seems strange to go back to those old days now; but once I meant to tell you all about it, Arthur." She paused for a moment and then went on slowly: "All the time I was engaged to that man I was wretched; and when I saw you the last time—that dreadful time by the road—it was almost more than I could bear; so I took back my wicked promise of marriage and came to see you and tell you all about it."

As the girl had been speaking the other had been staring at her with a look upon his face that was indescribable, a look that was more terror than anything else; he had staggered back, he grasped at a tree to support himself. Helen saw the look and stopped, frightened herself.

"What is it, Arthur?" she cried; "what is the matter?"

"You came to see me!" the other gasped hoarsely. "You came to see me—and I—and I was gone!"

"Yes, Arthur," said Helen; "you had gone the night before, and I could not find you. Then I met this man that I loved, and you wrote that you had torn the thought of me from your heart; and so—"

Again Helen stopped, for the man had sunk backwards with a cry that made her heart leap in fright. "Arthur!" she exclaimed, taking a step towards him; and he answered her with a moan, stretching out his arms to her. "Great God, Helen, that letter was a lie!"

Helen stopped, rooted to the spot. "A lie?" she whispered faintly.

"Yes, a lie!" cried the other with a sudden burst of emotion, leaping up and starting towards her. "Helen, I have suffered the tortures of hell! I loved you—I love you now!"

The girl sprang back, and the blood rushed to her cheeks. Half instinctively she drew her light dress more tightly about her; and the other saw the motion and stopped, a look of despair crossing his face. The two stood thus for fully a minute, staring at each other wildly; then suddenly Arthur asked: "You love this man whom you have married? You love him?"

The girl answered, "Yes, I love him," and Arthur's arms dropped, and his head sank forward. There was a look upon his face that tore Helen's heart to see, so that for a moment or two she stood quite dazed with this new terror. Then all at once, however, the old one came back to her thoughts, and with a faint cry she started toward her old friend, stretching out her arms to him and calling to him imploringly.

"Oh, Arthur," she cried, "have mercy upon me—do not frighten me any more! Arthur, if you only knew what I have suffered, you would pity me, you could not help it! You would not fling this burden of your misery upon me too."

The man fixed his eyes upon her and for the first time he seemed to become aware of the new Helen, the Helen who had replaced the girl he had known. He read in her ghastly white face some hint of what she had been through, and his own look turned quickly to one of wonder, and even awe. "Helen," he whispered, "are you ill?"

"No, Arthur," she responded quickly, full of desperate hope as she saw his change. "Not ill, but oh, so frightened. I have been more wretched than you can ever dream. Can you not help me, Arthur, will you not? I was almost despairing, I thought that my heart would burst. Can you not be unselfish?"

The man gazed at her at least a minute; and when he answered at last, it was in a low, grave voice that was new to her.

"I will do it, Helen," he said. "What is it?"

The girl came toward him, her voice sinking. "We must not let him hear us, Arthur," she whispered. Then as she gazed into his face she added pathetically, "Oh, I cannot tell you how I have wished that I might only have someone to sympathize with me and help me! I can tell everything to you, Arthur."

"You are not happy with your husband?" asked the other, in a wondering tone, not able to guess what she meant.

"Happy!" echoed Helen. "Arthur, he is ill, and I have been so terrified! I feared that he was going to die; we have had such a dreadful sorrow." She paused for a moment, and gazed about her swiftly, and laying her finger upon her lips. "He is asleep now," she went on, "asleep for the first time in three nights, and I was afraid that we might waken him; we must not make a sound, for it is so dreadful."

She stopped, and the other asked her what was the matter. "It was three nights ago," she continued, "and oh, we were so happy before it! But there came a strange woman, a fearful creature, and she was drunk, and my husband found her and brought her home. She was delirious, she died here in his arms, while there was no one to help her. The dreadful thing was that David had known this woman when she was a girl—"

Helen paused again, and caught her breath, for she had been speaking very swiftly, shaken by the memory of the scene; the other put in, in a low tone, "I heard all about this woman's death, Helen, and I know about her—that was how I happen to be here."

And the girl gave a start, echoing, "Why you happen to be here?" Afterwards she added quickly, "Oh, I forgot to ask you about that. What do you mean, Arthur?"

He hesitated a moment before he answered her, speaking very slowly. "It is so sad, Helen," he said, "it is almost too cruel to talk about." He stopped again, and the girl looked at him, wondering; then he went on to speak one sentence that struck her like a bolt of lightning from the sky:—"Helen, that poor woman was my mother!"

And Helen staggered back, almost falling, clutching her hands to her forehead, and staring, half dazed.

"Arthur," she panted, "Arthur!"

He bowed his head sadly, answering, "Yes, Helen, it is dreadful—"

And the girl leaped towards him, seizing him by the shoulders with a thrilling cry; she stared into his eyes, her own glowing like fire. "Arthur!" she gasped again, "Arthur!"

He only looked at her wonderingly, as if thinking she was mad; until suddenly she burst out frantically, "You are David's child! You are David's child!" And then for fully half a minute the two stood staring at each other, too much dazed to move or to make a sound.

At last Arthur echoed the words, scarcely audibly, "David's child!" and added, "David is your husband?" As Helen whispered "Yes" again, they stood panting for breath. It was a long time before the girl could find another word to speak, except over and over, "David's child!" She seemed unable to realize quite what it meant, she seemed unable to put the facts together.

But then suddenly Arthur whispered: "Then it was your husband who ruined that woman?" and as Helen answered "Yes," she grasped a little of the truth, and also of Arthur's thought. She ran on swiftly: "But oh, it was not his fault, he was only a boy, Arthur! And he wished to marry her, but they would not let him—I must tell you about that!" Then she stopped short, however; and when she went on it was in sudden wild joy that overcame all her other feelings, joy that gleamed in her face and made her fling herself down upon her knees before Arthur and clutch his hands in hers.

"Oh," she cried, "it was God who sent you, Arthur,—oh, I know that it was God! It is so wonderful to think of—to have come to us all in a flash! And it will save David's life—it was the thought of the child and the fate that it might have suffered that terrified him most of all, Arthur. And now to think that it is you—oh, you! And you are David's son—I cannot believe it, I cannot believe it!" Then with a wild laugh she sprang up again and turned, exclaiming, "Oh, he will be so happy,—I must tell him—we must not lose an instant!"

She caught Arthur's hand again, and started towards the house; but she had not taken half a dozen steps before she halted suddenly, and whispered, "Oh, no, I forgot! He is asleep, and we must not waken him now, we must wait!"

And then again the laughter broke out over her face, and she turned upon him, radiant. "It is so wonderful!" she cried. "It is so wonderful to be happy, to be free once more! And after so much darkness—oh, it is like coming out of prison! Arthur, dear Arthur, just think of it! And David will be so glad!" The tears started into the girl's eyes; she turned away to gaze about her at the golden morning and to drink in great draughts of its freshness that made her bosom heave. The life seemed to have leaped back into her face all at once, and the color into her cheeks, and she was more beautiful than ever. "To think of being happy!" she panted, "happy again! Oh, if I were not afraid of waking David, you do not know how happy I could be! Don't you think I ought to waken him any-way, Arthur?—it is so wonderful—it will make him strong again! It is so beautiful that you, whom I have always been so fond of, that you should be David's son! And you can live here and be happy with us! Arthur, do you know I used to think how much like David you looked, and wonder at it; but, oh, are you sure it is true?"

She chanced to think of the letter that had been left at her fa-ther's, and exclaimed, "It must have been that! You have been home, Arthur?" she added quickly. "And while father was up here?"

"Yes," said he, "I wanted to see your father—I could not stay away from home any longer. I was so very lonely and unhappy—" Arthur stopped for a moment, and the girl paled slightly; as he saw it he continued rapidly: "There was no one there but the servant, and she gave me the letter."

"And did she not tell you about me?" asked Helen.

"I asked if you were married," Arthur said; "I would not listen to any more, for I could not bear it; when I had read the letter I came up here to look for my poor mother. I wanted to see her; I was as lonely as she ever was, and I wanted someone's sympathy—even that poor, beaten soul's. I heard in the town that she was dead; they told me where the grave was, and that was how I happened out here. I thought I would see it once before I left, and before the people who lived in this house were awake. Helen, when I saw *you* I thought it was a ghost."

"It is wonderful, Arthur," whispered the girl; "it is almost too much to believe—but, oh, I can't think of anything except how happy it will make David! I love him so, Arthur—and you will love him, too, you cannot help but love him."

"Tell me about it all, Helen," the other answered; "I heard noth-ing, you know, about my poor mother's story."

282

Before Helen answered the question she glanced about her at the morning landscape, and for the first time thought of the fact that it was cold. "Let us go inside," she said; "we can sit there and talk until David wakens." And the two stole in, Helen opening the door very softly. David was sleeping in the next room, so that it was possible not to disturb him; the two sat down before the flickering fire and conversed in low whispers. The girl told him the story of David's love, and told him all about David, and Arthur in turn told her how he had been living in the meantime; only because he saw how suddenly happy she was, and withal how nervous and overwrought, he said no more of his sufferings.

And Helen had forgotten them utterly; it was pathetic to see her delight as she thought of being freed from the fearful terror that had haunted her,—she was like a little child in her relief. "He will be so happy—he will be so happy!" she whispered again and again. "We can all be so happy!" The thought that Arthur was actually David's son was so wonderful that she seemed never to be able to realize it fully, and every time she uttered the thought it was a sweep of the wings of her soul. Arthur had to tell her many times that it was actually Mary who had been named in that letter.

So an hour or two passed by, and still David did not waken. Helen had crept to the door once or twice to listen to his quiet breathing; but each time, thinking of his long trial, she had whispered that she could not bear to disturb him yet. However, she was getting more and more impatient, and she asked Arthur again and again, "Don't you think I ought to wake him now, don't you think so—even if it is just for a minute, you know? For oh, he will be so glad—it will be like waking up in heaven!"

So it went on until at last she could keep the secret no longer; she thought for a while, and then whispered, "I know what I will do—I will play some music and waken him in that way. That will not alarm him, and it will be beautiful."

She went to the piano and sat down. "It will seem queer to be playing music at this hour," she whispered; but then she glanced at the clock and saw that it was nearly seven, and added, "Why, no, we have often begun by this time. You know, Arthur, we used to get up wonderfully early all summer, because it was so beautiful then, and we used to have music at all sorts of times. Oh, you cannot dream how happy we were,—you must wait until you see David, and then you will know why I love him so!"

She stopped and sat thoughtfully for a moment whispering, "What shall I play?" Then she exclaimed, "I know, Arthur; I will play something that he loves very much—and that you used to love, too—something that is very soft and low and beautiful."

Arthur had seated himself beside the piano and was gazing at her; the girl sat still for a moment more, gazing ahead of her and waiting for everything to be hushed. Then she began, so low as scarcely to be audible, the first movement of the wonderful "Moonlight Sonata."

As it stole upon the air and swelled louder, she smiled, because it was so beautiful a way to waken David.

And yet there are few things in music more laden with concentrated mournfulness than that sonata—with the woe that is too deep for tears; as the solemn beating of it continued, in spite of themselves the two found that they were hushed and silent. It brought back to Helen's mind all of David's suffering—it seemed to be the very breathing of his sorrow; and yet still she whispered on to herself, "He will waken; and then he will be happy!"

In the next room David lay sleeping. At first it had been heavily, because he was exhausted, and afterwards, when the stupor had passed, restlessly and with pain. Then at last came the music, falling softly at first and blending with his dreaming, and afterwards taking him by the hand and leading him out into the land of reality, until he found himself lying and listening to it. As he recollected all that had happened he gave a slight start and sat up, wondering at the strangeness of Helen's playing then. He raised his head, and then rose to call her.

And at that instant came the blow.

The man suddenly gave a fearful start; he staggered back upon the sofa, clutching at his side with his hand, his face turning white, and a look of wild horror coming over it. For an instant he held himself up by the sofa, staring around him; and then he sank back, half upon the floor, his head falling backwards. And so he lay gasping, torn with agony, while the fearful music trod on, the relentless throbbing of it like a hammer upon his soul. Twice he strove to raise himself and failed; and twice he started to cry out, and checked himself in terror; and so it went on until the place of despair was reached, until there came that one note in the music that is the plunge into night. Helen stopped suddenly there, and everything was deathly still—except for the fearful heaving of David's bosom.

That silence lasted for several moments; Helen seemed to be waiting and listening, and David's whole being was in suspense. Then suddenly he gave a start, for he heard the girl coming to the door.

With a gasp of dread he half raised himself, grasping the sofa with his knotted hands. He slid down, half crawling and half falling, into the corner, where he crouched, breathless and shuddering; so he was when Helen came into the room.

She did not see him on the sofa, and she gave a startled cry. She wheeled about and gazed around the room. "Where can he be?" she exclaimed. "He is not here!" and ran out to the piazza. Then came a still more anxious call: "David! David! Where are you?"

And in the meantime David was still crouching in the corner, his face uplifted and torn with agony. He gave one fearful sob, and then he sank forward; drawing himself by the sheer force of his arms he crawled again into sight, and lay clinging to the sofa. Then he gave a faint gasping cry, "Helen!"

And the girl heard it, and rushed to the door; she gave one glance at the prostrate form and at the white face, and then leaped forward with a shrill scream, a scream that echoed through the little house, and that froze Arthur's blood. She flung herself down on her knees beside her husband, crying "David! David!" And the man looked up at her with his ghastly face and his look of terror, and panted, "Helen—Helen, it has come!"

She screamed again more wildly than before, and caught him to her bosom in frenzy. "No, no, David! No, no!" she cried out; but he only whispered hoarsely again, "It has come!"

Meanwhile Arthur had rushed into the room, and the two lifted the sufferer up to the sofa, where he sank back and lay for a moment or two, half dazed; then, in answer to poor Helen's agonized pleading, he gazed at her once more.

"David, David!" she sobbed, choking; "listen to me; it cannot be, David, no, no! And see, here is Arthur—Arthur! And David—he is your son, he is Mary's child!"

The man gave a faint start and looked at her in bewilderment; then as she repeated the words again, "He is your son, he is Mary's child," gradually a look of wondering realization crossed his countenance, and he turned and stared up at Arthur.

"Is it true?" he whispered hoarsely. "There is no doubt?"

Helen answered him "Yes, yes," again and again, swiftly and desperately, as if thinking that the joy of it would restore his waning strength. The thought did bring a wonderful look of peace over David's face, as he gazed from one to the other and comprehended it all; he caught Arthur's arm in his trembling hands. "Oh, God be praised," he whispered, "it is almost too much. Oh, take care of her—take care of her for me!"

The girl flung herself upon his bosom, sobbing madly; and David sank back and lay for an instant or two with his eyes shut, before at last her suffering roused him again. He lifted himself up on his elbows with a fearful effort. "Helen!" he whispered, in a deep, hollow voice; "listen to me—listen to me!—I have only a minute more to speak."

The girl buried her head in his bosom with another cry, but he shook her back and caught her by the wrists, at the same time sitting erect, a strain that made the veins in his temples start out. "Look at me!" he gasped. "Look at me!" and as the girl stared into his eyes that were alive with the last frenzied effort of his soul, he went on, speaking with fierce swiftness and panting for breath between each phrase:

"Helen—Helen—listen to me—twenty years I have kept myself alive on earth by such a struggle—by the power of a will that would not yield! And now there is but an instant more—an instant—I cannot bear it—except to save your soul! For I am going—do you hear me—going! And you must stay,—and you have the battle for your life to fight! Listen to me—look into my eyes,—for you must call up your powers—*now*—now before it is too late! You cannot shirk it—do you hear me? It is here!"

And as the man was speaking the frenzied words the look of a tiger had come into his face; his eyes were starting from his head, and he held Helen's wrists in a grip that turned them black, tho then she did not feel the pain. She was gazing into his face, convulsed with fright; and the man gasped for breath once more, and then rushed on:

"A fight like this conies once to a soul, Helen—and it wins or it loses—and you must win! Do you hear me?—*Win!* I am dying, Helen, I am going—and I leave you to God, and to life. He is, He made you, and He demands your worship and your faith—that you hold your soul lord of all chances, that you make yourself master of your life! And now is your call—now! You clench your hands and you pray—it tears your heart-strings, and it bursts your brain—but you say that you will—that you will—that you *will!* Oh, God, that I have left you so helpless—that I did not show you the peril of your soul! For you *must* win—oh, if I could but find a word for you! For you stand upon the brink of ruin, and you have but an instant—but an instant to save yourself—to call up the vision of your faith before you, and tho the effort kill you, not to let it go! Girl, if you fail, no power of earth or heaven can save you from despair! And oh, have I lived with you for nothing—showed you no faith—given you no power? Helen, save me—have mercy upon me, I cannot stand this, and I dare not—I dare not die!"

The man was leaning forward, gazing into the girl's face, his own countenance fearful to see. "I could die," he gasped; "I could die with a song—He has shown me His face—and He is good! But I dare not leave you—you—and I am going! Helen! Helen!"

The man's fearful force seemed to have been acting upon the girl like magnetism, for tho the look of wild suffering had not left her face, she had raised herself and was staring into his burning eyes; then suddenly, with an effort that shook her frame she clenched her hands and gave a gasp for breath, and panted, scarcely audibly: "What—can—I—do?"

David's head had sunk, but he mastered himself once more; and he whispered, "I leave you to God—I leave you to life! You can be a soul,—you can win—you *must* win, you must *live*—and worship—and rejoice! You must kneel here—here, while I am going, never more to return; and you must know that you can never see me again, that I shall no longer exist; and you must cling to your faith in the God who made you, and praise Him for all that He does! And you will not shed a tear—not a tear!"

And his grip tightened yet more desperately; he stared in one last wild appeal, and gasped again, "Promise me—not a tear!"

And again the throbbing force of his soul roused the girl; she could not speak, she was choking; but she gave a sign of assent, and then all at once David's fearful hold relaxed. He gave one look more, one that stamped itself upon Helen's soul forever by its fearful intensity of yearning; and after it he breathed a sigh that seemed to pant out the last mite of strength in his frame, and sank backwards upon the sofa, with Helen still clinging to him.

There for an instant or two he lay, breathing feebly; and the girl heard a faint whisper again—"Not a tear—not a tear!" He opened his eyes once more and gazed at her dimly, and then a slight trembling shook his frame. His chest heaved once more and sank, and after it everything was still.

For an instant Helen stared at him, dazed; then she clutched him by the shoulders, whispering hoarsely-then calling louder and louder in frenzied terror, "David, David!" He gave no answer, and with a cry that was fearful to hear the girl clutched him to her. The body was limp and lifeless—the head fell forward as if the neck were broken; and Helen staggered backward with a scream.

There came an instant of fierce agony then; she stood in the center of the room, reeling and swaying, clutching her head in her hands, her face upturned and tortured. And first she gasped, "He is dead!" and then "I shall not ever see him again!" And she choked and swallowed a lump in her throat, whispering in awful terror, "Not a tear—not a tear!" And then she flung up her arms and sank forward with an incoherent cry, and fell senseless into Arthur's arms.

A week had passed since David's death; and Helen was in her father's home once more, sitting by the window in the gathering twilight. She was very pale, and her eyes were sunken and hollow; but the beauty of her face was still there, tho in a strange and terrible way. Her hand was resting upon Arthur's, and she was gazing into his eyes and speaking in a deep, solemn voice.

"It will not ever leave me, Arthur, I know it will not ever leave me; it is like a fearful vision that haunts me night and day, a voice that cries out in my soul and will not let me rest; and I know I shall never again be able to live like other people, never be free from its madness. For oh, I do not think it is often that a human soul sees what I saw—he seemed to drag me out into the land of death with him, into the very dwelling-place of God. And I almost went with him, Arthur, almost! Can you dream what I suffered—have you any idea of what it means to a human being to make such an effort? I loved that man as if he had been my own soul; I was bound to him so that he was all my life, and to have him go was like tearing my heart in two; and he had told me that I should never see him again, that there was nothing to look for beyond death. And yet, Arthur, I won—do you ever realize it?—I won. It seemed to me as if the earth were reeling about me—as if the very air I breathed were fire; and oh, I thought that he was dead—that he was gone from me forever, and I believed that I was going mad! And then, Arthur, those awful words of his came ringing through my mind, 'Not a tear, not a tear!' I had no faith, I could see nothing but that the world was black with horror; and yet I heard those words! It was love—it was even fear, I think, that held me to it; I had worshiped his sacredness, I had given all my soul to the wonder of his soul; and I dared not be false to him—I dared not dishonor him,—and I knew that he had told me that grief was a crime, that there was truth in the world that I might cling to. And oh, Arthur, I won it—I won it! I kept the faith—David's faith; and it is still alive upon the earth. It seems to me almost as if I had won his soul from death—as if I had saved his spirit in mine-as if I could still rejoice in his life, still have his power and his love; and there is a kind of fearful consecration in my heart, a glory that I am afraid to know of, as if God's hand had been laid upon me.

"David used to tell me, Arthur, that if only that power is roused in a soul, if only it dwells in that sacredness, there can no longer be fear or evil in its life; that the strife and the vanity and the misery in this cruel world about us come from nothing else but that men do not know this vision, that it is so hard—so dreadfully hard—to win. And he used to say that this power is infinite, that it depends only upon how much one wants it; and that he who possessed it had the gift of King Midas, and turned all things that he touched to gold. That is real madness to me, Arthur, and will not let me be still; and yet I know that it cannot ever die in me; for whenever there is an instant's weakness there flashes over me again the fearful thought of David, that he is gone back into nothingness, that nowhere can I ever see him, ever hear his voice or speak to him again,-that I am alone-alone! And that makes me clench my hands and nerve my soul, and fight again, and still again! Arthur, I did that for days, and did not once know why-only because David had told me to, because I was filled with a fearful terror of proving a coward soul, because I had heard him say that if one only held the faith and prayed, the word would come to him at last. And it was true—it was true, Arthur; it was like the tearing apart of the skies, it was as if I had rent my way through them. I saw, as I had never dreamed I could see when I heard David speak of it, how God's Presence is infinite and real; how it guides the blazing stars, and how our life is but an instant and is nothing beside it; and how it makes no difference that we pass into nothingness—His glory is still the same. Then I saw too what a victory I had won, Arthur,—how I could live in it, and how I was free, and master of my life; there came over me a feeling for which there is no word, a kind of demon force that was madness. I thought of that wonderful sixth chapter of Isaiah that David used to think so much beyond reading, that he used to call the artist's chapter; and oh, I knew just what it was that I had to do in the world!"

Helen had been speaking very intensely, her voice shaking; the other's gaze was riveted upon her face. "Arthur," she added, her voice sinking to a whisper, "I have no art, but you have; and we must fight together for this fearful glory, we must win this prize of God." And for a long time the two sat in silence, trembling, while the darkness gathered about them. Helen had turned her head, and gazed out, with face uplifted, at the starry shield that quivered and shook above them; suddenly Arthur saw her lips moving again, and heard her speaking the wonderful words that she had referred to,—her voice growing more and more intense, and sinking into a whisper of awe:—

"In the year that King Uzziah died I saw also the Lord sitting upon a throne, high and lifted up, and his train filled the temple.

"Above it stood the seraphims: each one had six wings; with twain he covered his face, and with twain he covered his feet, and with twain he did fly.

"And one cried unto another, and said, Holy, holy, holy, is the Lord of hosts: the whole earth is full of his glory.

"And the posts of the door moved at the voice of him that cried, and the house was filled with smoke.

"Then said I, Woe is me! for I am undone; because I am a man of unclean lips, and I dwell in the midst of a people of unclean lips: for mine eyes have seen the King, the Lord of hosts.

"Then flew one of the seraphims unto me, having a living coal in his hand, which he had taken with the tongs from off the altar:

"And he laid it upon my mouth, and said, Lo, this hath touched thy lips; and thine iniquity is taken away, and thy sin purged.

"Also I heard the Voice of the Lord, saying, Whom shall I send, and who will go for us? Then said I, Here am I; send me."

BOOMER BOOKS™

Readable Type
for People in their Prime

Boomer Books are not "large-print" books; they are books that are designed for comfortable reading, with ample line spacing, hanging punctuation, and superbly justified type. The typeface is Matthew Carter's Charter, which follows traditional old-style book types but with three differences: narrow proportions for economical use of space; a generous letter-height to improve readability; and sturdy, open letterforms that ensure legible printing in any environment. The result is a typeface that is handsome, versatile, and above all, readable. (The Boomer Books logo illustration is by Jazz Age artist John Held Jr.) We hope you enjoy Boomer Books! You'll find them all at www.boomer-books.biz.